BACK LASH

BACKLASH

GENEVA LEE

QUAINTRELLE

BACKLASH
Copyright © 2020 by Geneva Lee.
All rights reserved.

QUAINTRELLE
PUBLISHING + MEDIA

A branch of Geneva Lee, LLC.
www.GenevaLee.com
First published, 2020.

Cover design © Date Book Designs / Image © pvstory/Adobe Stock.
ISBN-13: 978-1-945163-52-4

To every teacher that reads this—
I appreciate you more than you know

ADAIR

PRESENT DAY

I thought my life was hell until the devil walked through my door. He wore a wicked smile and a familiar face. That day I looked into his blue eyes—the eyes of the only man I'll ever love—and all I found was hatred.

Baudelaire said the loveliest trick of the devil is to persuade you he doesn't exist.

He's wrong. Sterling Ford *is* the devil, and his greatest trick was convincing me we had something real. Five years ago. Last night. It doesn't matter. I fell for his lies.

One month. That's how long it took him to get under my skin and to get me back in his bed. Stupid doesn't begin to cover it. Reckless? Maybe. Self-destructive? Definitely. And now he thinks he can mess with my heart. Two can play that game. Let's see how he likes coming home to an empty bed.

That's why I'm sitting in my car at the stoplight on the corner, blinking back tears, as he jogs down the street with Zeus. Sterling looks as free as his adopted bulldog as they run toward his apartment building, Twelve and South. My insides twist and I consider ducking out of sight.

I don't.

I'm done hiding from this man. I'm not running from him or his lies anymore. I'm walking away. I should have set his house on fire. The message would have been loud and clear. Maybe then he'd stop toying with me. I eye his black canine companion and remind myself that I love him—the dog, not the man. Zeus deserves a good home. At least his owner is better with pets than people.

Despite that, I'm watching him in my rearview mirror. Sterling pauses at the entrance to open a door for someone with a baby stroller, and I wonder for an instant what would happen if he looked up. My car is directly in his line of sight. He's not about to mistake the Roadster for someone else's car. I imagine him spotting me. He'd walk over, and what? Ask me where I was going? What would I say? Would I explain myself? I can almost hear it: *Sorry your girlfriend texted you. I figured I should bow out.* That would be damn near civil. I can't have that. Maybe I would demand answers? Except I don't want to hear his excuses. Sterling doesn't deserve a second more of my time. He's stolen enough from me. Five years of my life gone like they mean nothing. Anger churns inside me until I wish he would see me. Maybe I should have stayed and confronted him. Gotten the answers *I deserve.*

He steps inside the building, and my fantasies dissolve. He's not going to come after me. There will be no reckoning. I don't realize how tightly I'm gripping the leather steering wheel until a loud honk sends me jumping in my seat, the wheel my only anchor. The light turns green and I gun it through the intersection, speeding away from the wreckage of us.

I'm glad he didn't see me. This time I'm not waiting around for Sterling to leave again. I refuse to look for a reason for his betrayal, because I already know why he did it. I need to accept the truth that's been right in front of me the whole time. Sterling Ford didn't come back because he loves me. He came back because he hates me.

This isn't a game anymore. This is war.

ADAIR

FIVE YEAR IN THE PAST

This is going exactly as I expected.

A surprise birthday party—the last thing I wanted tonight—and now an obviously pissed Sterling stalking back to me.

"Where are you going?" I ask.

He doesn't look up. He just keeps his hands shoved into his jeans, his glare directed at the driveway. "Too many people," he grumbles. "I just wanted to get out of here. I didn't think you'd care."

"You didn't think I'd..." How can he think that after I made it clear he was the only person I wanted to see today? A raw ache swells in my throat. "You were just going to take off. I was going to..."

I cut myself off again. The only way to be even more inexperienced in Sterling's eyes is to make a big deal over losing my virginity. That's so not how I want that to happen. I'm not some maiden waiting for my wedding night in a novel. It just seemed like a pretty good way to take my mind off my birthday. I thought he understood that. I guess I was wrong.

Sterling's head lifts and he studies me for a second, the look on his face inscrutable. Finally, he shakes his head. "You just seemed busy," he says, sounding more tired than mad now. "I'm not much of a partier. I didn't want to rain on your parade."

"I know that." I force a smile, the knot in my throat loosening a little. "We can sneak off after—"

"There you are!" Poppy's voice trills. "I've been searching everywhere for you."

I glance between my best friend and my boyfriend, torn.

Sterling bobs his head in her direction. "Go on. I'll stick around."

"No way." I pull on his arm until he slips his hand from his pocket and twines it with mine. "I'm not letting you out of my sight."

"Sure." He sounds anything but; however, he comes with us.

The party is moving inside to the ballroom, DJ included. A fresh champagne tower is already flowing, and the bar is open. The presents have been brought in, stacked high next to a table full of jars of candy and small plastic balls with a sign that reads 'Trick-or-treat.' Poppy's thought of everything my mom would have done, down to the Halloween candy and the party favors.

"Don't go anywhere," she orders me. "I want you to open presents in a minute."

I force myself to smile—to pretend like I'm enjoying myself.

"How are you doing?" Sterling asks when we're alone. He hasn't spoken once since we came inside, and he's no longer holding my hand.

I rectify that, clasping his again, and shake my head. "My mom loved to throw me birthday parties. Every year there was a theme centered around Halloween. I know Poppy meant well, but all I see are the ways this isn't the party my mother would throw."

"Like?" he asks.

"She definitely would have stuck with champagne and skipped the hard liquor," I tell him. "Mom didn't like underage drinking."

"But champagne was okay?" Behind his puzzled expression something darker flashes.

"She would say drinking is to escape." I can practically hear her speaking. "But champagne is to experience."

The ache is back, amplified by thoughts of her. I clear my throat, trying to get rid of it. "Candy?"

Sterling shrugs. He really doesn't want to be here. I can't blame him. Instead, I hold his hand tighter. We make our way to the jars on the table, and Sterling picks up a plastic ball while I unwrap a Belgian chocolate.

"What's this?" He holds it up.

"A trick or a treat. It is Halloween." I try to sound cheerful, but I wonder if he picks up on the strain.

He pops it open and his eyes grow wide.

"What did you get?" I angle my head to peek, discovering a folded up bill.

Sterling unfolds it to reveal the face of Ulysses S. Grant.

"Not bad." I grab one and pop it open to discover a condom. Panic seizes me and I snap it closed.

"Trick or treat?" he asks.

I swallow. "Hard to say. Definitely not as good as yours."

"You keep it." He holds the fifty-dollar bill out to me. "It's your birthday."

"No way. You chose it." When he scowls, I grab another prize and toss it to him. "Maybe you'll like this more." I drop the ball, holding the condom on the table nonchalantly while he opens the new one.

"That's more like it," he mutters and withdraws a rubber duck.

"It's cute," I protest.

Before I can grab another, Poppy glides towards us, smiling widely. "I can't wait for you to see what I got you."

"Come with me," I beg Sterling as she hooks her arm through mine to lead me off.

He waves off my request, shoving the plastic ball in his pocket. "Go open your gifts. I'm not going anywhere."

Why does he sound so resigned? I allow Poppy to lead me over to the gift table, daring a glance back just in time to see Sterling deposit one of his prize balls back into a jar. Poppy thrusts a package into my hands, and I slip into hostess mode. Not something I enjoy, but a trait that seems encoded in my DNA. The Southern woman's curse. My gaze darts back to Sterling to see if he's watching as I tear off the bow.

He's standing with Cyrus, talking. Or rather, Cyrus is. At least he's not alone. I relax and focus on the present, which turns out to be a Tiffany bracelet from Cyrus himself. Poppy gushes over the heart charm dangling from it.

"He's so thoughtful," she says meaningfully, and I wonder how much champagne she's had to drink.

I look up to thank him, but he's gone—along with Sterling.

3

STERLING

PRESENT DAY

Zeus acts like a puppy in the elevator, trying to jump up and lick me. I barely keep him off poor Percy, even if the old bellhop doesn't seem to mind.

"He's fine, Mr. Ford," he reassures me as I haul Zeus off him.

"Sorry." I gently grab Zeus's collar and drop to one knee to keep him contained. "He's had an exciting day. We've had company."

"Company?" Percy asks with a knowing smile. "A pretty girl, maybe?"

Of course he met Adair. He only runs the elevators during the daytime hours when people come and go more frequently. I can't keep a goofy grin off my face just thinking of her. I nod.

"She's been coming around a bit," he notes. "A little quiet this evening, but a looker. Will we be seeing Miss..."

"MacLaine," I give him the name he's fishing for. It's a matter of professional curiosity, I know. He likes to know his passengers, but I spy the way his eyes widen slightly under his bushy eyebrows when he realizes who is visiting me.

"Will we be seeing more of Miss MacLaine in the future?" he asks smoothly. That's Percy—a consummate professional. He'll be discreet.

"I don't know which one of us likes her more: me or the dog."

"If the dog likes her, she's good people," Percy advises me.

"She introduced me to him." I scratch Zeus's ears.

"So, you brought them together, huh, boy?" Percy asks Zeus who responds with an enthusiastic bark.

"Something like that," I murmur. The truth is that the dog did bring us together—back together.

"Well, I'll see you tomorrow. Maybe Miss MacLaine, too, if she comes back around. Shift's over," Percy says as we reach my floor. "You two will have to push your own buttons the rest of the evening if you're coming and going again."

I bite back a smile. There's something about the old-fashioned way Percy views the world. It's not often that I find that old Southern sensibility charming, but the thought of Percy waiting to deliver my lady caller to me during proper visiting hours is as sweet as Hennie's iced tea. If only he knew that I plan on pushing as many of Adair's buttons tonight as I can tonight. "I think I can handle that."

Zeus races to our door as soon as we're out of the elevator. We both know she's there, waiting for us. The second we're inside, we both stop dead as an eerie silence greets us. I toss my keys on the counter, bend to unhook the leash from Zeus's collar, and look around. Nothing is out of place, but everything feels wrong.

"Adair?" I call. Zeus shoves his wet nose into my palm and whimpers at the sound of her name. My stomach drops and I tell myself he wants a treat. That's all. Given how impatient I was on our walk—eager to get back to the woman I'd left in my bed—I can't blame him. I snag one from the canister I keep in the kitchen and toss it to him.

But Zeus doesn't go for it. That's the second sign something is wrong. Instead, he lopes toward the bedroom, tongue lolling from his mouth, and lets out a howl.

Panic seizes me, and I can't move. Déjà vu does that. It sticks you to a spot until dread forces you to move. I do that now as calmly as possible. "Lucky? You in there?"

She's probably in the shower or fallen back asleep. There's absolutely no reason to suspect anything is wrong. Other than the quiet house and worried dog—a dog that loves her as much as I do. I'm not stupid enough to believe that we've earned a happily ever after. There are things she doesn't know about me—things I need to tell her.

When she was a mark—a line on my blacklist—I didn't worry about that. Now?

Things are different now.

Now she's on a different list. One I reserve for my makeshift family. It's a list of people I'd die for. It's a select group. I didn't know until this moment that she'd not only made the cut, she'd worked her way up to the top.

I pause in the butler's pantry, opening a cabinet and reach toward the back, sliding free a Glock 19. The safety's already off. If I'm reaching for it, I don't have time to mess around. I know that from experience. What I don't know is what's waiting for me in my bedroom.

But whatever I expect to find, it isn't this. The bedroom is empty. There's no running shower. No clothes on the floor. No trace of her except the unmade bed I'd left her in twenty minutes ago and the slight hint of magnolia lingering in the air. I want to believe she's in the bathroom. I lower my gun, and not because I'm worried she'll surprise me. I lower it because I know I'm alone. The room feels cold, like all the light and warmth has been sucked from it. She's not here. I feel her absence as acutely as I would feel her presence. Something is missing. There's a gaping hole in this place now. I carved a spot for her without knowing it. Her absence makes me see that.

The imprint of her body lingers on the sheets. I can still see where her head rested against the pillow minutes ago. For one chilling moment I wonder if someone took her. I wonder if I've dragged her into a world she knows nothing about. I wonder if someone else is crossing her off their list right now.

Then I see the pages.

Words ripped from a book like the heart the sight rips from my chest, scattered with its remains across the bed. I don't need to check the book she's tossed on the nightstand. I know which book it is. Of course, she knew where it was. Heat swells inside me as I cross to the piece of torn page she's left in the spot she occupied when I left.

So we beat on, boats against the current, borne back ceaselessly into the past.

She tore up my favorite book.

She tore up my heart.

I don't know which hurts more.

More than that, I don't know what it means. When she'd come here tonight seeking shelter from her brother, I thought we'd turned a corner. I'd taken the first step with the flowers and the note. I'd given us a blank slate. I'd listened to my fucking heart instead of my head and this is where it landed me: a vandalized book and an empty bed.

She chose that line for a reason. Because it was the end? Because there's no happily ever after? No.

Into the past.

It's a message. We can't escape the current, the riptide will keep dragging us back out to sea—lost and separated, making it impossible to find our way back to one another. That's where we were in the past.

So that's how Adair sees it. I thought when she came here last night that she'd agreed with what I'd written on that note:

I'm all in, Lucky.

I was—until now.

"What the fuck, Lucky?" I growl. Zeus backs away a little and I force myself to take a deep breath. If I can scare him, what does she think of me? Is that why she left? Did I say something? Did I frighten her? Is that why turned away from me five years ago?

I look down at the gun heavy in my palm and realize if that's the case, she's smarter than I thought—and I've always thought Adair was brilliant. I flick on the safety and shove the gun in my waistband. There's no danger here, except me. I should have seen *myself* coming.

I spin around, rubbing my palm against my neck. She can't have gone far. I feel stupid thinking about my conversation with Percy now. He said she seemed quiet tonight. He meant when she left! I consider trying to catch him before his shift ends to see if he has a clue where she's gone. Then, I can go after her, demand an explanation. But I know Adair. She gave nothing away. Still, it's not like I won't be able to spot the Roadster, even in Nashville traffic. It stands out a little. I'll make her see that it's not like before. I'll prove it to her like I should have five years ago.

I reach for my phone and start to slip it into my pocket when the lock screen flashes a text notification. All the pieces fall into place in an instant when I see Sutton's name. The conversation I'd been having with her probably read a lot differently to Adair. She wouldn't know it was playful. She wouldn't know it was innocent.

Because she doesn't know Sutton is my sister, and that's on me. I pick and choose what I let Adair see about me and my life. I always have. So why did I hand her my phone so thoughtlessly?

"Fuck!" My phone hits the wall and crashes to the ground with a loud crack before I realize that I've thrown it. What the fuck was I thinking? There are a dozen people I wouldn't want her to read texts from and I just gave her my phone? Clearly, *I* wasn't the one thinking; my dick was. It's not the first time. It might be the worst time, though. Had Adair gone through them all? Snooped through my life? Does she know who I am now? What I am? I slide the message and read the thread.

Adair didn't need to read more than this. Without any context, it looks bad—really goddamn bad. It's a testament to how screwed up our relationship is that I'd rather she had found a message from one of my clients. That might have gone over better than me saying I love you to another woman. Anyone could have texted me while she had the phone, but it had to be Sutton. It's just like us to get the short straw.

Adair might be my lucky charm, but the thing about luck is that it's bad as often as it's good. And this time? My luck is as bad as it gets.

4

STERLING

THE PAST

Cyrus leans over the bar while the bartender flirts with a few of Adair's friends. Straightening to his feet, he holds up a bottle of West Tennessee Whiskey. He swipes a glass. "Want one?"

It's not the first time he's offered me a drink. I'm not sure why he keeps asking. Maybe he expects that one day I'll take him up on the offer.

Today's that day. "Sure."

He grins and grabs another glass. Then, he tilts his head toward an archway. I follow him away from the party, down a hall, and into a large study. Built-in bookshelves line the walls, filled with a neatly organized library of leather-bound volumes. They're beautiful books, their titles stamped in gold on their unbroken spines. There's not a speck of dust to be seen as I wander around, perusing.

"Adair's dad is a reader, too," I note as Cyrus hands me a tumbler of amber liquid. I hold it for a moment, aware of its weight in my palm.

Cyrus laughs. "No clue."

"He has a lot of books," I point out, admiring his collection of Hemingway.

"So does my Dad," he says with a shrug. "His home office looks a lot like this, and I've never seen him read a book. He's too busy with contracts and stuff. I think shit like this comes with a house on Magnolia Lane."

I start to pull out a copy of *Exit to Eden*.

"Don't, man," Cyrus warns me. "There are cameras everywhere. Her dad goes nuts if people touch his shit."

No one touches the books, let alone reads them. I force a tight-lipped smile. That explains their pristine condition. Pretty objects to fill empty places. Books mean something else entirely to me. Mr. MacLaine doesn't deserve this library. He doesn't deserve this life.

"I can't believe he left on her birthday," I say.

"It's better, though," Cyrus points out. "All our parents take off so they can pretend they don't know what we get up to." He taps his glass against mine. "Cheers to absentee parents."

It's a weird thing to toast to, but I guess if daddy pays the bills and keeps you in luxury cars, you don't care.

"What about you?" Cyrus asks.

"Huh?" The glass is hovering near my mouth, but I can't seem to take a drink.

"Your parents. You never talk about them." A shadow passes over his face and his eyes widen. "Fuck, I forgot. I met your, um, adoptive mom, right?"

"Foster mom," I correct him. Suddenly, it's easy to take a sip. The whiskey burns down my throat, igniting a deeper thirst. I take another drink.

"Sorry, none of my business." But I can tell he's curious.

"They're dead," I say flatly. It's almost the truth. I'm only half lying, and they both might as well be dead for all I care.

"Fuck." He rakes a hand through his hair. "I'm sorry. That's rough."

Given the worst thing that's ever happened to Cyrus Eaton was probably dinging his BMW, I doubt he can relate. I don't hold it against him. Why would I want another human to live through the death of their mother— let alone their mother's murder? But I wish he didn't feel the need to sympathize. He doesn't get it. He never will. His platitudes are meaningless.

Silence falls between us, and I think he expects me to fill it in with the story of their tragic deaths or some shit. No way am I falling down that hellhole.

"Another?" Cyrus asks, holding out the bottle.

I thrust my cup toward him, remembering what Adair said about her mother. *Drinking is to escape.* I'll drink to that, because I've never wanted out more in my life.

We make short work of the bottle. Cyrus provides the entertainment, telling me about every ridiculous birthday party he's been to at Windfall. He's just wrapping up the story of the year an interactive haunted house went terribly wrong as we polish off the last of the whiskey.

"You two have known each other a long time." I like the way my head feels, fuzzy like the old television set Francie kept in the kitchen—so old it used a shitty antenna to pick up the local news.

"We've known each other the longest, since like

diapers. Most of our friends moved here later, but we've always been here." He tries to pour himself more and frowns when a single drop plops into his glass. "We're out."

"Let's get more." There appears to be no shortage of booze at Windfall.

"I hated her," Cyrus says as we trip down the hall, the sound of the party growing louder with each step. "When we were kids, I mean. She was a snot."

"Ha! Was!" I clap a hand over my mouth, realizing I let this escape.

Cyrus only laughs. "She's better than a lot of them."

"Not as nice as Poppy," I remind him.

"You sure you don't want to date Poppy?" He raises two eyebrows. Or maybe it's only one. Or maybe there's two of him. It's hard to decide, because things are getting a little blurry around me.

"I belong to Adair MacLaine," I tell him, "for now."

"What?" he asks.

I wave him off. "Nothing."

Before he can press me for more details, we step inside the atrium to discover everyone is still crowded in a semicircle around Adair. She's smiling widely and holding something in the air. A purse, maybe? It's hard to make-out.

"She's still unwrapping presents?"

"A lot of guests. The girls always have to open every present and fall all over whoever gave it," he explains.

"And you don't?"

"No, fuck that." His answering grin is sly. "Course, we usually just get booze. We're lucky if anything makes it until morning. We tend to drink it all. Speaking of..." Cyrus points to the bar. "Be right back."

I study Adair while he grabs more liquor. Her smile is plastered on, dulling at the edges and nowhere near her eyes. There's a crease between them where she's worn a line from worry. Or is it anxiety? Frustration? Who the fuck knows? I don't get her. She claims to want nothing to do with all this, but she steps right up and takes all these gifts, laughs off fifty-dollar party favors, and gulps champagne.

I'm beginning to understand her problem. She wants to believe she doesn't fit in with this crowd, but it's just an indulgent fantasy, like the rest of her life. She's the heroine of her own story, choosing to see herself as a victim waiting to be rescued. But from what? The happy ending that comes along with a padded bank account? Already having everything handed to her?

Yeah, her life is so fucking hard.

"Here." Cyrus returns and thrusts a new cup in my hand, filled to the brim with whiskey. "The bartender is being a bitch about me swiping another bottle. Apparently, he's never heard not to bite the hand that feeds him."

I swallow the drink along with the words crowding in my throat. Of course, he sees it that way. Everything belongs to these people. The world exists for them to take.

"Ahh, this will be her big present." Cyrus elbows me and I turn my attention back to Adair. Poppy is tying a blindfold over her eyes. Adair looks fucking thrilled about it.

"Her big present?" Because half a department store's worth of shit isn't enough?

"From her parents. I mean, her dad," Cyrus corrects himself quickly.

I frown. "Her dad isn't here."

"Yeah, but he left a present." He looks at me like I'm from another planet.

Maybe I am. Maybe I'm from a planet where dads don't remember birthdays, so they can't leave town on them, where there aren't any presents or cake or music. There's booze, though, and plenty of it. It's just not for celebrating or escaping. It's just a fact of life.

As if I need proof this is the case, the next thing I hear is heavy foot falls, falling like claps of thunder on the marble floor. My head swivels towards the sound to find a jet black horse being led towards Adair.

"Is that a fucking horse?" I'm not sure why I need confirmation. Even with half a bottle of whiskey coursing through my blood, I think I still know what a horse looks like.

"Another one." He shakes his head. "I'm pretty sure that's the only thing Angus knows she likes. I think it's like" —he counts on his fingers— "the third one he's given her as a present. Maybe the fourth. She got one for graduation."

"Does he know you can only ride one horse at a time?" My mouth is dry. I take another drink to wet it.

"You can only drive one car. That doesn't mean you only own one."

That's pretty much exactly what it means. I keep this to myself, though.

Poppy tugs off Adair's blindfold, and she gasps, jumping up and down. But there's something hollow in her actions. I half expect to look up and find puppet strings dangling over her head. She doesn't need them, though.

She knows how all the steps, and how the beats work—she can put on her performance for memory.

God, I hope the horse shits in the foyer.

The man leading the horse takes it away, presumably to the stables, but I don't know. Maybe she sleeps with them. I no longer hold these people to any measure of sanity I'm familiar with.

"I think they want us," Cyrus says, nudging my arm with his.

I turn back to Adair, and she's waving us over.

I resign myself to joining her, but I can't stop thinking about what she said earlier. She'd told me I was all she wanted for her birthday. Now I know that probably meant on a silver platter, wrapped with a bow, and delivered to her with minimal effort. I'm just another toy—another object, like the presents scattered across the table. Something shiny. Something new. She'll play with me until she gets bored. If I'm lucky, she'll pass me off like a hand-me-down or donate me to a bitch less fortunate than herself. Standing in Windfall, I can safely assume even the richest girls here fall in that category.

Why did I ever let myself believe we had a single thing in common?

"Did you see?" Poppy's glowing with excitement. "An Arabian."

"A what?"

"An Arabian," she repeats. "Adair's always wanted one, and her dad got her one."

"Lucky girl," I say pointedly.

Adair's eyes flash, but she manages a tight smile. "I wanted one when I was like six, Poppy." She rolls her eyes as if this can offset the extravagant tribute made to birth tonight. "Like I needed another horse."

"Can you have too many?" I pass it off as a joke, but her forehead wrinkles as she laughs. Some part of her heard it for what it really was: a gentle reminder that she's being an ungrateful bitch. As usual.

"I promised Sterling some alone time," Adair says, grabbing my arm.

"Ohhhh." Poppy's mischievous wink tells me that Adair's been telling everyone about her plans to nail me. I wonder if Poppy's on the list of girls next in line for a piece of me.

"I should probably go." I hitch a thumb in what I think is the direction of the door. "You have a horse to attend to."

"Nonsense," Poppy cuts in. "He's being taken care of. You aren't going anywhere. Besides, don't you have a present for her?"

I don't know if she means the pathetic one I left in her car, the one wrapped in cheap paper I found at the student union, or my dick, which seems to be what Adair's really after. At least one of them's worth something.

"He gave it to me earlier," Adair blurts out.

Is she embarrassed at the idea of opening a present from me in front of her rich friends? She would be if she knew what was inside that stupid package.

"I should get back to the dorms," I repeat, my whole being wanting to walk away from this place, from her, from all of them.

"But my dad's out of town," she reminds me in a whisper. "I thought you would stay the night..."

So, she still expects her birthday treat. Poor little rich

girl needs to fill the gaping hole inside her. Maybe she'd be a different person if her dad actually showed up for her birthday. I don't know. But then how could he turn a blind eye? Of course, it's not like he can't watch all of this on security cameras, relive each happy moment he bought for her instead of being there. No wonder Adair uses people like she does. How can I expect her to think of me as a person when I have something of value she doesn't own yet? I wonder what her dad would think if he knew his little girl was planning to screw some poor kid from Queens. What would he think of his prize possession on her knees in front of me? I remember what Cyrus said about cameras and how Angus MacLaine hates when people touch his belongings.

I'll stay, but I'm going to make her work for it. She's going to beg for it, and I'm going to make sure Windfall's cameras catch every minute.

5

ADAIR

PRESENT DAY

S terling isn't my only problem—he's just the one that hurts the most. The whole shitshow that is my life is why I'm driving aimlessly through downtown Nashville, wondering if I'm crazy or stupid or some dangerous combination of the two.

I'm homeless. It's one of the many thoughts rattling around in my brain—and it's getting louder each second. Self preservation in action, I guess. It's a problem I can actually fix. The rest of my thoughts?

They're all about him.

Heartless. Evil. Bastard. I'm at least five miles away from Sterling's place and distance is not making the heart grow farther. My brain is shouting every insult it can come up with to drown out the whispering doubts vying for my attention.

I don't want to hear those. I scream the loud ones, the angry ones. I call him names. I shout so loudly another driver's head turns, a puzzled expression on his face. I feel badly until he flips me off. I turn some of my rage on him, but it doesn't silence the doubts. They scratch at my brain, tickle against my nerves, refuse to be ignored. The quiet thoughts are the dangerous ones.

I should have known better.

No one will ever love me.

I'm an idiot.

I'll never be anyone other than a MacLaine.

And the worst of all?

He loves her.

Sutton.

Sutton who called me a bitch. Sutton who begged him to come home. Sutton who usually gets her way. Sutton who implied this was all a game. Sutton, the woman I've never heard a thing about, and Sutton, the woman he loves.

I want to leave everything behind me. The old Roadster isn't very fast—not by modern standards—but it's always willing. I drop into second gear, sending the engine screaming towards the red line. A woman pushing a stroller along the sidewalk screams something at me as I pass, but I'm beyond caring if I woke her baby. I mash the throttle around a corner, sending the tail of the Jag sideways, and I have to wrestle the steering wheel into submission.

I knew Sterling had an agenda. I sensed it from the very beginning. He told me as much to my face. I let myself believe it was about money—about proving himself. I *wanted* to believe it, too. I wanted to believe he had returned to Valmont to show off what he's become.

I should have known better. He came back to hurt me. I didn't want to think it then, but refusing to believe something doesn't make it any less true.

And knowing that's what brought him back? It shreds

some semblance of propriety. I'm not sure either passes muster.

A giggling woman nearly steps into the revolving door compartment before I can exit. She's distracted by the man she's with. He pulls her out of the way and smiles apologetically. "Excuse us."

"Oops!" she adds. I can't tell if she's drunk or just intoxicated with him.

I force myself to nod but can't make myself return the smile. Stepping into the lobby, I discover it full of happy couples holding hands, whispering to one another—one pair is even touring the space with a wedding coordinator. I suddenly feel like I'm gagging on my own silver spoon. This is supposed to be my life. Dinner at a five star restaurant, drinks in the bar, small talk with the other elite members of Tennessee society—and a sexy, successful man at my side paying for it all. It's what I'm supposed to want. I never have—until now.

But I'll never be able to settle for this lie of a life. Not after tasting real life. Or, at least, what I thought was real at the time.

I make my way to the concierge desk, unsure exactly how this works, but desperate to get away from all the happy couples. I hadn't been given a key or anything of the sort. Several of my friends's families owned apartments in hotels in New York or London or Paris, the benefit being that at a hotel there was always someone available for maintenance and security. It would always be clean when it was time for an impromptu visit. Why settle for a housekeeper when you could have a five star staff at your disposal?

The concierge doesn't bother to look up when I

approach. He's a few years older than me and a few inches shorter, which leaves me staring at a thinning patch of hair as his attention remains on the computer screen. He's probably planning someone's dinner reservation with their mistress. "May I help you?"

Still no eye contact. I take a deep breath and speak directly to his bald spot. "I hope so. I'm Adair MacLaine, and I—"

His head whips up at the mention of my name. "Ms. MacLaine! My apologies!"

"It's okay, Geoff," I read the name engraved on the polished brass pin on his jacket. Judging from his reaction at the mention of the MacLaine name, he expects me to throw a tantrum. I dismiss the innocent snub because I don't have the energy to be offended, and because I'm tired of living up to my family's reputation—good and bad. "My family suite—I recently inherited it...um, I'd like to see it."

Use it. Live in it. Hide in it. I add the rest silently, unwilling to commit fully to the idea that I'm leaving Windfall behind for good. Too much has happened in the past twenty-four hours. I need to process. I need to be alone.

"Of course, let me get a key made." Geoff switches quickly into schmooze mode, but I can't help noticing a bead of sweat near his receding hairline. Then I realize his hand is shaking slightly.

I want to tell him that I don't bite, but something tells me he won't believe that. I try to put him at ease instead. It's not a trait that comes naturally to me. MacLaines are accustomed to demanding and receiving. We don't take time to apologize or ask kindly. The world comes to us, or else it can go fuck itself.

That needs to change.

"Sorry to put you on the spot." I plaster the warmest smile I can muster on my face. It takes effort given the gnashing anger roiling inside me. It's not Geoff's fault that Sterling is a bastard. Geoff is helping me. Geoff is a solution.

He's also a man, and after my brother's demands yesterday and Sterling's manipulation, I'm ready to lash out. Geoff is an easy target, but I won't let him be. I'm not that bitch that needs to be left behind. I'm not the girl who waited around for a man who only came back to throw her away again.

I don't know who I am, but I'm determined to decide my own fate from now on, starting with Geoff here.

"Will you be staying?" Geoff interrupts my thoughts, and I blink at him.

"Excuse me?"

He pulls a handkerchief out and mops his forehead as he repeats the question.

"Does it matter?" I don't feel like committing to anything. Not until I know if Malcolm will come looking for me. Not until I've seen the suite.

"We can set a key to expire," he explains, his fingers hovering over the keyboard. "We can also leave them open if you'd like to come and go or..."

Of course, that's why he asked. It makes sense.

"Leave it open," I say after a moment. "I have business in the city."

"Let me show you up," he offers. He's out from behind

the desk before I can refuse. Geoff glances around me. "Do you have bags?"

"No." I flush even as I lift my head up. "I thought I better check everything out first. For all I know the place looks like Miss Havisham's house."

He gives me a quizzical look, but customer service wins out. "Very good. If you have a valet ticket, I can see to that."

It turns out that living at the Eaton includes in and out privileges. That's a relief, since I have no idea how much is in my bank account or how long it will last. Sterling came here to ruin my family. That much is clear to me now. There's a certain poetic justice to it. He'll be living in his penthouse pedestal, staring smugly down at the MacLaines on the street below.

"You have use of the private elevators. We reserve them for our penthouse floors," he explains, leading me past the bank of elevators in the lobby to a discreetly hidden set of golden doors. "Your key will call the elevator."

When it arrives, it's mercifully empty. I need a moment away from the bustle of the lobby, away from the couple clinging to one another as they speak to a wedding planner, away from the mother lovingly chasing after her toddler, away from people. But Geoff fills the silence with a constant stream of information on the hotel. He tells me about the pool and the spa and the member lounge reserved for platinum elite guests. I guess owning part of the joint secures me those privileges.

"Are there many other families who own suites?" I interrupt a lesson on how to use the hotel's wireless internet.

"Only the Eaton family. The other suites are reserved for high profile guests."

Translation: people with more money than common sense and a desperate need to show off. I'd forgotten that Cyrus's family has a suite here. I'm not sure how that's possible given what happened the last time I was here.

I might not have set foot in my family's suite in the last ten years, but I have been on this floor since.

Then, I wasn't the one holding the key. I shake off the horrible memory as the elevator reaches our destination. The past is in the past. I need to leave it behind.

I need to leave him behind.

"Everything is fully stocked and refreshed daily." Geoff leads me to a door marked with a polished brass placard inscribed with the number 614.

I hesitate on the threshold after he unlocks the door with the keycard. Somehow stepping across it feels like I've drawn a line in the sand. The truth is that I don't have other options. At least, none that don't include willfully turning a blind eye to my brother's demands or running back to Sterling, a man who clearly hates me.

The suite isn't like I remember. Of course, it's been a decade since I came here. I stop a few feet in and stare at my new home. It's been redone recently. The television in the living area is the newest technology. The linen sofa looks like it's gotten less ass than a virgin. It's all lovely and tasteful—and so like my mother. I feel at home, and I hate it. There's little touches of her everywhere. I can almost swear I smell her perfume. I turn as a shadow passes in the corner, half expecting to find her there, but it's only my imagination.

"Is everything...okay?" Geoff asks, glancing around. "We'll send up housekeeping to freshen the sheets and towels."

"When were they last changed?" I murmur absently, beginning to wander around.

"This morning."

I stop and shake my head. "There's no need to send them up. I have everything I need."

"Room service is available, naturally. Anything you order will be included on your monthly bill."

"Bill?" I raise an eyebrow.

"Incidentals and residence fees are billed to the account on file," he explains. "It's part of the arrangement."

"Of course." That makes sense, although I can't believe my father kept this place all these years, paying fees on a penthouse we never used. No wonder our family is broke. "Where is that bill sent?"

The last thing I need is for Malcolm to know my every move, even if it's unlikely to be more exciting than knowing I ordered a club sandwich two days in a row.

"I'll look into that," he promises. "I do hope everything is up to your standards. It's been a while since we had a MacLaine in house."

"I know."

"Your father was a valued member here and we miss him terribly."

"My father?" I smile. "You must not have known him very well."

"Before his illness, he was here weekly. He was a demanding man but a generous one."

He didn't know my father at all.

Or maybe he knew him better than I did. Because I had no idea my father ever came to this suite at the Eaton. I only knew about it because of the slumber party.

"You're saying my father came here often?"

"Weekly," Geoff confirms. I see the recognition dawn on his face as this information sinks into me. He shouldn't have said a thing. The Eaton is a luxury hotel—the kind that turns a blind eye to the vices of their wealthy patrons. Those residence fees he spoke of—I'm guessing they have a different purpose: hush money. Tip staff well enough and they'll keep your secrets. Buy a penthouse, come and go as you please.

"Oh," I feign idiocy. "The Nashville apartment! The family has so much real estate. I didn't realize he was talking about this place. He did come here and stay when he had late meetings at the office. I haven't been here since I was a kid. I just thought of it as a hotel."

Geoff's shoulders relax as though I've lifted a weight from them. He probably thought he was about to lose his job, and then who would arrange romantic evenings for Tennessee's most spoiled mistresses?

"My brother comes here a lot, doesn't he?" I ask, realizing that I might have overlooked a critical component of this plan. Malcolm has a weekly date he likes to keep quiet, too. What if...? I don't want to think about my brother and his girlfriends being here.

"If he does, he doesn't use the suite. It was your father's," Geoff assures me, bypassing the question of Malcolm's patronage while still getting to the heart of the issue. I have to give it to him. He's smooth.

"And now it's mine," I murmur. "The decor?"

"We can arrange for it to be redone as you like. I can put you in touch with our in-house interior designer."

"Interesting."

I mean it. I need some place to call my own.

"If there's anything else..." Geoff trails away.

"Yes, can you call that designer? I just took a job in the city." I mentally cross my fingers that I can smooth things over with Trish. "I wasn't sure if it would be a good fit, but I think maybe I'm home."

"Then let me be the first to say welcome back, Ms. MacLaine."

Once Geoff leaves me in my new place, I find the bedroom, throw myself on the mattress, and scream into a pillow until my throat is raw. It beats crying. I once swore I would never cry over Sterling Ford again. It's one of those promises you make out of desperation, and not because you think you can keep it.

But today?

Today, I don't want to cry. Today, I want to be angry, because anger fuels. Crying saps. I need energy to steer this wreck of a life toward a stable future. When I'm done screaming, I order a fucking club sandwich and a bottle of champagne. I'm going to celebrate this moment.

I have a home.

I have a job.

I have a choice.

That makes today a diamond by any standards. I choose to see it that way.

Things could have gone on longer. I could have wasted even more time letting Sterling get the best of me. I could have let Malcolm dictate my entire future. I stood up to both of them. I walked away. If that's not cause for celebration, then I don't know what is.

The food arrives so quickly that I can feel my ass getting bigger. I might have to set some boundaries if they can get chocolate cake to me at this speed. Or not. It's my life now.

Tomorrow, I'll go to Windfall and pack while Malcolm is at work. Today, I settle for a silky Eaton robe I find in the master closet. But celebrating by myself turns out to remind me I'm alone. Usually, I'm okay with that. Even surrounded by friends, I've never quite fit. I'm always the odd one out. The one being dragged toward socialization. I've embraced that over the last few years.

But Sterling changed everything. He reminded me of what it's like to be perfectly understood. Even when we're at odds, he gets me. For a moment I was completely, utterly myself with him.

I let my guard down, and he attacked. I don't know why I expected anything different to happen. You can't blame a predator for striking. I practically laid down and begged for it. Just like he said I would.

Never again.

It's something to drink to, so I pop the bottle of champagne and pour myself a glass. Room service, in its infinite wisdom, sent two champagne flutes. It feels like an insult to see it sitting there empty, so I pour another glass and place it next to the framed photo of my mother.

"To being rid of bad men," I say to her and clink the rim of my glass to hers. I down the contents of my flute with one swallow. "You going to drink that?"

Great, now I'm talking to my dead mom. Maybe that's

because she's one of the few people I've ever known who never said a bad thing about people. She always saw the good in them, but not in the innocent way my best friend Poppy does. She saw flaws, but she didn't focus on them. People always say I take after her, but they mean in the looks department. I have her green eyes and fair complexion. That's where our similarities end. I'm nothing like her. I've got too much of my father in me.

"Why did you love him?" I ask her. "You saw what he was. What good could you possibly have found in him? I watched how he treated you for years and you always found a way to see past how he controlled you and used you. I mean, he probably brought other women to this very room! Why? Why were you in the car that night? Why did you let him drive? You knew! Why is this all I have left of you?" I wave my hand wildly around the hotel suite, forgetting my glass and sending champagne spilling across the desk. "Shit."

I slide open the drawer of the end table, looking for something to wipe it off with. All I find is a stack of paper and some pens. I try the next drawer, only to discover it's locked or stuck. For some reason, this puts me over the edge. The tears I've been fighting break loose and fall down my cheeks. I yank on the desk drawer, determined to get it open, but it won't budge. Definitely locked. It's not like it will have what I need anyway. I wind up grabbing a washcloth from the bathroom to soak up the mess.

"Don't cry over spilled champagne," I order myself.

But I'm not crying over it. I'm crying for my mom and the life I thought I would have. The life I will never have. I'm crying because I want to know the answers to those questions, because maybe if I did, I could figure out why I'm stuck—just like that stupid drawer—repeating mistakes, holding onto the past, never learning. Opening the top drawer, I reach to the back, feeling around for a key, but only find dust. It's the story of my life: there's always a missing key.

6

STERLING

Her phone goes straight to voicemail when I call, which means it's dead or she turned the ringer off to avoid me. I'm past being angry at her for jumping to conclusions, and now I'm in full-blown panic mode. If I can find her, if I can explain...

But I don't know where to start. Scrolling through my contact list, I stumble on Cyrus's name. He gave me his number weeks ago to set up a lunch date or whatever these rich fucks do to fill their meaningless days. Cyrus, for better or for worse, lives with Poppy. Poppy is Adair's best friend. It doesn't take a mathematical genius to put it together.

He answers after a few rings.

"Cyrus, it's Sterling," I cut him off mid-hello.

"I was wondering if you'd ever get around to calling me. We still need to get together. Charity galas aren't exactly—"

"Yeah, let's do that." I don't have time for idle chit-chat. "Listen, is Adair at your place? I'm trying to track her down. I thought she might be with Poppy."

"She's not here. I can ask Poppy," he offers.

"No, don't worry about it," I say quickly. The last thing I need is to spook her any more or to get all her friends involved. I doubt Poppy will take my side on this one. "Let's make sure we get together."

I hang up before I can waste more time on a dead end. Zeus wanders over and sits at my feet, staring up at me while I stare at my phone.

I call Jack because I can't think and he's pretty good at it. "Weird question," I say when he answers, "Have you seen Adair?"

"Misplace her?" I can hear the smile in his voice.

"Cute," I say curtly. "Seriously, she took off, and she's not answering her phone."

"Did something happen?" Jack's tone switches to all business. That's the other upside of calling him for help. Luca would still have three more quips on deck before he started taking things seriously.

"Doesn't it always?" I mutter. "She saw a text on my phone."

"So?"

"It was from Sutton. I think she got the wrong idea."

"I take it she doesn't know that Sutton is your sister?" He lets out a whistle. "You're in trouble. Look, I haven't seen her, but I'll keep an eye out. You might want to call Luca."

Calling him is the last thing I want to do. True, a hitman is pretty good at tracking people down, especially ones who are trying to hide, but their targets have a disturbing tendency to stop living. "I'd rather find her alive," I say dryly. "I'm just trying to figure out where she'd go."

"Um, home?" Jack suggests.

It's stupid that didn't occur to me. Maybe it's because I've never really had a home to run to. Maybe it's because Adair's always running from hers. "She had a fight with her brother. It's doubtful that she's there now."

"That place is the size of Versailles. If she wants she can avoid her brother for months. Look, if it was me and some guy screwed me over, I'd wind up at home." He makes a good point, but he's getting the wrong idea.

"I didn't..." I stop. Why bother trying to explain that we'd both screwed up? Right now, I need to be fixing things. "Thanks."

"So, I take it you've crossed her off your list?" Jack asks.

"You could say that."

"Where does that leave us?" Trust him to be direct. It's how we operate. There wasn't time on an operation for being passive aggressive.

I think about Malcolm and how he hurt her, about her father and how he used her. There's something rotten in Valmont, and it needs to be weeded out as much for me as for her. "Nothing else changes. Not until I talk to Malcolm MacLaine."

Jack doesn't try to argue the point. "I'll let you know if I see her," he says before we hang up.

Going to Windfall is a long shot by any stretch of the imagination, but maybe I'm wrong. Maybe a home is a place you run to no matter how much pain you've experienced there. I wouldn't know.

"Well, buddy, wish me luck. I'm going to track her down and make her listen to what I need to say." I lean down and stroke Zeus's head. He whimpers like he's hoping I have a better plan than that. Even a dog recognizes what sets Adair MacLaine apart. She has champagne taste and a whiskey temper—and I'm on the wrong side of both.

The sultry summer day begins to fade as I drive out of the city. The sun is beginning to set, purple seeping across the horizon, when I reach Valmont. Stopping at the gates of Windfall, I wait for the security guard to put down his sandwich. He steps out of the gatehouse, clipboard in hand, and motions for me to roll down the window.

"Name?" he says in a bored tone.

"Sterling Ford." I tap the Aston's steering wheel as his finger trails down his list. I wait for him to ask me why I'm here or call up for permission. Not that he or anyone else is going to stop me from getting to Adair if she's in there. It would be nice to do this the easy way, though.

Instead, he nods. "Thank you, Mr. Ford. One moment."

I made the guest permission list. That must mean that I'm still on Malcolm's good side. He's not the MacLaine I want keeping me around. I tear down the drive, swerving around to the back. Since I'm not here to see Malcolm, there's no need to walk through the front door.

No matter how much time passes, I remember every detail of this house. It's a bit like the ninth circle of hell—not a place that you forget if you make it out alive. I wasn't welcome here five years ago. I certainly never made a guest list. But I've been here plenty of times—each instance more memorable than the last. If Jack is right and Adair came home, she didn't bother with the front door. That's the first trick to surviving Windfall, keep a low profile. She would have gone around back, straight to the kitchen. I'll bet she's crying to Felix over a batch of cookies. The back entrance also has the benefit of being close to the servant's staircase. I can use it to get to Adair's wing of the house with little chance of running into anyone that I don't want to see.

I rap softly on the back door before letting myself in. The Windfall kitchen is huge, meant to accommodate multiple cooks and servers for parties and holidays. I've always been a little jealous of the pristine Viking appliances and marble counters. That was before, when I'd never had more than a closet-sized kitchen in Queens to use. Now, I wonder what the point of it is other than for show. Then again, that's the primary function of an estate like this. It's only here to show off the MacLaine wealth. I can see it for what it really is today: a family ego.

Felix looks up up from the pot on the stove. His hand, holding a wooden spoon, freezes in mid-air. He manages to cover his surprise well, but although his face remains blank, dislike narrows his eyes. I wonder how long he can keep up the charade of pretending I'm a stranger. He's done an excellent job so far.

"May I help you?" he asks. The sham continues, it seems.

"Don't act like you don't remember me, Felix," I said dryly. He played along before. We both know exactly who I am, and I'm guessing he knows why I came back. Adair always confided in him.

"You're Daddy's friend," a small voice pipes up and I turn to see Malcolm's daughter sitting at the kitchen island.

Large, blue eyes loom in her round face and she studies me critically. She obviously takes after her aunt.

"I am, but I came to see your aunt," I say to her. Felix might take Adair's side, but kids, in my experience, don't know how to go along with deception. They might hide a cookie behind their back, but guilt is usually written all over their face. That makes her my new best friend. If Adair is here, she won't be able to hide it. I'm not certain Felix will feel inclined to tell me if he's seen her.

The girl purses her lips and shakes her head. "Auntie Dair isn't here. She's been gone all night. Do *you* know where she's been?"

Now that's a loaded question.

"I don't. That's why I'm here," I say softly. I take a stool next to hers and turn my focus back to Felix. I suppose I have to sweet talk him now.

"Don't look at me," he says before I can press him for answers. "I haven't seen her since this afternoon. She spoke with Malcolm and left in... a hurry." Felix inclines his head, his eyes darting to the upper floors of the house. So he heard the fight. That's not a surprise. Felix knows everything that goes on in this house.

"I suspect you've seen her since I have," he says as he resumes stirring the pot. I don't miss the irony.

I start to tell him to have her call me, but he's unlikely to pass along that message. I can't blame Felix for not liking me. He's only ever heard Adair's side of the story, and I'm sure she painted me as the villain. I'm going to need a different ally. Someone she'll actually listen to. That's the trouble. Most of our mutual friends are loyal to her. There's no one in her family she'll listen to. She's too stubborn.

"Would you like hot chocolate? Felix is making me some," the girl says.

The answer is sitting right next to me. How didn't I see it? Adair loves the girl. I saw that the night I came to dinner. She might avoid her brother. Felix might not pass along a message. But a kid? She can make sure that Adair knows I came around. "What's your name again?"

"I'm not supposed to tell that to strangers," she says.

I see she has the hot and cold attitude of a MacLaine. Hot chocolate one minute, snubbing you the next. "I'm no stranger, remember? I know your dad and your aunt." I don't mind working for her trust. It will be good practice getting a MacLaine female to see past my flaws. I stick out a hand to her. "I'm Sterling. It's nice to see you again."

She takes my outstretched hand with a giggle. "Elodie MacLaine."

"That's a beautiful name," I say. I'm not above flattering this kid if it means getting closer to Adair.

"Everyone calls me Ellie," she says seriously, "but I think you should call me Elodie."

I raise an eyebrow. "Why is that?"

"You're in business with my dad," she says to me. "You talked about it at dinner."

"I see." I nod in understanding. "We have a formal relationship."

"Yes. Are you in business with my aunt?"

"Does she always ask so many questions?" I say to Felix.

"You have no idea," he says with a laugh. He pretends to focus on the pot of hot chocolate, making a show of acting like I'm not there, but I catch him stealing quick glances in my direction. He knows something. He probably knows where Adair has gone, but he's not going to tell me. He pours two mugs of hot chocolate, drops marshmallows into one, and places them in front of us.

"Is this your favorite?" I ask, picking mine up.

"*You* ask a lot of questions for an adult," she says pointedly.

"You're not exactly shy," I say to her.

"Scorpios usually aren't," Felix says. He holds up a finger when she reaches for her own mug. "Remember last time. We let it cool."

"Your aunt is a Scorpio," I tell her.

"I know." She's busy poking marshmallows like she can cool her drink faster if she plays with it. "We have a secret club."

"Can I join?"

She appraises me for a second, and I can already tell that I'm coming up short. "Are you a Scorpio?"

"I am not." There's no point in lying to her. That won't score me any points with her or her aunt.

She shrugs her tiny shoulders. "Sorry. Scorpios only."

"I understand." Elodie might be the friendliest member of the MacLaine family, but even she has the elitist streak necessary to call Valmont home.

"Can you tell your aunt that I was here?" I ask her.

She bobs her head. "I can do that, Mr. Ford."

We're back to formality. Honestly, it's one of the best business transactions I've had in a while.

"Thanks for the hot chocolate, Felix."

"I'd say any time..." He trails off.

"Understandable. I'm just going to pop up to her room."

"If you want, but she's not here," he says with a shake of his head. "I'm not lying to you."

"Would you admit if you were?" I ask.

He tips his head, conceding my point's valid. I don't bother to argue with him on this. Felix and I aren't likely to ever be best friends, and it's not like I need him to show me the way. I wind my way up the narrow staircase that leads into the family quarters.

The first floor of Windfall is all for show. A foyer that could house a tennis court. A sitting room meant to host cocktail parties. An atrium that's basically a ballroom. Upstairs is where the MacLaines live their lives, but that doesn't make it much homier. I pause at the top of the staircase, remembering the last time I was here. It seems like a lifetime ago. I guess that's because it was. Glancing to the corridor on the left, I see that they've taken down her mother's art. I can only imagine how Adair felt about that. I suppose that wing of the house is occupied by Malcolm and his wife now. I don't go that way. Instead, I take a right and find my way to the far side of the house. Adair's room overlooks the gardens below. It's not really a room. At least, not in the traditional sense. It's practically a condo. A living area, two bathrooms, a bedroom, a reading room. I wander through each, but she's not here, like Felix said. Still, she's everywhere. A lot of things might have changed since I left, but there are pieces of the girl she was littered everywhere. The clues paint a picture of her life while I was gone. Books are piled unceremoniously on the floor next to her bed, on the desk overlooking the gardens, shoved into shelves built into the walls. There's no rhyme or reason to any of them. She's never bothered with alphabetizing. These books are read. These books are loved. Somehow, seeing that—knowing that part of her survived—reminds me that, as much as she tries to act like there's nothing left between us, there's too much to be ignored. We'll always have this. This shared love. This shared language.

For one moment, I stand there, hands shoved in my pockets, and stare at all these pieces of her.

A different life flashes before my eyes. A little house with a covered porch and a wicker swing, somewhere far from here. Adair is tucked under a blanket on it, reading, I'm next to her with a book in my hands, and everything is right with the world. Some people want to believe in fairy tales. Those aren't real. I believe in real. I want us to be real.

I shake off the sentimental bullshit. It's not doing me any good to sit around and fantasize. That's not what got me this far, and it won't get me where I'm going. She's not here. I shouldn't be surprised. It was a long shot, no matter what Jack said. Adair has never felt at home here. It's not the first place she would run. I used to know exactly where she would go. The trouble is that I don't know where that place is anymore. Or do I?

She ran to me. She came to me. And for a few hours, I'd gotten everything I wanted.

Adair MacLaine's trust. Her desire. Her love? Maybe.

It gives me hope that we can get past this misunderstanding, but can I ever admit that's not what I came here for? All of this was part of my plan. I wanted her to trust me, to love me, to want me. I didn't plan on wanting her back.

Some things don't change. That's why she's not here. I knew she wouldn't be. She always wanted to leave this life behind. Was leaving me behind the first step in finally doing that?

What life does she want?

The publishing house. She wants to be an editor. It's the only concrete thing I know she wants. I whip out my phone, trying to remember the name. Bluebell or something like that. A quick search reminds me. Bluebird Press. That's the publishing house her father left her. The one she got a job at without mentioning her last name. It might have seemed conniving a month ago. Now I see it as a means of survival. Maybe her brother blew that, but if I know Adair, she's not going to give up on her dream that easily. She might not be there now, but I can sit out front and wait for her to show up tomorrow, or the day after, or however long it takes if she keeps avoiding my calls.

I'm halfway down the hall and on my way back to Nashville when Malcolm finds me. He's abandoned his suit in favor of a pair of khakis and a button-down with its sleeves rolled to his elbows. That's as casual as he gets. He holds out a hand. "Security informed me you were here. I thought you might have come to see me, but..."

I don't bother fumbling for an excuse as to why I'm down the hall from his sister's room. Malcolm has plenty of people stroking his fragile ego, I don't have to bother. There are more important things for me to focus on at the moment. "I'm looking for Adair." I slide my phone into my pocket. "Have you heard from her?"

"Not since this afternoon," he says coolly. He studies me for a moment, but seems to come up short in his analysis. It's the dance we've done since the beginning, turning circles around one another and waiting for the right moment to strike. I'm done with the sidestepping. It's time to upend his perfect, if false, reality.

"That's right," I say, taking a step closer. "She told me about that."

"She did?" He's surprised. I guess he doesn't have much experience with people confiding in him.

I smile widely and begin to walk away. "Adair tells me most things."

"You two have gotten close." Malcolm follows me as swiftly as his pride will allow.

He still hasn't put it together. He doesn't remember meeting me before. He doesn't recall how his family tried to ruin my life. If I ever had a moment's doubt about destroying him, it's gone now. He deserves whatever he gets. There's no need to hide now. I pause near the stairs down to the kitchens. "We've always been close."

"How close were you with her?" He squints as if trying to see me more clearly. Then he glances over to the servant's staircase, his face momentarily puzzled, as if he can't figure out why we're here.

"I came in through the kitchen," I explain.

"You came in through..." his words trail into a question. Maybe a few questions. "How do you know where the kitchen is?"

Malcolm MacLaine wants answers, but it's too fun to dangle them over his head just out of reach. I'm not giving him the carrot, he's going to have to jump for it. "I think if you try, you'll remember me."

There's a pause as his head tilts, his eyes still narrowed as he studies my face. All he saw when I showed up for his father's funeral was my Italian suit, my Breitling watch, my Aston Martin. He's never bothered to really stop and look at me. He saw as far as he needed to see to deem me worthy of sharing his air.

"You're..." He stops and stares at me.

Took him long enough.

"You were at my wedding," he says.

Now we're getting there.

"I used to come around here a lot," I say as I start down the stairs, Malcolm at my heels. The truth is that I never spent much time with him back then. We'd been introduced, but he was busy learning the family business, which as far as I could tell back then, meant covering up sins with money and with a powerful family name. He didn't have time to bother with taking out Adair's trash.

"My father didn't like you much." He shrugs as though it's not important.

"Your father never had much patience for the peasant class." Especially if one of those peasants was dating his daughter.

Malcolm doesn't deny it. He leans into it. "His opinion might have changed if you'd come back while he was alive."

"I'm afraid I've never cared much for Angus MacLaine's opinion." I would have come back a year ago if I had.

"And mine?"

"There's only one MacLaine I'm interested in," I say,

lowering my voice as we reach the floor below, "and if you don't start keeping your opinions to yourself when it comes to Adair's choices, then we're going to have a problem."

He blinks. "We are?"

"*We* are," I say.

We're back to the dance, debating our next moves. My gut says Malcolm will try to smooth this over. There's too much for him to lose, and he's never had the killer instinct his father had. I've watched the MacLaine family business dealings for years—in the newspaper and on television, through mutual business associates—Angus went for the throat. Malcolm wants the easiest path on offer.

"I want to buy your holdings in MacLaine Media," he says finally. "How much?"

"Believe me, you can't afford it," I say. I might be convinced to sell if Adair asks me to, but I made certain it wouldn't be that easy. Maybe I knew somewhere deep-down that I might fall for her again, and that's why I put a check on myself. Luca and Jack have to be convinced to sell as well. They'll never sell to a MacLaine. I made them swear. My holdings alone won't be enough to keep the family empire under his control. Even if the company and its ownership are private, he still needs to control over 50% of voting shares in order to control the company's Board of Directors.

"What about my sister? It sounds like you got what you wanted." So much for him claiming she wasn't for sale. He'd sell her body and soul right now if I handed him back the keys to his kingdom.

"I want Adair to be happy. If she wants to be an editor,

let her. If she wants to have her own place, let her. You don't own her."

"And you do?" he asks, crossing his arms over his chest. "Because you came here asking to *buy* her. You said you'd trade the company for her. Does she know that?"

"Yes," I lie.

Now I have to find Adair before he does. I need time to explain my plan before she hears it from him. Blood may be thicker than water, but MacLaine blood runs hotter than whiskey. My only chance of keeping this under control is to be the first person she hears this from. "Your father liked to think he owned people," I continue. "He was so obsessed with holding power over people that he never saw the bigger picture."

"What's that?"

"Power, wealth, control—none of it means shit when you're dead."

A muscle in Malcolm's jaw ticks. "I think maybe you should leave."

"There's nothing I want here, anyway."

"Really? You came back for a reason. Obviously, my father didn't pay you off well enough," Malcolm snarls.

So he doesn't know what happened. That's how meaningless I was in Malcolm's eyes. I assumed Adair felt the same until recently. Now? I'm no longer sure. What I do know is that there is no amount of money or status or power that his son can offer me to change my mind now. I may love Adair, but I hate the MacLaines and I always will. "He didn't pay me at all."

"Is that the problem? Is that what it will take for you to leave my family alone?"

"That depends." There's nothing he can offer me, but I'm curious what it's worth to him. "Are you lumping Adair into your family? She seems to have abandoned you."

"Adair will come back. She's a MacLaine." He sounds so sure of himself. It's the misplaced confidence of someone who hasn't heard the word *no* enough in his life.

But I know two things: Adair doesn't want to come back here and I won't let her. "Not if I have anything to say about it."

"She understands that her family is the most important thing—"

"Don't bother selling me the lies you've tricked her into believing," I interrupt before I can hear more of his egocentric bullshit. "I'm going to help her see that she has more— that she deserves more—than being held down by the MacLaine name."

"Adair will never burn that bridge," he says. "Neither will you."

"I'll help her light the match and then I'll pour gasoline on your funeral pyre. Don't fuck with me." I take two steps, bringing myself nose to nose with him. Adrenaline pumps through me. He thinks he knows me, because he thinks I'm like him: desperate to hold on to my wealth and my power. I took a risk coming back here, but the reward will be worth it.

Ginny waltzes past with a bouquet of freshly cut roses. She stops in her tracks when she spots us. There's a moment of hesitation — panic flickers over her face — but just as quickly she's composed and back to being a Stepford wife. "Why are you shouting?"

"It's none of your business," Malcolm snarls at her.

She winces but recovers quickly, lifting her chin in the air. Hatred burns in her dark eyes. Maybe she's not as beholden to him as I thought. "What happens in this house is my business."

"This is between myself and Mr. Ford," he says a bit more gently.

But she shakes her head. "If it has to do with this family, then—"

"Ginny, when I want your opinion, I will tell you what it is!" he roars.

"Is that so? Then you can run the whole house!" She shoves the roses into his arms, petals falling to the floor from sheer force, and storms away.

"Maybe she should burn some bridges, too," I say dryly.

"My wife is as loyal as my sister. I wouldn't expect someone like you to understand loyalty," Malcolm says. "Foster kid. College drop-out. Discharged from the Marine Corps. Most of your file is sealed, which means you did something wrong."

"All that work and the investigator didn't tell you I was at your wedding. You need better people." I flash him a smug smile. It looks like someone finally did his homework. He knows who I am — or what I let the world know about me, at least. Most of it is public record. Anyone can find out my mother is dead, and that I dropped out of school. That's only part of the picture, though. No one gets to see the rest. They don't get to know *why* I am those things, and they definitely don't get to know how much of my true identity resides there.

"At least I have people. At least I understand the importance of family."

"That's where you're wrong, Malcolm. If you want to know the importance of family, ask a man who's never had one. I know what it's like to have no one, which means I can recognize a man who's alone in the world, no matter how many people he surrounds himself with." I edge closer to him and lower my voice so that he has to strain to hear me. It will make it all that much harder for him. "You're mistaking loyalty for abuse. You don't think of your wife, your sister, even your daughter, as anything more than possessions. That's why you treat them the way you do, because they aren't worth the upkeep. But objects can be lost, Malcolm. They can be taken."

His mouth opens, but nothing comes out. I've managed to shock him into silence. Even the great Malcolm MacLaine has no retort, no snide order, no cutting aside. I've found his weakest point and buried a knife into it. He wants to see the women in his life as commodities, investment pieces, and bargaining chips, just like his father. They're not his family, they're assets on a list.

And what happens when a sister stops falling in line with the conditions of being a MacLaine? Or when a wife shows her true colors in front of a business associate? What happens when an asset becomes a liability?

"Don't worry. I'll show myself out." I leave him to piece back together the shreds of his worldview. He won't get far. I came here to destroy the MacLaine family. Now I understand there's no point in doing that. They destroyed themselves a long time ago, devoured themselves from within and left the rest to rot. All that's left now is to root out their poison from this place, this city, and the woman I love.

I just have to find her first.

7

ADAIR

THE PAST

I could kill Poppy. First, she can't take a hint and plans this stupid party. Then, she makes me open presents for an hour while Sterling apparently drank with Cyrus, and now, she brought up his present!

"But my dad's out of town," I say to him gently. "I thought you would stay the night..." I hope the implication is clear. My offer still stands. I wish he hadn't been drinking, but I can't exactly blame him. Plus, I've been pumping myself up for this all week. Poppy knows this. I confided as much to her when I decided I was ready to sleep with him.

There's a long pause. Sterling stares fixedly at me without saying a thing.

"Sterling—" I begin.

"Don't bother," he slurs the last words. "I think I better go, *Lucky*. You have enough new toys to play with."

"I don't want those," I coax, wrapping an arm around him and pressing my body against his. "Let me make it up to you."

His angry look turns blank, like his processing time has

slowed, then he shoots me a crooked grin. "That was the plan, wasn't it?"

"It can still be like that," I promise.

"How?"

"Follow me." I smile and take his hand. We head out the main entrance and toward the pavilion, now empty and cold despite the gas heaters. Everyone really has moved inside. Instead of cutting towards the pool house directly, though, I head toward the pavilion.

"This your idea of private?" Sterling mumbles. "Where are the cameras in here, anyway?"

"There aren't any," I say brightly. If I can get him away from my friends long enough, I know he'll come around. At least, I hope he will. "That's why we're here."

He narrows his eyes quizzically, and for a moment the brooding stops.

The sides of the pavilion are still covered by roll-down canvases, tied together to form a temporary wall to keep the heat in—they'll also keep curious eyes out. I undo a couple of knots and pull the canvas to the side. "After you, sir."

"What am I? Alice headed to Wonderland?" He shoots me a sloppy grin, seems to think better of it, and replaces the look with a scowl.

"You're not Alice. But I did plan on making a stop in Wonderland."

He's ducking through the opening, so I can't read his reaction. If that didn't cheer him up, probably nothing will.

I follow him through and we come out exactly where I planned, on a path winding between a garden and the garage. Sterling is walking ahead of me already, too far ahead.

"Stop!"

He turns slowly in the darkness. "What now?"

"That path has motion-activated lights. They're wired into the security system."

It takes him a moment to understand what I'm getting at. "Who lives like this?"

"Everyone I know, unfortunately." I point to the tall hedge that walls the garden. "It's through here."

"Your Wonderland has a lot of gates, Lucky." Before I can go any further, he grabs me and spins me into his arms.

For a second, I consider fighting it. I give in, instead. My body molds to his. I taste the sharp sting of whiskey on his tongue as a greedy hand moves from my hip to my ass. His fingers fiddle with my short hemline before dipping under it to fondle the curve of my buttocks. I'm so lost to him that it takes me a moment to process what he's doing—it feels too good. I'm painfully aware that he's touching me in places I usually only dream about. The floodlights wake me up, and I feel a cold rush of air against my bare skin.

Yelping, I jerk my skirt back over my ass. We must have stumbled back far enough to trip the lights, which means we've also tripped the security system. I reach for his hand to grab him and get him out of here, but he refuses to move.

"Now I can see you," he says silkily. He yanks me back against him, and I realize just how strong he is. I can't fight it. Not that I want to. This is what I wanted tonight. Just maybe with less cameras.

"We shouldn't," I murmur as his hand slips between my legs, bypassing the scrap of underwear I wore as a nod to propriety and dipping deep inside me. "Sterling!"

"Ask nicely." He kisses my neck.

"Not here." My eyes shutter despite my objection, my core clenching around his probing fingers.

"I didn't hear a question," he says.

"Can we please go to the poolhouse?" I pant, trying not to moan.

His tongue flickers along my earlobe. "Why? What do you want to do there?"

"You know what," I snap impatiently, but I can't seem to break free of him. It feels too good.

"I need you to say it, Lucky."

"So we can sleep together," I whisper, feeling heat explode on my cheeks.

"Like a nap?"

I groan and it morphs into something guttural as the pad of his thumbs finds my ticking center. "Fuck. I want to fuck."

He pulls aways, still kneading me, and raises an eyebrow.

"Will you please fuck me?" I pant. I'm not just ready. I'm bursting.

Sterling withdraws his fingers and lifts them to his lips. He sucks each one, a slow smile spreading over his face. "Lead the way."

I don't waste any time dragging him towards the hedge.

"My dad has tried to fix this hedge a dozen times," I explain. "He still hasn't figured out why he can't." I give Sterling a wink and step sideways through a gap in the hedge wall. A couple of branches snap as I pass, just like they always do. "Alright, you can come through. Make sure you don't get poked in the eye."

I hear a wordless grumble, followed shortly by an *ouch*,

but Sterling manages to force his way through. He takes a second to shake off the foliage and look around. "It's a garden," he says, surprised.

My mother's garden. I don't tell him. That's not what tonight is supposed to be. Of course, nothing tonight has turned out how I wanted.

"I hope you're not too drunk to climb through a window," I say, pointing to the pool house, which forms one of the garden's four walls.

"All this to avoid your own cameras?" he says, incredulous.

"Exactly."

The big picture window overlooking the garden can't be opened, but the one through the kitchen does. I push it up, straddle the bottom of the sill, one leg at a time, and I'm through.

"Welcome to Wonderland." I say triumphantly. "Now we can be alone." I give him a sexy smile, but I doubt he can see it through the darkness.

"Too bad I only rate the pool house," he says, his dark silhouette coming towards me.

Good. He's joking. We might be able to rescue my birthday after all.

"We'll see about upgrading you next time," I tease.

Our bodies collide awkwardly in the darkness, but as soon as he touches me it doesn't matter. I cover his lips with mine, and he responds instantly, hungrily. I explore the stubble along his neck, planting kisses and slowly making my way towards his chest.

"I suppose lights are out of the question?" he says with a deep purr.

"If you want there to be a sequel," I say, pausing to nip his earlobe before continuing, "we'd better not."

"Whatever you say, Lucky." He puts both hands on my hips and spins me away from him. His hands are greedy on my body, and his stubble scratches along my neck as he kisses me there.

"Oh, that's nice," I moan, rolling my head onto his chest.

"You know exactly how hot you are, don't you?" He sighs before planting kisses on my shoulder.

"Do I?" I whisper, melting into him.

His hands slide up slowly from my hips toward my breasts, which tighten in anticipation. Sterling's fingers glide over the tight points of my nipples and pinch slightly. The other hand wraps around my neck, and I gasp as he turns my head to the side and kisses me again.

There's nothing but him. I feel the bulge in his jeans against my ass, and I don't have to tell my body how to respond. I collapse backward into him, needing him to touch every part of me. My hands search for his body in the darkness, but he swats them away. He's in control. That's clear. I'd argue, but I have no complaints.

He trails kisses along the way from my shoulder to my neck. A jolt of lightning crashes through me when I feel the first nip of his teeth on my neck. He goes from sweet-and-soft to rough-and-demanding, and back again, until I have no idea what will come next.

He whispers in my ear, "Let's find somewhere more comfortable."

Our bodies break apart, and it takes a moment for my senses to return to normal. "Follow me."

I could lead him to one of the bedrooms, but the couch in the next room is much closer.

We stumble through the darkness and I push him onto the couch before he ever realizes it's there.

"I guess you know what you want, huh?"

The picture window overlooking the garden gives the sitting room a lot of natural moonlight, and I can see Sterling's features again. His eyes are narrow, but it's not because he's straining to see in the darkness. He's not even looking at me. I can feel the gulf between us widen.

But I won't let it. Not again. He's drunk. It's not ideal, but I'm ready. And besides, he's not too drunk to remember if the last few minutes are any indication. That's what matters.

I climb into his lap and begin to kiss his forehead, his cheeks, his perfect mouth. He's surprisingly slow to respond, so I place his hands on my ass and pull my top off. If he suddenly needs the paint-by-number approach I can oblige.

I kiss him again. Our bodies collide again. But there is no softness there, just hard tension.

"What's *with* you?" The words are out of my mouth before I can stop them.

He stiffens further. "It's nothing."

"Tell me."

"Sorry. I was thinking."

"You were thinking?" I repeat. How can he be thinking right now? I'm barely breathing.

"I was wondering how long it would be until the next one," he says, as if it explains everything.

"You're going to need to give me more to go on." I bend forward to kiss him again, but he stops me.

"What you were talking about earlier: the sharing."

The sharing? What is he talking about?

"Do you get me all to yourself for a while? Or maybe you plan to take turns?" He spits the words out like a bad taste. In the greyscale of the moonlight, his eyes are cold and accusing. "I'm just trying to figure out what the rules are."

My heart rate ratchets up again, but now it has nothing to do with his hands or his lips or his body. "What the fuck are you talking about, Sterling?"

The cursing turns him on like a switch. In a flash he spins me off of him and onto the couch. He leaps up, his face contorting in the moonlight and shifting to that of a stranger. Dangerous. Cold. A shiver runs through me. What have I done?

"I went to find you earlier. Here, in the pool house."

I remember. I was talking with Ava and Darcy. They were trying to get me to dish about Sterling.

"You promised you'd share me," he jogs my memory when I don't respond. "I just want to know what that's like. Do I sleep with you sometimes, but maybe if you're busy I throw them a bone?"

"What the..." Bile rises in my throat. I'm not sure if it's the idea of them touching him or the idea that he might be into it. Why else would he bring it up? I want to puke.

"You went along with it!" he rages. I try to interject, but he's already off again. "I don't get you people. Everything in your lives is just a toy waiting for you to get bored with it.

Including me. Why not share me now? Didn't they teach you that in school?"

"That's not fair. You know I didn't want any of this to happen. It was supposed to be just us." I'm ashamed when my voice quavers. How could I have been stupid enough to let him get close enough to hurt me?

"Don't be mad at me for finding out, Lucky. I'm smarter than you're used to." He turns to go, but stops at the kitchen door. "Admit it, I was supposed to be your birthday present. Because of course you are the type to get herself something. So let me spare you the trouble of *re-gifting* me."

My heart crashes inward like a black hole. When I look up, he's gone. *Some days are diamonds.*

But those days are never my birthday.

8

STERLING

I decide to major in philosophy.

It's a worthless degree, but one I can do on my own time. No classes required. So far, I'm working on what I call the invisible man theorem, which basically means that if I act invisible, I will be invisible. I'm testing it using two different methods.

The first is by skipping class. It turns out that in college, unlike high school, no one gives a shit if you don't show up to classes. No one. Not the professor. Not the administration. Not even your friends. I know, because I'm on my second week of testing the theory, and no one has even checked in, except Cyrus, who only stops by the room to grab shit a couple times a week. If I pretend I'm not there, he goes right along with it, only speaking when spoken to.

The other method of testing involves social invisibility, or the belief that if I show up at a party, say nothing to anyone, grab a bottle of booze, and take off, no one will even notice. But is this because I'm invisible or because people are shit-faced? I don't know. But I'll keep testing the theory until I can be certain.

There's one more theory, but I haven't given it a name yet. It's basically that a son can't ever escape becoming his father. I might not be the first to think of that one. I'd ask a professor, but I can't be bothered to actually enroll in a philosophy class. Not if it means skewing the findings of my first theory, which I'm dedicating myself to completely, and have been since the night of Adair's birthday party.

The door cracks open and Cyrus steps inside. His gaze sweeps over the room before landing on me.

"Hey," I grunt, grabbing a t-shirt off the couch and pulling it over my head. Today, we'll talk.

"I just needed to grab something," he says, as if it's some sort of revelation.

"Cool." I pick up a few bottles to check their contents, but each of them is bone dry. Cyrus stands there, watching me.

"When was the last time you even went to class?" Cyrus asks. "I haven't seen you in Econ in two weeks."

"What do you care?" I drop onto my bed and stare at the ceiling. If he noticed I wasn't in class, it undermines my working theory. He shouldn't notice my absence, and he definitely shouldn't care. I'm going to have to reconsider some things.

"No reason. I just thought you were on scholarship." He waits for me to respond, when I don't, he continues, "You okay, man?"

"Don't worry about me," I say flatly. "I'm living my best life."

"I can see that." He looks around our dorm room. "You want me to have my maid stop by?"

"Doesn't bother me," I say.

"I can see that, too." He sighs, and it's a sound I recognize. Disappointment.

I must have achieved a new standard of disappointing, if full-time party animal and part-time roommate Cyrus Eaton thinks I'm underachieving.

"Look, have you talked to..." he trails off as my phone begins to buzz on the coffee table. "Your phone is ringing."

"I hear it."

"Are you going to answer it?" he asks.

"Nah. It does that a lot. Nobody I want to talk to." I shift away from him, considering a nap.

The phone stops ringing, but then I hear Cyrus say, "Hello? Yeah, hold on."

I roll over and glare at him. So much for my nap.

"It's Francie," he says, holding it out to me.

It's too late to pretend that I'm gone, and he knows it. Cyrus is putting me on the spot. So much for being the cool roommate who's never here. Now he's definitely sticking his nose where it doesn't belong.

I jump off my bed and swipe the phone from him. "Hey."

"Sterling!" Francie's voice is a curious mix of relief and annoyance. "I've been calling you for a week."

I can picture her standing in her small, outdated kitchen with its shabby, seventies wallpaper and notched cabinets. She's probably leaning against the beige fridge, tapping her foot. I'd seen her do that a million times on the phone with whatever bill collector was on her ass that month. Now she's busy tracking me down.

"Sorry. Been busy. Classes and stuff."

Cyrus shakes his head at the lie and wanders into his side of our small closet. It's about the only thing he comes around for: a fresh change of clothes. He spends the rest of his time bouncing between random beds and rooms at his family hotel. This place is just his oversized suitcase. I can't remember the last time he actually slept here.

"I bet you're busy," she says. I think she hopes this will prompt more conversation.

"Yep." I, on the other hand, prefer to keep our chat as short as possible.

"I've been thinking," Francie says, and a warning bell goes off in my head.

In my experience, it's never a good thing when a woman says she's been thinking. "Yeah?"

"I'm going to drive down for Thanksgiving!" she says excitedly. There's a pause. "Sterling? Did you hear me?"

I think I'm supposed to jump up and down, but the idea of Francie coming to Valmont opens a pit in my stomach. "Sure, whatever."

"Unless you don't want me to…"

Great. Now I'm hurting her feelings. I do my best to drum up some enthusiasm, but the result is a lackluster: "No, it's cool."

"Will your roommate be around?" she asks.

I glance over to the closet Cyrus is still rummaging around in. "Doubtful."

"Then I can sleep on your couch. This is going to be

fun. I can't wait to see what you've been up to and meet your friends."

She's going to be pretty disappointed on both counts.

"Yeah, can't wait." We say goodbye. She promises to email me details later this week, and I hang up the phone. "Fuck."

"Something wrong with your m...Francie?" Cyrus corrects himself. He pokes his head out from the closet, eyebrow raised.

"She's coming for Thanksgiving," I say flatly.

"And you aren't happy about that." He steps out and studies me. "I thought you were dreading leaving her alone."

"I was, but that doesn't mean I want my foster mom bunking with me for half a week." I scope out the floor, my eyes landing on a bottle of cheap rum that's still half-full. Jackpot. I grab it and unscrew the lid.

"She's going to stay here?" Cyrus asks.

"Is that a problem?" My response comes out a bit more ferociously than I intended. "I'll sleep on the couch."

I don't know why he'd give a shit. He's never here anyway.

"Not for me, but..." He glances around the room.

I follow his lead. My clothes are strewn around the floor, there's a box with a half-eaten pizza next to the couch. I don't even bother trying to count the empty bottles.

"Maybe she should stay in a hotel," he suggests.

"This is going to come as a shock to you, but not all of us have a big vault of gold at our disposal," I say.

If I know Francie, she's using all her extra money to drive down here. Two one-thousand-mile trips in one year is too much of a strain to expect her to have anything left over for a luxury like a cheap motel. Why did I say yes when she asked if it was okay?

"You're a bit of a dick," Cyrus says.

I shrug. Who cares what he thinks? Being nice didn't work out for me. It's how I wound up here. Being a dick is easier, and it comes naturally. "So what?"

Cyrus rolls his eyes. "I own a hotel."

There's no way I'm asking him for help.

"Use my family's suite. We'll be out of town anyway."

"Nope."

"Why do you make it so hard for people to like you?" Cyrus asks. "Look, think about it. In the meantime, do you want to come to a party? It looks like you could use something to drink."

I'm not sure if he's mocking me or if he's serious. I glance down at the nearly empty rum bottle. It hardly matters since he's right. I might not be willing to accept his help when it comes to Francie, but I'll take him up on free booze. It will save me the time of finding a party on my own, and any party Cyrus is going to is sure to have top shelf stuff.

"What time?"

"Around eight." He runs his eyes up and down me. "That gives you time to take a shower."

"What are you saying?" I ask.

"You stink, Ford." He kicks a wadded t-shirt near his feet to mine. "And find something clean to wear."

Tomorrow, I need to deal with Francie's visit. I'll get my shit together then. Tonight? I might as well escape.

9

ADAIR

PRESENT DAY

So maybe I'm obsessing. Chances are, the locked drawer has a few expired credit cards, maybe an old checkbook, and, if I'm lucky, a bottle of whiskey stashed in it — probably nothing more. But that's the thing about growing up in a house built from smoke and mirrors: I'm always looking for the solution to the mystery, always trying to understand why.

Why my mother married my father? Why she stayed with a man that cheated and lied? Why he had to rule over all of us with an iron fist? Why? Why? Why? I'm always full of more questions, and there are never answers in sight. If there's even a possibility that the answer to one of those questions is in that locked drawer, then I have to find it.

It helps that it's a distraction from Sterling, too, because it turns out that I'm not very good at wallowing. I can't stand it. I can't stand the lingering, raw sensation of tears in my throat. I can't stand the self-recrimination. I can't stand not knowing which one of us to be more angry at: him or me. I just want to feel anything else, and right now, obsessive curiosity is winning out. Tying the robe tighter, I abandon my room service and grab my keycard. Stepping into the hall, I walk right into a man heading the opposite direction.

"Sorry."

"It's okay. Hey, are..." He trails off as I continue past him with nothing more than the apology. I'm heading in the direction of the elevator before I get caught chatting with my new neighbor. I'm not looking to make friends at the Eaton. I step inside the elevator in time to see his back disappearing into a suite on the opposite side of the corridor.

Geoff isn't at the concierge desk, so I grab a passing bellboy.

"Excuse me," I stop him. "Is there any way I can get a screwdriver?"

"Is something broken?" he asks in confusion. I'm guessing your average hotel guest doesn't ask for a screwdriver.

"I'm in suite six-fourteen, and my father left a drawer locked. He passed away. I'm just trying to sort through his things."

Maybe it's too much truth, because he seems to shrink an inch, like he wants to retreat to a safe hiding place. "I'm not certain I should" —

"Is there a problem, Anthony?" Mr. Randolph, the manager, steps in, adjusting the cuffs of his suit jacket. His eyes widen when he glances my direction. "Miss MacLaine. I didn't know you were staying with us. Anthony, get whatever the lady asked for."

"But she asked for" —

"Whatever she asked for," he hisses through his teeth before plastering on a slippery smile and turning back to me. "I'm Mr. Randolph, you may call me"—

"I remember you, *Mr. Randolph*," I cut him off before things get too friendly. You don't forget a man who glued his face to your family's ass at every opportunity. Randolph will find out I'm staying here, so I might as well get this over with. It will be good practice for telling people that my address is changing. "I'm moving into my family's apartment. I hope that's not a problem."

"Not at all!" He looks genuinely pleased at this announcement. Given how his eyes skim down my body, I'm not sure that's something I should be happy about. "That's delightful news. We'll be pleased to have you, and I will be certain the staff understands who you are."

I guess I won't have any trouble getting a screwdriver in the future.

"What do you require?" He asks. "I'd be happy to ensure it arrives swiftly."

There's no way I'm using the word screw in front of Mr. Wandering Eyes. "There's a drawer in my father's desk. He left it locked and I'm trying to sort through his things before I move in."

"We can call a locksmith," he suggests.

"I prefer to do it myself." I shake my head. Forget *prefer*. I *need* to do this now. I need answers. I need closure. It feels as though I've been standing still for the last five years, and I can't do it a second longer. I need to free myself from the past, whether that means cutting ties with my brother, walking away from Sterling, or breaking open a stupid locked drawer.

Anthony returns with a Philip's head screwdriver and hands it to me reluctantly. His eyes dart to his boss.

"A flathead would be better. I don't want to damage the wood." I pass it back to him and smile apologetically. Anthony forces one in return and leaves to find the correct tool.

"Perhaps Anthony can help you?" Mr. Randolph suggests. "I would hate for—"

"That's unnecessary," I back up a few steps, hoping he doesn't follow me. "Thank you."

"Once you're settled, perhaps we could have dinner," he suggests before I can make a clean getaway.

"Um, sure." I have no idea why I agree, even super-ficially.

"To acquaint you you with our services," he adds, reading the skepticism on my face. "As one of the Eaton's oldest patrons, it's the least we can do to welcome you."

"That will be nice." I force myself to say. Something occurs to me then. Mr. Randolph has always been the type to show up at the table when my family is dining at the hotel restaurant. He's present for every function we've attended in the hotel ballroom. He's got an over-inflated sense of self-importance and a serious obsession with being close to the wealthy elite of Nashville. That means he might remember why my father bought the apartment in the first place. "Do you know how long the apartment has been in my family?"

"I don't recall," he says. "But I'll look into it and we can discuss it over dinner."

"Of course." And like anyone who spends their time worming into the upper rungs of society, he knows he needs to be important to stay there. He's not going to tell me anything until he gets his reward. That's a problem for another day.

"Well, I better head back. I have a lot to sort through."

Like years of emotional baggage.

"Do call down if you need help," he says. "I'll make sure someone gets you the proper tool for the job."

"Thanks." I can't say I like the sound of that. Mr. Randolph must see me as another way to get in with the Valmont crowd. I'm just another heiress in his eyes. If he only knew. It's not as though I'm too helpless to jimmy open a locked drawer. I learned the fine art of getting past a lock in my early teens, back when my parents bothered to lock up the booze. My mother's idea. My father, like most of the other Valmont parents, could have cared less about what me or my brother was doing with their friends. I'll get dressed, go to the store, and get one along with some basics: a change of clothes, toiletries, a toothbrush. At least then I can avoid returning to Windfall for a few days.

Chances are that I don't even need a stupid screwdriver to open the drawer. I'm brainstorming other ways to get the drawer open as I step off the elevator, and my focus is so intense I don't even see him.

"Got somewhere to be, Lucky?" Sterling's voice rushes over me like a surge of cold water, sending chills dancing along my spine. It's not the effect he usually has on me, but it's no less dizzying.

It takes effort to face him, especially since I'm in a robe and tennis shoes with no socks. Oh, and because the last time he saw me I was sprawled naked on his bed. There's that, too. "What are you doing here?"

"I think that's my line." He moves toward me and I move backward instinctively. Sterling stops, a frown marring his perfect face. "We need to talk."

I can't help snorting. People in couple's counseling need to talk. Friends need to talk. Whatever we are? It requires more than talking. We need to scream. We need to throw shit. At least, I do. But I settle for agreeing with him. "Yes, we do."

"Those texts aren't what you think," he begins.

That's how he's going to play it? No way. "Did someone named Sutton call me a bitch?"

"Yes, but—"

"Did she beg you to come home to her?" I can hardly blame her for calling me a bitch. I am a bitch, and I'm damn proud of the fact. It's his part in this that bothers me.

"You don't understand—"

"Did you say loved her?" My voice cracks on this last question.

He sighs, pinching the bridge of his nose as though he's getting a headache. "I did, but I had a good reason."

Tears smart my eyes and I whirl away from him. There's no way I'm giving him the satisfaction of seeing me cry. He doesn't deserve my tears, but that's the thing about a broken heart, the person that deserves it is never the one who gets theirs broken. "I don't think I need to hear an explanation. I think the message was pretty clear. You can't explain saying I love you to another woman."

"If you think that, that proves how wrong you are." Strong hands grip my wrist and he spins me toward him before I can pull away. "I can explain."

"Don't let me stop you." I yank myself free and cross

my arms over my chest. Pasting on my best poker face, I do my best to look unimpressed even though I can't ignore the tingling that lingers where he touched me. I can't trust myself around him any more than I can trust him. That much is clear.

Then he drops a bomb on me.

"Sutton is my sister."

"*Oh.*" That explains the *I love you*. I've spent the last few hours planning exactly what I would say to him the next time I saw him. I didn't prepare for the possibility he'd have a reasonable explanation.

"You did remember that I have a sister, right?" he asks, a smirk tugging up the corners of his mouth.

He's got me cornered—physically, emotionally—and he knows it.

"I thought you didn't know where she was," I say stupidly.

"I didn't know where she was five years ago."

"I guess you found her." Suddenly, it seems I have a gift for stating the obvious. Sutton is his sister. That does make sense. But like so much of Sterling's life, I don't know much.

Sterling doesn't seem to hold my newfound observational skills against me. "I did."

It's less that I forgot about his sister and more that, in the past, talking about her was like flipping his asshole switch. "I thought you didn't want to find her."

"I didn't. She found me."

"And why does she think I'm a bitch?" Sutton being his sister might clear up why he said I love you, but it doesn't change how they seem to talk about me. I'd seen the message with my own eyes. Not only had she said it, he hadn't corrected her.

"She's not your number one fan," he says, shifting away from the wall.

Now we're getting somewhere. Somewhere uncomfortable for both of us, but where we need to go. "And why would that be?"

"There's a lot you don't know about me," he says. "About my life."

No shit. Now who's stating the obvious? "Enlighten me."

"You're unbelievable," he says with a laugh that sounds anything but amused. "You read my messages, jump to conclusions, and then—"

"Jump to conclusions?" I repeat in disbelief. "What am I supposed to think about you saying I love you to another woman *and* it's not like I was snooping. *You* gave me your phone."

Now he looks cornered. Good. "I did give you my phone."

"Don't you dare paint me as some psychotic girlfriend who is nosing around in your business." I poke his sternum with my index finger. That turns out to be a mistake because it's like hitting a launch button.

"Aren't you?" he storms. "You're always sticking your nose where it doesn't belong."

"Because you won't tell me anything!" I'm the unbelievable one? There are a lot of ways that he's changed. There are a lots of ways that I've changed. But the lies and mystery he likes to keep as armor? It hasn't changed.

"There's nothing to tell."

My jaw unhinges and I hastily close my mouth with a glare. If I started writing down all the things I don't know about him, it would rival Santa's Christmas list. All he does is keep secrets. It might even be what came between us before. I can't be sure, because I don't even know what that was!

"I think there's a lot to tell. Like why she wants you to come home or why you said *not this time*," I quote the text back to him.

"You memorized it?" His eyebrows raise.

I can't tell what he thinks about that, except that I'm in real danger of actually being a psycho girlfriend despite my intentions.

"It's kinda burned in my brain," I say. "I mean, I fucked you thinking I could trust you, and then before I could put my panties back on, another woman was sending you texts."

Sterling sucks in a deep breath and I'm not sure if he's preparing for a shouting match or finding his zen. He releases it slowly, stroking his chin thoughtfully. "You can trust me, Adair."

"Okay, prove it," I challenge him. "Tell me how you made your money."

I'm tired of being on the outside. I'm tired of looking at him and seeing as many questions as I do possibilities.

"I don't see what this has to do with anything." He shakes his head and I get the distinct impression he's lying to himself as much as he is to me.

I watched a marriage built on lies. I lived it. There's no way I'm settling for less than all of him, even if it means getting none of him. "It has everything to do with it. Where have you been the last five years? Why did you come back? I'm tired of only knowing half of your life. How do I know things are real between us?"

Sterling's perfect eyes wince in pain. If it hurts him to be misunderstood, why doesn't he make himself clear? I see the little muscles in his jaw twitch as he takes a step toward me. I back up reflexively, bumping into the wall. There's nowhere to go.

"Lucky," he tries to say it evenly, but his tone is a complete betrayal of the storm on our horizon.

Isn't that how it's always been with us? We crave the breeze that blows in while we ignore the blue-black thunderclouds. For us, it's easier to pretend it's not coming. We tell this lie. We believe it. We turn our backs to the wind. It's what makes the squall impossible to overcome. The storm grabs hold before we can break free, capsizes us, drags us below the surface. We drown in each other. I'm tired of it. I want to sail into the storm—standing on the bow, back straight, head unbowed. I want to face what we are and see if I'm strong enough to survive the truth of it. "Tell me I'm wrong."

"You're beyond wrong." His intensity is breathtaking and now it's in his eyes: the hurricane I'm determined to face. That's when I realize that he is my storm. He is the danger. I can either sail through him or turn back. There's no other way to survive him. So why do I melt against the wall? Why do my eyes close, my lips part?

His hand flashes towards me and unties the knot of my robe. It falls open before I've processed his intentions. One impossibly strong arm reaches under my right, around my back, and grabs my upper left arm. His body presses me against the wall, his knee pins my legs apart.

"Does this feel real?" he says. I can sense how hard he is fighting to keep control of himself. It should frighten me. Instead, I feel the fabric of my panties soak. He holds me fast against the wall, waiting for my response.

I nod.

His mouth finds mine, desperate and hungry. Frantic to claim me. He takes my bottom lip into his mouth and nips down hard. The sharp metallic tang of iron floats across my tongue.

"Is this real?" he growls between all-consuming kisses. There's no hesitation. He touches me like he owns me. And that's when I realize it. He does.

I can still pull away. I can still stop this. I can sail to safe harbor, but I haven't made it this far to give up now. On myself. On him. On us.

I bite back.

Sterling betrays little of the pain. Instead, he simply grunts. He is primal. Animalistic. He takes as he gives. His possession liberates me until I can feel it. I can feel every raw, aching nerve in my body.

The fingernails of his free hand scratch me slightly as his hand makes its way to my waiting, bared breast. "And this?" My nipples stiffen painfully, and I moan in spite of myself. "Tell me this isn't as real as it gets."

Meeting his gaze as evenly as I can, I shake my head. I can't tell him that.

"That's right, Lucky," he says through gritted teeth.

As if to underscore his point, he bends to take my right nipple between his teeth. He doesn't bite down, but I feel the threat he will almost hysterically. His hand soothes my left breast, rubbing gently in counterpoint to his mouth, which begins to suck on my breast, hard. I can feel blood rushing in, engorging the nipple, making it more tender.

When at last he releases it from his mouth, the feeling is dangerous and exquisite. Relief at freedom gives way to a painful stab of absence, which itself gives way to a deep ecstasy, throbbing in time with my heart. It feels like he has connected me to the resonant frequency of the universe.

"I know what's between us is real, Adair. It's a feeling I have when I look at you. Would you like me to show you how it feels?"

My eyelids flutter, an approving moan slipping past my lips. A wicked grin lights his face, and I realize my head is bobbing furiously, though I don't think I sent that instruction.

The arm pinning me in place disappears. My body reacts intuitively, attempting to close the distance between us, but Sterling pushes me back against the wall with a palm to my belly. He kneels before me, kisses my navel. His fingers pinch the black lace fabric of my panties, pull it away from me. He lets the fabric go, and the elastic threads snap back into place, giving me a jolt. He does it again and again, always kissing my belly.

Is this what he feels? That I'm a tease, or that he needs to tease me? Or is it just torment? Delicious torment? He doesn't need to show me that. He always tormented me.

Suddenly I feel the rough skin of his knuckles brushing between my legs. Then, the lace of my panties bites into my hips, followed by the sound of ripping fabric. I feel the shredded lace dangling loosely around my hips, exposing the rest of me. Cold air floods across my sensitive sex and couples with my wetness to send shivers up my spine.

He stands, his wild look reflecting how I feel. Arms wrap around me, holding me close to him. My body finds its shape in him, my curves filling the open space that should never be allowed to exist. Then, his hands move to the last band of fabric hanging off my hips. He finds the seam and slowly pulls it apart. I feel every thread give way. When he rips the last few threads from my body, my breath explodes out of my mouth. Sterling puts his mouth near my ear and whispers, "*This* is real."

"Yes." It comes out in a squeak as I struggle to take in oxygen. My hands grope feebly at the button of his jeans.

"We should be careful, Lucky, we don't—"

"I'm on the pill."

It's his turn to react instinctively. He lifts me from the ground and pins my splayed hips between his chest and the wall. He looks up at me, his face full of naked lust and wonder and reverence. Had it always been there? Had I been too stupid or too consumed with my own pleasure to see it? I feel something fundamental shift—realign. But I don't have time to consider what it is or what it means, because Sterling frees his cock and plunges inside me.

My arms hook around his neck. My ankles cross above his buttocks. I hold on to him. Sterling's hands cup the bottom of my ass, supporting my weight but also pulling me wider, so that he can fill more of me.

Restraint has left the building.

He looks into my eyes—and for a moment, he shows me he has nothing to hide, and that I have nothing to fear—and I want this to last forever.

"Don't," I pant, "stop...don't ever stop!"

Sterling smirks and shifts slightly until I can't find the words to make demands. "*Ohhhh—*"

His long, strong strokes become quick and powerful, punctuated by the impact of his pelvis on my clitoris. He's my anchor point. My body shatters around him, safe in the eye of the storm. I am free. I am tethered. I am everything and I am only this. When Sterling arrives a moment later, his eyes roll up to the ceiling, and at last the missing element is found. I dissolve into him, and he into me.

This has always been the easy part.

Sterling's sweaty forehead presses against mine as we untangle ourselves. He adjusts my robe, covering my body again. "Have dinner with me."

It's not a question. I swallow to give myself time to come up with a reason to say no, but I can't find one that outweighs how much I want to say yes. I gesture down to the robe. "I should change."

"I like you just the way you are." He brushes his thumb over my swollen bottom lip.

"You tore off my panties," I remind him, "and the last time I checked the restaurant had a dress code."

"Well, when you put it like that." He releases his hold on me, and, bending down, he gathers the lacy remnants of my panties from the ground before shoving them into his pocket.

"Don't tell me you're going to keep those." Why do I hope he says yes?

He winks at me, turning his smile up until it's blinding. "Consider it a trophy."

"If I find them mounted on the wall at your apartment, we're going to need to talk."

Sterling twines his hands through mine, leading me down the hall. I'd forgotten for a moment that we never made it inside the suite.

Now that he's no longer occupying every ounce of my attention with his body, my surroundings remind me. It's the first time in a long time that I've done something as reckless as that, but the flush of shame I expect to heat my cheeks never arrives. I don't care that I have no business screwing Sterling in the hall of the Eaton. Because I'm already thinking about Sterling's hands and how much I want them on me again. I'm shaking so badly I can't get my keycard to work.

"Allow me." He reaches for it, but I hold it away.

"I've got it," I snap despite all evidence to the contrary. It's too much. He's too much. I can't even think with him this close. Not after that. Not still reeling from how he makes me feel. It takes every ounce of discipline I have to shut the door to the suite in his face with a quick "I'll be right out."

If that's what happens when he catches me outside my door, I can't risk allowing him inside. We need to talk. He needs to come clean, and I need to hold him accountable. With a locked door between us, I remember that I don't even have underwear here. I settle for cleaning myself up in the bathroom as best I can. I'm going to have to get some clothes soon, particularly if he's going to keep shredding mine.

There's not much I can do without makeup or a hairbrush. My reflection looks as reckless as I feel. My hair is a tousled wildfire, flames swirling uncontrollably around my shoulders. My lips are still swollen with blood from the brutality of his kisses. I ditch the robe and see the imprints from where his fingers dug into my hips. It takes some finessing, but I manage to make my dress look presentable by ditching the torn sash and using a safety pin I find with the complimentary sewing kit provided by the hotel. It's not exactly dinner at a five-star hotel apparel, but it will have to do. There's nothing to help my unruly hair, but I find I actually like it like this. I want Sterling to look at me and remember what it felt like to pin me against the wall — to control me. I want him desperate to get me back into bed. I'm going to distract him, so that he lets his guard down. Because tonight — no matter what happens — I'm winning this round. I'll either get my answers or give him marching orders. Sterling won't know what hit him.

10

ADAIR

THE PAST

The perk of not starting classes again until next term is that no one seems to notice I've gone into hiding. At least, not at first. Following my disastrous birthday party, I found myself more than happy to avoid the Valmont campus, along with my friends. My dad's been in and out of town on business or busy with the latest personal trainer that assures him he'll walk again someday. Malcolm is busy with his campaign and wedding plans. The only person to show any interest in me is Felix, but now he has stopped making cookies every time I show up. Apparently, this is one heartbreak chocolate chips can't cure.

Maybe because—despite everything—I won't let myself fall to pieces. After the way Sterling treated me, I just couldn't let myself fall apart again. I thought he was different, and the fact he was a grade-A asshole and I failed to notice it falls squarely on my shoulders. Even if he misunderstood what he overheard—and he did—I'm not about to let him treat me like that, drunk or not. In fact, in my experience, a person shows you who they truly are when they've been drinking. I have a lifetime of memories to back that up.

I'm on my second binge of *The Vampire Diaries* when Poppy bursts into my room with Kai. My first sign that she's up to something is her sly smile and the tight black jumpsuit she's wearing. Normally, I wouldn't put the words sexy and jumpsuit together, but this one dips low in the front, showcasing the swell of her cleavage, and hugs her rear so tightly she almost looks like she has an ass. Her shiny, dark hair bounces around her shoulders, setting off her ruby lips. Kai looks more casual but equally cool in a pair of black jeans and a slim-fitted button down, sleeves rolled up. His hair is combed strongly to one side, a swatch of jet black.

I pause the television. "Why do I feel like I'm on a reality TV fashion intervention?"

"Because you are," Kai says with a grin.

At least I'm not hallucinating.

"You cannot stay in bed forever." Poppy wastes no time. She marches to the window and pushes open the drapes I've refused to open all week.

Twilight streams into the room, and I wince, grabbing a pillow to block it.

"I think she might be a vampire now," Kai says. "It's practically dark out and she can't handle any sun."

I reach for another pillow and toss it at him, missing entirely. Despite my objections, it feels good to see them. Trust Poppy to know exactly when to force me to come out from my shell.

"We're going to a party tonight," Poppy says, throwing open my closet doors and walking inside it.

She lays the blazer on the marble counter, tucking the bralette under it. "Sexy but comfortable."

"I was thinking t-shirt," I mumble. She shoots me a look that tells me I better not push my luck.

Rolling my eyes, I strip off my satin pajama shorts and wriggle into the jeans. I forgot how tight they are. They come up high on my waist, covering my belly button, which is a blessing given that I'm not allowed an actual shirt. Poppy tosses me the bralette, and I put it on, thankful to discover it's not sheer enough to show my nipples. Finally, I slip into the white blazer.

"So?" I turn for their inspection.

"You look amazing," Kai says.

"Seriously." Poppy takes me by the shoulders and guides me to the mirror. She bunches my hair up on top of my head, lets it fall down, then repeats the process. "I can't decide."

"Up," Kai says.

I feel like a paper doll being dressed up by two gleeful children, but I can't deny that I actually look pretty cool. It's not something I would have come up with on my own. Poppy piles my copper hair on top of my head while Kai offers critical analysis.

"Can I wear sneakers?" I ask as Poppy holds up a pair of thin hoop earrings.

Neither of them answer, which is a response in itself.

Twenty minutes later, after I talk them down from a pair of gorgeous—but impossible to walk in—Louboutins, opting instead for ankle booties with a stacked platform heel, we head out through the kitchen.

"Going out?" Felix asks, coming around the corner.

Poppy and I both jump, earning a laugh from Kai. "You scared me!"

"I'm not the one creeping through the house like a burglar," Felix says dryly. He busies himself with a notepad. "Will you be home late?"

"Um..." I'm not sure how to answer that. It's not like my dad will notice or care that I'm gone. We only went through the back so we could take the Mercedes without him noticing—something he *will* care about. "Don't know."

Felix glances up from his notes and studies the three of us for a moment. Then he sighs. "I'll make cookies."

The party is off campus, which is a nice change because I'd gladly never set foot in another fraternity. The house sits a few blocks from the quad in a neighborhood of homes mostly occupied by groups of upperclassmen looking to get away from campus restrictions. It's your typical fixer-upper converted into a rental unit. A hundred years ago, it was probably a stately home for a professor and his family. Now it's mostly barren, which leaves plenty of room for students to cram into it. Tye dye tapestries hang on the walls, and the furniture looks like it was bought secondhand decades ago. But there's a keg in the living room and the night is fairly warm for November, so the party has spilled outside into the back yard.

"Want a beer?" Poppy asks as we weave our way inside.

I shake my head and hold up the keys. "I'm driving."

"We can walk to campus," she calls over the crowd. "You can crash in my room or..."

"Or what?"

"I'm sure Sterling would let you sleep at his place," she says meaningfully.

I've been waiting for this. I'd been purposefully vague about what went down with Sterling and me the night of my party, saying we had a fight. Poppy hadn't pushed me for answers, and part of me was beginning to hope she might let it go, especially once I agreed to return to the land of the living. No such luck.

"Sterling Ford's bed is the last place you'll find me," I yell back, adding, "Ever!"

"Got it," a harsh voice growls behind me. Poppy's eyes widen in response. She looks to Kai, and then they both look at me, mouths open.

This can't be happening. Again. What is it they say about repeating past mistakes? I guess where Sterling is concerned, I'll never learn.

"I'll find you in a minute," I promise my friends. Gathering up my shredded dignity, I put on my gameface, and turn to glare at him. My knees weaken immediately, my body betraying me, but I lock them and do my best to avoid his piercing blue eyes. "You might as well know, since you couldn't be bothered to end things face to face."

"I think I did." He smirks, lifting a bottle to his lips and taking a swig.

"Wait! Are you drinking again?"

"Never stopped," he says sloppily. "Turns out that booze is nearly as easy to score on this campus as ass, if you know the right people. Guess I was wasting my time before."

I recoil like he stabbed me in the stomach.

"You're a dick," I hiss at him.

He leans closer, and I smell stale beer and the sharp tang of old liquor on his breath. Up close I realize he hasn't shaved for a few days and his shirt is a wrinkled mess. "There you go thinking about my dick again. I know I told you no before, but if you ask nicely, I might just give you a free pass tonight, Lucky."

"Don't call me that." The nickname that was once endearing now feels like a ploy at best—a slap in the face at worst. "And find someone else that will put up with your shit."

"I always do," he slurs. "Every single night."

I storm away, pushing through the crowd. I need to put as much distance between us as possible before the tears come. There is no way I'm crying over him *in front of him*. He doesn't deserve it. I hear Poppy call to me, but I keep going until I reach the back door. Outside, I suck in a long, steadying breath.

"Adair!"

I look up to see Cyrus standing with some guys. He says something to them and heads toward me.

"Hey," I say weakly.

"You okay?" He puts a hand on my shoulder, his eyes squinting with concern.

"Fine. I just ran into your roommate."

Cyrus frowns, glancing behind me. "He's a bit of a mess."

"He's a dick," I say. "I can't believe you put up with it."

"I stopped sleeping in the room," Cyrus says.

"How could you sleep with a carousel of girls coming and going?" I tighten my jaw like I can bar the raw ache from working its way to the surface. Why did I let my friends talk me into coming here tonight?

"Girls?" he repeats, shaking his head. "More like a perpetual happy hour without the happy part. I only stop by to make sure he hasn't died of alcohol poisoning."

"He said..." I blink a couple of times trying to process this new information. "He's just sitting there, drinking?"

"Like a fish," Cyrus confirms. "You were probably smart to drop him when you did. At this rate, he won't make it past his first semester. He's got to be failing all his classes. I feel bad for him, though. I thought maybe going out would help him get it out of his system. I didn't know you would be here."

Suddenly, I'm on information overload. It's not like it's my fault that Sterling is pouring his life away one drink at a time, but I can't deny that this all started the night of my birthday. And worse than all of that is the tiny, wicked glimmer of satisfaction I feel learning that he's a mess without me. I'm sure it makes me a terrible person, but still not as bad as he is.

"Come meet the guys," Cyrus says.

I'm grateful for the distraction. I need to take a break from all of this, get it off my mind, and just relax. For the last two weeks, I've been zoning out and rewatching old television shows—the kind of stories where the guy and the girl always make up in the end. Maybe it's past time to admit that's just a fantasy. Reality is much uglier, and there's no script heading things toward a happy ending.

Cyrus introduces me to the guys, who turn out to belong mostly to Beta Psi, the fraternity he pledged earlier this fall. They all say hello and return to their discussions about the football team's chances in their upcoming game.

One of them, tall with sandy brown hair, edges closer to me. Leaning down, he confesses, "I know nothing about football. Don't tell them."

"I grew up in the South. I know too much about football," I say with a laugh.

"Is that my problem?" he asks. "I mean, we have football in Vermont, but it's not like this."

"Vermont, huh? A hockey town?" I ask.

"Now you're really emasculating me," he teases. "I thought when I came here I would never have to fake hockey talk again."

"Your secret is safe with me," I assure him. "What are you into...?"

"Jeremy," he reminds me.

"Sorry." I glance at the ground, embarrassed to have forgotten his name already.

"That's okay. You'd be a genius if you could keep all of us straight." He tips his head toward the house. "Can I get you a drink?"

I think back to my earlier promise about being the designated driver and hesitate.

"It's cool, if you don't want to," he says. "I just want to be hospitable."

"Is this your place?" I ask.

"Yep. Me and a few guys decided the frat house was a bit too crowded. We can control parties a little easier here," he confesses.

"I'd love to grab a drink," I decide. I've learned my lesson about accepting drinks from anyone I don't know, no matter how hospitable they are. But I've met Jeremy, and he knows Cyrus, who has been around since before I formed memories. Besides, I'll watch him like a hawk.

We make it into the kitchen, and Jeremy butts in to the keg line to pour a beer from the tap. I watch him the whole time and grab it as soon as it's out. This cup isn't leaving my sight the rest of the night.

"Took that freshman orientation tip about watching your cup pretty seriously, huh?" he says with a laugh as we find a quiet spot by the door.

"Unfortunately, I learned that lesson the hard way," I tell him.

"Oh, I'm sorry," he says instantly. "That was a stupid joke."

"It's okay. I was lucky." I curse inwardly at my choice of words. "I had friends there and made it home safely."

"But you learned your lesson."

"Yep." I take a drink, realizing that the lesson I'd forgotten was that beer tastes gross. I smile at him over the rim of my Solo cup. "So, not into sports."

"I'm more of a thinker. I'm going into engineering."

"Cool." I pray that this doesn't trigger a conversation about engineering, because I know nothing about it and I'm interested even less.

"What are you majoring in?"

Well, that subject is nearly as bad. "Right now? Nothing. I took a semester off."

"Right on."

"I'm coming back in January, though," I say quickly. "I think I'll major in English."

"Cool."

I guess he doesn't know much about my preferred field, either. We linger for a moment in awkward silence before a new song starts in the living room.

"Want to dance?" he asks, just as I spot Sterling's brooding face behind him.

"Yes!" I abandon my beer on the counter and grab his hand.

I drag Jeremy toward the unofficial dance floor. So, it's not my finest moment, but a girl can't be held accountable when the guy who broke her heart is a few feet away, especially if said heart is still in pieces. Plus, Jeremy seems like a nice guy and I'm determined not to let Sterling's presence ruin my night.

Jeremy suffers from the typical male problem of mistaking grinding for dancing, but since I want to make it clear I'm not waiting around on Sterling, it works out in the end. The crowded room is sticky from so many bodies being packed so tightly into the small space. After a few minutes, I feel Jeremy's hands on my hips. I lean into it, letting my body take over. I lose track of the number of songs we dance to. At least Jeremy has stamina. His hands turn me around so my back is against his body. Then his arms wrap around my waist, holding me closer to him, and I realize that stamina isn't the only thing he has—he's also got an erection. I wiggle, trying to put a little distance between us. The message he's sending is coming through loud and clear. It's time to send a response.

I must be responding too subtly, because instead of giving me space, he yanks me back again, pressing himself harder against my butt.

I pull away, pushing sweaty strands of hair out of my eyes. "Maybe we should go outside. It's hot in here."

"No, that's just you," he says, his eyes hooded. He reaches for me and pulls me back into his arms. "Let's keep dancing."

"I really need air." How much clearer can I be?

"In a minute." His face angles down, and I realize a second too late that he's aiming for my lips. They close over mine, and my palms flatten against his chest, shoving him. He breaks away and turns confused eyes on me.

"Stop!"

"Fine," he says, grinning like this is all a misunderstanding. "We'll keep dancing." The hands on my hips tighten their hold on me.

"I need to find my friends." I look around, squirming against his hold, hoping that I'll spot Poppy or Kai in the crowd. I'd even settle for Cyrus.

"They're around. Don't worry." Jeremy is not getting the message.

"I really need to go find them," I repeat more firmly.

"Adair," he starts, but before he can finish the thought he is thrown backwards like he's a yo-yo.

Jeremy crashes against the wall, knocking a few people over along the way, before I process what happened. He slides to the floor, but as soon as he tries to scramble to his feet, Sterling is there.

Someone arrives at my side, and I look over to see Poppy. She clutches my arm, but before she can ask what happened, Sterling lifts Jeremy up by the collar of his shirt and slams him against the wall again, knocking loose dusty plaster.

"She said she wants to go," Sterling says, dropping him on to his feet, only to shove him hard in the chest.

"Who the fuck are you?" Jeremy brushes off his shirt.

"Her boyfriend," Sterling roars.

"Oh!" Poppy's fingernails dig into my arm. That's the moment I decide to intervene.

"Enough." I grab the back of Sterling's shirt, and he turns toward me.

"He was touching you." His eyes blaze with unrepressed fury.

"That's none of your—"

Before I can finish. Jeremy grabs Sterling by the collar, spins him around, and lands a right hook square on his jaw. It stuns Sterling, but only momentarily. He recovers and slams into Jeremy, and the pair crash onto the ground. A few seconds later, more guys jump in to pull them apart.

"Get that asshole out of here," Jeremy shouts.

Two of his friends drag Sterling out the front door. I'm torn between following and staying.

"That's your fucking boyfriend?" Jeremy comes over, wiping blood from his lip.

"No. I mean, yes. I..." I say, then realize he's the last person I'm going to explain this to.

"Well, it's not going to matter much longer." Jeremy stalks out the door after him.

I rush after, arriving in time to see his friends holding Sterling by the arms. Jeremy moves to hit him, and I scream. The porch light goes on at the neighbor's, and someone opens the front door.

"Hey, we called the cops. A party is one thing, but I draw the line at this shit!" A disembodied voice calls out.

Instantly, it's chaos. The guys drop their hold on Sterling and he stumbles forward, taking another swing at Jeremy but misjudging and landing on the ground.

"Christ," Cyrus says, tearing out the front door and skidding to a halt next to me. Everyone else at the party comes streaming out behind him as the distant sound of sirens pierce the night. "Should we leave him? A night in jail might sober him up."

Sterling can't afford bail or a fine, and I know it. I square my jaw and shake my head. I can't believe I'm saving his ass.

"Come on. Let's get him back to your place," I say to Cyrus.

"Are you sure?" Poppy asks, as Kai and Cyrus go over to gather Sterling off the grass.

I stare at him. Boyfriend or not—and it's definitely not at the moment—I owe him. "He wouldn't leave me here."

"That's not the same," Poppy points out. "Someone drugged you."

"Yeah," I say in a hollow voice. Sterling did this to himself, but that didn't make the idea of leaving him to get picked up by the police any more appealing. "I guess sometimes you help people even if they don't deserve it."

And Sterling Ford doesn't deserve it. I know that. That's why I'm going to make him pay for his mistakes, just as soon as he sobers up.

11

STERLING
PRESENT DAY

It's not the first time Adair has shut the door in my face. It probably won't be the last. Ten minutes later, I'm still standing in the hallway when a harassed-looking bellhop scurries down the hall, heading in my direction at breakneck speed. He stops a foot from me and his eyebrows knit together as if I'm some sort of puzzle. After a few seconds of silence, it's clear I've fried some circuitry in his brain.

"Can I help you?" I ask, leaning casually against the doorjamb.

"Miss MacLaine requested a screwdriver." He peeks around my shoulder to check that he's in the right place.

"She's changing," I explain.

"And you are..." he fishes.

"Waiting." Jesus, I've seen less interrogation sitting at an Afghani prison. I hold out my hand. "I'll give it to her."

He looks like he's trying to decide if that's a good idea. "Maybe I should..."

"Do I look like I'm going to steal a fucking screwdriver?" I slip a hand from my pocket so he can get a view of my Breitling as I reach for my wallet. Drawing out a fifty, I hold it out. "For your trouble."

His attitude improves predictably. "I'm sorry. I didn't mean to—"

I wave off the apology and tuck the bill next to the pocket square on his uniform. Then I hold out my hand. He drops the screwdriver sheepishly into my palm, and I slide it into my pocket.

"I'll make sure she gets it." It's not like I would deprive Adair of a good screw.

He disappears back to the elevator, and I'm left wondering what's taking her so long.

Finally, she emerges in the dress she wore last night. Her hair is still loose around her shoulders, artfully mussed from where I held it minutes ago. I stare for a moment at her full lips, which look even more inviting than usual. It only takes me a moment to see what she's been up to.

"Sorry," she says, smoothing down her dress, and I see she's artfully pinned it to the side. "My dress is torn, and I don't have anything else to wear."

I tore her dress last night. I also tore her underwear, but I hadn't given those back to her to fix. If she doesn't have anything else to wear...

Backing her against the door, I run my hands over the soft curve of her hips. There's definitely nothing more than one silky layer of fabric between my hand and her skin. "*Fuck*, Lucky. How am I going to concentrate knowing you're walking around without your panties?"

"Maybe it will teach you not to rip them," she says as I press the call button on the elevator.

I arch an eyebrow. "That's what you think I'm going to learn? Hate to break it to you, but knowing you're bare down below only provides an incentive to keep ripping your panties off you."

She swallows, a rosy blush painting her cheeks. "Don't get ideas. I'm hungry."

"Me, too," I say meaningfully, trailing a finger across her stomach.

She shudders, her eyes closing for a second, before shaking her head. "Food, Ford, unless you want me to waste away."

"I don't want that." There's always dessert, I remind myself. "Do you want to eat here or go somewhere else?"

"I'm starving," she says. My eyes glint mischievously and she holds up a finger in warning. "Don't even think about it, Ford."

The elevator doors open as soon as I press the call button, and I hold my arm across the threshold. "After you, Lucky."

"How did you find me?" she asks.

"Luca is staying down the hall from you," I explain.

"So much for privacy," she grumbles. Adair presses against the far side of the elevator, holding the rail like a life raft, as if the small distance can protect her from wanting me. I can't have that. I run my tongue over my lower lip before biting down on it, hoping she can read exactly what I'm thinking in my eyes. She manages to look unfazed, but I can't help noticing her knuckles are white.

Maybe she needs a little break before she implodes from self-denial. "I accepted a delivery on your behalf."

"A delivery?" she repeats in surprise.

I pull out the screwdriver. "Maybe I'm wrong, but I think they have a maintenance staff to fix things."

She hesitates, staring at it. I can tell she's torn between explaining why she needs the screwdriver and wanting to punish me more for the misunderstanding about Sutton. Now who's keeping secrets? She tries to take it from me, but I hold it back. "What do you need this for?"

"I have things that need screwing." She crosses her arms defiantly.

"I can help with that." I don't try to hide the suggestiveness of my tone. She walked right into it.

She snorts but won't allow herself to laugh. She swats at the screwdriver, but I hold it higher. "Get your mind out of the gutter, Ford. There's a stuck drawer in the suite."

"That's all? Disappointing. Of course," I say thoughtfully, "I wouldn't mind helping you unstick your drawers."

"I'm sure you wouldn't." Her mouth twists with the effort of holding back a giggle. She knows better than to reward this behavior, especially since she's planning to grill me with questions over dinner. I know when Adair is on a mission.

The elevator comes to a stop and I glide out, screwdriver still in hand. "All you have to do is ask."

"I don't need your help," she repeats.

I lean closer and whisper, "Bullshit. If you need help with a screw—"

"Well, you *are* a big tool." She manages to keep a smile off her face, but her lips twitch at the corners.

I'm about to remind her about the size of my tool and its many uses, when we pass a man in a suit at the front desk. His head turns just enough for me to see his profile. A jagged scar runs from his temple to his cheekbone. I stop.

He doesn't belong here. Noah Porter.

I know it's him without bothering to get a good look. Some faces you don't forget, especially the ones with scars you gave them. Instantly, my training kicks in. I know where all the exits are, exactly where to duck for cover, and how many bystanders are likely to die if weapons are drawn. But there is one new variable I never considered— never needed to consider—before today.

Adair.

I can't calculate her reaction. I don't have a plan that includes her. Partly because, until this moment, I thought I was a step ahead of my *problematic* acquaintances. But also because I hadn't planned on needing to protect her.

There's only one option. I need to get her out of here without drawing attention to us.

"Let's go out," I say, taking her elbow and steering her back in the direction we came from moments ago. "Or, better yet, let's order room service."

"I think we should stick to neutral territory." She tugs free of my grip, shaking her head. Of course, she thinks this is about getting her back into bed.

Actually, that might be exactly what I need to distract her and get her moving. Grabbing a handful of her dress, I pull her gently toward me and angle my mouth to hover over hers. Adair sinks her teeth into her lower lip, staring up into my eyes uncertainly. For a single moment, I'm lost to her. I kiss her and everything fades into the background.

There's only her taste on my lips and a fleeting feeling of calm.

Then I remember and my head snaps up, the spell broken, and I see Noah is gone. One lapse—one critical moment of distraction—and I lost him. Now we really need to get out of here.

"Sterling?" Adair says my name before her head swivels to see what I'm staring at. She turns back, confusion furrowing her eyebrows. "What is it?"

"We need to go." I can't wait around to see if he spotted me. It's not a coincidence that he's here. Nashville is a big city, but Noah Porter is here because we're here. The question is: who tripped his snares?

"What are you—"

"For once, don't fight me on this," I say gruffly as I guide her across the lobby.

"Let go of me." She yanks her arm free and stops in her tracks. "What is going on?"

"We need to go somewhere private before I can tell you that." There's not a chance in hell that I'll actually tell her who I saw or what's going on. Not until I know whether he spotted me with her. The less she knows, the less trouble she's in. I doubt she'll see it that way, but apparently I'm becoming an optimist.

"I'm not going anywhere with you until you tell me—"

I don't wait for her to finish the sentence. Instead, I pick her up and carry her the last few yards to the elevator. She's too stunned to put up a fight. It must look like I'm carrying her off to bed because a few drunk college students coming from the hotel bar catcall us as I haul her inside the compartment. I grin, playing the part of the dashing groom, and punch the button to her floor with my knuckle.

Adair glares up at me, her plump lips smashed into a thin line. That line of effort is all that stands between me and an explosion. If I were smarter, I'd put her down and run in the opposite direction. I know to get as far from a blast radius as possible. The trouble is that her trigger is linked to me. One wrong move and she'll blow.

"Put me down," she orders.

I release her slowly and brace for impact.

As soon as she's on her feet, she reaches to press the lobby button. "I don't know what's wrong with you, but I'm hungry."

I move between her and the control panel. Her nostrils flair, and I swear I can hear an actual countdown to detonation.

"Order room service," I say tersely, slipping my cell phone out of my pocket and pretending not to care that her glare radiates fury.

"Are you going to tell me what's going on?"

"In a minute." I dial Luca's number as we arrive on the sixth floor. He answers on the second ring.

"Find her?" he asks.

"Yeah, thanks for the tip," I say.

Adair's eyes narrow, and she points to the phone. "Is that Luca?"

"That's not why I'm calling." I ignore her. Right now my priority can't be her feelings. "I just saw an old friend of ours in the Eaton lobby."

"Yeah. Who?" His voice is muffled, like he's chewing

something. I wonder if he's in his room. That would be convenient.

Adair clears her throat, we've made it to her door, and she stands there tapping her foot.

I shift the phone.

"Open it," I mouth.

"If you think I'm letting you in—"

"Open it," I growl, leaving no room for interpretation.

"Sterling, who was it?" Luca repeats, sounding more alert. He must have heard the alarm in my voice.

Adair slams open the door, and I step inside, pulling her along with me. As soon as we're through, I throw the deadbolt and pace to the end of the room.

"Noah's here," I tell Luca.

"Noah Porter?" Luca asks in disbelief.

"No, the guy with hundreds of animals. Prepare for a fucking flood," I snap. My free hand rubs my temples as I feel the first pangs of a headache. "Find out why he's here."

Luca doesn't argue with me. He already shifted to our contingency plans. "Will do. You sticking around?"

I turn an analytical eye on Adair. She hasn't moved from the door. Her arms are crossed, and I can almost swear actual smoke is coming from her nostrils.

"Unclear," I mutter, pivoting away from her.

"I'll let you know when I have something," he promises.

Ending the call, I take my time pocketing my phone while trying to come up with an excuse for my bizarre behavior. The trouble is that Adair isn't like a lot of women I know. The few other relationships I've had were purely transactional. Sex. Dinner. Conversation not encouraged. They didn't care who I did business with or if plans changed. Adair? She cares, and conversation is definitely mandatory. It's why I'm in love with her. It's why I don't know if we'll ever work.

"I'm waiting," she reminds me.

"It was just an old friend. I was surprised to see him, and I wanted to make sure Luca caught him," I say. I'm trained to withstand enemy interrogation, but I'm no match for Adair MacLaine.

"Do you always run from your old friends?" she asks flatly.

"Lucky, this is complicated."

"Actually," she storms, "it isn't. It's simple. Tell me the truth. Who is he? Why is he here? Where have you been the last five years?"

This is spiraling out of control so quickly I'm not sure there's a way to reverse course.

"Those questions might seem simple, but the answers to them aren't," I say, searching her face for some sign that she'll let this go, but I know Adair better than that. She's too stubborn to let anything go, especially when it comes to our relationship.

"Let me put it another way," she says, "that's the door." She points to it. "Why don't you go catch up with your *friend*? Come back when you're ready to be honest with me."

"I can't tell you everything," I say, adding quickly, "not yet."

"And I can't let another man lie to me, manipulate me, and treat me like I'm an idiot," she seethes. "*Not ever.* Goodbye, Sterling."

"Adair—" I begin.

"Goodbye." There's no room in her voice for further argument, so I do what she wants, hope it's a sign of good faith to her, and leave.

Adair thinks she wants answers, but that's something she has never understood. Sometimes a lie is kinder than the truth. Sometimes ignorance is salvation.

12

STERLING

THE PAST

The earthy scent of coffee wakes me. I open one eye to find a mug being held in front of my face. It's at this point I discover someone has started a jackhammer in my brain. I wince, closing my eyes again and flopping against the couch.

"Leave it," I groan to whatever saint has come to care for me in my final hours, because I have to be dying. "Actually, find me something harder to drink."

The trick, I'm learning, is to not stop drinking long enough for the hangover to catch up with you. Some people call it hair of the dog. I just think of it as survival skills.

"That's going to be a hard no," Adair says sharply over the pounding in my head. "You're drying out."

Oh fuck. I roll to the side and open my eyes just enough to peek at her. She's in one of my t-shirts, and damn, it looks good on her. The frown she's wearing is meant to display her disapproval. Instead, the downturn of her lips forms a tempting pout. I should have known I couldn't avoid her forever. I was stupid to think I could resist Adair. She's not a temptation. She's an inevitability.

"Did you..." I search the fuzz that is last night's memories for her. "... stay the night?"

"You mean, did I watch over your drunk ass so that you didn't die in your sleep? Yeah, I did that." She places the coffee mug on the table and walks over to the window. A second later, the blinds open, and I blink wildly.

"Please, no," I croak. "Less light or more booze. Your choice, Lucky."

She huffs dramatically, but twists them closed again. "I don't think you should call me that anymore."

"It's your name."

"It's not," she snaps. "It's the kind of thing that a boyfriend calls his girlfriend."

Something swims back to me from last night. It involves that word—boyfriend—my fist and some guy. Sitting up, I realize that it's not just my head pounding. I reach up to discover my eye is swollen. I don't need a mirror to know I have a black eye.

"I guess my streak is over," I mutter.

"What streak?" Adair crosses her arms and glares. It's probably a move to look less interested, but I know she is. Why else would she still be here?

"Fighting. It's been..." I do some quick mental math. "... almost a year and a half since I kicked someone's ass."

"Your streak is still intact. You mostly got your ass kicked," she tells me.

"That's not how I remember it." More is coming back to me. I definitely gave as good as I got. Not that I expect her to know the parameters of what successful ass-kicking entails. People in Valmont probably still settle arguments with a gentlemen's duel.

"Trust me," she says. "I wasn't impressed."

Ouch. That hurts. Maybe she does know the perimeters, because impressing the girl? That's pretty much the point. At least, when it comes to fights over girls.

"You told him to stop," I say, recalling what triggered me.

"I didn't need you to punch him."

I throw my legs over the side of the couch. "I think that's exactly what you needed."

"No," she says. "The last thing I need is some drunk guy causing trouble and nearly getting arrested."

"Some drunk guy?" I repeat. "I hope you're talking about..."

"Jeremy," she fills in the blank. "I'm not. He wasn't drunk."

"What are you saying?" There's a reason I've been avoiding her, because somehow, despite everything, we haven't actually ended things. Sure, it was implied, and, yeah, I'd been the one to walk out on her.

But seeing her now, in a t-shirt that's two times too big for her, her creamy legs on display, and her attitude turned up to eleven, I'm not sure I'm ready to commit to that.

"Look, I owed you one." She grabs her jeans and starts to pull them on. "That's all this is. I should get going."

"Don't," I blurt out. She's so surprised that she drops her pants, which is better for so many reasons. Standing, a sharp pain pierces my skull, and I grab my forehead.

Adair takes a step closer, remembers she hates me, and stops.

Now that I'm on my feet, I realize that the floor is oddly clear. I look around my dorm room. The empty bottles are gone. There are no dirty clothes on the floor. My books are back on the coffee table.

"Did you clean?" I ask in a confused voice.

"I am capable of cleaning, and I wasn't about to sit around in your personal garbage dump all night." She blows a strand of hair out of her face. Probably so she can focus her murderous gaze more intensely on me. "What is wrong with you?"

Where to begin? I have a choice to make. The best thing for both of us is to push her buttons until she walks out my door and never looks back. I don't belong in her world. That's clearer every second we spend together. I'm not even sure why she bothers if she's just using me to get back at her father. In the long run, I'll hurt her, and she'll wreck me. Why not skip to the shitty part now?

Except that I'm as selfish as she is. I don't want to save her the pain. I don't want to save myself the pain. I want her for as long as I can have her.

"I told you I don't drink." I try a grin on her. Her face remains stony, but I think I see her eyes soften. "Can I have that coffee now?"

She picks it up and passes it to me. "Ready to dry out?"

"That's probably a good idea," I admit. "Look, you don't have to stick around."

Please do, though, I add silently.

"I have a little expertise in seeing someone through a hangover," she says quietly.

"Me, too."

"You should stop drinking. Please." The pain in her

voice hurts worse than my headache. We've danced around the topic of our fathers, but it's clear to me that Adair knows an alcoholic when she sees one.

"I know. I'm back on the wagon." I place a hand over my heart. "Promise."

She shrugs.

"You've heard that before, haven't you?" I ask.

"So many times I've lost track," she says, "so, forgive me if I wait to believe it until I see it."

"I wouldn't expect anything less. But I am done. You'll see. I don't want to be like my dad." I wait, giving her a chance to decide how she wants to proceed. I've opened the book to my backstory. It's up to her if she wants to read.

"Your dad promised you to stop drinking, too?"

Decision made. "No. He never bothered with us. Me and my sister," I clarify. "He didn't give a shit what two little kids thought. But my mom? Yeah, he promised her a lot. He'd get drunk, tear the place apart or worse, and then the next day, he'd promise to stop drinking. Sometimes, he went as far as to go to an AA meeting. But as soon as she forgave him, he started right back up."

"Or worse?"

She wants the whole story. I can't blame her. It's just that I don't particularly like to share it. I've had to a couple of times—for social workers and judges and lawyers. I take the mug of coffee and go back to the couch. "You sure you want to know?"

Adair bites her lip, tugging on my t-shirt nervously, before finally nodding. She moves closer, staring at the couch for a second before carefully sitting at the other end.

Tucking a leg under her, she arranges my shirt to make sure she's covered.

"The worst times were when he'd beat her." I pause to take a sip of coffee. I swallow it along with my pride. "Once I got old enough, I'd jump in and pick fights with him, so he'd take it out on me."

"He hit you?"

"His abuse came in all shapes and sizes. The more he drank, the more physical it was," I admit to her. "My kid sister was the only one he never touched, I made sure of that."

Her eyes close for a second. Is she pitying me? Imagining me as some poor kid being shoved around? That's the last thing I want. But when she finally speaks, it's to tell her own secrets. "My dad never gets physical. He just reminds us exactly how much or how little we're worth to him, and of all the ways we disappoint. He was nicer to my mom. At least, when we were around. I guess it didn't matter in the end."

"I'm sorry about your mom," I say, and every bone in my body means it.

"Why does the shitty parent always make it out alive?" she asks, then quickly covers her mouth like her own words horrify her.

"Because men like our fathers are rats. They run from danger. They'll do anything to survive."

"Sterling," she says in a gentle voice, "why were you in foster care?"

She's skipping ahead, but I can't blame her for not wanting to hear about the years of abuse. It's not easy reading. "I ran away," I tell her. "At first I was able to crash with friends, but their parents' patience ran out pretty quickly. One even tried to get me to go home."

"Did they know why you left?"

"Yeah, but they all had problems of their own, and having a kid around eating more food and taking up more room wasn't helping anyone. Pretty soon, I just moved to the streets."

"You were homeless?" Her words are brittle, like she's on the verge of tears.

"Hey, it wasn't so bad," I say, trying to play it off. "I learned to fight—that came in useful last night." I wink at her, but she doesn't laugh. She doesn't even smile. "There's a lot of places to go in New York when you're on the streets. It's not so bad."

"Where did you go?" She scoots an inch closer to me on the couch.

"During the day, school or the library."

"You still went to school?" she asks in surprise.

"Not the runaway fantasy of most kids, right? But there was always a hot breakfast and lunch there. Food's food." I shrug.

Her lip trembles and she bites down on it again.

"I went back and checked on my sister a couple times a week. I couldn't help it," I say. "Dad was usually out at whatever bar he hadn't been banned from yet. One night he stayed home instead. I didn't know he was there until I climbed in the window and heard him raging. My sister she was in her room, crouched between the bed and the wall."

Suddenly, I'm back there.

. . .

Stale cigarette smoke lingers on the wallpaper. No one's bothered to change Sutton's sheets again, and her clothes are dirty. Usually, Mom is more on top of taking care of her, but judging from the shattering glass and cursing coming from the kitchen, she's occupied with Dad. I kneel down next to Sutton and lift the chin she's tucked against her knees. "Hey kid, you okay?"

"Mom didn't feed me dinner tonight," she whispers.

A cold chill races up my spine, but I force myself to smile at her. "I'll get you dinner. Why don't you find some clean pajamas?"

She shakes her head, shrinking down again.

"Come on, kid. I'm here. It will be okay. Let's just find you some pajamas."

"Sterling..." Her eyes are as round as the moon outside and shining with tears. "I had an accident."

"It's okay," I say softly. "All the more reason to get cleaned up. I'll stick around tonight, okay?"

She bobs her head and timidly gets to her feet. I notice the smell then.

It's been a few days since I came to see her. I'd managed to snag a bed at a good shelter across town and hadn't wanted to lose it. It looks like she hasn't had a bath since then. Her hair hangs in stringy strands around her shoulders. There's a slight rumble and I realize it's her stomach.

"What did you eat for breakfast?" I ask her.

"I snuck out yesterday and got some cereal." She bites her lip before carefully pulling a small box of cereal out from under her pillow. It's the tiny, individual size they give out for school breakfast some days. I take it and see she's eaten

maybe half of it. My own stomach churns on the full meal I'd gotten at school this afternoon.

"Is this all you've had?" I ask. "Did you eat at school?"

"I haven't gone to school."

Something begins to pound and I realize it's my heart. "Sutton." I take her by her thin shoulders. "This is important. When was the last time you went to school?"

"A few days. I don't know. Daddy says to stay in my room."

How could I have left her this long? Usually, our mom can be trusted to take care of her and Dad? He never touches her. He just pretends she doesn't exist. "And Mom hasn't checked on you?"

"She's sleeping. Daddy says she's sick," Suttons says quietly.

My heart is beating so fast it feels like it might burst through my chest. I force myself to stay calm. "Okay, let's find those jammies and then I'll get you some real food."

"Don't!" Sutton squeaks. "Daddy is really, really mad. If he sees you..."

"Hey, I can take care of myself, right?" I proved that too well. I'm as bad as he is—always looking out for myself. I should have been here for her.

We find her a big t-shirt. Most of her clothes are dirty. From the looks of it, mom hasn't done laundry for a while. She changes into it and some fresh underwear while I stare out the window. I know why Sutton doesn't want me to go out there. She might not have experienced one of his rages herself, but she'd seen me bear the brunt of one.

But I can't ignore the sick, nervous feeling in my belly. Mom isn't doing laundry. She's not feeding Sutton. I can't ignore that. I can't stick around either. Dad will kill me. I'm absolutely positive. And Mom? It looks like she's finally given up. How sick is she?

I take the dirty sheets off Sutton's bed, find a blanket, and tuck her in with a teddy bear. "I'm going to bring you dinner in bed."

"Dinner in bed?" She giggles. "There's no such thing."

"There absolutely is," I say. "You know those big hotels we see when we go to Central Park?"

She nods, hanging off my every word.

"When you stay at one of them, they'll bring you anything you want in bed."

"Anything?" she repeats in awe. "Even ice cream?"

"Oh yeah." I nod.

"Have you eaten ice cream in bed? Is that where you stay when you aren't here?"

I fluff the pillow behind her head and grin. "Yeah," I lie. "Of course, I do, and someday, it will be me and you staying at one of those hotels and eating ice cream."

"Promise?"

I hold up a pinky and she hooks hers through it. "Promise." I stand up. "I'm going to go get you something to eat."

Sutton sinks down, pulling her covers up and clutching the shabby dollar store teddy bear I bought her last Christmas. "Be careful."

She shouldn't have to warn me to be careful when it comes to our father. She shouldn't live like this. I need to get her out of here. There's a social worker who keeps showing up at the midtown shelter. Maybe she'd help me.

I open the door a crack and peer out. Instantly, the scent of old garbage and something worse—something rotten—hits

my nose, and I gag. Mom must really be sick to let it get this
bad. I turn and hold up a finger to my mouth, reminding
Sutton to be quiet. She pulls the covers over her head.

Dad has passed out on the couch with a full bottle of
beer, a cigarette hanging limply from his mouth, the smoke
flickering with his snores. I should take it and put it out
before he burns the place down. I will, but after I make sure
Sutton gets something to eat. If he wakes up, I'll be in no
condition to make sure she gets food.

The fridge is mostly empty, except for half a carton of
milk that expired last week. I open it and smell it. It's not too
sour and if she eats it with the cereal, she probably won't
notice. It's a trick I've picked up over the years. You have to
make do with what you've got.

Flies are buzzing around the garbage can, which is probably home to whatever disgusting smell is radiating through
the apartment. I carefully open the kitchen window to let
some air in. It's snowing outside, so I can't risk letting too
much cold air. I can't assume the heating bill has been paid
this time of year.

I find a bowl and dig a spoon out of a drawer of
mismatched silverware. A quick perusal of the cabinets
yields nothing more to bring her. Tomorrow, I'll get to school
early and charm the lunch lady, Gladys, into giving me two
breakfasts. I can make it back here and get Sutton fed and
dressed and to school myself if Mom's not up to doing it.
They'll feed her lunch, and that will buy me time to figure
out what to do next. Dad usually works an afternoon shift at
the plant. I can come back and check on Mom, force her to
see that she has to take care of Sutton or see a doctor or
whatever.

Tiptoeing down the hall, I pause at her bedroom door. I can't risk surprising her, because it might wake up Dad. I head back to Sutton instead. Between the cereal in her box and the milk, it's close to a meal.

"I'm going to get you breakfast in the morning," I tell her, "so you can finish this now."

"Something hot?" she asks hopefully.

"Definitely." I give her the bowl. "And you're going to school tomorrow."

"I miss school." She takes a bite of cereal and screws up her nose. "This milk tastes funny."

"It's special milk," I tell her, making up something on the spot to account for its sourness. "It has special minerals in it, so you don't get sick like Mom."

She buys the explanation and finishes it up, even forcing herself to drink the remaining milk in the bowl. When she's done, she licks her lips. "Sterling, I'm still hungry."

There's something hot and wet sliding down my cheeks. I swipe at the tears, feeling betrayed by own body. "I didn't have anything else to give her," I tell Adair. "She was fucking starving—they told me later. And I was just going to school and living my life, and my baby sister was starving to death."

Adair is quiet for a second, then she crawls over and climbs onto my lap. Her arms wrap around my shoulders, a hand cradling my neck, and she draws my face to her chest. "You were a kid," she says softly. "You shouldn't have been dealing with any of that."

"Who else was going to deal with it?" I ask the question

I'd asked a million times since then. "Nobody cared. The school saw me showing up every day in the same clothes. They didn't say anything. The shelter gave me a bed and tried not to ask questions. You know why?"

Adair waits, as if she senses that this is a conversation I need to have alone.

"Because as long as people can say they're trying, they don't have to feel badly. I mean, I had food and somewhere to sleep most nights thanks to them. They couldn't do anything else, right? Some parents are shitty. Some kids have to get stuck with them. I thought I was doing my sister a favor. Being invisible is a helluva lot better than watching your dad beat the crap out of your brother every night. Most of the time, Mom was pretty good at lying low. At least, I thought she was." I laugh, and the sound is so distant it's almost like it's coming from somewhere else. "Until..."

"She got sick?" Adair guesses.

I shake my head, my brain trying to stop the words from coming out. "She wasn't sick. That was the problem."

The sound of children screeching wakes me, and I sit up to see a blur of white outside the window. My limbs are stiff. Not just from sleeping on the ground, but also from the chilly air. I guess the heating bill didn't get paid. Getting up, I discover a blanket of snow on the fire escape outside. Another joyful scream rises in the air as my heart sinks. If the kids playing below are any indication, it's a snow day.

No school. No breakfast. No lunch. No safe place to stash Sutton while I figure out what to do next.

Sutton sits up in bed, rubbing sleep from her eyes, and grabs her blanket. She clutches it to her tiny body. "It's cold."

"Yep, but it snowed." I grin widely to distract her from her chattering teeth.

"Am I going to school?" She glances at her alarm clock, and her face falls.

"No school today," I say quickly. "We're having an adventure instead. We're going to see the city."

"Where are we going?" she asks as I look for the warmest clothing I can find in her drawers, then toss them on her bed. It takes me a minute to find her winter coat. It's still shoved in the back of her closet. The coat is two sizes too small, but it's better than nothing.

"Let's see." I search for places that will definitely be open and warm. "The library?"

"Yes" She lights up. Sutton loves reading almost as much as I do. "The zoo?"

"It's a little cold for the zoo, kid." I grab two pairs of socks.

"Not for the polar bears." She pulls on the first pair.

"I'm going to leave Mom a note," I tell her. With any luck, there's a little money in the stash Mom keeps hidden in the cabinet. It's for emergencies, but I'm pretty sure this qualifies. Sutton needs food, and maybe I can check on Mom, get her some medicine.

Dad's chair is empty, and I breathe a sigh of relief. He went to work, which means I don't have to sneak around. I open the kitchen cabinet next to the oven and stretch my fingers to the back of the shelf until they skim across cold metal. It takes me a second to get the old coffee canister down. When I pop open the lid, I find three dollars. It's *enough for a hot dog. Maybe a slice if Tommy at the place on the corner is in a good mood. At least it will be hot, and to Sutton it will seem like a treat.*

I pocket the bills and head back down the hall. Mom's door is cracked, and I poke my head in, calling a soft, "Hello?"

She doesn't answer. I can see her on the bed, even though the room is still dark. I hesitate. Maybe I should let her sleep, especially if she's sick. I glance toward Sutton's door across the hall. It takes me a second to realize that if mom is really sick, she might need to see a doctor. If she's just avoiding reality, then she needs a wake up call. I can't stick around all the time, not when Dad is on the warpath.

"Mom," I say more firmly. I walk over to the bed and sit next to her. "You feeling okay?" I wait for her to answer, but she's still sleeping. "Mom, Sutton needs you to get out of bed. I can take her for the day, but..." I reach to shake her, but when my hand touches her shoulder, it's ice cold. Of course she's cold. She's on top of the covers, laying on her stomach. Maybe she had a fever and fell asleep like this.

"Come on." I try to pull the covers up and over her, but she doesn't budge. "You're just going to feel worse if you don't warm up."

Reaching over, I twist on the lamp by her bed, hoping the light will wake her. That's when I notice the blood.

Adair gasps and my hands clutch her hips, feeling the soft, warm skin. I want to bury myself between them and escape, but I can't escape the past any more than I can change it.

"She was dead," I say flatly. "Had been for days. Dad hit her with something. They never found out what."

"And your sister?" Adair asks. "What happened?"

"I took her out for her snow day," I say.

Her eyebrows knit together. "Did you call the police?"

"Not at first," I admit. "I didn't want Sutton to...to see that."

I close the door behind me, my hands trembling. I feel as cold as she did. Sutton appears in her doorway, beaming like a ray of sunshine. Her jeans are an inch too short and her sneakers have a hole in the toe.

And she's got no mother.

I push the thought aside and grab her hand. "Ready for our adventure?"

"Yes!" she squeals. She pauses and looks at Mom's door. "Did you tell her where we were going?"

"Yeah," I lie. "She knows. Where do you want to go first?"

"The library!"

"Big surprise." I lead her down the hall, away from the nightmare she's been living, away from her old life, away from everything she knows, and say a prayer that whatever comes next is better than the hell she's leaving behind.

"You went to the library?" Adair trips over the words like she can't fathom it.

"There were computers there, and it's always warm," I

tell her. "I looked up some addresses. We spent the day together, and then I walked into the closest CPS office."

"And told them what?" she asks.

"I pulled them aside and said my sister needed to go into custody, that she wasn't safe at home. There was a really nice woman who got my sister hot chocolate and talked with her."

"And you?"

"When no one was looking? I left."

"You left?" Adair repeats like she misheard me. "Where did you go?"

"Where do you think I went? I went home to kill my dad."

The arms around my neck loosen, and Adair draws back to study my face. "But your dad is alive."

"What can I say? I'm a crappy murderer." My attempt to lighten the mood falls flat. It's not surprising, I guess. "He came home, and I confronted him. I stabbed him with a kitchen knife, but it wasn't very sharp. He probably would have killed me if the cops hadn't shown up. CPS alerted them, and they came to do a wellbeing check. I didn't see my dad again until I testified in court a year later."

"Is he in jail?"

"Yeah. He deserves to be in hell."

Adair doesn't argue against this. She just lowers her face against my hair and holds me close to her. "What about your sister?"

"She was young and adorable, and CPS found her a place to live right away. The family didn't want an older kid."

Adair gasps. "So they split you up?"

"It was better for her, anyway. I basically spent the next three years jumping around the system. Anytime things got too comfortable, I'd pick a fight and get sent somewhere new."

"Until Francie?" Adair guesses.

"The nice woman at CPS with the hot chocolate? Francie's sister. I kept winding up back at her desk. Finally, she got Francie to take me, and I've been with her ever since."

"She cleaned up your act."

"It took a while. I caused as much trouble as I could," I say.

"Why?"

"Because I had this ache inside me and nothing soothed it, but hitting something distracted me. Then, at a party, I discovered drinking," I confess. "It was like escaping. I found rock bottom at the bottom of a bottle."

"Francie didn't give up on you, though?"

"Yeah, I have no idea why." I still don't. I never deserved her patience, and I've tested it too many times to count.

"Maybe she sees what I do," Adair says softly.

"A worthless orphan?" I ask. "Or not an orphan, I guess. My piece of shit father is still alive, serving his sentence in upstate New York. I guess I'm a bastard?" I laugh feebly, but she doesn't join in.

"Don't do that."

"What?"

"Talk shit about yourself," she says. "I forbid it."

"It's one of the few things that I'm really good at," I tell her. "I mean, I'm just like my dad." I turn my face away, unable to look at her. She deserves love and magic and wonder and a life I can never give her. I'm a black hole, destroying every good thing I encounter, swallowing them up and leaving nothing behind.

"You're not." She grabs my chin and forces me to look her in the eyes. "You just have to let yourself believe it."

"I'm sorry, Lucky. I guess I learned a long time ago to expect the worst in people, especially myself."

I look into her eyes and find understanding. No, more than that: *acceptance.*

"We all have our faults," she murmurs, "and our baggage."

"Some of us more than others."

"Tell you what," she says. "How about when yours starts to feel heavy, you let me help you carry it for a while?"

I stare at her in wonder. She surprises me at every turn. I don't look at Adair and see someone perfect. I see someone real. Maybe the first real person I've ever known. Her faults are glaringly obvious. Her temper? Well, it's scary. She sticks her foot in her mouth every other sentence. And she quotes books and calls me on my shit and holds me during the dark moments. "Why would you do that?"

"I think that's what you're supposed to do," she whispers, "when you might love someone."

"Might?" I murmur, the pounding in head drown out by a rush of blood.

"Definitely, maybe." She kisses me softly with her sweet lips.

"I don't want you to go." I want to trap her in my arms

and keep her here with me—safe and flawed and beautiful
—forever.

"I'll be here as long as you want me," she breathes.

"That's going to be a very long time," I warn her.

Adair smiles and warmth seeps into me like I've
stepped into the sun. "Good."

13

ADAIR

The next day a dozen roses arrive at my suite, followed by an arrangement of magnolia blossoms the day after, and by a large arrangement of wildflowers the next. I leave them all in the hall for maid service to take away, but no one does. Since I refuse to even acknowledge their existence, they just linger like funeral flowers.

Here lies the remains of our relationship.

I'm debating ordering breakfast to my room to avoid seeing them when someone knocks on the door. Checking the clock, I see it's unusually early for deliveries. I brace to find him on the other side, but when I peek through the chain lock, Poppy's pursed frown stares back at me.

"Shit, hold on." I slide the lock free and fling open the door to discover her and Kai on my doorstep. He's dressed down, a cap pulled low on his head, likely to avoid recognition. In a pair of worn jeans and a vintage Johnny Cash t-shirt, he still exudes too much coolness to avoid notice. Poppy, on the other hand, is dressed for battle in a skintight, black leather dress and sky-high black pumps. She wears the ensemble like armor, and I know exactly what weapon she's brought along: a sharp tongue. She marches into the room, a vase of flowers in her arms, and deposits on the small table in the living area.

"These were outside," she announces, wiping her palms together as if to congratulate herself on a job well done.

"I don't want—" I begin, but Kai shakes his head.

"Don't try to argue with her. She's on a tear."

"I am not on a tear!" Poppy exclaims, whirling on us. "I mean, why would I be? It's not as if my best friend moved out of her house without telling me and then moved into my boyfriend's hotel without telling me and then avoided my calls for three days."

"I'm in trouble, aren't I?" I whisper to Kai.

"You are," Poppy answers for him, blowing a strand of black hair from her face with unnecessary force. "What were you thinking?" She pauses and runs her eyes down me. "And what are you wearing?"

"I got it at Target," I say defensively. I pat the silky-soft knit jumpsuit affectionately. If I'm going to hunker down in a hotel, I might as well be comfortable.

"I like it," Kai offers and I shoot him a grateful smile. At least he's still in my court.

"Target?" she repeats like I'm speaking a foreign language. "Adair, what is going on?"

"You better sit down. Do you want me to order breakfast?" I ask.

Poppy drops onto the sofa and crosses her arms. "I'm not hungry."

"Mimosas?" I coax.

She glares at me and looks away. I order the mimosas anyway. By the time they arrive, I've filled them in on the last few days.

"So, the flowers are from him?" Kai says. I nod.

Poppy remains silent but reaches for a glass. She skips the orange juice and pours a full glass of champagne. "This isn't a time for moderation," she informs us. "Why didn't you call me?"

I see the battle in her dark eyes. She wants to understand, but she's hurt that I didn't reach out. I shake my head. I can put her mind to ease on that front. "I left my phone at his place. It's dead as a door nail, which is probably why he hasn't realized he has it."

I have no doubt Sterling would have brought it to me himself if he knew he had it.

"Do you want me to go get it?" Poppy asks.

I shrug and down half a mimosa. "I don't need it."

She exchanges a look with Kai.

"What was that?" I ask.

"You don't need it?" Kai repeats. "Are you sure you aren't waiting for him to bring it to you?"

"The last thing I want is to see Sterling Ford," I fume. Just saying his name sends blood rushing to my cheeks—and to other places.

"Yes, you probably would much rather be shagging him in the hall." Poppy's lips twist into an impish smile.

I hold up a hand. "I confessed! Now can we drop it? I need a break from the Sterling roller coaster."

"That means you haven't talked to Felix!" Poppy gasps, and my heart plummets into my stomach. For one never-ending second, the world stops. She seem my terror and her eyes widen. "Nothing's wrong, darling! Oh, I'm sorry. We went by looking for you when we couldn't reach you. He mentioned that Ellie got into preschool at Valmont Preparatory."

Pressing a hand to my chest, I take a deep breath and feel my heart rate drop. "You scared me!"

"Oops." She shrugs her slender shoulders with a sheepish smile. "However, he did say to ask you to call him. Ellie is asking questions."

Neither my heart nor my stomach takes this news particularly well. There's only one reason to stay at Windfall: to protect Ellie. "I shouldn't move out."

"Nonsense. You can protect her without being there," Poppy says. "She sees the way they treat you. Show her that a strong woman doesn't stick around when she's treated like that."

"What if they turn on her?" I ask so quietly that I'm almost surprised they hear me.

"They won't." Kai sounds so sure. I wish I shared his optimism.

"We won't let them," Poppy says. "Felix is there ,and he's in charge of her inheritance. He'll make them toe the line. He already made Ginny attend dance lessons with her."

"He did?" I ask hopefully. Ginny tended to skip out on little things like that, reserving her attention for charity functions and luncheons—whatever Malcolm would want.

Poppy nods her head. "He's got them in check."

"Are they that bad?" Kai asks.

"Worse," Poppy says. "I never understood how a

woman so desperate to have a baby could be so disinterested in her child." It's unlike Poppy to criticize someone, especially a family member. By her terms, this is the height of judgment.

"It's part of the terms of their prenup," I explain, gulping against the guilt surging in my throat. I was taught never to air family business that might reflect poorly. "My father told me once. If Malcolm divorces her before she gives him a child, she gets nothing. Having Ellie ensured she would be taken care of for life."

"She had a baby to crack the terms of a prenup?" Kai asks. "Your lawyers are terrible. I would never sign that."

"The lawyers can be a bit backwards when it comes to middle-class wives and billionaire husbands," I say dryly.

"And middle-class men? Or, for that matter, poor guys?"

"We're taught from a young age that they don't exist," Poppy says. "I'm not joking! You can marry into money if you're a woman, but marry down and you're out."

"Really?" Kai turns to me for confirmation. "Is that where things went wrong for you and Sterling?" He winces when he realizes that he just brought up a painful topic.

Before he can apologize, I jump in, "I have no idea what happened with Sterling and me. I have no idea why he betrayed me."

Kai opens his mouth again, another question in his eyes.

"Change of subject!" Poppy says. Her head tilts, and she grabs my hand. For an awkward minute, she studies it. I half expect her to start telling my fortune. When she finally looks up, she shakes her head with disapproval. "When do you start your new job?"

I bite my lip. So maybe Sterling isn't the only call I've been avoiding. "I'm supposed to pop in to do paperwork, but after what Malcolm did..."

"Nope!" Kai interrupts loudly. "You aren't letting your brother wreck this for you. She hired *you*. Do you think that offer is going to be around forever?"

"I doubt it's around at all. I own the business. I'll never be there because she wants me, not now," I say, looking for some inkling of understanding. Instead, I'm met with tough love.

"I'm with Kai," Poppy says in a firm voice. She pulls out her phone.

"Who are you calling?" I can't help my suspicion. I can't trust her not to intervene if she think's she's helping me.

"Elsi," she says.

"No!" But I know it's too late to stop her. She holds a finger and mouths: *shush*. "Are you available? It's an absolute emergency."

"Who's Elsi?" Kai whispers.

But Poppy's off the phone before I can answer. "She's my miracle worker."

"Her stylist," I say to him.

"Miracle worker," she says, "and she deserves the title. She's on her way. We need to get you ready for your first job."

"I don't need to do any of that. It's going to be awkward and terrible. I should probably just sell."

"No!" Kai and Poppy yell in unison.

"I'll take this one," Kai says to her. He puts an arm around my shoulder. "They know you own the place. So what? Own it. Treat people well. Do the work how you think it should be done. People will think what you let them think—until you show them differently. Trust me."

Kai would be an authority on the matter. I understand what they're trying to tell me, but it doesn't make me feel that I'm making the right choice. "The truth is that when Sterling showed back up, I was ready. Ready to claim my life. Ready to be on my own."

"And that hasn't changed! So, they know who you are. Go show them you deserve their respect," he adds.

"Yeah?" He makes it sound so easy. "How?"

"I'll tell you what Simon Cowell told me: fake it until you make it," he says with a laugh.

"And that's where Elsi comes in," Poppy adds. "And while we're on the subject, are you planning to... um... decorate?"

"Is there something wrong with this place?" I pretend to be offended.

"Not for a fifty year-old woman," Kai says.

"You need someplace—""Sexy," Kai finishes.

"And chic," Poppy says.

"And minimalist," Kai adds.

"Bright and airy."

"Okay! Okay!" I surrender. "I already told them to send the house decorator."

"I'll speak with her," Poppy says seriously. "Now take that onesie off before Elsi gets here."

"It's not a onesie," I argue as she shoves me into the attached bedroom.

"Whatever you have to tell yourself, darling!"

When the familiar knock comes from the door there are cucumber slices on my eyes and my nails have just been painted a smokey purple-gray. Poppy darts off to answer it. She reappears holding a large box. "More gifts from Sterling."

"Get rid of it," I tell her, but she's already opening the box.

She lets out a little moan when she sees what's inside. "It's chocolates from La Bonne Bouché."

"Get rid of it," I repeat.

She ignores me, dropping the box on the entry table before plucking a truffle from the pink tissue paper inside. "You can throw away flowers, but a girl never throws away chocolate."

"I agree with her," Kai calls through a sheet mask.

I shrug, pretending that I have no interest in them. The truth is, part of me enjoys torturing Sterling. I don't want the gifts, but I don't want them to stop coming. My stomach does a flip when I realize why.

"Has he called today?" Poppy asks.

"He will."

She looks far too pleased at the prospect. Since I finally hooked up with Sterling, she is feeling either vindicated or hopeful. I'm not sure which is worse.

"Who do you think he was?" Poppy asks, popping another truffle into her mouth.

"Who?" I blink at her in confusion. "What are you talking about?"

"The guy Sterling didn't want to run into in the lobby," she says.

If we're going to talk about Sterling, I might as well have some chocolate. It will soften the blow. I hold out a palm and she places a truffle in it. I pretend I'm not enjoying it. "I don't know." Whoever he was, Sterling totally freaked out when he saw him.

"Do you think he's in trouble?" she asks.

One of the best things about Poppy is her beautiful naiveté. Poppy is innocent. She sees the good in everyone. This also means she overlooks the bad. It doesn't take a genius to figure out that Sterling is involved in some questionable businesses. There's no way he could've made the kind of money he's flashing without doing a little dirty work. Somehow, this seems never to have occurred to Poppy.

"I think he is in trouble," I say. "Which means trouble is going to follow him until he leaves town."

"Don't be pessimistic," Kai advises.

I pull up the edge of a cucumber slice to make sure I aim my glare at him.

Poppy senses my anxiety and switches the subject. "Have you thought any more about what patterns you want to use?"

In the time it took Elsi to arrive, she called down to the front desk and had the house interior designer drop off fabric samples. If I had half her determination, I might be running MacLaine Media.

"Honestly, I don't care." I drop into a chair, wishing it would swallow me up and give me a break from my new life.

"You were so excited to have your own place," she reminds me.

"I know." I hold a throw pillow to my chest. "It just doesn't seem important now."

"That will happen when you're lovesick," Kai says. He strolls over, adjusting his hotel robe and sits next to me on the bed.

"Love—what?" I splutter.

"You know what he said. What about these?" She asks and I flip up the cumber slices to see her rifling through a stack of fabrics before pulling two and setting them side-by-side. She peers down at them, seeing some special difference that eludes me.

"Those are fine," I say dismissively, and return the cucumbers to their mission. I'm not sure this place can ever feel like home. It's somehow both full of my mother and lifeless at the same time.

Poppy plucks the cucumbers off and tosses them on the table. I hear Elsi cluck with disapproval from the bathroom, but Poppy ignores her.. "This is your first place. I don't want fine. I want spectacular. When Sterling comes banging down your door , I want to know that he's going to find a strong, confident, worldly woman."

"You have an apartment of your own," I say to her, "I don't know how you can manage to be here all the time."

"I'm not talking about me." She huffs and drops onto the foot of the bed. "You told him that you didn't want a man to control you anymore. Show him that. But don't let everyone make choices for you, either. Pick one." She points to the samples.

I'm not entirely certain this proves what she thinks it

does, but I can't argue with her logic. I can't keep saying I want a life of my own without making any progress towards it, without working on making my own choices. I grab a stack, toss aside her choices, and rifle through until I land on a bottle-green velvet. "This one."

Poppy raises one perfectly lined eyebrow. "Oh."

I can't tell what she thinks of my choice, but honestly it doesn't matter.

"I love it," I tell her.

"Excellent. Now let's decide on—" she is cut off by the ring of the suite's phone.

"Let's see what excuse he came up with for today," I grumble as I accept the call from the front desk. Part of taking control means not avoiding my problems either. I listened to the messages he left but avoided answering. That ends now. "Hello?"

"I'm so glad you answered," he says in a rush.

"Oh yeah?" I lounge back in the chair and check my watch. Actually, he's calling a little later today. Probably part of his plan.

"It's Zeus," he says.

I sit bolt upright. "What's wrong?"

"I don't know. He's acting oddly," Sterling says, his voice coated with worry. "I can barely get him to go out on a walk."

"What?" I knew his adopted dog for months before Sterling adopted him from the shelter, so I know exactly how odd that is. Zeus loves his walks.

"Look, I know you're avoiding me, but could you could come over here and see what you think? You know him better than I do," he says.

"I'm on my way." I don't bother to say goodbye. I wipe the creamy mask off my face and begin searching for my purse. "I need to go."

"How did he finally hook you?" Kai's tone sparkles with laughter.

"Something is wrong with Zeus," I explain to them. I grab a pair of jeans and a shirt from the dresser drawer and dash into the bathroom to get dressed.

"I hope everything will be okay," Poppy calls after me as I run toward the door.

"Me, too," I say as I leave.

I can almost swear I hear her whisper to Kai as the door swings closed, "He used the dog. Brilliant."

Poppy's theory has me thinking. By the time I arrive at Twelve and South, I'm sure she's right. I'm already prepping my lecture for him on using an innocent animal when I reach the penthouse. Sterling opens the door before I can knock. "He's in here."

He doesn't bother to linger. He barely looks at me. Instead, he heads straight back to the living room. Sterling disappears, and a few steps later I realize he has laid down on the floor next to the dog, his dark head resting on him like he's listening to his heartbeat.. Zeus is in the middle of the floor, barely moving. He lifts his head when he sees me and lets out a small whimper.

"How long has he been like this?" I ask, dropping to the floor beside him. Something shifts in Zeus's demeanor when I reach to scratch behind his ears. He's not his usual playful self, but he moves closer, almost climbing into my lap to kiss me on the face. After a few seconds, he practically vibrates with joy. Maybe Poppy was right. "Did you train him to do this?"

"Honestly, I would have shamelessly used the dog if I had known it would work," he says, exhaling in relief. He props his head on his elbow and watches us.. "He just misses you."

"What's up, Zeus?" I continue scratching behind his ears before leaning down to whisper. "Did he talk you into this?"

"I can still hear you." He sounds happy, and my heart skips.

"Okay," I whisper, "nothing is wrong with your dog."

When I glance over, Sterling is studying him with concern. "I still want to take him to the vet."

"Hey, I really do think he's okay," I say, finding myself wanting to reassure him.

"I'm supposed to take care of him." The statement is loaded with self-recrimination.

"And you are," I promise him. Something sticking out from the seam of the couch catches my eye. I point to it. "Is that my phone?"

Sterling tears his eyes from us, rolls to the side, and pulls it out. "You mean, this whole time you haven't been answering because your phone was here? I thought you were avoiding me."

"Trust me, I was." I reach and grab it from him.

He just stares dumbly at his empty hand. "You really were," he says quietly. "You didn't even come for your phone."

"I didn't need it." I do my best to sound casual.

"What about your job?" He looks up, concern deepening the blue of his eyes.

"It's fine. I haven't started yet." I console myself that it's not really a lie. I scratch Zeus on the chin before pushing to my feet. "I should go."

Sterling gets up and blocks my clean getaway. "Let me buy you dinner."

"It's two o'clock," I say, crossing my arms and trying to look disinterested in the offer. "that's hours away."

He stalks a few steps closer. "If only we could think of something to do until then..."

"Like talk about your mysterious friend Noah?" I ask pointedly, trying to ignore the tingles breaking over my body.

"I already told you it's complicated," Sterling says, pulling up a half step before crashing into me.

My body responds to his proximity, longing for the release only he can give me. But I won't repeat my past mistakes, even if all I do is make new ones. "And I already told you it isn't. Either I matter to you or I don't."

He flinches as if I slapped him. "Of course you matter to me."

"Not enough to tell me about the last five years of your life. Not enough to tell me who Noah is and why he scared you."

"That's not fair," Sterling insists. "It's not like—"

"Well, I won't really know until you tell me, will I?"

It's an excellent point, and he knows it.

"Lucky..." he trails off, his eyes wild, like a cornered animal's. "I won't lose you."

He reaches for me, and I don't stop him.

I tell myself I could, that I'm the one steering this runaway train of a relationship—but as soon as his hands are on me, I know it's a lie. He leans down to kiss me, and it takes every ounce of self-control I can muster to keep the train on the tracks.

"I'm not going anywhere." His face is inches from mine, and his eyes, beginning to close, snap open. It's like I've breathed life back into him. "But I'm also not waiting around for you to get your shit together."

"So where does that leave us?" His sense of relief fades, replaced by a sly, hopeful look. His hands, wrapped around my shoulders, begin to slide down my back.

That's exactly what I'd like to know.

When I don't answer, he moves his face closer to mine —close enough to kiss me, but he doesn't. "Is this the part where you break my heart?"

Is it? In order to survive Sterling Ford, I told myself I had to slam the door in his face. And it was easy enough to believe when we were apart. But in the same room? With his hands on me? We're both powerless. We hurtle forward, faster than we can see the way ahead, because this thing we have—whatever it is—is better than the darkness of our lives. Our passion throws sparks to light the way, but sparks only last so long. There's always another bend in the tracks ahead, too far for the light to reach, and once we round it, the darkness swallows us again.

I know this and it doesn't matter.

"Just put your fucking hands on me, already," I breathe. Sometimes a girl needs freedom from the dark, even if it's a stolen thing. Even if it's all I can rely on Sterling to provide.

He doesn't hesitate. Pulling his t-shirt off with one

hand, he uses the other to force open my jeans. He doesn't bother helping me take them off, instead shoving his hand between my legs to find his prize.

My own hand slides to his jeans, unbuttoning them to free his swelling cock. It falls heavy and hot into my palm, and his vocal cords spasm, collapsing his sharp grunt into a deep moan. He pushes them down and steps out of them. Sterling spins me the opposite direction, his left arm under my ribcage, bracing me tightly, his right hand buried in my panties.

He slides one finger into my gushing sex, then two. I can feel my clit between his knuckles, like a vise there's no hope of escaping. The pressure is so intense that, for a moment, I'm afraid I might pass out. My head rolls back onto his chest as he lifts me off the ground and starts to carry me to the bedroom? The wall? I can't think well enough to process the particulars, and I care even less as long as he doesn't stop. I lose my sandals along the way and possibly my mind.

I give my body completely to him, not knowing what the future will bring besides the escape I so desperately need.

When he lowers me to my feet, he doesn't release me. His hand slides away, but only so he can grab the waistband of my jeans and frantically jerk them off me. He moves closer, angling his body until my seam rests against the shaft of his cock. My body responds, my hips swiveling and twitching, trying to get him inside me.

"Not yet," he murmurs, drawing his crown across my aching cleft until it throbs with expectation.

My eyes have been closed since the moment he first put

his hands on me: I wanted to lose myself from the real world, to escape to somewhere else, to be consumed by him. But I can't help my eyelids fluttering as some distant part of my brain tries to discover the reason for my denial.

We're in the bathroom, facing the mirror. I'm naked from the waist down, my t-shirt pulled halfway up my stomach under his strong arm—and Sterling? Every inch of him is naked, but I can only enjoy the parts not hidden behind me: the massive swell of his biceps, the strong slope of his shoulders, the slab of abs peeking from the curve of my waist.

Sterling's face is waiting for my eyes to open, for me to process where we are. He counterbalances in order to kick the door closed, and I distantly register Zeus's skittering nails on the tiles outside.

"I want you to see what I see when I love you," he says, fixing me with a relentless gaze.

I watch, now completely unable to close my eyes, as he coaxes my seam back and forth along his shaft, the head of his cock bumping against my clit only to slide back away. My legs tremble under me from the effort of holding out for more.

"You're fucking perfect, Lucky. Christ, just look at you." His eyes are possessive, but there's something selfless in his attention to my body. He could take me any moment, but he seems obsessed with making this linger.

He spreads me open, wide enough that I can see where his cock is stroking against me. I want to see what he does, but my eyes stray to the dimples on my thighs, the thickness of my hips. It's too much and I turn my head from the reflection.

"No," he says. The hand wrapped around my torso reaches up to point my chin back toward the mirror. "You need to understand."

I train my eyes on our reflection, finding his own gaze burning into me. Sterling slides his arm down and around my waist, lifting me off my feet, just high enough that his cock springs upward, banging against the open target his other hand created and sending convulsions throughout my body.

"I will never stop giving to you," he says. "Because you won't let me."

He takes his cock in his hand and centers against me. My breath catches when he begins his slow, excruciating slide inside.

"Are you watching, Lucky?"

When I don't respond he begins to slide out of me, and I sputter my reply, "Yes."

He allows my weight to slide down along his chest, his cock disappearing inside me as I fight to focus on how he makes me feel and not my body. It gets easier with every glorious inch. He holds me like that, his cock half-buried inside me, so that I can see it all.

"This is what I need to show you." He only mouths the words, but I hear it like a booming command.

I watch, absent any conscious direction on my part, as my body takes over. My hips roll back and forth. Somehow, another inch of him slides into me. I feel the pressure increase, but also the ache for more of him.

I've stopped breathing. My lungs burn, but my body seems to think his cock is more important than air. My hips begin to wiggle, then to spasm, jerking down onto his shaft.

When his shaft is fully engulfed, the clenched knot in my throat disappears, sending sweet air back into my lungs. I shudder and gasp, my eyes finding his in the reflection.

"Do you see?" he asks. "You don't need to be saved. You never have. You need to be found, so understand what I'm saying now—I see you. I want you. I always have. I always will."

Strange, shimmering lights float in my vision. Thoughts are fuzzy, words getting lost between my brain and my lips.

Sensing my confusion, he leans to kiss me, then nips my ear. "I noticed it the first time we made love."

I nuzzle into the hollow of his neck, beneath his jaw. The spice of his cologne is warm and calming. Relief floods me, my body shivering at the release of so much tension. I've found the place I *need* to be, and I want to stay there forever.

"You need me more than air, Lucky." He isn't bragging or teasing.

I don't bother trying to correct or object. They are foreign concepts, held by a version of me who only exists in a different place than the one we've just created. I don't care what she thinks. I only want this me—the one he's showing me. The Adair he sees. I want to exist in his eyes alone.

So, I allow my body to go limp in his arms.

His stroke is long and slow, hitting against my g-spot and releasing waves of warmth and drawing hollow moans from my lips. Our tempo increases steadily, building alongside the pressure of taking all of him.

I spy flashes of us in the mirror, a rapture of limbs and flushed-red skin. My shame is gone, back with the other parts of me that don't belong here. I feel only light and heat, air and flame, the spark of us.

"Come for me, Lucky," he orders, his fingertips finding my clit and stroking furiously until all I see is a blur and all I feel is pleasure. It builds, grabbing holding of me, until he frees me, my body surging with wave after wave of release. My eyes close, lost to it.

"Fuck. *Fuck*." I repeat the word so many times I lose track.

Sterling's voice adds to my chorus of *fucks*, and I can feel his cock jolt as he comes inside me. After a few moments, the waves fade in frequency, then die, but I can't bring myself to open my eyes. I know what comes next.

"Look at me, Lucky."

I do. I can't resist him.

He stares back at me, worshipping me with eyes, even as he turns on the faucet, still holding me up. He slides out of me, and I replace his absence with a whimper. He washes me off, carefully and gently, like he knows how tender I am now.

Why can't it be like this back in the real world? I wonder.

When he finishes, he shoots me a deeply satisfied grin before releasing me to my own feet.

My legs behave like a newborn foal's, and he puts a steadying hand on my hip. After a couple moments I nod at him, still a little short of breath.

He finally lets go of me, turning towards the shower and flipping the faucet handle to *hot*. "I'm glad you came over, Lucky," Sterling says, flashing me one of his patented

I know exactly how irresistible I am looks over his shoulder. "I'm glad *it's* not over."

He's in danger of getting the wrong idea. Of course he would think more sex would fix things. I shoot eye daggers at him as I yank my jeans on and button them. There's no time to find my panties. That's another pair lost to him.

"I came over for Zeus," I say, edging toward the bathroom door. I need him to be completely clear on this point. "And it can't *be over*, because it never really started."

"I love you."

This stops me for a minute, but it's not enough. "Saying I love you is meaningless. Show me! Prove it!"

"I will every damn day," he growls, lunging for me.

I dodge him, shaking my head. "It's too late."

"Lucky," he splutters, but I'm already out the door. I swipe my sandals from the floor outside his bedroom and grab my purse from the counter. I don't turn even as he keeps calling my name. I practically run into the elevator.

"Lobby, please!" I tell the bellhop, reaching past him to jam the door close button just as the door to Sterling's penthouse flies open.

The door slides closed, giving me one flash of a very naked and very angry Sterling stepping into the hallway. The bellhop turns away, a smile ghosting across his lips.

"Sorry about that," I mutter before falling into an awkward silence. I take a deep breath and allow myself to relax. Sterling knows what I need when we manage to shut out the real world—that much he made absolutely clear. But it doesn't change what I need from him in the real world or my determination to get it.

By the time the elevator reaches the lobby, it's being

called back to the penthouse. I turn pleading eyes on the bellhop. "Do me a favor—" I read the name on his badge "—Percy? Stop on a few floors before you take him to the parking garage?"

He winks at me. "Yes, Ms. MacLaine."

"How do... never mind." I realize my tempestuous encounters with Sterling have probably drawn a fair bit of attention to both of us among the building staff. "Thank you."

"If you don't mind me asking," he says as he holds open the doors for me, "are you sure you're running for the right reasons?"

My eyes flicker upward, as though drawn towards where Sterling is. Every inch of me wants to go back up there. That's how I know. "I am."

Percy nods and steps into the elevator. "Going up!"

The panel above the elevator begins to light up, climbing back to him without me. That's my cue to get away before I find myself falling right back into Sterling's arms. It doesn't matter if that's what I want, because I can't risk having him now if ignoring our problems tears up apart forever.

14

STERLING

THE PAST

Econ 101 has 220 students and seven teaching assistants. As soon as Professor Jones releases us all to our Thanksgiving break, I find myself struggling through a hoard of bodies toward the front of the class, where my eight sub-instructors are arranged like courtiers attending their king.

"See you Sunday," Cyrus calls over his shoulder, off to some island with his family for the holiday. He left the keys to his family's suite with me, as promised, but unlike for him, the arrival of Thanksgiving only means we're getting close to finals.

I've been back on the straight and narrow for a week, thanks to Adair's gentle, if fierce, dedication to my reform. She's even going to help me study over break. Now, I need to find out exactly how far I managed to fall during my two-week bender. Surely, it can't have been enough to jeopardize my grades seriously.

My assigned teaching assistant, Shannon, a short, fierce grad student from Boston, left through the faculty exit almost immediately. Probably on her way back to the Northeast for the holidays. Apparently, I'm not the only one worried about my grade because two dozen others stop for an audience. By the time I reach the front, there is only one T.A. left to bother. His pinched face is adorned with black, wire-rimmed glasses that reflect his laptop screen so perfectly I could probably read Cyrus's grade as well as mine.

"Hey." I shoulder my bag higher. "I was wondering if you could let me know where I'm at."

He sighs, his eyes flickering to the long line of students, waiting to ask the same question, behind me.

"Name."

"Sterling Ford," I say. "Thanks. I have to maintain a certain GPA for my scholarship. I have to get a B."

This goes a considerable way toward softening her attitude. I'm guessing someone stuck grading papers and tests for a professor is in the same boat I am. He's got to earn his keep here, too.

"Well, bad news, Sterling. To get a B, you'll need to score an A on both your final essay and your final exam," he says with a grim, but sympathetic smile.

I do a quick calculation and realize the situation is worse than I expected. "So right now I have a...?"

"You would receive a C minus," he takes a moment to gauge my reaction before continuing. "I've seen you in class. You're bright, so you probably don't need me to tell you this, but—"

"Taking zeroes has ruined my grade."

"You only have A's and zeros on our grade sheet. But look," he punches in two numbers on his laptop, swivels it around towards me, and I can see how the weighting of our last two assignments might turn my C- into an A-.

"Thanks. Have a nice break."

He nods and waves the next student forward, preparing to deliver the next bit of bad news.

Suddenly, I'm not so sure I should have taken Adair up on her offer to help me study. Between that and Francie arriving in a couple hours for her visit, I doubt I'll get the time I need to do it properly. I spend the whole trip back to my dorm considering ways to tell Adair it's probably not a good idea.

"Don't you know it's bad form to keep a lady waiting?" She's leaning against the doorjamb of my room as I come off the elevator.

"Damn, you're beautiful," I say, suddenly forgetting my plan to reject her help.

And it's true. She's wearing tight-fitting black leather pants and a lacy top that allows glimpses of a black bra. Her bun is set with lacquered black chopsticks, and her lips are full and glossy. A well-worn jean jacket completes the ensemble. She looks like one of her magnolias, just waiting for the world to come along and admire her.

"Not a bad apology. What took you so long?"

"I was considering our study arrangement and whether you'd be helpful or distracting." I fumble with the keys for a moment as she gives me a slight frown.

"What did you decide?"

"You're definitely going to be distracting. Leather pants? Really?"

She sweeps into the room as soon as I open the door,

taking Cyrus's chair by the window. "They are remarkably difficult to get off and on, actually."

"Is that a challenge?"

"Already forgotten about studying, have we? That won't do." Adair does her best impression of a schoolmarm, pursing her lips and tutting softly. "Which grade is most in need of rescue?"

"Econ."

"Let me see your notes."

I slide them out of my bag and open to where the final exam notes begin, then I hand it over.

"This looks more like Latin. *Ceteris Paribus*?"

"It's a fancy way of saying that all variables not under consideration will remain constant."

"When you say it like that, I wonder how you're *not* getting an A."

"Well, I actually went to that class, but I missed a few assignments when..." I don't need to finish that statement. She knows exactly why my grade is tanking. "I can't believe it only took two weeks to fuck everything up."

Adair tilts her head. "What do you mean? You're behind, but I bet everyone is their first semester."

"Everyone doesn't have to earn a 3.0 GPA to keep their scholarship. I'm at a steady B in my other classes, but Econ?" I sigh. "It's a C minus. That's just low enough to lose my scholarship. So maybe..."

"Are you telling me to leave?" she asks.

"I'm not sure I can risk it." Not if I want to stick around Valmont, and the last week with Adair has proven to me that I do.

"Listen, I'm not going to let you lose your scholarship,

but I think I can actually help." She pauses, her lips twisting into a wicked smile. "And to make it worth your while, I'm not sleeping with you until finals are over and you've aced them all."

"I, um, what?" I find myself looking everywhere but her face, which is unfortunate because my eyes land on her breasts.

"I've given this a lot of consideration," she says, re-assuming the air of a teacher. She snaps her fingers and I tear my eyes away from her chest. "Please make yourself comfortable before we begin."

"Yes, ma'am." I sit cross-legged on my bed, leaving just enough room for Adair to join me.

Instead, she wheels a chair a few feet from my bed and flips through my notes until she reaches a section I photo-copied from Cyrus. Obviously, they're from a class I missed. "Let's begin. Markets increase overall welfare via the concepts of consumer and producer *blank*."

"Surplus."

"Well done." Adair kicks off her shoes and fires off another question, which I also get correct. She pulls off her socks.

My dick twitches in my pants at the sight of her bare skin, even if it is only her feet. "Do you have warm feet or something?"

She ignores my question in favor of another quiz. "With every purchase they make, a consumer experiences what measure of satisfaction?"

"Utility."

"Very good." Adair fixes me with an impish smile and takes a good 20 seconds slowly removing her jacket.

Now I can make out the entire outline of her bra beneath her top, and suddenly my jeans feel extra tight. "Are you—are we doing what I think?"

"What two functions limit the production of businesses?"

Shit. I can't think. "Uh, cost, and..." I trail off sheepishly.

"Diminishing returns," she says with another tut. She shifts in her chair as she puts the jacket back on.

"No." The word escapes my mouth reflexively. If every class involved a striptease, I'm sure I'd never miss one.

"The antithesis of the unregulated market is what other model?" she asks.

"The monopoly model?" I say, trying to sound casual.

Adair pauses a moment, clearly enjoying herself. She begins to re-remove her jacket, but pauses at the last second. "Is that your final answer?"

"Yes." I am absolutely sure I'm right. I lick my lower lip.

"Good boy." The jacket comes off quickly this time, pulling against the satin fabric of her top and revealing part of her breast.

I can actually feel the amount of blood reaching my brain decrease. I uncross my legs in order to make more room in my jeans. Adair notices the growing bulge and gives her glossy bottom lip a coquettish nip.

"I took psych my last year of prep. I got an A," she brags.

"*This* is what they teach in psych?"

"Not exactly. But we did cover techniques for the reinforcement of desirable behaviors. This is just a practical application."

"And all of the blood leaving my brain for other places?"

"A regrettable side effect, unfortunately. Let's continue." She flips over a page of notes and now the impish side is back. "Oh! A tough one. The Nash Equilibrium is considered the ideal solution to what thought problem?"

"The prisoner's dilemma!" I say, embarrassed by my own enthusiasm.

Adair places the notes on the edge of the bed, crosses her left arm over her right, and slowly pulls up the hem of her top.

I lean forward, slack-jawed, as Adair pretends to struggle with getting it to slide up and over her breasts. Her timing is impeccable.

At last, she puts me out of my misery, her top popping off suddenly and sending her breasts colliding into each other. I scoot forward on the bed, manually readjusting my jeans yet again. I really think it would be better to just to get the fooling around out of the way.

It takes me a moment to realize Adair said something.

"Fuck, you're so gorgeous." I say in response.

"I'm afraid that answer won't work on your professor." Adair grabs her top as if to put it back on.

"Double or nothing?"

Something about the smile she gives reminds me of a large cat playing with its dinner. "Very well."

I get the next question right, and Adair throws the top behind her without looking. By luck it catches the lever door knob and hangs there, which reminds me of something. I hop off the bed, and Adair, who evidently thinks I am moving in to jump her, rolls her chair away from me. I stoop to retrieve one of her socks. I pop my head out the door, careful to block the view inside, and stuff the sock on the outside door knob. This way, if Cyrus comes back unexpectedly, he will know to fuck off for a bit.

We return to our earlier arrangement, and Adair begins asking harder questions. Suddenly I know things I'm not sure how I know. I'm unclear on the rules of this little game, and my responses are an equal mix of right and wrong. Eventually, after a correct answer, and in my best earnest student voice I ask, "Do I get any say in what you take off?"

"Hmm." She taps her finger pensively on her chin. "I'll allow it."

"Let's see how hard those pants are to remove. Call it scholarly interest."

She meets my gaze evenly. "They are so hard to remove it will take three questions, I think. Otherwise, the reward system might get out of whack. So one down."

"And the bra?"

"Two. One for each little clasp."

"You're killing me," I grouse. "Let's start with pants."

"Aren't we ambitious?" She grins. "It looks like the next few notes are pretty complex."

"Ask me."

She rises slowly from her chair, slides a thumb under the waist of her pants and begins to fumble with the button. With her other arm, she holds the notebook and looks for another question. When the button finally gives way, I have to stifle a low moan. A tiny red flower is embroidered on the top of her panties, the only thing visible past the slit of black leather.

She asks a question about game theory as it relates to

microeconomics, and I surprise even myself with the correct answer. She pauses a moment, and it occurs to me for the first time that this might be getting uncomfortable for her.

"You don't have to if—"

"Hush. Close your eyes."

"I thought the point was that I got to watch."

"There's nothing graceful about this, I promise," she says. "Now, close your eyes."

"Right." I acknowledge. "How do I do that? I can't seem to remember."

She laughs softly, leans forward, and brushes her hand softly down my face. I close my eyes, which immediately heightens my other senses. Her perfume wafts across me, a faint floral aroma that gives me dark thoughts. I hear her zipper take five long seconds to come undone, hear the faint *whish* of fabric sliding over fabric. A floorboard creaks. I hear her settling into the chair.

"Open your eyes."

I do, and well before she finishes her first word.

There's teasing, and then there's torture. This is the latter. She sits sidelong in the chair, one leather-clad leg arranged nearest me. One glorious naked leg is folded up in front of her, and her arms reach around either side of it to hold the notebook.

"I'm not sure how much longer I can stand this," I say with perfect honesty.

"Nearly there. Focus. Utility is used to measure a consumer's optimal rate of *what*?"

"Consumption. Easy." I try not to sound smug.

"Maybe it shouldn't count, then?"

Fuck. No. No. No.

"It'll definitely be on the test," I argue.

"Eyes. Closed."

I oblige with a grin.

I hear the squeak of the plastic office chair, the even, smooth sound of her other leg coming out, followed by total silence. I'm on the verge of insanity when I feel two palms on my shoulders. I inhale deeply, taking in her scent. Then I'm shoved onto my back as she straddles me.

I feel like an attack dog let off its leash. My eyes snap open. I grab either side of her jaw in my hands and see her soft, glossy lips part in anticipation. I bolt upright and she responds by wrapping her legs around my torso. The bulge in my jeans grinds against the fabric of her panties and she whimpers.

"Teachers aren't really supposed to do this kind of thing with students," she says, eyes closed, cheeks stained crimson on alabaster white.

"I think I'm going to ace that final. Maybe we can skip the chastity clause?"

"I think that would undermine the reward system," she pants, but presses her body closer. "Don't you want to focus?"

I answer by pushing her hips against mine, our bodies slowly grinding as our hands explore. There are a lot of things I want to focus on.

"Sterling." The call is soft, barely audible over the blood pounding in my ears.

"Yeah, Lucky?" I respond, my teeth nibbling her ear. Adair tenses. I pull away. "Did I do something wrong?"

"I didn't say anything," she whispers. "I think there's someone at your door."

"Sterling!" This time there's no mistaking it. Someone's calling from outside the door which is, thankfully, locked.

"Francie!" I hiss quietly. We've been studying for longer than I thought. "Get dressed, quick."

"Easy for you to say. You're the one who wanted me to take off the pants!" Adair picks them up and dashes for the bathroom door. "Shit! It's locked!"

"Sterling, are you there?" Francie calls on the other side of the door.

Adair is on the bed, desperately trying to pull on her leather pants, her legs stuck straight up, like she even needs gravity to help with the process.

I tiptoe to the door, retrieve her top, and throw it at her. That's when I hear Cyrus. Cyrus, who is supposed to be on his way to the Bahamas or the Virgin Islands or somewhere I'll never be able to afford to visit.

"Francie? I'm Cyrus." he says. "Sterling told me you were coming."

"I didn't think I would get to meet you." I can hear her hug him, the smoosh is audible.

Yes, keep up the small talk, I pray.

"I need to hit the road soon, but I forgot my phone charger."

Keys jangle. *Come on, Cyrus. Figure it out.*

The key goes in the lock. *The sock is universal, shithead.*

The door opens inward, and I am greeted by my foster mother and my soon-to-be ex-roommate. I'm going to kill him, or maybe roast him alive. My own Thanksgiving turkey. I slide over to block their view of the bed and try to seem like I was hurrying to the door. Cyrus brushes past me, a shit-eating grin sparking on his face as he catches sight of Adair standing up from the bed, her top on inside out.

"Well," Cyrus says flatly. "I guess that explains the sock." He tosses it to her.

"Francie, I'm so sorry. I lost track of time," I say. Adair appears at my side, somehow already more composed than me. "This is Adair. Adair MacLaine. My, um, friend."

Adair's eyes dart in my direction at the sudden demotion, then smiles warmly at Francie. "Pleased to meet you."

Come on, Francie. Be cool.

"I'm pleased to meet you, too." Francie gives me a small, inscrutable frown before returning to Adair. "I wish I could say Sterling has mentioned you, but Sterling hasn't told me much of anything since he began school."

"He's a bit of a mystery sometimes," Adair says knowingly.

"Well, she's got your number." Francie laughs.

I can always tell how Francie feels about a person. If she dislikes someone, her face gets pinched and her tone snappy. But she sounds like she's reconnecting with an old friend as she says, "I've had years to get used to it, hon." She grabs Adair and hugs her like a mama bear claiming a lost cub.

Adair looks a little ruffled by the affection, and I remember she doesn't like hugs.

"Will you be joining us for Thanksgiving?" Francie asks her.

"Oh, um, I'm supposed to have dinner with my family."

She spares a glance at me. "I'd invite you to our house, but, honestly, I think this year will be a little rough."

"That's okay," Cyrus steps in, saving the day. "The Eaton always delivers a meal to its guests."

"The what-now?" Francie asks. "I figured we'd hit the grocery store and cook in the community kitchen. The dorm brochure said there was one on the ground floor."

"There is?" Cyrus shrugs. It's not like he's ever bothered to check the Valmont dorm amenities. Why would he, when he has a five-star hotel at his disposal?

"Surely Sterling has cooked for you." Francie clucks at me when she sees their vacant expressions. She pins her eyes on Adair. "Not even you?"

"No, ma'am." Adair bites back a smile.

"I raised him better than that. No wonder you look so skinny," she says, skimming my form. "You can't live off dorm food."

"Are you from the South?" Cyrus asks. "Because I feel like you will fit in here."

"I'm from Queens," Francie says as if that settles the matter.

Cyrus checks his watch. "I have to get going. You have the keys?"

I nod, carefully avoiding Adair's eyes. I'd mentioned my arrangement with Cyrus casually, but I don't want to linger on it. Adair MacLaine has never had to borrow a friend's place to house her family. Because her house is the size of a castle and features multiple guesthouses on property?

"I should go, too." Adair pops onto her tiptoes and kisses my cheek. "It was really nice to meet you."

"Will I see you again?" Francie asks her.

"Um, that's up to Sterling."

Two sets of demanding eyes land on me. Nothing like being put on the spot.

"If you can get away from your family," I say. The thought of spending the whole week without Adair sucks, even though I'm genuinely looking forward to showing Francie around. But I'm not certain Adair will enjoy being dragged to every free exhibit in Nashville, or eating whatever we can concoct in the hotel suite's kitchenette. Not when she's used to country clubs and multi-course dining.

"God, I hope I can," Adair mutters. Our eyes meet, and I remember that for every way we're different, there are a bunch more that we're exactly alike.

"I'm going to walk Adair to her car." I look to Francie for permission, and she beams with pride.

"I wouldn't expect less. I'll just be here," she says.

I grab Adair's hand and lead her into the hall.

"Your m... she seems nice," Adair says breathlessly as I rush her out of the dormitory. "Sorry, I don't know what to call her."

"Just stick with Francie," I advise her. "I struggled with what to call her when I first got placed with her. The other foster families I'd been stuck with before had insisted on titles and surnames. All that formality went out the door the second I stepped into Francie's house. That didn't mean she wasn't tough, though. She was easily the strictest foster parent I ever had."

"She straightened you out, huh?" We step out of the building into the crisp, breezy Tennessee twilight. Adair's favorite car, a Jaguar Roadster, is parked dangerously close to the no-parking zone. I doubt anyone would have the guts to tow a car belonging to a MacLaine.

I walk her to it and open the driver side door for her.

"What a gentleman," Adair murmurs.

"Don't let that fool you," I warn her, angling my mouth over hers. "I'm thinking very dirty things about you. I might need a second study session."

"That can be arranged."

I nip her lower lip. "We should be careful or I'm going to wind up pinning you to the hood of this car."

"Campus is deserted."

I groan at the invitation in her voice. "Seriously?"

She laughs, shaking her head and loosening her makeshift bun. "There's no way you could get these pants off, remember?"

"I *am* willing to try." I hook my index finger in her waistband and tug her closer. I kiss her slowly, savoring one final taste of her.

"I'm going to miss you," she confesses. "I think I'd rather do Thanksgiving at the Eaton than my house, but Daddy would throw a fit."

"I'm a phone call away," I promise.

"Will you call me?" she asks. "I'd like to hang out with you and Francie, but I don't want to intrude."

"Sure," I say swiftly, but I don't know if I'm telling the truth.

She slides into her car and blows me a kiss. I watch as she drives off, feeling like my own heartbeat grows fainter the farther aways she gets.

"Cyrus took off. He told me to tell you that his car is

parked in the lot behind Tucker," Francie says after the walk back to my room. "You were gone a while."

"Hmmm?" I shake my head. "I mean, what?"

"You have it bad for that girl." Francie laughs and pins me in a hug. "Why didn't you tell me about her?"

"It's kinda off again, on again," I admit.

"I want to know everything," Francie demands. "But first, what is this about not staying here?"

"Cyrus thought you might be more comfortable if we stayed at his family's place. They own a hotel in Nashville, but they're going to be out of town." I fill her in on the details as we make our way to the parking lot.

Francie packed light. She has to, in order to avoid baggage fees. My stuff fits easily in one duffel bag. There's only one car left in the lot. Francie stops when we reach the edge of the sidewalk.

"Wait, your friend is letting you drive that?" She stares at the BMW.

"Yeah, he loaned it to me a couple of times."

Francie raises her eyebrow so far it disappears behind the coil of her bangs. "Are you sure that's a good idea?"

"Usually, I am the designated driver," I explain, "and I drove Adair to the hospital in it once."

"I think you better start catching me up." Francie pauses at the passenger door even after I open it for her.

"It's okay, really," I tell her. "Cyrus is an okay guy."

"He must be." But she doesn't sound convinced.

I fill her in on the night I met Adair, leaving out the nastier fights we'd had along the way. Francie isn't the type to take sides, but I want her to like Adair. More importantly, I'd rather she not know about some of the bad choices I've made since coming to Valmont.

"That poor girl," Francie says quietly when we pull into the circular drive of the Eaton. "Her first Thanksgiving without her mama. You make sure you check in with her."

"I will."

A parking valet opens her door. "Welcome to the Eaton, ma'am."

I follow Cyrus's instructions, handing off the keys and giving his name. Inside, I head straight for a bank of elevators with golden doors. Even though this was Cy's idea, I still feel out of place. I want to get up to the room and out of the opulent entrance with its gleaming marble floors and domed, stained glass ceiling. When I reach the elevators, I turn to find Francie standing in the lobby, staring around her.

"Francie," I hiss as the elevator in front of me dings.

She hurries over. A few others board with us. The suite is on the sixth floor, the very top level of the hotel. Everyone else gets off on other floors. When we reach the suites, I see why. There are only four, apparently numbered randomly between 600 and 614. In small letters under each number is the word 'penthouse.' The first one we reach, number 614, is also marked as a private residence.

"It's the one at the other end. Number 600," I tell Francie, shouldering our bags.

"People live here?" she says.

"Guess so." I might have thought that was far-fetched until I met the Valmont elite. Now, nothing surprises me about this town.

"This wasn't what I was expecting when you said your friend's family owned a hotel. I thought it would be like that place we stopped outside Roanoke. The one with the mini-fridge and the broken ice machine." She falls silent when I open the door to the suite.

It's easily twice the size of our place in Queens, and a far cry from the Drive Rite Inn we stayed at in Virginia.

No expense was spared for the Eaton's private suite at their hotel. Plum velvet sofas with turned arms face each other, perfectly spaced around a large stone hearth. A chandelier drips crystal above us, its light sparkling around the richly papered walls. Cyrus mentioned a kitchenette, and it turns out to be larger than our room and appointed with luxury appliances, including a refrigerator with French doors. An oak table that seats twelve stretches between it and the living room, with each place already set for a dinner party. I spot a note on the counter.

Make yourselves at home. Order what you want. Don't worry about the bill. It's on the house.

Francie wanders throughout, pausing before continuing down a hall. There are two bedrooms, each with its own private bathroom. I drop Francie's bag in the biggest one and turn to her with a grin. It fades as soon as I see her face.

"I don't know about this," she says. "This is an expensive place, Sterling."

"I guess I have friends in high places now." The joke falls flat.

"That girl? Adair? She has money like this?"

"More, I think," I admit. I drop onto the bed, knowing there's more we need to talk about.

"Why didn't you tell me she's rich?"

"Does it matter?"

"If you have to ask, it does," she says. "Do you know what you're getting yourself into?"

Resentment bubbles inside me. Francie was the one that pushed me toward the private, affluent university. Who did she expect my classmates to be? I fight the urge to boil over. She's voicing the exact same concerns I had when I first met Adair and her friends.

"Adair's different," I promise her.

Francie studies me before forcing a smile. "I hope you're right."

15

ADAIR

PRESENT DAY

"This will be your desk."

I trail my finger across the top of the cheap office chair. It's not much. A desk shoved into the corner of the room with a beat-up filing cabinet next to it.

The offices at Bluebird Press are a half-story underground. The vibe is exactly the opposite of most offices I've been in. Instead of a fluorescent-lighted, taupe-cubicle hellscape, Bluebird shows signs of actual life. Along the two exterior walls, high windows give the cramped space a surprising amount of natural light. Piles of books and loosely bound, coffee-stained manuscripts gather on well-worn wooden desks. The air is slightly stuffy, except when I walk through a stream of air blown down by the ancient, belt-driven ceiling fan system. The stale, wet-cardboard smell of cheap coffee wafts through the room, but it's unclear if this is from an actual coffee machine, or if the aroma has simply always been here.

A few steps from my desk there's a community copy

machine liberally plastered with instructions on how to coax it to do one's bidding. It's definitely not the executive office I imagined sitting in one day.

I don't care, because there's a stack of manuscripts waiting for me on my desk. Who cares about the cramped space? Books take you all over the world. No passport required. Trish watches me nervously, probably wondering if I'm going to demand a corner office.

Thanks to Poppy's intervention, I'm overdressed for my first day on the job. Where Trish looks comfortable in a pair of slim-legged khaki trousers, canary-yellow ballet flats, and an oversized white tank top, I'm in a black pencil skirt that hugs my ample hips and 3-inch black crocodile-leather heels that Poppy deemed "tame enough for work." My saving grace is the soft denim shirt I insisted on. Knotted in the front, the outfit was classic but sophisticated. Even Poppy approved.

Now, I wonder if I'm sending the wrong message. I don't want Trish to think I'm here to take over. There's a lot I need to learn from her before I'll be ready to be a real editor, let alone oversee the entire company as its owner.

"Is it okay?" she asks when I'm quiet for too long. "We can move your desk anywhere—"

"No!" I stop her. I don't want her to ruin the moment. "This is perfect."

"I know it's not fancy..." Trish glances around as if she's afraid someone might hear her. "But we can't afford much."

"About that." I take a deep breath and prepare myself. "My salary."

"Obviously, it's not very competitive," she says, tugging

her honey blonde hair into a messy bun. "I can see if we can afford more."

"Are you kidding? It's my first real job. I'd probably work for free coffee," I confess to her. Now that she knows who I am, there's no need to hide that fact. "But I also own the place, so maybe I shouldn't take a salary at all."

"Of course you should take a salary." Trish looks at me like I've grown a second head. "If you think you're gonna make any money as the owner, then you're deluding yourself."

"But Bluebird can afford this?" I should have seen how difficult this was going to be. As much as I want this job on my own terms and as much as I want to be treated like everyone else, I can't divorce the fact that I'm responsible for all of them. Why I thought I could come here to play editor and pretend I don't have the power to make or break this publishing company, I don't know. Standing here now amid my new coworkers, I realize they're more than that. They're my company's backbone.

"Look, you should get paid for what you do. It's only fair. But you might want to check with accounting—and by accounting, I mean Meg." Trish grins and hitches a finger toward a woman sitting on the far side of the room. "She's pretty much in charge of keeping the books. It's a really sophisticated operation we have going here."

"I can see that." I return her smile. If she can have a good attitude about all of this, I can as well. I'd expected to come here and find a pity position, but Trish isn't acting any differently than when I saw her last week. "I want to do whatever I can to help Bluebird succeed. But, honestly, I really want to work with books."

"Let me clear about this. You earned the editorial job," Trish reminds me. "I had no idea who you were. Not that it matters."

"It doesn't?" I mutter.

Trish mistakes the look on my face. "Don't worry. I haven't told anyone that you own them."

"I don't," I say quickly. Something about the way she says it reminds me too much of my father.

"I'm just teasing."

"Sorry, sore subject," I admit. "Being a MacLaine is a lot like having a big, old albatross hanging around my neck."

"I would think it opens a lot of doors," Trish says thoughtfully.

"It does—but mostly to cigar lounges and boys clubs and private meetings with lots and lots of old men."

"When you put it like that." Trish gives me a rueful smile. "I have no idea why your dad kept Bluebird for all these years. I'll be truthful. We kept waiting for him to decide we weren't profitable or that we needed to publish different kinds of books. It was a relief when..." She trails off, clamping her mouth shut.

"It's okay. Actually, it's refreshing to know I'm not the only one who felt a little relieved when he died." I can't believe I said those words out loud, but Trish doesn't look shocked.

"We're just glad to be in good hands now." She winks at me. "So, anyway, we aren't very formal here. Come and go as you please. I just ask that you get the manuscripts and notes back to me by the dates on the Post-it notes." She taps a yellow sticky note dated July 18 attached to the front of the manuscript. "If you're not going to make a deadline, let me know. If one of your authors is being a pill, let me know. If you need anything—"

"I'll let you know," I promise her.

"I need to make a few calls. You're welcome to hang out or start whenever. I think you'll like these manuscripts." She hesitates a second before giving me a quick hug. Pulling back, she gives me a thumbs up. "Welcome to the team."

The team. I like the sound of that. I settle down at my desk at my job and pick up my first manuscript. I always thought my dreams were out of reach, but it turns out they were just down the street.

I'm so absorbed in the Valmont grad's manuscript that I skip lunch and keep reading. The premise is unlike anything I've ever read. It's a thriller, but somehow romantic and dreamy at the same time. I want to linger on every word and savor every sentence. It's so good that I nearly jump out of my chair when Trish taps me on the shoulder. I hastily drop the page onto the top of my stack.

"Sorry," she says with the hint of laughter in her voice, "but you have a *guest*."

For a split second, I'm embarrassed, wondering which of my friends has come down to take pictures of me like it's the first day of school or prom night. Then I catch the dazed expression on Trish's face. My gaze moves from her wide eyes to the front door, already knowing exactly who I'd find. Sterling is standing near the door, looking a bit too much like a male model for his own good. Glancing around the office, I realize that everyone is staring at him. But Sterling? He's looking directly at me and the intensity of his gaze scorches through me.

"Thank you. Is it okay?" I ask Trish, half-hoping she'll tell me about some heretofore unmentioned visitation policy preventing hot men from distracting the entire office during work hours.

"Look, if you don't want him to visit you, he can come and hang out at my desk," she whispers.

I wave him over and she flashes me a quick smile before she disappears back to her own desk. I can't help noticing that she's still watching him. Sterling winds through the maze of desks with the confidence of a man who knows exactly where he's going and sees no obstacles in his path. He let his five o'clock shadow grow a little longer, leaving a sexy bit of stubble on his jaw. His hair is slicked back, showing off the strong line of his nose and his almost unnaturally blue eyes—eyes that haven't left me yet. Each step closer sends my heart rate ratcheting up.

"Lost? Or did you feel the need to distract the entire workforce from their jobs?" I ask, dropping my chin into my hands and staring up at him.

"Me? A distraction?" His head swivels around like this is news to him. Throughout the office heads drop, trying to avoid being caught ogling him. He shrugs when he looks back to me. "Everyone seems busy. Maybe I'm only distracting you, Lucky."

"Fat chance." I snort and hope it comes off believably. The truth is, as much as I want to return to the manuscript, my body is actively rebelling against me. I squeeze my thighs tighter, trying to control the ticking pulse that started between them when I saw him. I need to get Sterling out of here before I leave a puddle on my seat. "Why are you here?"

"It's your first day. I brought you a present." He holds up a brown paper bag.

"You didn't have to do that." I hesitate and lean back in my seat. I need to be more direct—more forceful. I can't let him think that he can smooth talk his way into my heart. "You *shouldn't* do that."

"I know," he stops me before I can ask him to leave. "I've been thinking about what you said and maybe you're right."

I clutch the arms of my chair because I need solid proof I'm not dreaming. "Come again?"

"There are things I need to tell you," he lowers his voice so that no one can hear us. "I can't tell you everything—" I open my mouth to protest, but he shakes his head, "—not every story is mine to tell."

"But you'll tell me about the guy in the hotel and the last five years?"

"Yes," he says.

"And you thought, hey, this isn't a big day for Lucky, I'll just pop by and be as distracting as possible while she tries to make a good first impression...?" I open a desk drawer and rifle through the papers in it.

"Err, sorry," he asks, looking boyishly sheepish, "What are you doing?"

"Looking for a contract. I want this in writing," I say.

"Very funny." He drops the present on top of the manuscript on my desk. "What are you doing tonight?"

I bite my lip. I want answers and I don't want to wait for them, but Sterling often promises more than he delivers.

"Don't overthink it," he says. "Just say you'll have dinner with me so that we can talk."

"Okay," I agree slowly, "but on one condition. Not your place. Not my place. Neutral territory."

"Deal." A wide smile steals across his face, momentarily rendering me awestruck. It's rare to see him genuinely happy, but when he is, I can't help the swell of joy I feel. He seizes the opportunity to lean down and brush a kiss over my forehead. "I'll pick you up at five-thirty, Lucky."

It takes me a second to recover, and he's halfway to the door before I process what he said. "Six," I call after him.

He nods, his back on the door, as he pulls out a pair of aviators and slides them on. When he's finally out of the building, I realize I'm not the only one with my eyes glued to the door. Trish is already back at my desk. "Who was that?"

My biggest mistake? My biggest regret? How do I describe who Sterling is?

"Uh-oh," she says, dropping to sit on the edge of my desk. "I know that look."

I manage to tear my attention from the exit. "What look?"

"The look of a woman who's in love with a man but wishes she wasn't."

"Is it that obvious?" I ask with a sigh.

"Only to those of us with eyes," she assures me. "Word to the wise? Men are like manuscripts, if you love one, fight for it before someone else snatches it up."

"Is there a lot of competition here?" I ask dryly.

"For manuscripts," she says before tipping her head toward the door. "But I saw the look on his face. He is one hundred percent in love with you."

I glance up to her. Is she right? She does pretty much study human nature for a living. "I'm not sure that's enough."

"Girl, love is the only inexhaustible resource in this world," she says. "If you need more, demand more. You deserve it. And that man? He wants to give it to you."

She heads back to her desk, leaving me with a half-read manuscript and a vice grip of emotion coiling around my heart. Maybe she's right. Turning my attention back to the book and hoping I can clear my head after Sterling's impromptu distraction, I find the present he left me. Digging past the tissue, I find a note.

Lucky,

I thought about getting you a fancy red pen, but there's no room for mistakes with that. So here's your very own editorial pencil. Shape your story however you want and don't be afraid to make mistakes. You can always erase them.

At the bottom of the bag, there's a single, sharpened red pencil. I twirl it in my fingers before laying it next to the manuscript. I can't help reading more into this gift and his note. I've made plenty of mistakes. He knows that. If only it was as easy to erase them as a bad sentence. I don't know if I can trust Sterling, but I do know that this thing between us—it can't be erased, mistake or not. He's right. It's time to revise my situation.

I've been waiting my whole life—waiting to be free, waiting to be wanted, waiting for him. I'm done waiting. It's time to do some editing. Because this is my town, my life, my heart—and he's going to have to earn his place in each of them.

16

ADAIR

THE PAST

On Thanksgiving morning, I follow the scent of pumpkin and cloves to the kitchen where I find Felix pulling a pie out of the oven. Most of today's cooking is being handled by Sadie, our cook, and her staff, but Felix always handles the desserts. He's in the holiday spirit, sporting an apron embroidered with orange and yellow leaves.

"Tell me you made one for breakfast," I beg, breathing in the heavenly scent.

"You're predictable." He pulls a cookie sheet holding a small hand-pie out of the lower oven and places it on a trivet on the counter.

"And you're the best." I grab it greedily, but regret it when it singes my fingertips.

"Every year." He shakes his head.

"Speaking of, who are the guests of honor this year?" I blow on the hand-pie, knowing from experience that I'll burn my tongue if I don't wait.

The holidays are a time for the MacLaines to show off

our wealth, under the premise of hospitality, of course. The season starts with inviting someone—usually a business associate of my father's—to share Thanksgiving dinner. Then, a week before Christmas, we host a huge party at Windfall, the scale of which grows larger and increasingly ludicrous every year. On Christmas Eve, we open presents, so that the next morning we can fly off to a family vacation planned by my mother. Last year, we spent the week leading up to New Year's Eve in London. This will be the first year I'll wake up on Christmas morning with nowhere to go. Suddenly, I don't feel like eating my pumpkin hand pie. It's usually the perfect start to the holiday season, but now everything's different.

"Your in-laws, or future in-laws, will be here for dinner. I expect they'll be around for most holidays now," Felix says.

I wrinkle my nose. "Fantastic."

Felix shoots me a look.

"What?" I say defensively. "They're so boring. Ginny's dad spends all his time telling vaguely racist jokes, and her mom is like a walking game show. She just tells you how much everything she owns costs her. 'See this bracelet,'" I mimic her, "'Ronald paid five-thousand dollars for it. We just bought a new Lexus and upgraded the trim.' Ugh, it's so weird."

"Why do you think she does it?" Felix asks gently.

Ginny's family is well off by most standards. Her dad is a prominent doctor in Nashville and her mother a homemaker. They were probably at the top of their social rung before their daughter met my brother. "I don't know. To impress us?"

"To fit in," he says. "Consider how overwhelming all of this is."

My shoulders slump, not because I'm inaccurately describing the Higginboth family, but because I've spent the last few months having Sterling open my eyes to just how extreme our family's wealth is. "I just wish..."

"Don't wish. Act," he advises. "Maybe you can make them feel more comfortable."

"Okay," I promise. I grab my hand pie and head back to my room, wondering what would make Sterling more comfortable. Honestly, I can't imagine him ever feeling like he fits here—and that's a bigger problem. I'm not sure I want him to fit in here.

Dinner is a formal affair held every year at three p.m. sharp. This allows the women to starve themselves all day in preparation for consuming so many calories, while ensuring the men have time for cigars and brandy. Some things never change. I opt for a deep red dress with long sleeves that end in dainty bell cuffs and a full skirt, but forego the standard heels in favor of the pair of gold velvet flats I wore for last year's Christmas party. Opening the drawer to my nicest jewelry, I freeze when I spot the small ivory notecard. Familiar curly handwriting is scrawled across it.

Darling, I'm so proud of you and I can't wait to see you graduate from Valmont in four years. These are probably a little much for campus, but I thought of you.

My hand shakes as I lift the card to find a pair of delicate golden earrings shaped like flower blossoms. On a thin wire hook in the center of the blossom's bell, a brilliant opal dangles. My birthstone. How long had these been waiting for me, untouched? Since August, at least. Mom must have put them there around the time I was getting ready to start at Valmont. I tuck the card back in the drawer. It will be the last one I ever get, I realize. Staring at the earrings, I finally pick them up and hook them, one at a time, into my ear. I check the mirror, discovering that they catch the copper of my hair, reflecting a dozen shimmering hues.

The alarm on my phone goes off, warning me that I need to head down to the table. I drag my feet on the way. When I reach the landing to the stairs, my father is at the base, glowering at me from his wheelchair.

"Three sharp does not mean five minutes later," he barks before wheeling away.

I don't know why we have to go through any of it. Why do we have to pretend like everything is normal? Why does it matter if it's three sharp—the time my mother set—or half an hour later? Why act like we have anything to be thankful for this year at all?

Plastering a smile on my face, I enter the dining room to discover everyone else already in their seats. Most years I'm sandwiched between guests, left to make small talk on topics I know little about and care even less for. This year, I stop when I see there's no place for me.

My father clears his throat and nods toward the end of the table opposite him. "You're the lady of the house now."

My gaze lands on my mother's place, the spot where she would sit and charm everyone, redirecting arguments before they could occur, seamlessly keeping track of when courses needed to appear, and making certain no one at the table wanted for anything.

I don't move. I'm not up for the task.

"Adair," my father says with a smile, but there's a sharp edge to it.

"Maybe Ginny should," I stammer.

"Nonsense. Ginny sits across from Malcolm, not me," he says.

"Maybe they should sit at the ends of the table," I blurt out before I can stop myself.

A dangerous silence falls over the table. Eyes flicker between the two of us as our dining companions try to stay clear of the approaching storm.

"They are not the heads of this house." His words are terrifyingly quiet. I strain to hear them, even though the implication is loud enough.

"Neither am I! We can just leave the spot to remember Mom," I begin to suggest.

"Sit down." He slams the table with his fist.

I don't know where it comes from or why. It would be easier to just agree. It's what my mother would do. She'd sit and quickly distract everyone from the unpleasantness with a witty story. I've never been any good at putting on airs. Instead, my hands ball to fists and I shake my head.

"What?" My father asks like he doesn't understand.

"No," I say in a quiet, but firm voice.

"You will—"

"No," I shout, losing control, "I won't sit here, fill her spot and pretend nothing's wrong. I won't act like I'm okay that she's gone, not when we all know it should have been you!"

"Go to your room," he roars.

"I thought I was a head of the house," I spit back. "I guess that means I can do what I please."

I dash out the side door, down to the kitchens. I don't know why I'm running. He can't follow me. Not in his wheelchair. I just know I need to get out—away from him, away from Valmont, away from the secrets slowly tearing me apart inside.

Just like my mother should have done while she had the chance.

17

STERLING

"Turkey time!" Francie calls in a sing-song voice, so full of joy I can feel it warm me up.

I miss how excited she gets over the little things. Food is a passion we share, mostly because we were always too broke to order out or eat at the new, hip places in Manhattan or Queens. Instead, we found the best hole-in-the-wall restaurants and food carts and learned how to make the things we loved. I'd been secretly glad when she announced she was cooking Thanksgiving and to 'not test her patience on the matter.'

We earned more than a few side glances from the guests of the Eaton when Francie and I crammed into the elevators with grocery bags full of supplies. She'd taken one look at the hotel's idea of catered dinner, laughed, and began looking for a local grocer. It had taken a little work, but we finally found one with fresh turkeys and most of the items she considered essential to the holiday. To her dismay, there wasn't a fresh cranberry to be found in the whole store, so we settled for some of the canned stuff.

"It smells okay," I tell her, leaning onto the counter.

She swats at my head with the spatula she's using to scoop fresh whipped cream out of a bowl, sending dots of it onto my shirt. Neither of us can stand the stuff in the plastic vats, and since we agree it's a prerequisite for pie, we had to make our own.

"So, do we get to eat now? Before I die?" I ask, swiping some of the whipped cream with my finger.

"Don't test me. You didn't even help me cook."

"Not fair." I grab the empty bowl and carry it to the sink to wash up. "You kicked me out, remember? Something about being alone with a Viking?"

She banished me earlier in the day, about the time she decided she needed some one-on-one time with the granite counter tops and sleek, stainless-steel Viking oven. I pretended to be grossed out when she splayed across it like she'd developed genuine feelings, but inside, I felt like I'd finally given her something. Maybe it was only for a few days—but sometimes an experience is worth more than any gift you can unwrap.

"A woman has needs," she says, patting one of the knobs on the range affectionately.

I gag again, harder.

"It didn't look like you thought those needs were gross when your girlfriend's shirt was on inside out."

"Harsh," I say, "but fair."

"Get out of my way," she orders me, "before that turkey burns."

"She complains that I don't help, then she kicks me out again. I worry about you, Francie."

She's sliding the bird out of the oven when someone knocks on the door.

"Oh lord, I hope that roommate of yours didn't order us that sad dinner."

I laugh and head to the door, wondering if I'm about to turn away two-hundred dollars worth of food. But it's not room service on the other side.

"Lucky." I swing the door open wider and grab her hand. She's white as a sheet of paper and startles a little when I touch her.

"I'm so sorry," she says in a rush. "I should have called, but..."

"That better not be green beans almondine and cranberry apple pie," Francie calls. "Send it back to the kitchen. They can eat that. Cranberry apple pie on Thanksgiving!"

"I should go." Adair swivels away, but I don't let go.

"We have enough food for an army. Come in."

"What are you doing over here?" Francie comes to the door, wiping her hands on a towel. "Oh! Adair. Sterling didn't tell me you were coming."

"I'm intruding," she says, trying to tug her hand free. Color returns to her cheeks in two red blooms.

"No, come in! Someone should appreciate my effort," Francie says, swatting her inside. "This one watched me cook all day."

"The lies you tell." I grin at Adair, hoping she realizes that we're just joking. She manages to return a small smile as I pull her along, closing the door behind me.

"I just couldn't deal with my dad," she confesses in a whisper.

"We're glad you came." I wrap an arm around her waist and tilt her chin so I can kiss her.

"Save that for after dinner," Francie calls.

"We'll be too stuffed then," I say.

"Exactly!"

A giggle bursts from Adair, and she untangles herself from me with a shy smile.

"It smells really good," Adair says. "Can I help with anything?"

Francie and I share a look. "Do you cook?"

"Um, not really," she admits.

"Why don't you grab another place setting for yourself? I stacked all the extras over there." Francie points to the end of the kitchen counter. "They set the damn table like it was Buckingham Palace."

"The Eatons can go a little overboard," Adair says, carrying over a place setting and arranging it precisely.

"I want to hear all about them," Francie says, brandishing a carving knife a little too dramatically. "I need to know who my Sterling is hanging around. Do you know them well?"

"You could say that."

My Sterling? She's never called me that before. Never claimed me like I was hers. I shrug it off, trying not to get attached to the idea, and help Adair finish adjusting the table.

We eat at one end only, so we can actually talk,. Although we DO agree that we should have a very formal dinner and pretend we're aristocrats, before our time in the suite is up. Adair probably attends dinners like that regularly, but she's the most enthusiastic proponent of the plan.

If I had any qualms about what Francie thinks of Adair, they're all gone by the end of dinner, mostly because they discover a common ground: trying to embarrass me. I play the part, pretending to be horrified at every revelation, from the time I got stuck sneaking out a window when I first moved in with Francie—a story she mortifyingly refers to as the Winnie-the-Pooh incident—to Adair's impression of me riding a horse for the first time, which sends Francie into a fit of howling laughter.

"City boy on a horse. Next time take pictures."

"I promise," Adair laughs.

After pie, Francie opens a bottle of wine.

"I'm going to get acquainted with that bathtub," she tells us.

"Already cheating on the Viking?" I ask, earning a quizzical look from Adair.

"I'm too old to settle down," she says with a wink. "Behave yourselves."

I settle onto the couch and pat the spot next to me. Adair slides off her shoes and sits, curling her legs up and molding against me. My arm drops around her and lands on her pooling skirt.

"There is a lot of dress here," I say.

"Thanksgiving is a formal affair at Windfall," she says with a groan. "I didn't really think when I left. I just took off."

I pause. We've studiously avoided talk of what sent her running to my door tonight. I'm not sure if that's because Francie was around. "Do you want to talk about it?"

"Honestly? No." She peeks up at me, dark lashes framing her eyes. "Is that okay?"

"Yeah." I kiss her forehead, earning a soft sigh. "Is it selfish that part of me is glad, because it means you're here now?"

"Terribly selfish." She grins. "But that means I'm selfish, too, because I'd much rather be here with you."

"How would you feel about getting out of that dress?" I ask her.

"Sterling Ford, you were told to behave." Even as she teases me, her warm hand slides across my thigh.

It takes some mental—and physical—adjustment to remember what I was saying. "I have something you could put on."

I untangle myself from her and go into the bedroom I'm using. Digging in my duffel bag, I find a clean, ribbed undershirt and boxers and toss them on the bed. She watches from the doorway.

"Here. Get comfy. You can sleep here tonight," I say.

Her eyes flicker past me, and I know what she's seeing. Not the clothes I've found for her, but the king-sized bed.

"I'll sleep on the couch," I say quickly.

"No," she blurts out, "I can sleep on the couch."

Part of me wants to pick her up and carry her to the bed and undress her myself, putting to rest our feeble attempts at propriety.

"Why don't we both just sleep in here?" she suggests. "The bed is huge. We can still *behave*."

"I am shocked." I pretend to be offended. "Do you think I'm that kind of guy?"

Adair crosses to the bed and grabs the clothes, sticking out her tongue. She darts into the bathroom to change. I stare at the closed door between us. A vivid fantasy takes hold of me.

I walk over and open the door to find her stripped to her bra and panties. She doesn't even fake surprise. Adair's in my arms in an instant. A second later, she's pinned to the wall, my lips on her neck as she rocks against me. I reach behind my head, grab my collar and pull my shirt over my head. Her skin is soft and inviting against mine. She runs her hands across my chest.

"Sterling," she whispers.

"Sterling!"

I blink and see her standing in the doorway.

"Sorry," I say. "I was thinking."

She smirks, and I wonder if she can actually read my mind. Now that I've come back to earth, I discover the reality is better than the fantasy. She's in my clothes, my boxers hanging loosely off her hips and my ribbed tank clinging to her curves. Her nipples poke against the thin fabric. She moves across the room, showing no self-awareness of how incredibly sexy she looks.

"Are you going to sleep in that?" she asks.

"Um..." What are words? "No." I hook my collar and tug my shirt off. I toss it on the floor to discover Adair is now the one staring. My pants follow, turning her cheeks pink.

"Let's watch something," she says quickly, grabbing the remote.

We climb into bed, both hesitating about how close to each other we should be. Adair scoots next to me, until our bodies are brushing, and flips on the television. She scans through the channels with a focus usually reserved for brain surgery. Finally, she lands on an old film adaptation of *Wuthering Heights*.

"I've never read this," she admits. "I can't get through it."

"Heathcliff is a dick," I say.

Adair laughs while giving me a pointed look.

"What?" I roll over and pin her to the bed.

"I was just thinking it takes one to know one." Her eyes gleam, and despite being the butt of her joke, I find myself moving to kiss her. It's long and slow, but our bodies soon get the idea. Adair's legs fall open, allowing me to center myself between them. A soft hand runs along my abs, gliding around to my back and dipping below the elastic of my boxers. I break the kiss, moving lower and planting kisses down her neck. I skim over her collarbone and slowly move to the valley between her breasts. She moans softly, melting against the bed. I take this as a sign to continue, so I move to the peak of her nipple, closing my mouth over the thin fabric and sucking gently.

"You're going to pass that Econ exam, right?" she pants.

I release my suction and kiss the swollen pebble. "Why do you ask, Lucky?"

"Because this is a very big bed," she whispers, "and it would be a shame to..."

"Yeah?" I coax. "It would be a shame...?" I need to hear her say it—ask for it. It's her first time. I can't rush her, even if the blood rushing to my groin has other thoughts.

"Sterling, I want to—"

She's cut off by the door to the bedroom flying open. I roll off her, grabbing the sheets to cover her, and yell, "Close the fucking door!"

But it's not Francie there. A man in an expensive suit marches into the room, fury radiating from him. He's tall with graying hair, and he looks down at us past a long, hooked nose. "Who the fuck are you?" he says with a snarl.

"Who the fuck are you?" I repeat.

"I am Nicholas Randolph, the manager of the Eaton," he says in a clipped tone as he takes a walkie-talkie from his pocket and flips it on. "Have security meet me at Suite 600."

Fuck!

"There's been a mistake," I say in a rush. "We're friends of the Eaton family."

"I wasn't informed the family had placed guests in the suite. We'll have to sort this out with the police."

"What? No? I'm Cyrus Eaton's roommate. He gave me the keys. You can check." This is spinning out of control so quickly, I feel dizzy. "Don't call the police."

"It is hotel policy, and furthermore, it is not up to Mr. Cyrus to give the keys to strangers. It has to be cleared with his father. We'll need to contact him, but in the meantime..."

Cyrus and his family are off at some private resort on an equally private island. It could take hours to reach them. Long enough, I'm certain, for me to get thrown in jail.

"What is going on?" Francie appears in a bathrobe, tightening the belt.

I stare helplessly as security guards arrive behind her and grab her arm. That snaps me out of it. I jump up. "Let go of her. This is a misunderstanding."

"You are trespassing," Randolph says, as though this settles the matter.

A guard grabs me, but before they can drag me off, Adair shouts, "Wait!"

She pushes out of bed, holding her head up with more dignity than her clothing choice should allow. "We can move to my family's suite if there's a problem."

Randolph pauses mid-order and turns a careful eye on her. "And you are?"

"Adair MacLaine," she says. "My family's suite is down the hall. We would have stayed there, but since there's only one bedroom and my boyfriend's family was in town, Cyrus wanted us to have more space." She picks up the phone on the nightstand. "You won't be able to reach the Eatons. They always spend Thanksgiving in Saint John. We can call my father. He's home entertaining his future in-laws. I'm sure it won't be a problem. Of course, I could text Cyrus as well. He can have his father call. I'm certain they aren't busy as this time of night."

"My apologies, Miss MacLaine. Of course, there must be a mix-up. We wouldn't dream of asking you to change suites, but we're happy to open your family suite if you'd like the additional space." Randolph backtracks so quickly he's practically out of the room. He snaps his fingers at the guards and hisses, "Let the guests go."

Francie glares at the guard who grabbed her. "Shame on you."

"I am so terribly sorry for the mistake," Randolph says, but he's not speaking to me. He's talking to Adair.

"I'm not the one you should apologize too," she says.

"Yes, of course. Mr...." It looks like it physically pains him to look at me.

Is it that obvious that I don't fit in here?

"Ford," Adair prompts smugly.

"Our apologies, Mr. Ford. May we have breakfast sent up tomorrow morning to show how sorry we are for our mistake?" he asks.

"No need," I say through gritted teeth, daring a glance at Francie. "I think after *your* mistake, we'll go elsewhere for the rest of our stay."

He tries to argue with me, but my mind is made up. He continues bowing and scraping until he's out the door along with the hotel security team. I slam the door after them.

"I need to pack," I say, stalking back toward the bedroom.

"We don't need to go," Adair says in a confused voice.

I can't bring myself to look at her. Instead, I continue back to the bedroom. I hear Adair heading my way, but Francie stops her in the hall.

"Let him be," Francie says. "We don't want to take advantage of anybody's hospitality."

"But you aren't," Adair says. "You have every right to be here."

"Part of that is having the right to walk away when someone treats you badly," Francie tells her. "We'll be more comfortable somewhere else. Why don't you get dressed and we'll figure out where to go next?"

Adair is quiet as she comes back into the room. She disappears into the bathroom, while I shove my things in my duffel bag. I pull on my clothes, sit down on the end of the bed, and wait for her. My brain plays the last few minutes in a loop. Not the good bit with Adair in bed, but everything after. Adair's terrified shriek when the door flew open. The pinched disapproval on the manager's face.

Francie appearing in the hall. But the images aren't the worst bit—it's the cycle of shame that accompanies them.

It hadn't mattered that it was a mistake—not until Adair stepped in and used her family name to prove it. I might as well have been speaking in Latin. Nothing I said mattered, because I was nobody.

I am nobody.

"Hey," Adair says softly. She's in her huge dress again.

"We should go." I don't trust myself to say more. It's not her fault that this happened. I shouldn't have been so stupid as to think I could fit in enough not to raise questions.

"I'm sorry that happened," she says. "They had no right to treat you like that."

"Don't they? I don't belong in a fancy suite at the Eaton. I don't belong in Valmont. I certainly don't belong with you."

"Don't," she orders me. Adair strides to me and grabs my chin. "You don't get to decide who belongs with me. I do! And I choose you. The rest of them can have their vapid cocktail parties and keep score of how important they are. They have to, because they have nothing else to offer the world."

"And I do?"

"Yes, you do," she says. "You're smart and kind and better than all of them combined, and I would trade all of this to be with you."

"You say that now, but wait until you're stuck in a studio apartment in Queens trying to keep the lights on. I can't give you this life."

Her eyes close, and she takes a deep breath.

"Why can't you see what I do?" She holds a finger over my lips when I start to answer. "I don't want this life. I want you."

I don't know what to say to that, so I kiss her instead. When I finally release her, she says, "I'm going to find my shoes. We can go to your dorm or my place. Whatever."

She disappears into the hall and I follow, spotting Francie's silhouette waiting by her door. Our eyes meet and it's clear she heard everything Adair said to me.

"I don't know what to do," I admit to her in a low voice.

"Believe her," she says softly, "and believe in yourself, because she's right about you."

18

STERLING

PRESENT DAY

The last thing I want to do after seeing her is deal with business, but this situation with Noah can't be ignored. Plus, I've just agreed to do the one thing I promised I would never do, and that means it's time to talk to my brothers.

The Barrelhouse is only a few blocks from Adair's office, so I text Luca to meet me there. I find Jack behind the bar, prepping for the evening crowd. His shirt, bearing the blues bar's iconic logo, stretches tightly across his chest, the fabric blacker than his skin. He greets me with a smile and guilt surges through me.

"You look like a man who needs to confess," he says as I take a seat at the bar.

"Luca is already on the way," I say, bypassing his preternatural greeting. Maybe he can sense what I've come here to tell him. "We need to talk about Noah and stuff."

Jack raises an eyebrow before nodding and grabbing another glass from the sink.

"Why do you think he's here?" he asks as he dries the

tumbler. He adds it to the stack of clean ones at the end of the bar.

"You always do your own dishes?" I ask.

"It's distracting," he admits. "I keep waiting for Noah to walk through that door. Better to keep busy than go crazy."

None of us should be that surprised over Noah's appearance, but that doesn't mean we're excited to see him. Luca's been tracking him all week, without much to report, and he doesn't seem concerned. But Luca could stand in the eye of a hurricane and not look ruffled. Jack, on the other hand, tends to worry. I see it on his face now. He didn't buy this bar, effectively planting roots in Nashville, to hide. He won't be willing to run. He did it to move on and start fresh.

"Jack, he's here for me," I say. "Maybe Luca."

"The last I checked," he says, leaning down to the bar and lowering his voice so that the handful of his employees setting up for the night's performance don't overhear him, "I'm just as responsible for what happened in Afghanistan."

"Yeah, maybe," I say with a shrug. "But he can't do anything about that. He already tried, remember? Now he's just going to try to punish us in other ways, and you've kept your nose clean since then."

"*I have*. Maybe you should get out of town," Jack adds. I know what he's really saying. Maybe I should disappear. Start a new life. Leave all this behind. That might've been an option a few months ago. To be honest, I'm not entirely sure I would have returned to Valmont if I'd known Noah might come sniffing around again. I cover my tracks well, but it will only take one mistake—maybe not even my own

—to give the FBI the excuse they need to investigate further. That begs the question: did I fuck up? Did someone else? Or is this just a courtesy call to remind me that he's not giving up?

"I need to know why he's here," I say. "Until I do, I can't move on anything."

Jack groans and reaches for another clean glass. "How do you know he's here for you, anyway? Last I checked, Luca is just as much trouble—if not more."

"That is the nicest thing anyone's ever said about me." Luca drops onto the bar stool next to mine. "He's right, you know. Noah might be looking for me. Then again, it doesn't really matter who he's looking for, because he wants to take us all down."

"That's what I'm afraid of," Jack says.

Trust Luca to be sensitive to Jack's anxiety. It's not that he can't read the room, it's just that he prefers chaos to order. "Just keep minding your own business," I tell Jack. "He's got nothing on you."

"What could he have on you?" Jack asks.

"That's a good question." I have a list of possibilities in my head already, and it's not getting any shorter. "But I actually want to talk to you about something else."

"Here it comes," Luca mutters, but I ignore him.

"So, things have changed with Adair," I begin.

"We noticed," Jack says.

"But we're not exactly on the same page," I continue. "She's got questions."

"That's not a surprise," Jack says. "What does she want to know?"

"It would be shorter to list what she doesn't want to

know. I already told her that I can't tell her everything, but—"

"I can't believe you're going to be the one to break the pact," Luca interjects. "Wasn't it his idea?" Jack nods, but, unlike Luca, he doesn't look angry, he looks like he's holding down laughter.

"I told you that he would," Jack says.

"Wait, what?" I ask. "I had no intention of telling her anything when we came here."

"That's just it," Jack says. "It might not have been your intention, but like I told Luca, a man doesn't spend five years obsessing over a woman just to throw away another shot at her."

"I didn't come back for a second chance," I protest.

"Then, I guess you're lucky she's giving you one, anyway," Jack says.

"Can we focus on the fact that he's planning to break his sacred vow?" Luca asks, but the edge is gone from his voice. That doesn't mean he's pleased about my change of heart.

"I'm leaving you two out of it," I promise.

"Like hell," Luca says, spinning on his stool to jab a finger into my chest. "You aren't taking all the credit for our success."

"Is that what you call it?" Jack asks dryly.

"Okay, I'll leave Jack out of it," I clarify.

"And you make sure she knows that Cairo was—"

"Tell her what you need to tell her, brother," Jack says quickly. The last thing he needs is another fight breaking out over what happened in Egypt, especially since this time it would be his bar taking the damage.

"Whatever. Listen, want to grab lunch?" Luca asks. He checks his Rolex. "Or maybe early dinner? Whatever you eat at three in the afternoon."

"High tea," Jack offers dryly. "Aren't you going to ask me?"

Luca rolls his dark eyes. "I'd ask you, but let's face it, you're married to this joint."

"And it's true love," Jack says with a grin.

"I've got plans tonight and I need to prepare," I say with intentional vagueness.

"Plans? With whom?" Jack bats his eyes in feigned innocence.

"I had no idea you needed to check my schedule," I say, dodging the question.

"We're just curious," Luca says. "It must be important if you can't buy lunch for the man who saved your life."

"You're getting your stories mixed up," I tell him. "I thought I saved your life."

"Boys," Jack interrupts us. "Let's not fight, especially since I'm the one that saved both your asses." He slides a glass to Luca. "Stay and have a drink with me. We can mourn the taming of our dear friend, Sterling."

"And the loss of his balls," Luca adds, while Jack uncaps a bottle and begins to pour.

"I have no idea why you two are still single," I say flatly.

"It's a mystery, right?" Luca agrees. He takes a sip of the whiskey Jack just poured him. "Celebrating her new job?"

A primal urge awakens in me and I take a step closer. "How do you know about that?"

"She lives down the hall from me, remember?" He

waves his napkin in surrender. "Don't worry. I'm not sniffing around your girl."

"I never said you were," I say stiffly. I need to get this whole caveman thing under control or I'm going to catch more hell from both of them. "Or that she's my girl."

Luca sniffs his glass and looks up at Jack, continuing to sniff the air. "What's that smell?"

"What smell?" Jack asks, looking around the bar quickly, his forehead wrinkling with concern.

"Something stinks." Luca swivels back to face me. "Some kind of shit. A bull's, maybe?"

I hop off the barstool. "Well, this has been fun, truly. The next time I need to talk about a woman, I will call my sister. I have somewhere to be."

"Stalking is illegal, my friend," Luca calls after me, but I ignore him.

I'm two steps onto the sidewalk when a familiar figure blocks my path. Like the rest of us, Noah Porter has filled out since our Army days. His wallet hasn't, however. The suit he wears is a typical FBI affair: black, boring polyester. His hair is still cropped closely to his head, and he makes no effort to hide the angry scar that runs down the side of his face. But unlike most FBI agents I've encountered—and I've encountered quite a few—he looks like he might burst through its seams at any moment. Staring at him now, it's hard to remember that we used to have so much in common. Now, we're as far apart as night and day. We don't even exist in the same time.

"It's been awhile," Noah says. He slides his gas station

sunglasses off and looks me up and down. I wonder what he sees. Is it the same funhouse reflection that I see? A version of his life he decided against? It could have been different. I could be standing in his shoes if I'd made different choices. He knows it. I know it. It's what makes it so hard for us to look at each other, let alone coexist. We are one another's *might-have-been*.

"I didn't know you were in town." I shove my hands in my pockets and tell myself this is just two old friends catching up. But I still check my periphery for signs of other officers. The street is empty and quiet. He's come alone, which means he doesn't plan to arrest me. Whatever he has on me must be flimsy. Not that it matters. Anything is blood in the water where he and I are concerned. Noah will circle and wait. I've lost him a few times. Shaken him a few more. But, like a bad penny, he always turns up. I'm not sure why I thought he might let me go when I came to Valmont. Because it would mean I was keeping a low profile? Because I'm not actively working for any clients? Because as far as he knows, returning to Valmont is like the un-prodigal son finally coming home?

"Didn't you?" He flashes a cold smile full of straight teeth, perfectly aligned by some Midwestern orthodontist. "After you went to all the trouble of carrying your girlfriend off to her room?"

Fuck. He *had* seen me that day. I keep my face carefully neutral and shrug like I'm drawing a blank. "Girlfriend?"

"The pretty redhead."

"She's not my girlfriend." I sell this easily, because it's true. Adair has made that clear.

"Why did you come back, then?"

"I had a business opportunity," I say, knowing that's as bad as admitting to any of my dealings. Just that statement alone is like throwing chum in front of a great white. But it will distract Noah from Adair, and that's all that matters.

"So you didn't come home for Adair MacLaine?"

Of course, he knows who she is. He has access to files full of information I'd rather he didn't see. But, as careful as I am, the FBI usually manages to collect a few. That's the trouble with lying to former best friends—sometimes they know too much about you. Noah Porter used to be one of us, which means he heard all about the girl who broke my heart. I can't believe he remembers her name all this time later. It becomes a problem when that old friend works as an FBI agent, and you're his number one target.

"Buy you a drink?" he asks.

"I don't drink," I remind him.

"That's right. I got confused when I caught you stepping out of a bar." He manages to play it like he actually forgot, but I know it's a test. "Lunch?"

"I was actually on my way to meet someone."

"I'll come with," he says, calling my bluff.

"You win." We could do this two-step all day, but I'm not wearing my dancing shoes. I start walking forward, away from the Barrelhouse. At least I can lure him away from Jack and Luca. "How about coffee?"

"That works." He glances to the Barrelhouse sign swinging on its post. "Maybe we should invite the guys."

"Does this concern them?" We might as well get to the bottom of this now.

"Not really." He frowns as if delivering bad news.

"Don't look so disappointed," I say.

"It's okay. I just have to remind myself that patience is a virtue. I'll find a reason to catch up with Luca and Jack later."

I hope that's not the case.

"It was ballsy," he continues. "Coming here—all three of you."

"Feeling left out?" I ask.

"A little," he says as we begin to walk.

I lead us a block over and shoot off a quick warning text to Luca. Noah claims he's not here for either of them, but they need to know he made contact. He wouldn't risk our leaving unless it somehow served his purpose. I might as well get as much information as I can.

"Tell them I said hello," Noah says before I can slide my phone into my pocket. He pauses in front of a coffee shop and points to it. "This okay?"

I don't care where we go as long as we get it over with soon, so I nod. We take a seat at a high-backed booth in the back and a waitress with purple hair skips over, laminated menus in hand. She plops them in front of us. "What can I get you?"

"Two coffees," I say before Noah can answer her.

"You want to grab a bite?" he asks me. The waitress hesitates, waiting for a response.

"Two coffees," I say again firmly. I'm giving Noah exactly as long as it takes me to get to the bottom of this cup before I'm back out the door.

"Don't worry, I'll be quick." He settles against the red vinyl booth, dropping his massive arms along the top of it as he assesses me for a moment. "You've changed."

"And you haven't?" I ask, as the waitress reappears with two mugs.

"Don't take it so badly," he says. "You look good. Successful."

"Let me guess, you'd like to know what I've been up to recently."

"Nope." He blows steam off the top of his mug. "I already know what you've been up to lately."

An alarm rings inside my head, but I ignore it. "Buying a house. Investing in a media conglomerate. Boring stuff, really."

"In my experience, Sterling Ford and boring don't go in the same sentence."

"And yet. All I'm doing here is walking my dog and catching up with old friends." I drain half the coffee in one gulp, ignoring the way it sears the back of my throat. I may not want to give anything away, but I'm not going to sit around here all day making small talk, either.

"Among other things." Noah abandons his mug, along with the other pretenses of our conversation. "Look, I don't know why I am telling you this."

I narrow my eyes. Noah has tried to play me before. The difference between those times and now is the concerning level of sincerity in his voice. "Telling me what?"

"You deserve to be in jail," he says with a terse shake of his head.

"I didn't need you to tell me that," I say dryly. It's a fact I'm well aware of.

"But be that as it may, you don't belong six feet under," he says.

My eyebrows shoot up and I stare at him, waiting for a punchline that doesn't come. "Finally, something we can agree on."

"Someone flipped on the Koltsovs," he explains, "and your name came up."

I can't believe what I'm hearing. Not about the Koltsovs. That was just a matter of time. "Wait a minute, are *you* actually warning *me*?"

"I'm giving you a chance. You can still do the right thing here," he says. "Clear your name. Be the guy I used to know."

Does he think it will be this easy to reform me? Maybe I'll buy a few bad suits and join the FBI with him? The trouble with Noah is his American Pie earnestness. He always saw the world through red, white, and blue glasses. He joined up to serve his country. I don't think he ever really believed the rest of us when we told them it was our only option. Jack wanted to get out of town. Luca needed to dodge the family business for a few years to get his head on straight. I—well—I was running from a girl. Noah was a believer, an idealist. Black and white. Right and wrong. There was no in between to Noah Porter.

"And you think that's what I want?"

"You came home," he says, like this clears matters up. "You came looking for your girl. Do you really think she fits into your life? We both knew the Koltsovs were going to come looking for you."

"They've got no beef with me." I mean it. I delivered on every job they ever sent me. We left everything just fine.

"It's not that simple. They're cleaning house. Half the list—courtesy of our friendly informant—is dead already."

"And you think I'm next?"

"You're not hearing me. They *know* you've been named by someone who flipped—"

"Which means *your* office fucked up," I hiss, trying to keep my voice down enough it won't be overhead. "And now you're talking to me, which will only make me more of a target. So leave off pretending you're here to do me any favors."

Noah's expression sours, but he doesn't give up. "Now *I'm* to blame for the Koltsovs trying to clean house? Look, I don't know if they're working through their list in fucking chronological order, but they'll get to you, eventually."

"Thanks for the warning." I toss a twenty-dollar bill on the table.

Noah reaches for it and tosses it back at me.

"Can't let someone like me buy you a cup coffee?" I ask.

"I try to keep my ledger clean."

"You did me a favor. Told me what to expect. Consider this making us even," I say and drop the bill back on the table. "I'll see you around. Thanks for the warning."

"You have a chance to do what's right here, Sterling. Don't waste it," he advises me.

"I can always make new chances," I tell him, as I button my suit jacket. "What you're talking about is closing doors."

"And this is the door you really want to keep open?" He gestures to the city outside the café's windows.

"For now." I'm not giving him the satisfaction of any more of my time, even if he's given me a lot to consider. It's one thing to have the FBI sniffing around town. If I keep my nose clean, he can't touch me. The Koltsovs? That's another story. If he's right, then I'll be hearing from them soon enough. "See you around."

He tips his head in acknowledgment before tapping the corner of his eye. "I'll be watching."

"I bet you will." As soon as I'm outside, I dial Luca's phone. There's no time to waste.

"Bail Money 'R Us," Luca says when he answers. "Did you punch him again?"

"Shut up. This is important." I fill him in on what Noah said.

He lets out a low whistle before he responds. "Looks like Nashville is getting more interesting."

"Tell Jack," I say, ignoring his misplaced humor.

"Will do," he says.

"You know he'll go after her," Luca adds quietly.

"Yeah," I say in a clipped tone.

"Watch your back, brother."

"I always do."

What have I gotten her into? Valmont isn't big enough for all of us. Not if my past mistakes are going to move to town with me.

"And, Sterling, better watch hers, too," he says before hanging up.

I thought Valmont needed a reckoning, but now that one is on its way, I'm wondering not only if I made a mistake coming back but who's going to pay or it?

19

ADAIR

THE PAST

"I'm going to sleep with Sterling."

Poppy's Audi swerves into the next lane, and she quickly jerks it back to the right side of the road, narrowly avoiding a head-on collision with a mini-van.

I instantly regret my decision to tell her while she's driving.

"I thought you already did," Kai says from the backseat.

"What? Of course she hasn't!" Poppy cries in a shrill voice, turning off the radio. She throws an exasperated look over her shoulder at him.

"Eyes on the road!" I grab the steering wheel and straighten it until her focus has returned.

"We would know if she slept with him. She would tell us," Poppy lectures him. "It's part of the rules."

"There are rules?" I ask.

"Yes, and they're so ingrained that you didn't even know it. You just knew you needed to tell us!" Poppy claps and then grabs the wheel. "Oops! Sorry."

We pause the discussion until we reach safety, but the

moment our feet are on solid ground, they pepper me with questions.

"When?" Poppy asks.

"Where?"

"Friday, and I don't know." I wring my hands together. That's the part that's been weighing on my mind. Part of me wishes we hadn't been interrupted that night at the Eaton. Then it would already be behind me. Sterling has been focused on his finals since Francie left, leaving little time for romantic interludes. "I told him that I'd sleep with him if he got an A on his Econ final."

"You incentivized your virginity?" I can tell Poppy doesn't approve.

"Look, I know I want to lose it to Sterling, so I figured I'd kill two birds with one stone."

"Romantic," Kai says with a chuckle.

"Actually, I think it will be." I bite my lip, wishing they could see in him what I do. Unfortunately, the pair has been privy to enough bad behavior on his part to make that harder than I'd like. I take a deep breath and drop the bigger bombshell. "I think I'm in love with him."

I know it, actually.

Poppy spins and grabs my hands. "Oh my god, did he say it?"

It doesn't matter if she likes him or not. She knows that a moment like that is bigger than her personal objections. Her face falls when I shake my head.

"We keep hinting at it," I admit. "We've definitely used the L-word but not actually said I love you."

Even speaking the words to them ties my stomach in knots.

"Don't say it first," Poppy advises.

"Why not?" Kai is clearly not on board with her old-fashioned views about relationship etiquette.

"We'll say it when it's right." I really do know it's about what's right for me and Sterling. I just needed to share before I imploded, trying to keep all the nerves and excitement locked inside me. "But I don't know what I should do. I mean, how do I tell him I want to have sex without actually having to say it?"

"No panties," Poppy says seriously. Kai and I burst out laughing, and she shakes her head. "Nothing sends a clearer signal. A garter belt and nothing else."

"I'll keep that in mind, but I'm not sure I'm ready to jump from virgin to vixen."

"You want to know the truth?" Kai asks.

I nod, hoping one of them has some real advice.

"It's like any other day of your life. There's not a lot of ceremony about it—unless you're going to wait until your wedding night," he adds.

"No way."

"Then find something you feel good in, tell him you want to hang out, and... "

"And what?" That can't be the end of the instructions.

"Kiss him," Poppy says.

"Kiss him? That's all."

She shares a wicked look with Kai. "Kiss him," she repeats. "The rest will take care of itself."

I tell myself I'm not nervous, but my hands are slippery on the steering wheel of Mom's Roadster as I pull into Sterling's dorm parking lot. I'm running late, which isn't a surprise after the number of outfits I tried on. We're supposed to be getting together to celebrate the end of finals. Despite my friends' assurances that a kiss will send the message I want to send, I'm hoping he remembers the promise I made. I don't want to make an idiot out of myself.

I *want* everything to be perfect. I teased him during our pre-Thanksgiving study session, but the truth is, I don't have a lot of stuff from the Victoria's Secret front window. I spent hours combing my closet for the perfect outfit. Kai said to be comfortable, but I doubted showing up in yoga pants was going to send the right message. I needed to look hot, but I understood I'd gone overboard on my birthday. I couldn't show up in a mini-dress to hang in his dorm room without feeling out of place. In the end, nothing felt right, so I ended up in a gray t-shirt with a deep cut v-neck, jeans, and a black gasoline jacket with boots to match. I thought I looked like a badass. Now, I just need to channel that energy into some self-confidence.

I make a kissy face in the rearview mirror, then check my teeth for any of my blush-red lipstick. All is well.

Sterling had one of the latest finals on campus, and the parking lot is mostly empty. He's sticking around through the week to attend my family's Christmas party before leaving to spend the holidays with Francie in New York. That's why this needs to happen tonight. I want to be able to spend as much time with him as I can before enduring Christmas without him.

His dorm is a ghost town, so I'm surprised when the elevator slides open and he's inside. His eyes widen when he sees me. "Damn, Lucky. You. Look. Perfect. I was just stepping outside to wait for you."

Is it possible for a heart to actually explode over a guy? Because mine feels like it's on the verge of bursting.

Wait for me? I can't help feeling like he's as eager to see me as I am to see him. A casual sexiness rolls off him. Sterling might not spend thousands on his wardrobe like most guys I know, but that works in his favor. His faded t-shirt with its well-worn fabric only accentuates his muscular torso and wide, strong shoulders. The leather coat he's wearing was vintage twenty years ago, but that only makes it better. He's clean-shaven for once, drawing attention to his electric-blue eyes. There's even a little piece of paper where he must have nicked himself with the razor.

"You're not so bad yourself," I say, plucking off the paper.

He grins sheepishly, biting the edge of his lip, and rubs the spot.

I'm in love with him. I feel it every time he looks at me. It fills me so full that I have the strangest sensation of floating whenever I'm near him. I only want more of him.

"How'd the Econ final go?" I ask.

"Pretty good, I think. I wasn't sure on a couple answers, but that's not bad when there are 30 questions."

"Ready to celebrate? And by celebrate, I mean avoid books for a night?" He doesn't know how important his answer is to me, how much I need him to myself tonight.

"For ever and ever," he says, sighing. "Cyrus is gone for break. In fact, it looks like we pretty much have the entire dorm to ourselves. I was thinking we'd start with a movie.

But I can't remember Cy's Netflix password, so we should to go to the library and grab one."

"It's open?"

"I think there are a few more finals going. They won't close it until every student's brain is fried from studying," he says with a grin. "Don't worry. I checked the hours."

So he's been planning tonight, too. The library to grab a DVD? It's not the first time I've been reminded of how different our lives are. I'm about to tell him we can use my account when I realize it might hurt his pride. I smile brightly, even though I'm ready to get back to his room and be alone with him. No movie required. "Lead the way."

Eaton Library is a couple blocks down from Sterling's dorm. The librarian at the desk glares at us when we enter. Apparently, she's as ready for finals to be over as the students.

"This way." Sterling seems at ease at the library, weaving in and out of the stacks before leading me up a staircase. It's clear he spends a lot of time here.

On an upper floor, we find ourselves looking at Valmont's meager collection of DVDs. Nearly all of them are marked *Criterion Collection* or *AFI Top 100*.

"So this is what film students do?" I guess.

"I doubt they study classics like *Waterworld*." He picks one up. "What do you want to watch?"

"Whatever." Honestly, I don't plan on watching much of the movie.

"Francie likes old movies," he continues. "*Philadelphia Story. Arsenic and Old Lace*. Cary Grant is great."

Is he really not thinking about... ? I expected us to pick up where we'd left off in the suite at the Eaton.

"Cary Grant it is then." I grab every title I can, making a small stack. If we get them all, we'll have no reason to leave his dorm again for a while.

"I've heard of this one," says Sterling, flipping one of the cases over to read the back. "Charade. Cary Grant. Audrey Hepburn."

"Perfect." It could star a banana and a bit of shrubbery for all I care.

We take the DVDs to the front desk and check them out, and Sterling slides them into the large waist pocket of his coat. I'm a couple steps ahead of him when we exit, and I'm surprised when I feel his heavy coat land on my shoulders.

"Oh, no. Don't," I say. "It's freezing out."

"Hush. I'll be fine, Lucky." He pauses as we reach the food court. "It's only going to get colder. Why don't we get something from the food court on the way back? That way we don't have to go out again."

Now he's thinking. I can get behind stopping for food if it means we get to stay put later. But when we reach the food court, we find it closed.

"Fuck," he says, reading the sign.

"Let's just order a pizza or something. My treat," I say.

"It's not that. I probably should have stocked up before it closed. I didn't think about it, and I'm here for another week before I head to New York."

"Don't worry about it. We can go by the grocery store," I say without thinking.

He flinches at the suggestion. Sometimes I forget how sensitive he is about being on scholarship. That's not going to stop me from making sure he eats, even if I have to decorate my naked body with food to trick him into accepting it.

"Or... " With a furtive glance, Sterling walks over to the market section of the food court, where students buy the kind of stuff they can take back to their dorms. The lights are off, but there's nothing stopping someone from taking things. There's just no way to pay. He picks up an apple and a couple of bananas, then he grabs a tiny box of cereal.

"Here." I grab them and shove them in the oversized coat he put on me.

"No way. I can't let you steal for me," he says, his face a mixture of stubbornness and concern.

"If you get caught, you will end up in big trouble," I say firmly. "If I get caught, they'll end up apologizing to me. So just let me do this."

His face remains a stony mask, and I regret bringing it up.

"It's all going to go bad. We're doing them a favor," I say.

"Fine," he says, softening a bit, "but if campus cops stop us, I'm telling them it's all mine."

We shove the stolen food in his coat pockets, and, feeling suddenly reckless, I swipe a cake slice in a plastic container.

"Uh, what do you think you are doing, Lucky?"

"I want cake. And I shall have it."

"Not in my pockets you're not."

"And this," I say, ignoring him and grabbing a brownie. I stride towards the exit, my pockets loaded with contraband. "You'll thank me later."

Sterling has to hustle to keep up.

"You're so hot right now," he says appreciatively.

"I know." I try to say it evenly, but a wicked grin finds its way to my face. Is it the thrill of stealing something for the first time? Or am I riding high on embracing my bad girl side? First, stealing. Next, sex. Maybe he's rubbing off on me.

Because my hands are full, Sterling opens the door for me. I nearly bump into a couple professor types, and despite telling myself moments ago that I didn't care about the consequences, my heart skips a beat. One of the professors, a kindly looking uncle-type with bushy white eyebrows, does a double take when he sees me carrying the brownie. After a moment, though, he seems to conclude I am a student worker taking home old food, because he gives me a bright smile and says, "Looks yummy."

"It better be," I say.

Sterling's dorm is across the street, and it's not until he's putting the DVD in the player that my heart slows down. I no longer feel like a fugitive. Now, I just feel like a girl about to make the biggest decision of her life. I distract myself by arranging the stolen food on the coffee table, like it's a feast.

"You hungry?"

I shake my head. I'm too nervous to be hungry. "Maybe later."

He lies down on the couch and beckons me with his finger to join him.

"Are you hungry?" I ask, trying to think of anything to say and coming up short. I lounge back, and he folds his right arm into a V, and my head falls on it like a pillow. His other arm he wraps around the bare skin of my midriff.

"I'm good."

I consider asking him to forget the movie and put his hands all over my body, but manage to bite my tongue. He turns it on, and I try to pay attention, but all I can think about is the way he feels pressed against me, how strong his arms are, how good he smells.

"I'd love to take you there," he says.

I focus on the screen. Paris is gold-tinged in the evening light, and the characters are on a boat somewhere along the Seine, bickering.

"Paris?" I say dreamily, thinking of walking with him, hand in hand, under the Eiffel Tower.

"You've been there, haven't you?" he guesses.

"Yeah, but I think it would be better to go with you." I think every experience would be better with him at my side.

"Someday," he promises, his breath tickling across my ear lobe. A tremor races through me. "Someday, I will give you Paris and London and every dream you've ever dreamed."

"I only want them if you're there." I watch Audrey Hepburn for a moment. It's not exactly a standard romance. She seems to be spending most of the movie trying to figure out if he's only after her for money. "Do they fall in love?"

"I don't know." His lips brush my ear. "Do they?"

Are we still talking about the movie?

I want to turn into him and discover every unexplored bit I can. But I can't seem to find the courage. Instead, I sit up and reach for the piece of chocolate cake. There are no forks, so I pinch a piece off and stick in my mouth. The rich, creamy frosting is a balm to my fragile nerves. Apparently, chocolate is the answer to everything, even pre-coitus stage fright.

"I think the stealing makes it taste better," I say through a full mouth.

Sterling chuckles and swipes a bite. "Definitely better."

We're nearly finished with the slice, and I'm eying the brownie when Sterling leans over. "You have frosting... "

His thumb swipes over my lip, then he sucks the chocolate off his thumb.

I nearly choke on a bite. I'm officially jealous of an appendage. I recover and turn my face for his inspection. "Did you get it?"

"Damn. I missed some." His hand reaches for me, but this time, he draws my face closer and presses a kiss to the corner of my mouth. "Hmm. You taste even better than cake."

My lips part in expectation and I toss the cake container away. Sterling's mouth covers my own, his hands gripping both sides of my face. Then, he spins me underneath him and all thoughts of *Charade* go out the window. He kisses my lips and the curve of my chin, and I do the same to him. Our pace is slow as we explore with our mouths. I tangle my fingers in his hair as he kisses my collarbone, holding him close. It should be like this always.

Soon, when I start classes in January, I'll have every excuse to be near him. The challenge will be doing anything but this.

Because this? It's all I want. This glorious, full-bodied awareness his touch provokes in me. I want to feel this aching, delicious hunger for his touch, for his kiss. It's all I want.

His hand brushes my breast, but he moves it away quickly, no doubt testing where the boundaries remain between us. I respond by sliding my hand under his jeans and grabbing his ass. That ought to get the point across.

"The bed," I say, breaking away. I don't have a lot of expectations about where this goes, but I'm not losing my virginity on a couch.

He releases me and I stumble to my feet, holding out my hand. He grabs it, but the second he stands up, he drops it. Two strong hands cup my ass and lift me into the air. I respond with a gasp that is quickly quieted by his mouth. I am weightless in his arms. Blood pounds in my ears, matching the beat of my heart and the pulse between my legs. I need him. Only him. Nothing else will do.

The pull of gravity shifts as he lowers me gently on the bed and sits next to me. I want him to go faster. And slower. Should I lay back on the bed? Or wait for him? Why isn't he just taking control? He's the one with all the experience. My hands move down to the button of his jeans.

"Woah, Lucky," he says, and a frisson of alarm tenses my whole body. Does he not want this? After everything, is this the part where he breaks my heart?

"Don't you... " I search his face for a clue as to why he's putting on the brakes.

"You don't have to ask. God, I'm going to regret this." He turns his head away. "If you're not ready, it's okay. This probably isn't like you planned. Not special, I mean."

"What?" I say. "I don't care about that. I want you—no,

that's not right. I *need* you, Sterling. Like I've never needed anything."

"Here? In my dingy dorm room?"

"What's wrong with it?" I say, meaning it.

"You deserve a penthouse in Paris. Champagne. There should be—"

I place my fingertips on his lips. He kisses them.

"I only want you." I look into his eyes and for a moment I see a whole world there. "Okay?"

"You don't have to ask twice." He kisses me, resting his forehead against mine. "I'm all in."

My hands reach for the hem of his shirt, but he pulls away.

"Wait." He twists around and opens a drawer in his bedside table. My breath hitches when he drops a condom on top of it. Sterling turns back to face me. "I thought we better... "

"Good idea." Can he even hear me over how loudly my heart is beating? How is this supposed to go again?

A kiss.

I crush my mouth to his, and Sterling's hand cradles the back of my head, maintaining contact. I reach to pull off his shirt, and he helps this time. Under it, two perfect pecs trail down to the V of his abs. There's no trace of boyish fat, just hard muscle. As soon as it's off, his arm hooks around me, lowering me to the bed.

His hands are on me at once, firm but patient. We kiss, our tongues now exploring along with our mouths. I can't take it. I need the feel of his skin on mine. I pull off my t-shirt, and Sterling is ready. His left hand undoes the clasp of my bra in one fluid motion as his right squeezes my breast. The flesh there tightens, and I moan in pleasure.

He peels the bra off of me slowly, drinking in every moment as if he were dying of thirst. He looks up into my eyes and I know, somehow, that it's to make sure I'm not having second thoughts. I smile shyly, shrinking against the pillow a little.

Reaching out, he brushes hair away from my shoulders. "You're perfect."

"Kiss me." It's not a demand. It's a wish.

His answer is to coax me down onto my back. He starts at my ear, nipping and sucking, and slowly works his way to my breasts. When he takes my nipple into his mouth, my hips thrust towards him. I don't remember that particular reflex being covered in health class. But even if all of this is new, it's somehow effortless. It just feels... right.

Sterling won't let me go. He holds me tightly but leaves me time to breathe. Every time I look at him he is studying me, his face a mask of desire tempered with concern. He pauses at the button to my jeans, and I nod. Taking his time, he draws them off me before tossing them to the ground. He groans when he sees my red panties.

"I am the luckiest man alive," he says against my mouth. "But—"

I still his mouth with a kiss and begin to undo the button of his jeans. His breath catches as I slide my hand beneath his boxers, closing my fist over him.

"Oh fuck," he says, releasing a deep sigh.

His shaft is already large, but as soon as I touch it it begins to grow. He wrenches down his jeans with a sharp tug, and by the time he finishes kicking them off, his hand has slid between my legs.

He's gentle at first, rubbing slowly on top of my wet panties. My hips begin to gyrate—I don't remember telling them to—trying to create more friction. My hand grabs his shaft and I give him a small stroke. I want to make him feel good, too. I just wish I knew whether I was doing it right.

It takes us a little time to figure out the give and take. When his hand touches down there, it takes all my focus to keep stroking him. Suddenly I can feel my body shake, and Sterling stops to check on me.

"You alright?"

"Yes. God yes," I say. "It's just the cold."

"Here." He helps me off the bed, and when he turns around to pull up the covers, I slide my panties off. Somehow, it's easier to do it when he's not looking.

He slides into the bed and holds the covers up like the flap of a tent. "Come here."

I climb in quickly, aware that I'm standing in front of him naked. It's the first time he's seen my whole body. It's the first time any guy has seen my whole body. Sterling wastes no time exploring the new territory. A fingertip presses past my seam, centering over the pulse there, and I jolt. Every sensation in my body feels like it's been turned up. I didn't know anything could feel like this, and I wonder if it's always like this, or if it's just this way with us.

Sterling takes his time, allowing me to adjust to the new sensations. Then a finger coaxes inside me and he begins to gently massage.

"Please," I moan. Ready for more. Ready for him.

"We need to take it slow," he whispers. "I don't want to hurt you."

He rolls on top of me, still watching me like a hawk. I bring my knees up and open as he leans down to kiss my breasts. I hear the foil wrapper on the condom tear, watch him reach down to put it on. He moves between my legs, positioning himself carefully, but then he stops.

"I love you."

His words sink in slowly past the haze in my brain. *He loves me.* I try to find my voice, but there's a knot of emotion where it should be. My whole world revolves there on a tiny dorm room bed with a beautiful, broken boy. I'm being swept away to somewhere new—and it's terrifying and exhilarating all at once.

And then I finally find the right words. The ones I've been holding back. The ones he's given me. "I love you."

Impossibly, his answering smile is shy, and I realize that this is his first time, too.

Not with a girl.

With love.

He props himself on the same arm that gathers my shoulders. His other hand carefully guiding himself inside me. He watches me, careful but relaxed, as his tip pushes inside me. I feel pressure. *Insane* pressure. It feels like I'm being split open, and I gasp.

Sterling freezes, and I clutch his shoulders, worried I've done something wrong.

Stop it. You're ready. You want this.

I hook my heels around his waist and try to force him deeper, but he resists.

"Slowly," he warns. "It gets easier, but the first time... Just trust me, okay?"

I bite my lip and nod.

He slides in more and the pressure increases, a searing pain growing until he begins to move. Each stroke draws a line of pain in its wake, then erases it, until the pain fades to a dull throb. I close my eyes and cling to him.

Sterling pauses. "You alright, Lucky?"

"Keep going," I whisper.

He begins with slow, steady thrusts. I'm so full of him there doesn't seem to be room for the air I need to breathe. And always he watches carefully, like he's holding his needs at arm's length. Slowly, Sterling destroys me and rebuilds me, until I'm no longer the girl that walked into this room. I'm someone else entirely.

When his breathing becomes ragged and uneven, he kisses me, and I hold on as his body tenses and spasms.

"That was amazing." He says, brushing my lips with his thumb.

I can tell he's waiting for me to say something, but I can't find the part of my brain that speaks. Everything is new and raw and possible.

"Yuh... yeah," I fumble, and the only words I can find are the only ones that matter. "I love you."

"I love you, too."

He wraps me in his arms, holding me close as my body shakes. When it quiets, he kisses my neck. "Be right back."

Sterling returns with a washcloth and runs it gently between my legs. I sit up on my elbows and spot a crimson stain on the sheets.

"Oh my God." I stare at it in horror. "I'm so sorry." I

flop back and cross my arms over my face, willing myself to be invisible.

"Hey." He pries them away, but I refuse to open my eyes. "That's normal. You have nothing to be sorry for."

"I wrecked your sheets," I say.

"You can buy me new ones for Christmas."

I lift one eyelid. "So was I terrible?"

"Honestly?" He pauses, and I wish the bed would swallow me up. "Nothing has ever felt better than being inside you. I just wish you enjoyed it more."

"I did!" For some reason, this sends me shooting up in bed. I grab the sheet to cover up, a little self-conscious. "It was the best. I don't regret anything."

"I mean that I want to make you come," he says with a laugh at my reaction.

"Oh," I say shyly, biting my lip. It turns out that I want that, too. "We could try again."

"We will," he promises, lifting my hand and kissing the inside of my wrist.

"Now?" I ask hopefully.

"How about we watch another movie and give your body a minute?" he suggests.

That makes sense. "So after the movie?"

His answering laughter echoes in the room. "It's my fault."

"What?" I ask, confused.

"I did nickname you Lucky."

20

STERLING

PRESENT DAY

I take longer than I should at the store, picking up ingredients for my date with Adair. She requested neutral territory. I can do that, but it doesn't mean I'm going to play fair. She wants to know more about where I've been the last few years? I'll show her by highlighting the good bits and glossing over the bad. It's not the best plan, but it's all I've got.

"Dinner party?" Percy asks when I step into the elevator with two overstuffed grocery bags.

"Something like that. I have a date."

"Did you learn your lesson?" he asks me seriously.

I stare at the old man, drawing my eyebrow into a question mark. I can only guess what he's referring to, given that he sees everything that goes on at Twelve and South.

"I assume Miss MacLaine was trying to teach you a lesson when she ran off the other day," he says, shrugging his shoulders.

"I forgot you were there for that," I say with a rueful smile. I can only imagine how it looked—or what he saw. I raced after Adair sans clothing in an attempt to stop her, only to spot the elevator doors closing with her inside. It hadn't occurred to me that Percy was in there, too. "Wait, that's why you stopped on all those floors going back down," I realize. "Did she ask you to do that?"

"A gentleman never tells," he says, placing a finger on the side of his nose to show I'm right on the money.

"And a lady wouldn't ask," I mutter. Adair is keeping me on my toes. I might enjoy the chase more if I didn't have other concerns preoccupying me, like the FBI's golden boy and an overly cautious Russian Bratva hitman being in town.

"Your new dog walker is quite charming," Percy changes the subject, perhaps sensing that I'm not exactly happy about his role in aiding Adair's escape.

"Thanks, I guess." I don't exactly know the girl, but she probably spends as much time with Percy as I do, given Zeus's walking schedule. "The dog is clearly getting comfortable. He demands two walks a day, but I think he's just trying to get treats."

"He's a good dog," Percy confirms. "I think you gave him exactly what he needs to thrive."

"What's that?" I ask as the elevator reaches my floor.

Percy tilts his head quizzically, as if this is an odd question. "A home, Mr. Ford."

"Oh, yeah." I shake my head like this should have been obvious. To most people, it probably would be. It hadn't even occurred to me. Yeah, I'd taken the dog in and adopted him. I liked to pretend it was out of pity after that dumpster fire of a charity gala, but as I shift the groceries to dig out my keys, I stop and stare at the door to my house.

My house.

But more than that, it's my home. I'm not even sure when it happened, but I've put down roots. That wasn't part of my plan, and yet here I am. The closest thing I've ever had to a home was Francie's place, but even then, something was always missing. And the house I grew up in before foster care? The only label it ever deserved was hell. A strange sensation lingers as I turn the lock and step inside.

I'm home.

I carry the grocery bags to the counter and call for Zeus. When I don't hear his paws skittering on the tile, I check my watch. He shouldn't be out for a walk now, but maybe Carly's running late today.

"Hey, I got you a bone," I yell, pulling it out of the bag and walking into the living room. "You better not be in my bed or—" My words die on my lips when I see Zeus on the couch, his head in someone's lap. "He's not allowed on the couch."

"Does he know that?" Sutton asks, flashing me a mischievous grin. "Where's my bone?"

I toss it on the ground, and Zeus finally breaks free of my sister's spell. He jumps to the ground after it. "If I'd known you were coming... not that you go in for that kind of thing."

"Never say never." Her blue eyes flash as she jumps up to greet me. Before I know it, I'm locked into a Sutton-grade hug. Sutton never lets go first. She squeezes extra tight, and she doesn't give a shit whether you want a hug or not. I pretend to hate them, but really I just don't know what to do. I don't have much experience in the hugging department. Unlike me, Sutton received a permanent placement with a wealthy foster family. She'd been young enough to benefit from their stable family environment. She even called her foster parents Mom and Dad. None of that makes her any less of a Ford, in my mind. "I came to rescue you."

"I don't remember needing to be rescued," I tell her, "but it's good to see you."

"Well, you stopped responding to my texts a few days ago," she says, referencing the now infamous—in my mind—conversation Adair had accidentally read.

"I've had my hands full," I say, moving into the kitchen to put things into the fridge. I leave out the cheese and fruit I bought and begin unloading the rest.

"I know. Jack caught me up." Sutton snags a grape, flashing her bright purple manicure. "Sounds like you've really stepped in it this time, big brother."

"I have," I say, trying to sound casual, "which is why you should get your ass back to New York."

"I can handle myself," she says defensively.

I shoot her a look. We've had this conversation before. Ever since she showed up at my place in Manhattan, I've done my best to keep Sutton away from the less savory aspects of my life.

"I did just fine when Noah Porter came looking for you," she says.

I drop the knife I'm using to chop tomatoes.

"Noah found you."

"Showed up at my dorm." She pops another grape, like the FBI showing up at NYU is a daily occurrence.

"Why didn't you call me?" I ask. The last thing I need

is him dragging her into this, even if she thinks she can handle herself.

"It's not like he was honest with me." She rolls her eyes, propping her feet on the barstool and hugging her knees to her chest. "He told me he needed to ask me about my family. I figured it had something to do with when we were kids. I told him I'd been in foster care since I was eight. Then he asked me about that and if I had any contact with my family. I thought he meant dad, so I said 'nah,' and then he left. He did give me his number."

I stare at her through the entire rambling account. "He gave you his number? Or his business card?"

"His number," she says, leaving no room to doubt what she means. "I have it somewhere. Do you want it?"

I'm going to kill him. Of course Noah would hit on my baby sister. Trust Sutton to attract a man like him. She's too pretty for her own good, and she's got a pistol for a mouth. It's just the combination an alpha male like him goes for. If he only knew.

"It's not like I'm going to call him," she says, misreading my face. "Not the same team, remember?"

"How did you figure out he was looking for me?" If I spend another second thinking about Noah trying to flirt with Sutton, I'm going to find myself in jail for murder by nightfall.

"Luca told me." She freezes, grape in hand, then winces.

"Weren't supposed to tell me that, were you?"

"If you would keep me updated, I wouldn't have to! But you went radio silent. What was I supposed to do?" Her shoulders square as she gets fired up. In another minute, she'll be a five-foot-three, one-hundred-and-ten pound fireball.

"You're not the one who's in trouble," I say calmly before she explodes.

"Luca just told me you had your hands full with MacBitchFace." Sutton screws up her nose to remind me exactly where she stands when it comes to Adair.

I take a deep breath. This isn't going to go over well. "About that..."

"Yeah," she stops me. "Jack told me about that, too. What the fuck are you thinking?"

"I'm in love with her." I might as well face the truth, and the sooner Sutton accepts it, the better. The last thing that will help me get into Adair's good graces is Sutton unleashing chaos on our relationship.

Sutton shakes her head like she's not buying it. "Your dick's in love with her."

"Nice," I mutter, returning to the Jerusalem salad I'm making. I check the clock, trying to guess whether I'll have time to manage my sister's fire and prepare all the food for a picnic date. "I don't expect you to get it. I barely get it myself, but it's real, okay?"

"Sounds like she doesn't know it."

"Yeah, she's got questions." I wipe my hands on a towel, finished with the salad. I turn to hummus next, blitzing chickpeas, garlic, tahini and lemon together with my secret weapon, picked up from a Greek YaYa: smoked paprika..

"About?" Sutton presses.

"The last five years," I admit.

"What have you told her?"

"Nothing."

"Wait!" Sutton spins the stool around and hops to her feet. "I know more than she does?" She claps and begins bouncing around in her socks. I do my best to ignore her happy dancing at this revelation, but I can't keep a smile off my face. For as much trouble as she's going to cause being here—and I know she will—I missed her.

"Sit down," I order her when Zeus begins to howl out of concern.

In fairness, he never encountered this particular brand of insanity before. Some people burn energy by fidgeting, but Sutton would die if she had to keep still.

"So, what are you cooking for me?" she asks with bright eyes, peering across the counter to watch me work.

"Get takeout," I tell her. "This is spoken for."

Her lip sticks out. "And who is getting your sausage?" When I don't respond, she groans. "Not fair! I came all the way from New York to see you!"

"Without calling to tell me you were coming," I point out.

"As a surprise!" She feigns devastation. "Only to discover I've been replaced by MacBitchFace."

She watches, faux-wistfully, as I use a mortar and pestle to grind fresh za'atar, a dizzyingly fragrant mix of thyme, sesame, and a dried berry called sumac.

"No one can replace you," I tell her, and I mean it.

"Unless it comes to dinner," she mutters.

Adair opens the door to her suite just wide enough to slide through, purse in hand, wearing a loose linen sundress. Her hair is pinned into an artful mess on top of her head, revealing her long porcelain neck. The straps of her dress are thin enough that I can see every delicious freckle on her shoulders.

"Something wrong with your door?" I ask, leaning in to kiss her. It's swift, a brush of my lips, before she can stop me. When I pull back, her cheeks are flushed pink.

She swallows before saying in a business-like voice, "I thought it best we keep a safe distance between us and a bed."

"If memory serves, the wall suited you just fine." I pat the wallpaper for good measure.

"Don't even think about it," she warns me, "or I'll start bringing a chaperone with us on all our dates."

Dates? As in plural? That's a good sign. I try to keep my face blank, but she must see something hiding there, because she sighs.

"Keep it in your pants, okay?"

"Happy to," I promise, offering her my arm. I'm already dreaming up all the things I can do to her with my pants on. I don't mind being generous.

"I don't like the look on your face," she says, but she loops her arm through mine, anyway. "So, where are we going?"

"Guess."

"Hennie's," she says.

"As much as I will live and die for hot chicken," I say, "—and I will—I thought something more romantic might be in order."

"I thought we were going to talk." She stops in the middle of the Eaton's lobby so abruptly that a bellhop nearly runs over her with a baggage cart.

"We are." I tug her forward, calling an apology to the guy who's collecting suitcases from the floor and shoving them back on the cart.

"About you," she says, "not us."

"There's not a me without you," I say without thinking. She stops again and I turn to her. Cupping her face in my palm, I look into her green eyes. "I'm really trying here. I promise."

Uncertainty flickers across her face, but she finally nods. "Okay, let's go, but it better be neutral territory."

"It doesn't get more neutral," I promise her, closing my free hand over the one hooked around my elbow. Neutral or not, she's not getting away again.

It's a typical, sultry summer night in Nashville. Neon signs glow under the waxing sun. There's still a couple of hours until sunset, but the light has already begun to fade to the rosy glow of twilight as we drive away from the city and towards Valmont.

"Neutral territory?" she says with a raised eyebrow when we pass the first mile marker.

"There's not a lot places in Tennessee that are neutral for us," I remind her. If I was doing this perfectly, I would take her out to the far reaches of Windfall's grounds like we did on our first picnic. That's not going to happen. I'm not going to risk going anywhere near her family estate at the moment. Besides, the last time we did that, we rode horses, which Adair doesn't do anymore. The thought jogs my memory. "Why don't you ride anymore?"

"There was an accident," she says tersely, suddenly taking an intense interest in the scenery outside.

"You said that." I wait for more of an explanation when she doesn't continue, I add, "If you don't want to talk about it."

"I don't." I can tell by her tone that she means it.

Apparently, Adair can demand all sorts of information about me, but I'm not allowed to ask about something that changed her life dramatically. "I just remember how much you loved to ride horses. Do you miss it?"

"I try not to think about it." She turns to me and reaches for my hand. "Can we drop it? It's not a good memory and there's nothing you can do about it."

"Why does that matter?" I ask.

"Because you'll try to fix it for me," she says, "like you always do, and this can't be fixed, which only makes it worse. I did something stupid—-really stupid—and I can't take it back. That's all you need to know."

"For what it's worth, I'm sorry," I say, squeezing her hand. She falls so silent afterwards that I nearly drive off the road turning my attention to her. Her face is stricken—white as a magnolia petal—and the moment our eyes meet, she blinks and shakes the look off her face.

"It's worth a lot," she says at last.

"But it doesn't change anything," I guess. "Okay, happier topic. Have you figured out where we're going yet?"

"You really aren't going to tell me?" She twists in her seat and turns wide eyes on me.

"No. You'll see."

"What if I guess?" she asks.

"You haven't exactly been playing that game."

"We're going to Valmont but not Windfall, so the quad? Or to Market Street for dinner?"

I grin. "Terrible guesses. I want somewhere private, but neutral," I add quickly. "Besides, I already have dinner." I hitch my thumb to the back seat.

Adair peeks into the back and spots my carefully prepared picnic basket. "A picnic? Is that a good idea?"

"The weather's right."

"It's hot as hell," she says in disbelief.

"It's cooling off." I dismiss her concern, because I know the real reason she's against the idea. A picnic might take place in neutral territory, but there's a good chance we'll wind up alone.

"You're the worst," she says as if guessing my thoughts.

"No, Lucky, I'm an opportunist," I tell her, turning the car down a narrow lane.

"Wait, where are we going for this picnic?" She looks out the window and groans when she processes the scenery outside. "You're shameless."

"It's a public place. Outdoors. *Suuuuuper* neutral."

"Little Love isn't what I had in mind," she says dryly.

"You only said neutral," I remind her.

"You're shameless." Despite her objections, her hand stays warm and soft in mine as the car climbs up the winding road to the highest point in Valmont.

Little Love is named after its much more impressive cousin Love Circle, which overlooks the whole of Nashville. Love Circle is a spectacular spot for seeing the entire city, the kind of place where someone is always proposing marriage or taking couple's portraits. That means it's not exactly off the beaten track.

Little Love, on the other hand, looks out over Valmont University. During the academic year, couples visit it for slightly more debauched reasons. It's a place to get away from your roommate or smoke pot. But right now Valmont is between summer sessions, and hardly anyone sticks around for classes during the summer, anyway. That means there won't be many people here. Not only will it get me alone with Adair, it also will make certain the wrong people don't hear something they shouldn't. Adair wants to know about the past few years? Fine. But I can't take the chance that Noah Porter is around, or that someone from the Koltsov family is following me.

When we reach the top of the hill, we don't just find it quiet, we find it deserted. Lights twinkle in the dusky orange sky above us, the university sprawls below us. If Love Circle is the quintessentially urban romantic spot in Nashville, Little Love is the country dream version. Small sparks pop in and out of the air around us as the lightning bugs come out for the evening. They're joined by a symphony of cicadas. It should be magical, but Adair sits in protest in the passenger seat while I lay out a wool blanket and start setting things up.

I pour a glass of wine for her and pop open a Pellegrino for myself, then I hook my index finger, beckoning her to join me. Her eyes narrow and her mouth flattens as if she's seriously considering staying put.

"Lucky, come on, let's talk!" I call.

She throws her hands in the air, but finally climbs out

of the car. She stops on the edge of the blanket and stares down at the feast I've laid out. "What is this?"

"I settled on a picnic because a lot of the really good food I discovered the last five years is just as good if it's not hot." I'm about to launch into a description of each item, but she cuts me off.

"But where did you get it?" she asks, carefully joining me on the picnic blanket. She spreads her skirt, carefully as though she has anything to hide from me.

"I made it." I grab a chunk of cheese—the fruit and cheese assortment is standard for all meals throughout the Middle East. I'm not entirely certain how Adair will react to the Sujuk, a dry, spicy beef sausage, but it's possible she has had everything else.

"You cooked?" she says.

I frown. Why is she acting like this is weird? "I love to cook, remember?"

"I know, but I've never had a guy cook for me like this before," she says, her words strangely strangled.

"I've cooked for you."

"With Francie," she says, recalling the meals we shared with my foster mom five years ago. "Never like this."

"I can't tell if you're scared to eat my cooking or not, Lucky."

"It's not that." She shakes her head and a copper strand falls into her eyes. "It's...really nice."

I reach over and tuck the strand of hair behind her ear. Then I brush my thumb across her cheek. "I want to take care of you."

We stare at one another, neither of us speaking. There's

a whole world stretching out around us, but she's the only thing I see. I wouldn't have it any other way.

"So, what is this?" She points to the covered bowl containing an oily paste of herbs..

"That, Lucky, is za'atar. And I'm glad you haven't tried it before." I tear off a hunk of barbari, a kind of Persian flat-bread similar to pita, but crispier, and bathe it in za'atar before popping it in my mouth.

Adair mimics my technique, and her eyebrows try to bounce clean off her face. "Where did you learn to make this?" she asks between ravenous bites.

"I was in Turkey for a while. For them, this is like having ketchup on the table." I shrug like it's no big deal, but I know better than that. I just opened the door she's been trying to unlock since my return.

"You were in Turkey?"

"For a while, after I left the Marines," I explain.

"So, you were in the Marines?"

I pause, momentarily surprised. That fact isn't exactly top secret. It wouldn't have taken much for her to dig that up. "I assumed you knew that. I told Cyrus."

"I heard you joined up. That's all. I left for London shortly after you enlisted," she says softly. "I needed to get away."

Not for the first time, I want to ask her why? Why she didn't stay in London? Why she came back here? Why she never reached out? But I'm the one who has promised to give answers tonight. My own will have to wait.

"What happened when you left?" she asks.

I suspect she wants to know about *why* I left, but I avoid that part. Adair has suffered enough without knowing what her father did to me—to us. There was a time when I thought I could never forgive her for siding with him, but now I realize leaving her the way I did only made it harder for her to break free from her family.

"I enlisted. Francie was furious," I begin.

"I bet," Adair says with a knowing smile. "I hope she chewed your ass out."

"Don't worry. She did," I confirm, before continuing, "but I couldn't stand to go back to New York and take advantage of her anymore. So I joined up and went through boot camp. My drill sergeant said that I had a killer instinct and a willful disregard for human life, particularly my own."

"Harsh, but I imagine that's what they like," she says, pouring herself a second glass of wine. If I'm lucky, it will soften her up for the rest.

"It was true. I just didn't care. I figured I had nothing to lose, so I just went for it. Every training exercise. But she liked me."

"She?" Adair says. "Your drill sergeant was a girl?"

"Don't be jealous."

"Oh, I'm not." She holds up her wine glass. "I just can't believe she liked you."

"Women find me charming."

"I thought she found you reckless, with a death wish," she says.

"It was a very charming death wish," I explain. "*Anyway,* she pulled some strings and got me transferred to a special forces unit. That's where I met Jack and Luca."

"What were they doing there? Neither seems the type," she says thoughtfully.

She's not wrong, but I've seen other sides to my best friends—sides I hope she never even glimpses. "Not my story to tell, Lucky."

"It's okay. Sorry I asked."

"Luca might tell you if you flatter his ego enough," I advise.

"I can only imagine how much flattery that will take given the size of his ego."

"That's the thing with egos—the big ones don't take much to flatter." I can't help laughing at her astute observation. She's got his number, alright. "So, we got sent to Afghanistan with a special forces unit. There were rumors the Taliban was running guns from an unknown source and we went in to find that source."

"And then what were you supposed to do?" She's stopped eating entirely.

"Kill them," I say matter-of-factly, daring to look her in the eye.

"And did you?" From her tone, I'm not sure she wants the answer.

"Yes, and that's where things went wrong."

She frowns, carefully setting down her wine glass. "How?"

"Remember the guy at the hotel?" I ask.

She nods, licking her lips. It's what she's been waiting for, and I can only hope she looks at me the same way after she knows.

"He was also in my unit. He was our fourth. As close a friend as Jack and Luca. His name's Noah Porter."

"And you aren't friends anymore," she guesses.

"That would be an understatement. Noah's FBI now."

There's a long pause. She knew this was coming. Adair is too smart not to see the truth that's sitting in front of her. That I'm a bad guy. That my money came stained with blood. She might not know the details, but she gets the big picture. That's not going to stop her from making me paint it for her, though.

"And why is that a problem? Why did you hide from him? Call Luca?"

"Because the FBI, or rather Noah, has been trying to nail our asses to the wall since Afghanistan, and he's come damn close a few times. It's his version of payback." I search her eyes for a sign of how she's taking all this.

"Why would he want revenge?"

"Because the other three of us got him hauled in front of a disciplinary committee. He probably would have been discharged like the rest of us if we hadn't sworn he wasn't involved."

"Involved in what?" she asks slowly.

"We'd been there a couple of months, trying to avoid getting blown up, but getting no closer to figuring out where the guns were coming from. Every lead went nowhere. Then Jack overheard something, and we did a little digging. We kept it to ourselves and eventually brought Luca in on it."

"What about Noah?"

"Let's just say that Noah's always been better at taking orders than thinking for himself. We knew that until we could prove anything, he wouldn't believe us."

"Prove what?"

"Jack discovered that our lieutenant was smuggling the guns, even running drugs."

She stares at me, mouth wide. "Wait, what?"

"Yep, so we had a dilemma. We could try to turn him in and hope someone higher up believed us. But we also knew he couldn't be doing it alone, so we had no clue who to tell. You have no idea how seriously the military takes breaking the chain of command, on any pretext. Plus, it's not exactly easy to get messages past your commanding officer when you're in the middle of a war theater."

"So what did you do?"

"We decided to steal the next shipment," I say with a shrug. Adair gasps, and I can tell what she thinks of this plan already. "It would be proof, and then we would have leverage. Of course Noah was onto us, but he got the wrong idea. He turned us in—and that's how the lieutenant knew. So he hauls us in for a chat along with Noah and that's when we realize who's helping him."

"Who?"

"Everyone. Turns out the rest of the section is crooked, too, and they plan to kill the new guys to keep it quiet. They have to make it look right, of course. But the lieutenant gets mixed up on why Noah turned us in. He thinks Noah wants in, and, for once, Noah is smart enough to play along. He makes a big deal about his loyalty and they drag us off to a cell. That night, Noah breaks us out and tells us to run."

"Did you?"

"Where the fuck are we going to run in the desert? We told him that and before he could stop us, we took care of the situation."

The silence that falls between us is deafening. She's

doing the math, putting two and two together. "Oh," she finally says.

"I didn't have a choice, Lucky." Can she see that? Does it matter?

"You killed them." She says the words aloud like she's trying them on.

"We didn't have a lot of options." I wait for some sign that she understands that, but she doesn't speak. She just stares fixedly at her glass. "They were going to kill us. We would have been killed by the Taliban if we tried to run. We couldn't exactly make a phone call and get anyone to help us out."

"How many?" she asks softly. "How many people did you kill?"

"Does it matter?" It's a question I've asked myself a lot. How much blood is on my hands from that night? Did I make the right call? There is one thing I know. One thing I have to confess to her before she gets any idea that I made an impossible, but noble choice. "Once you kill a man, it's easier to kill another one and another. It's still easy."

"You've..." she trails away.

"Yes," I admit. "That's not the last time I've killed a man. I didn't make it a profession or anything, but I've had to make some shitty choices. Me or them choices."

She doesn't say anything for a moment, when she finally looks up she studies me for a second. Does she still see the same man? "What happened after that? How did you explain it? Why does Noah hate you?"

"We're getting to that part," I say grimly.

I take it as a good sign that she is still listening after what she learned so far.

"So, everyone was dead," I continue, "and an entire new platoon arrived to investigate and to take us into custody. They start looking into matters and thankfully, our lieutenant was a real piece of shit, because they found plenty of evidence against him."

"So you weren't charged?" She's biting on her nails and I gently take her hand away from her mouth.

"They found we acted in our own defense. Noah corroborated our story, but we took the fall for killing everyone."

She shakes her head, confusion shining in her eyes. "Then why were you discharged?"

"Believe me, the Marines don't want to keep around a bunch of guys who'd kill their own unit, even if it's in self-defense. I guess we were supposed to die to prove our loyalty. Noah would have if we hadn't knocked him out before the gunfire began." I pause, knowing that's not the whole story but knowing she'll accept it.

"And that's why he hates you." Her lips twist into a grimace. "You saved his life."

"Don't tell him that," I advise her. "As far as Noah is concerned, we ruined his life by putting a mark on his pristine record."

"But why come after you?" she presses.

I draw my hand away and take a sip of my sparkling water, which is warm and flat from the summer heat. "The team investigating the incident found evidence that the lieutenant was planning to unload a large shipment of contraband. At that point, the date set for the delivery was still in the future. They couldn't find any weapons. No drugs. But there was no evidence that the deal had taken place early. So suspicion turned on us. We all swore we didn't know anything, but Noah suspected we were lying and told them that. In the end, they couldn't find any proof, so they discharged me, Jack, and Luca, slapped Noah on the wrist and transferred him to some hellhole, and that was it."

"And Noah still thinks you had something to do with the missing contraband?" she guesses. "Why didn't he believe you?"

"We used to play poker. There's not much else to do at night in the desert. According to Noah, I have a tell when I bluff," I admit to her with a bemused grin. She's not going to find this funny. "He swears I was bluffing to the investigation unit."

"And Jack and Luca, what do they think?" There's a softness in her voice that says she already knows the answer. It's not accusatory or judgmental. She's giving me a choice. I can lie to her and she won't push it, but I have no doubt I'll lose her. Or I can tell her the truth and probably lose her anyway. There's no way to win.

I turn my head away from her just long enough to reconsider what I'm about to say. In the end, it's not really a choice. "They know I was lying, Lucky."

"What did you do?" she asks, her words turning to stone.

"We had a couple days before anyone reached us. I waited until the others were asleep and I was on watch and I hid it."

"You hid...the guns?"

"I knew we were facing discharge. I knew no one was going to give two shits what happened to us." I suck my lower lip into my teeth, wondering if I made the wrong call. It's not the first time I've considered that.

"How could you do that?"

I expected this response. It's not as though I could ask her to look past my crimes. "For a long time, it didn't seem to matter. I had nothing to lose. Then Sutton showed up on my door and everything changed."

"You had a family," she says distantly. "What about Francie? Does she know?"

"I told myself I was doing it for her—that I'd be able to take care of her—" there's something thick swelling in my throat that makes it hard to speak "—like she took care of me. But she didn't want anything to do with me."

"What?" Adair shakes her head like she can't believe this. "She loves you like a son."

"Maybe she did," I say, "but when I showed trying to buy her a new place, get her a new car, she had a lot of questions."

Adair sighs and crosses her arms over her chest. "Let me guess. You didn't answer her questions."

"What was I going to tell her? I told her I got discharged because my commander was a piece of dirt and that they gave me my enlistment bonus anyway."

"An enlistment bonus doesn't buy you an Aston Martin and a penthouse," Adair says dryly. "She knew that."

"Neither did one shipment of small arms. Francie might have believed me. She told me to keep the money and set myself up. She didn't expect me to go back to the Middle East. I think that's what tipped her off that there was more to this story."

"You went back?" She seems genuinely shocked.

"I've been all over the world for the last three years. Jack and Luca, too. We had our own little operation. With Luca's connections it was easy to stay under the radar. Plus, we had a plan. Once we hit a certain amount, we'd pull out, go in our own directions, and let the chips fall where they may."

"But they're all here," she says, blinking, "so that means you're still doing whatever you were doing."

"Not exactly. Jack wanted to open a blues bar. Always has. Luca tends to come and go as he pleases in our lives. We're all doing our own things now except one last mission."

"What on earth could you be doing in Nashville?"

It's a charmingly naïve thing to say. If Adair knew half the organized criminal activity that went on down the street from her privileged enclave, she'd never see the city the same way. "I had a list," I tell her, realizing the only chance I have at keeping her is to be painfully honest. It's the only way to prove to her that I'm all in.

"What kind of list?" She sits back on her heels, shifting the smallest bit away from me. Maybe it's a coincidence. I doubt it.

"A blacklist of people who ruined my life," I confess. "A list of people I wanted to hurt, and every name on that list lived in Tennessee."

There's a pause so heavy I swear it brings the night crashing down on us. Maybe I hadn't noticed the sky fading to midnight blue, or the stars coming out overhead. Or maybe darkness finally caught up with me. She doesn't speak. She only studies me, her face as blank as fresh paper.

When she finally opens her mouth, her voice hitches on her question. "Was I on that list?"

I tell myself it's the only way to keep her, but I know it's not true. There's nothing I can say that won't cost me Adair MacLaine's love, so I choose the path I should have taken years ago. "You were on the very top of it."

21

STERLING

THE PAST

The rest of the week is spent in my dorm room, failing to watch any movies. We put them on, but we're distracted before the opening scene. We pause for bathroom breaks and food delivery, which Adair keeps ordering behind my back.

"You need your stamina," she tells me.

And I never want it to end. I don't know where her family thinks she is, but no one has checked on her. That only proves she belongs here with me, instead of there with them. When Friday rolls around, I'm dreading the Christmas party at Windfall for two reasons. The first is that it involves getting dressed, and I've grown pretty attached to Adair's naked body. I'd rather she never put clothes on again, actually. The second is that the party marks our last night together. I leave on a redeye for New York in the morning.

Adair manages to pry herself away early that afternoon, to return home to get ready.

"It will not take you six hours to get ready," I say, grab-

bing her around the waist and dropping her on the bed. I
pounce on top of her, pinning her to the spot.

"I need to run an errand, if you must know." She cranes
to kiss me, and the next thing I know her pants are off and
I'm buried inside her.

The girl is a serious over-achiever, because she can't
keep her hands off me. When I suggested it would take
time for her body to adjust to sex, she initiated it every
second she could. Crawling on top of me in the night and
waking me up with her pretty mouth on me. Refusing to
wear a stitch of clothing for entire days. I have to give it to
her. By day three, we fit together like our bodies were
carved from the same block of marble.

Her head lolls back against the pillow, her breathing
coming in shallow pants, small whimpers escaping her lips
until she cries out, her legs snapping around me like a
spring. I don't make it long after that—I never do.

She seizes the opportunity to grab her clothes while I
pull off the spent condom and toss it in the trash. A quick
look in my bedside drawer shows me I only have one of the
bounty provided by Campus Health Services left. Apparently, I need to run an errand, too.

"You'll be there at seven?" she asks, pulling on the
clothes she wore over here last Friday. It's the first time
she's bothered to pick them up off the floor since then.

"Cy is picking me up at six-thirty." My roommate did
us the courtesy of staying away for the week to apologize
for the mistake at the hotel. I'm pretty sure that I got the
better end of the deal.

Adair pauses, her hand on the door knob. "I love you."

I start toward her and she squeaks. We both know

she'll never leave if I kiss her goodbye. She already tried leaving twice this week and somehow wound up right back in my bed. She even went as far as to have new sheets delivered to the room, so we didn't have to go out for them.

"I love you," I say, stopping at a safe distance.

The door closes, and the room feels empty without her. For the first time in a week, I have a moment to process what has happened between us. Adair MacLaine loves me. Impossible, but true.

I'm still mulling that over when I pull out the old suit Francie brought me during her trip. I'd left it in my closet in New York. The truth is, I hate the thing. It's a hand-me-down from her brother-in-law. He gave it to me so I could attend a parole hearing for my father. I testified against him in this suit. May he rot in prison. But I don't have anything else appropriate for the spectacle of a MacLaine Christmas party.

I put it on at six and stay away from a mirror. When Cyrus walks in, I know I was right to worry. His look says it all.

"That all you got, Sterling?" Cyrus says, taking one look at my polyester navy suit before going to check his closet.

I check my watch. We need to leave in a few minutes, and it's not like I have options. Even if I had his money, I doubt there's a place to pick up a tailored tuxedo that's open at this time of night, even in Nashville.

"That bad, huh?" It must be if he's saying something. Cyrus usually tries to massage my ego where money is concerned.

"Trust me, you'll want to make a good impression with these people."

"It's this or jeans, man." I wait for his response. "Which will her dad prefer?"

"A tuxedo." He emerges from his closet holding a gray garment bag. Cyrus might be better than most of his clique of Valmont trust-funders, but he isn't immune to obsessing over appearance. Naturally, he stashed a tux here.

I'm not sure why? In case of a black-tie emergency? "Really?"

"It should fit you. We're about the same size. Just be sure to get it dry-cleaned before you give it back. In fact, remind me to have my maid clean this whole room." He shoots me a knowing grin. "Poppy says she hasn't seen either of you all week. Did you two ever come up for air?"

I ignore him. Most guys want to chat about their conquests. I can't even claim that I've never bragged in a locker room. But Adair is different. I'm not sharing her. Not even with my words. I slide down the zipper of the garment bag to discover a black tuxedo radiating the smell of moth-balls. "You sure this will fit me? It smells like an attic."

"Yeah, well, I haven't actually worn it before," he admits sheepishly. "It was my dad's, and my mom had it tailored to me before I left for college. In her mind, there might have been a scenario in which I desperately needed one, but didn't have the 30 minutes needed to drive over to where they live."

Wait, are there actually black-tie emergencies?

"Naturally." The truth is, I would do almost anything to stop having this conversation. Men don't talk about clothes, or keeping up appearances. And part of me wishes

I could just go as I am, that I truly didn't care what these rich people think of me.

"Adair will prefer the tuxedo," he says, eerily up on where my head is at.

He's got a point. I know she's nervous about me meeting her family. I'm not sure if it's because she's worried I'll embarrass her or vice versa, but I'm not going to give anyone an easy excuse to look down on me.

I change as quickly as I can, dreading that there will be some button or cinch or component that is entirely alien to me, and will therefore require asking for help. But in the end it's all simple enough, just a standard cummerbund tux, black-on-white, with a bowtie which I have no idea how to tie. I shove it in my jacket pocket, resolving to call Adair on the way. Something tells me she will be able to help.

A quick glance in the mirror confirms that the tuxedo fits and looks much nicer than my cheap suit. I join Cyrus in the hall and we hop in his Jaguar for the ride to Windfall. I'm sure he noticed I'm not wearing the bowtie, but he doesn't say anything. Clearly, sharing clothing was as traumatic for him as it was for me.

When we're halfway there I call Adair, but she doesn't answer. I immediately call again, but it makes no difference.

"Shit," I mutter, pulling down the sun visor so I can access the mirror.

"I got you," Cyrus says without sparing me a glance. He punches up something on the vehicle's screen, and the phone starts ringing through the car's speakers.

"Hey, you there yet? I'm on my way," Poppy's voice says, bright as ever.

"Nearly. Listen, I've got Sterling with me. He needs someone who can tie a bowtie." Cyrus can't completely suppress a grin, but I'll forgive him if it means I don't have to be the only asshole missing one.

"I'm your girl." She sounds absolutely thrilled at the prospect, as though she's been waiting her whole life to be asked. "I just pulled in. Find me in the parking lot."

Cyrus and I ride in silence another few minutes before we pull through security at Windfall and into a large parking lot hidden behind one of Windfall's ubiquitous, manicured hedge rows. He parks next to Poppy, who replaces him in the front seat. She's wearing a pink satin dress overlaid with a white fur shoulder wrap, and it's easily the most expensive-looking thing I've ever seen someone wear.

Cyrus was right about my needing to change. A strange mixture of gratitude and resentment floods me, and it takes a second to realize Poppy said something.

"What? Sorry, I was distracted. You look lovely, Poppy."

I can tell from her reaction that whatever I said wasn't a response to her question, but she blushes at the compliment, anyway. "Lean over here, darling."

She slides her hands around my collar and begins tucking the tie into place. "Bowties are much easier than neck ties," she explains as her industrious hands make subtle adjustments that would probably be lost on me even if I could see them

"Is a bowtie not a kind of neck tie?" I wonder.

"Don't be silly." Poppy's grin widens, before her face suddenly sinks into a frown. "Damn."

"What is it?"

"It's too small for your neck," she says, holding up a finger and placing her phone next to her ear. "It'll never work."

"Felix? It's Poppy. Yes, I'm looking for Adair. Yes, it's an emergency." She pauses for a long time, and I can hear sports highlights start playing on Cyrus's phone in the back seat.

I can't help but note that there *are* actually black-tie emergencies. I'm so out of my element.

"Poppy?" I hear Adair's voice say through the phone.

"Adair, listen. I've got Sterling here in your parking lot, and we need the largest black bowtie you can find. Stat."

"Got it," she says before I hear her thanking Felix.

The back door opens, and then the front door. "Come on, Poppy. We don't need to be here for this. I want to stand by a fire with some Windfall nog. God, it's fucking cold."

She beams at him adoringly, taking his proffered hand and using it to pull herself out of the car. I guess that's working out. I can't help wondering for how long. Their heads bob off around the hedge, and about five minutes later Adair practically dives inside the car, shivering from cold.

"Lucky, why didn't you wear a coat?" Surely she has something warm and furry, like Poppy.

"No time," she says, straightening up and adding her foggy breath to my own.

"I had to take this off one of the staff," she explains,

looking harried. She reaches around my neck and begins fiddling with the tie.

"You took it off a human being?" Did I hear that right?

"I was told it was an emergency."

"About that," I begin.

She rolls her eyes. "I know it's ridiculous."

This is why we work.

"You look ravishing," I say, admiring her emerald-green velvet dress. Its spectacular, plunging neckline shows a delicious amount of cleavage. My cock twitches also admiring it. The rest of her dress is more conservative, having no slit and covering everything above her ankles. It does, however, show off the curves of her hips.

"Thanks," she gives me a brief smile which dissolves back into concentration as she puts the finishing touches on the tie. "There. You look very debonair. Very sexy."

"Good. It's Cyrus's tux," I admit.

"I figured it was something like that," she says, and I notice her blinking away the hint of watery tears.

"How are you doing? You seem incredibly stressed." I take her hand in mine and squeeze it gently.

"Oh, it's my father. It's the first Christmas since..." she trails off as her throat closes up. "I'm glad you're here."

Stupid, Sterling.

"I'm sorry. I didn't mean—"

"No!" She forces the word out. "It's nothing to do with you. My father, he wants everything to continue like she's still here, but he doesn't want to take any time doing the stuff Mom used to do for this party. A couple hours ago he shoved a bunch of stuff in front of Ginny and me, and we've been going a million miles an hour ever since."

"Gotcha." It sounds like a cop out, but I don't know what else to say.

"Let's go in," she says, her teeth beginning to chatter.

We hop out, and I toss my tux jacket around her shoulders. She leads me into a side entrance, which opens on the busy Windfall kitchens. We continue on through three more rooms before emerging into a long, narrow hallway with minimal decoration.

"It's just through those doors," she says, pointing to the end of the hallway. She slides out of my jacket and hands it back to me, then gently presses me against the wall so a servant—so quiet I hadn't realized he was there—bearing a large silver platter of canapés can get by. "I have a couple more things I need to manage. I'll be out as soon as humanly possible."

Then she tucks her hands under the lapels of my tux and pulls me down for a kiss, tossing me a wink before heading back towards the kitchen.

I follow her directions. I hadn't gone this way on the day of her mother's funeral. Considering Windfall is the size of a castle, that's not surprising. I don't know just what I expect to find when I push through the door at the end of the hall, but it's not to walk into a scene from *The Great Gatsby*. The atrium at Windfall is the most impressive room I've ever been in. Two-story, carved stone pillars support a domed roof of wooden arches, which stretch a further story into the cloudless, starry sky. The apex of the room is a wooden cupola set with gold-stained glass, and containing a well-concealed bank of lights that bounce off the mirror finish of the glass, filling the space with artificial, twinkling starlight. I'm pretty sure there is more walnut burl here than in every Jag, Rolls and Bentley ever made. Large planters the size of dinner tables hold exotic trees that twist carefully around the room like bonsai trees. Red and green festoons hang throughout, and on the floor there is a large family crest cut from shades of exotic marble, just in case anyone forgot whose house it is.

I don't see Cyrus or Poppy—or anyone I recognize. I make my way around the room slowly, trying to avoid conversation, and check the darker corners for someone to talk to. Eventually I reach a tiered platform set in front of the outer glass wall of the atrium. Wondering what it could be, I stop to take a closer look, which turns out to be a mistake.

"Choir risers," a man's voice calls from just over my shoulder.

He's about five years older than me, with a pinched, disapproving face that contradicts the fatuous smile he has tried to plaster there.

"Ah." I say, trying to sound the right mixture of polite and disinterested.

"Malcolm MacLaine." He offers his hand.

I take it firmly, but not crushingly. It probably wouldn't be a good idea to alienate my girlfriend's family. "Sterling Ford."

I watch his eyes flit back and forth, like he's reading from some file of notable persons, and, failing to find me there, shrugs. He studies the cut of my tuxedo, then sniffs loudly and frowns slightly. That would be the mothballs. "What business are you in, Ford?"

"I'm a student," I say evenly, glancing at him while he speaks, but otherwise continuing to scan the room.

"Business?" he asks before quickly taking another stab. "No, law. You look like a lawyer."

"No." I think he just insulted me, but I can't be sure. "Undeclared major. I just started at Valmont."

"Of course," he says, taking one more look at my clothes and giving another small sniff. "Enjoy the party." He catches the attention of someone else in our radius and makes a show of going to greet his old friend.

It takes maybe ten more minutes to complete my circuit of the crowded atrium, and I'm forced to repeat the same conversation I just had with a few gaffers who greet me warmly, like the son of a friend, before realizing I'm no one important and moving on. I'm just about to take out my phone and ask Cyrus where he snuck off to when I hear a rage-filled voice carrying down the corridor I used to enter the room. Another servant bearing canapés opens the door, and I hear Adair's voice respond, too soft to make out.

"If I wanted your fucking opinion, I'd have asked for it. I don't care what your mother did, I'm not filling these people's gullets with Cristal. Waste of money!"

It can only be Adair's father. What an asshole. I fight the urge to knock his head off by imagining how it would end up landing me in jail, never to see Adair again. I don't hear her response, but it mollifies him a little.

"I said, 'make sure it's to your mother's standard,' not fucking bankrupt this family. Go fix it and then get to the atrium and starting making sure people feel welcome."

I don't hear any response from Adair, but instead foot-falls coming toward me. I turn my back to the door and study a painting on the nearby wall, wanting to avoid seeming like I've been eavesdropping. It's an irrelevant gesture, though, because Angus MacLaine explodes out the door in his wheelchair in a hazy, whiskey-scented cloud. I notice the naked hatred in his eyes as he looks at the people in the room. His gaze passes my way, but he gives no indication he registers my presence.

"Malcolm!" he roars to no one in particular, and Adair's brother appears, hustling over with a worried look on his face. He bends down to the chair.

Angus whispers something to his son I can't make out, but I overhear Malcolm's reply. "I'm sure Ginny's looking into it."

"She's a stupid cow!" hisses Angus, and a few heads nearby turn in surprise, though of course no one says anything.

"There you are," Adair's voice calls softly. I turn to find Adair, a look of relief on her perfect face, and for a moment I'm lost for words. I had no idea her family was so abusive. She always said they were terrible, but I imagined cold and stoic, not pure venom. I wonder if Angus is normally like this, or if it's just harder for him because his wife is gone—not that it would excuse his behavior.

"Here I am, Lucky," I pull her to me, wrap my arm around her, well above her butt, and give her a hug. She could use one, even from someone as bad at it as I am.

"I'm so glad I found you," she says, reaching up for a kiss which I gladly give her.

"Adair!" hisses her father's voice behind us, and he wheels over to us, his cheeks and nose red from the spidery web of blown blood vessels all drunks eventually get. "What did I tell you to—"

The service corridor doors burst open, and a long file of

servers holding trays of champagne streams out.

"'Bout time you did something for a change," grumbles Angus.

Adair's hand finds mine, her nails biting into my palm from the effort of not screaming.

"My friends! Find a glass of champagne and let us have a toast!" Angus calls loudly, bringing the bustling room to a sudden hush.

People snap up the champagne in moments, and Angus rolls in front of the choir platform. He raises his hands above his head like a carnival barker, champagne flute in hand. "Another year come and gone. Another Christmas party here at Windfall."

A number of people in the crowd clap politely and off in the corner someone with a drunk's swaying gait actually whistles sharply, which puts a self-satisfied smile on Angus's face.

"For Windfall and for God!" He swigs deeply from his champagne flute as nearly everyone in the room follows his example.

"Wow," I say as a server passes us. I refuse a glass of champagne, but Adair takes one.

"Now, I've got a little entertainment in store for you all tonight. The Collegium Chorale of Valmont University will be performing a selection of Christmas carols for your enjoyment. Merry Christmas!" he shouts before clapping sharply twice. The doors a few feet from Adair and me swing open again, and a line of college students in tuxes and sequined dresses makes its way to the stage.

In a flash, Adair grabs my hand and pulls me against the throng of people headed toward the performance. As the first carol—O *Come All Ye Faithful*—starts, we manage to slip out of the atrium and into a long corridor less well decorated than the one we entered through.

"Another service corridor?" I guess.

"Yes," Adair says, pushing me against a storage cabinet and pulling me down for a kiss.

"Aren't you worried someone will say something to your father if we get hot and heavy in the hallway?" I'm not sure I'll ever understand the rules of Adair's world. If she keeps kissing my neck, I'm not sure I care.

"They like me better than him," she says, covering my mouth with a hungry kiss. Her hands reach around to grab my ass and I'm not sure how much longer I can resist taking her, party be damned.

I scan the corridor as she pulls at my bowtie, desperate to expose more of a target for her lips.

"Let's find somewhere more private," I say, and pull her towards a small swing door near the atrium entrance. Inside, I find a narrow stairwell leading both down and up. From below I hear the sounds of clanking glassware—no doubt the servants in the cellar are hard at work getting everyone drunk enough to enjoy the stuffy party. I lead us up, landing after landing, until I begin to feel the cold walls suck the heat from our bodies.

"I think this leads outside," she says, trying the knob.

She doesn't know?

A blast of cold air whistles loudly through the opening, and I hear the sound of footsteps ascending the stairs below us, although it's impossible to tell if the person is coming all the way up. Adair pulls us through the door and onto a small, flat section of roof overlooking the atrium below. The door catches the wind and begins to slam shut, but I'm able to grab the knob in time.

It's lucky I did, as I notice the door is designed to stay locked from the outside. I don't relish the thought of yelling down to the party below for someone to let us in. I spot a piece of broken roof tile near the door and prop it open so we can get back in.

When I turn back to Adair, I can see how cold she is, so I take off my jacket and throw it around her shoulders again. "That better, Lucky?"

"A little." She says, teeth chattering. A wicked grin lights her face. "I'm afraid it will take all your skill to keep me warm."

"Yes, ma'am," I reply, drawing her close to me.

Below us, the carol ends to a round of applause. Golden light spills from the hundreds of glass panes that form the walls of the atrium, bathing the grounds in a warm glow. It's so much darker outside than inside that I know there's no chance of anyone below seeing us.

"I'm getting cold," Adair says with a pout, and I feel her hands unclasp my suit pants.

My need takes over as I spin Adair around, pulling up the hem of her skirt and bending her over the half-wall overlooking the party below. The sight of her perfect ass greets me, and I can feel myself grow hard.

"Jesus, Lucky. No panties?"

It takes a second for the implications to fully register. She planned this all along.

I've never seen a woman wear a garter before. Very sexy. A garter and no panties, though? It's the promise of heaven itself.

She shoots me a feline grin. "Do you have a condom?"

My cock bursts out of my boxers, pointing the way. It takes a few seconds for my rapidly freezing hands to pull the condom from my wallet and get it on. I quickly slide into position, and when I bump into her sex, her body flinches and her mouth emits a moan that's almost a purr. Her body shivers in the cold, quivers in anticipation. When I make my first thrust, her body immediately stops shaking, and suddenly we're both warm enough.

I thrust into her, pinning her against the low wall.

"I'm going to have you screaming by the time we're done," I promise as I crash into her again and again. "The police will come. Everyone will know."

"Worth—*Uhhh*—it," she sobs around my thrusts.

My words are a self-fulfilling prophecy. She grows louder with every thrust until I really do begin to worry the people below will hear us. The carol changes from *We Wish You A Merry Christmas*, to a soft, quiet rendition of *Silent Night*. I match pace with the song.

"No, don't slow down," she demands.

I reach around to the front of her hips and my fingertips find her clit.

"*Ohhhhhhh*." The syllable rips through the air, discordant with the music below.

I pull back, and her next sound is full of deflated longing. I spin her around and lift her off the ground, placing her hips above mine. Her arms fumble with the fabric of her dress, attempting to get it out of the way. She leans back too far, and I struggle to keep her from falling. I stumble towards the broad wall next to the door, and we crash into it, too cold—and too hot—to care.

Her hips are beyond her ability to control them. They dart downwards again and again, trying to find their home. When at last she crashes down onto me, her moans become shrill gasps. She pushes my lips towards her cleavage, which looks as perfect as new-fallen snow.

"Harder," she pants.

My thrusts send shockwaves across her body and more long, low moans out of her mouth.

Some distant part of my brain must still be functioning normally, because I eventually recognize the sound of foot-steps on the stairs below us. Probably a member of the wait staff headed to the atrium. But when the number of foot-falls hits twenty, I know someone is on their way to us.

"Someone's coming," I say, slowing down.

"Don't care," she says, her hips goading me to return to our previous pace.

Dammit.

I double my pace, desperate to reach our climax before it's ruined.

"*Ahh. Ahh. Ahh.*" Adair repeats the sound again and again. Whoever is on the stairs can definitely hear us.

I see a silver-haired head appear below, its owner's back to us. Adair unleashes her loudest moan yet, and I clamp my palm over her mouth in desperation. I can hardly think, and the distant, still-rational part of my brain screams that it's a bad idea.

I don't care.

I kick away the tile propping the door before the figure on the stairs rounds to where he will see us, and slide against the far side of it. We're all in now.

Adair's orgasm echoes through the grounds, mixed with

the finishing strains of another carol. Mine follows just after, pulling every last bit of heat out of my body and syncing with the shivers I've managed to ignore so far.

A sharp rap on the door jolts us back to reality. I set Adair back on her feet and, keeping my weight against the door, furiously clasp my pants.

Another rap follows, this time accompanied with, "Adair?"

Adair's nervous look is replaced with relief.

"Felix," she whispers.

Thank god. If it had been her father...

We step back from the door when we hear the old butler try the knob. It opens slowly, and—although it's stupid to even try—we pretend as if we were simply taking in the performance from above.

He scarcely bothers looking at me, although he definitely sees me. Instead, he addresses Adair. "The performance will conclude soon. You'll be missed if you don't return now."

"Thank you, Felix," Adair says, the crimson of her cheeks betraying the evenness of her tone.

Had she arranged it with him? Or is he simply so good at his job he always knows where his charges are? It's impossible to tell by judging his expression. I suppose a good poker face is something of a job requirement for butlers.

Adair takes me by the hand and leads me down the stairs. We arrive back in the atrium half-frozen, and thankfully all eyes are on the final flourish of the choir's performance of *O Holy Night*.

Adair spends the next twenty or so minutes making

in silence back to Nashville. I didn't say a word when he dropped me at the Eaton. And since?

For the last week, Sterling has been keeping a low profile. There have been no gifts or flowers delivered to my door. He hasn't visited my office on a whim. He hasn't even called.

And somehow that makes everything worse.

"Then I will be your bodyguard," Poppy promises.

"Fine." There's no point arguing now that we're halfway there, and she's right. It's not like we get to see Kai perform in a local bar all the time. Usually, he's selling out the Staples Center.

"And tomorrow," she says, "you're going home to get your clothes."

"What's wrong with this?" I ask. I happen to think my yellow floral maxi dress is comfortable and pretty. "It's not like we're going somewhere fancy."

"Um, think about this for a second. Kai Miles is performing in Nashville at a place with no cover charge."

She's right. The Barrelhouse will be packed, and if I know anything about Kai's popularity, people will crowd around on the street outside just to get a free listen. Local news will be there, and I'll definitely talk with Kai. A picture of me in this dress will probably end up on the cover of tomorrow's newspaper.

"Are you embarrassed to be seen with me in this dress?" I say it teasingly, but the truth is, even with everything at Windfall, I don't have a quarter of what Poppy does in my wardrobe. She's probably secretly mortified.

"What? No," she stammers, "Well, it's a little plain is all. You definitely don't want to be the most-clothed person at a club, you know? Especially one that's going to be 80 degrees inside."

"I am plain, Poppy. Plainer than you, anyway."

"Baloney," she says brightly, "you're fabulous. And don't let anyone tell you any differently. Especially yourself."

I wish I saw myself as beautifully as Poppy does. Or as Sterling does.

Sterling.

Whenever he comes popping up in my thoughts, I feel paralyzed. I haven't begun to reconcile the different versions of him. The naïve one I knew before my brother's wedding. The foolish one who left for the military and wanted to do the right thing—but ended up killing his squad-mates. The vindictive one who came back to ruin me, but couldn't. The broken one who lost Francie.

They are all Sterling, but none of them is the real Sterling. My Sterling.

And that's the problem in a nutshell. Sterling may not really be who I thought he was.

When we pull up to the Barrelhouse, it takes us a few minutes to find a parking spot because a crowd has already gathered. Poppy strides straight past everyone waiting in line and right up to the security team. I'm pretty sure that even if we weren't on the VIP list, she would have no trouble getting in. Not with her toned, brown stomach on display in a champagne sequined crop top, her legs streaming from a tight leather miniskirt down to strappy stilettos. A few people grumble when we pass them, but no one tries to argue. Why would they? She looks like she owns the place. Her inky hair swings around her shoulders as she flashes the guard a sweet smile.

"Poppy Landry and Adair MacLaine."

"This way." He holds open the door, running his eyes down us appreciatively.

The Barrelhouse is still nearly empty. A few stage-hands are setting up the mic and lighting, with Jack over-seeing the process. He turns as we approach, his face breaking into a wide, warm smile. I try to return it as natu-rally as possible. He killed a dozen men? Maybe more? If someone had told me that when we first met, I might have laughed at them.

Jack doesn't seem to notice if I'm acting oddly. That might be because he's buzzing with excitement. "You came!" He reaches for a hug before I can stop him. His arms are as strong as Sterling's and my thoughts drift to images of him in fatigues in a desert. When he pulls back, he raises an eyebrow. "Sorry. Am I too excited?"

"She's not a hugger," Poppy explains, "but I am." The two of them embrace warmly and I'm left wondering what it must be like to feel that at ease around people.

Someone calls over to him with a question, and Jack waves us toward the side door. "Kai's in the green room. I'll see you two later."

We wind our way past the tables and into a hall that leads to the small room in back, which seems to function as a one-size-fits-all solution for performers. Despite the cramped quarters, it's amazing to see the names scrawled on the wall. It's a bit of Nashville history.

"He's cute," Poppy says in a low voice as we knock on the door.

"Who?"

"Jack," she says, "and he can't stop looking at you."

I want to tell her that's likely because he knows that I know that he's a cold-blooded killer. But it's not my secret to tell, so I just roll my eyes. "I think he was checking you out, actually."

"Yes, but I'm off-the-market," she says significantly. I know Poppy is fishing for information as to what happened between Sterling and me. I've been tight-lipped about our date so far. All she knows is what I know: things have changed for us—maybe forever.

The door swings open, and Kai grabs our hands. He hauls us inside and shuts the door, slumping against it. He's already dressed for tonight's show in a worn pair of Levi's and a black t-shirt. Only he could make something so simple, so hip.

"Are you okay?" Poppy's question mirrors the concern I feel. Kai is so pale that he looks like he's about to be sick.

"I just fired my agent," he says, pressing a hand to his chest like he's checking for his own pulse.

"What? Why?"

"Because I'm going to move to Nashville and work with Jack." He bites his lip, waiting for our reaction.

It takes a second for me to process. That's exactly one second longer than it takes Poppy. She's already screaming. The next thing I know, I'm being smashed into a group hug.

"I'm so glad you came," Kai says, squeezing us back. "But tell me—have I lost my mind?"

"Absolutely not," Poppy says. "Right?"

"Yes!" I force myself to sound excited and plaster a grin on my face. Inside, I can't help thinking about what Jack did all those years ago. Sterling said Jack is on a different path now, but should Kai know who he's working with? I'm not sure.

"Adair!" Poppy snaps her fingers near my nose, and I startle. "I was telling Kai that we're going to celebrate next weekend at Maison Blanc. Attendance is mandatory."

"That sounds great," I say in a feeble voice.

"No one has ever sounded so depressed at the prospect of a spa day," Kai says, eying me with concern.

"She had a fight with Sterling," Poppy tells him.

"We didn't have a fight." I blow a stream of air out of my lips, searching for the right word for what happened. "I had a wake-up call."

"Uh-oh." Kai shakes his head. "When will that boy learn?"

Poppy glances at me, barely suppressing a smile. "He'll learn when she teaches him."

An hour later The Barrelhouse is packed and Cyrus has arrived. Thanks to Jack, we've got a small table near the bar. It's close enough to keep the whiskey flowing and hear the music, but far from the crowd mashing their way closer to the stage.

"Hey, you ready?" Jack appears at our table, rubbing his palms together. His enthusiasm is infectious.

Poppy, who has stolen a cowboy hat—probably from Kai himself—whistles loudly. "Already losing control of your artist? Let's get this going!"

Jack's eyes sparkle. "He told you?"

"Yeah, congrats." I mean it. If Sterling is right, and Jack

is trying to change, I want the best for him. Maybe he made some mistakes, but he seems to have moved on.

The lights dim, and the audience begins to thrum with excitement. A few seconds later, the stage lights fall on Kai as the first notes of "The Liar" start. At least he's not making me sing it with him this time.

A grin splits Jack's face, but as he turns to yell something over the crowd, he pauses and waves at someone near the door. My eyes follow his to find Sterling entering along with Luca. I consider whether I can melt onto the floor with no one noticing, when a pretty girl in cut-offs and a nearly sheer tank top follows behind them.

"He didn't," Jack says, shaking his head.

My stomach plummets to my feet, and I fight the urge to vomit. I knew Sterling would show up. He couldn't resist. But I didn't expect him to bring someone else. A hand closes over mine, and I look up to find Poppy staring at me in concern.

"Bathroom now," I mouth.

For all the work that Jack has done on bringing the Barrelhouse into this century, he is yet to touch the ladies' room. There's a line, but Poppy pulls me along right past the others. "Sorry, ladies, this is an emergency. She just saw *him*!"

There's a collective murmur of understanding from the women waiting in line. No one has to ask who *him* is or tries to interfere as we press our way to the sinks, partly because we aren't jumping the line to the toilets, but mostly because every single one has *a him* of their own. No explanation is necessary.

"He brought someone," I say miserably.

"She might have come with Cyrus."

I ignore this rational observation in favor of self-pity. "She can't even be nineteen. How did she get in here?"

"She knows the owner's best friend," Poppy points out. "Or, maybe, she just walked in after them!"

I stare at her. "Is it perpetually sunny in your version of reality? I'd like to visit. The real world sucks."

"It is not always sunny," she says, "but it never rains long!"

"Must be nice," I grumble.

"Nope. You will not let him get to you," her voice rises, competing with the music seeping through the bathroom door. "Chin up. Tits out. Never let him see you cry."

A few girls shout their agreement, and I close my eyes. She's right. Part of being stronger is choosing stronger, even when I'm not sure I really am. It's the only way that—one day—I will be.

I do as directed, following her out of the bathroom and back into the bar. But now Cyrus isn't the only one at our table.

"Bloody hell," Poppy mutters. "I'm going to murder him."

I don't know if she means her boyfriend or Sterling. He's sitting, talking with his old roommate, and I'm struck by the memory of the first time we were here. They sat and talked about something I couldn't hear that night. Then, the Barrelhouse was a total dive joint. The kind of place minors aren't carded. Someone had been playing blues that night. That memory is a million miles away from the remodeled bar and the catchy song Kai is crooning on stage.

"Sorry," Sterling calls, spotting us. "Did I take your chair?"

"Nope." I swing onto a stool across from him and turn my attention to the stage.

"I should get back to my sister. She can't be trusted for long." Sterling tips his head. "Catch you later, Cy. Poppy." A hand closes over my shoulder and lingers a second too long to be a friendly gesture. "Adair."

I hate how my name sounds on his lips: regret mixed with longing and something that sounds dangerously like hope.

As soon as he's out of earshot, Poppy grabs my arm. "His sister!"

I wish this felt like a victory. Once, I might have wanted to meet Sutton, but that was before I discovered she thought I was a bitch, and before I found out about Sterling's plan.

"It doesn't matter," I call to her and turn my attention to the stage, where Kai is performing a new song I haven't heard. Try as I might, I can't keep my eyes from sweeping the bar until they land on Sterling. He's completely absorbed in the show. He's not looking for me—not wasting his time. Maybe he senses that it's really over. My gaze flickers away and locks with the girl sitting next to him.

Sutton is staring at me, and, from the looks of it, her opinion of me hasn't changed. I force a smile. She flips me off. Obviously, we're meant to be best friends.

The rest of the show, I feel her eyes burning into my back, and I force myself to focus on the stage. I'm not about to let Sutton Ford win this round. I survived Sterling. I can survive his kid sister.

When the set ends, I dare a glance to discover she's sitting at the table alone, still glowering at me.

"I'll be right back," I say to Poppy. She nods, continuing her conversation with Cyrus.

I take a minute to work my way through the crowd, but when I reach the table, she's waiting for me.

"I'm Adair," I say. I consider holding out my hand, but that feels a bit too friendly given that she looks like she would bite it off.

"I know."

I've encountered this brand of disdain before. It runs in the family.

"You missed the show," I say to her.

"It's hard to pay attention when you know there's a rapid bitch on the loose."

"My thoughts exactly," I say. "What exactly is your problem?"

"I don't like you." Sutton takes a long draw off her beer bottle and flashes me a toothy smile. It's incredible how much she looks like her brother. Right down to the wicked intent gleaming in her eyes.

"You don't really know me." I don't know why I'm bothering to argue with her. She made her mind up about me before she stepped into the Barrelhouse. The texts she sent Sterling proved that.

"I know my brother," she says.

"Do you?" I blurt out. Instantly, I regret it.

Sutton glares at me, her fingernails scratching off the label on her bottle. "Better than you do."

"I doubt it." There are a lot of things I'm not sure of anymore. I am certain that I know Sterling Ford better than anyone else alive. Better than Jack and Luca. Maybe better than he knows himself. That's not saying much. But part of understanding him is seeing how much he walls himself off from the world—how much he shuts it out.

"He's my brother," she says. "He's my family. My blood. Do you know what that means?"

"Family only means as much as you let it." It's a truth I understand all too well. "Blood doesn't mean much more."

"Maybe not to you, MacBitchFace." She practically spits the insult at me, but I find it strangely fitting. "It means everything to us."

"I don't expect you to understand." I turn to leave before this gets worse.

Sutton jumps off her barstool and blocks my path. "What does that mean?"

She thinks she wants the truth. We'll see if she can handle it.

"You want a family so badly you will do anything—anything—to get it. You'll cater to every expectation. You'll turn a blind eye. You'll make excuses. You'll defend them. You'll protect them," I say. Why force her to learn this lesson the hard way when she can have the benefit of my experience? "But family doesn't ask you to do that. Family accepts you. Family protects you. Family expects nothing. Family doesn't cost. Family gives."

"Like Sterling gave when he paid for my tuition at NYU a few months after we first met? Or maybe you mean give like the time he showed up at 3 in the morning at some house in Queens to pick me up when my date tried something at a party and I was too drunk to drive? Or like how he's paying Francie's bills before they even make it to her mailbox because he knows she won't take the money? He takes care of his family," she says. "He gives everything he can to us."

I close my eyes, wanting to shut her out, but all I find is Sterling. She knows him. Maybe not as well as I do. But she knows the side of him I fell in love with—the part of him that gives so completely. "Do you know why he's like that?"

"Because he's not a piece of shit, rich heiress?" she guesses, crossing her arms.

"That probably helps," I admit. "He's like that because he loves you. He shows up because he loves you. He takes care of you because he loves you. He does it because he wants to be loved. That's all he's ever wanted."

Her familiar eyes burn. "If that's true, why does he think he loves you? Because he doesn't act like it. He came here hating you, and now he thinks you hung the goddamn moon! Or is that it? Are you just keeping him on the hook, dangling love in front of him? Making him think he can finally have it? He doesn't need you to love him."

She might be right. I think I've always needed Sterling more than he has needed me.

"Hey! What are you doing?" Sterling's angry voice cuts into our conversation, but he's not mad at me. "Are you drinking? Do you want Jack to get busted? Do you want to wind up in jail?"

"It was one bottle of beer." She rolls her eyes and places it on the table. Then she holds up her hands like she's being arrested.

"And you promised me that if I let you tag along, you'd behave. I don't want to see you get in trouble."

I back away while he continues his lecture. It's a side of

him I've never seen before. Big brother Sterling is fiercely protective, and not because he's trying to save face, like Malcolm. Because he's looking out for her. Because she's his family.

Maybe Sterling finally got what he needed. Maybe the best thing I can do is finally let him go find happiness.

I find Poppy and Cyrus sitting near the bar, heads bowed together, deep in conversation. "I'm going to head home."

"What? But Kai should be out soon and then we're going to grab a bite," Poppy says with a pout.

"I have a deadline," I lie, "and a massive headache." The last part is true, even if it's only a metaphorical headache.

"Do you want a ride?" Poppy asks, elbowing Cyrus in the ribs.

"Yeah," he jumps in. "I can call my car."

"It's only a few blocks away, and it's still early. I think I'll walk."

Poppy's lips flatten like she's holding back her thoughts on this plan. She keeps them to herself, but she forces a hug. "Call me when you're home."

"I will. Tell Kai he sounded amazing."

"Will do." She blows me a kiss goodbye before returning to her conversation with Cyrus. I feel a stab of envy. Most of the time, I'm not jealous of their relationship. It's not exactly rock solid. But tonight I feel alone. It's a marrow-deep ache, reminding me I'm always just one more than is needed. The second child my father didn't need after Malcolm was born. The sister who never left home. The friend always tagging along with the happy couple.

I weave around the back of the club, doing my best to blend in to the crowd.

No one stops me. As soon as I step out the door, I release a breath I didn't realize I was holding. Even the sticky summer air feels cooler than it was inside the jammed bar. I dig in my purse and find a hair-tie. Lifting my hair off my neck, I sigh with relief. I've got it halfway up when a hand taps my shoulder, sending me jumping.

"Whoa, it's me, Lucky." Sterling's voice washes over me, and I calm down.

"Don't sneak up on me," I demand as I finish tying up my hair, spinning to face him.

He doesn't apologize. Instead, he frowns. "Were you just going to leave?"

Is he serious?

"We didn't come here together," I remind him, planting my hands on my hips. "In fact, I think your under-aged sister is inside. Why don't you worry about her?"

"Because right now she has two over-protective ex-Marines watching every move she makes," he says, the frown deepening. "You, on the other hand, are walking home alone in the dark."

"The neon lights will guide my way," I say dryly, but he doesn't laugh.

"I'm walking with you," he decides.

I open my mouth to argue but realize there's no point. Sterling is as stubborn as...well, me.

"What were you talking with Sutton about?" he asks.

"That?" I shrug my shoulders, carefully keeping a few feet between us as we walk. "We were just talking about girl stuff." There's no reason to repeat what she said to him.

It will only get one of us in trouble. Plus, I need to mull it over. Maybe she's right. Not about everything, but about enough.

"What kind of girl stuff?" he asks.

"Boys," I say casually. He won't want to hear about that. Not if it involves his sister.

"Really?" There's a challenge in his voice.

"Really." My eyes dart to him. Did he hear us discussing him? Does he know we were fighting?

"Must have been a one-sided conversation, since Sutton is a lesbian."

"She is? Oh." I blink, and he smirks at my surprise.

"You didn't see her staring at Poppy all night?" he asks.

"I guess..."

"You guess what?"

"I thought she was staring at me," I confess.

"How narcissistic of you," he says.

"Hey! What was I supposed to think? She's not my biggest fan."

"That's an understatement," he mutters. "Don't worry about Sutton."

A crowd spills out from Tootsie's and we dart across Broadway to avoid the drunken tourists. We continue down 5th avenue in silence until we've nearly reached the Eaton. It's all very civil. Sterling is on his best behavior. I doubt he'll even shake my hand at the door. That means he's learning his lesson. So, why do I wish he would pick me up and carry me to bed?

I'm caught in my imagination when he breaks the silence. "What else do you want to know, Lucky?"

"About?" I ask absently.

"Me. Before. Whatever."

"Now you're dying to tell me the truth." I take a deep breath. "It's late. I'm tired. It can wait."

"It can't wait!" Patient, gentlemanly Sterling vanishes in an instant. His eyes storm with barely suppressed frustration. His hand lashes out like he's going to grab me, but he thinks better of it. Instead, he rakes it through his hair, leaving a tousled mess behind. I hate myself for liking this primitive version of him.

That doesn't change our fundamental problem, though.

"You came here with a plan!" The words claw out of me, each one as painful to say as the truth. "You can't change that. You can say you're sorry. You can come clean. But you planned this. So tell me, why should I forgive you?"

Sterling steps closer. My body reacts to the proximity of his, and I want him to touch me. I want him to find some magic words that make this okay. Because I want to forgive him. I just don't know how I ever can.

"I love you. I didn't plan on that," he says in a soft voice. "I can't take back what I did. Five years ago. Yesterday. Those moments are gone. I can't change them. I can only stand in front of you and offer the moments I have left."

"How many of those are there? Between the FBI and god-knows-who-else after you?" I ask. He looks frustrated again, which sends my pulse racing. "How many of those moments do I get?"

"All of them." Confidence radiates from him. He believes what he's saying. He means it.

But I know how time has a way of changing people. "Until you tire of me. Or you meet another woman." I think of my father. I think of Malcolm. My whole life has been a parade of ending marriages. "Everyone believes in forever when they say it, but I don't actually know anyone who understands what it means."

"You want to know what forever is, Lucky? Forever is built on moments. This one. The next. Love means never living another second without you. Love is you and me— now, tomorrow, and every day after. That's forever." He dares to brush the back of his hand across my cheek. His touch scorches me to my core. "I'm not giving up on our forever."

But even I can't deny the budding hope inside me that he will. "Honestly, I hope you don't." I shake my head, backing away from him and his white-hot touch. "But saying something doesn't make it happen, Sterling. Action does."

"Then I'll prove it to you."

23

ADAIR

THE PAST

The flight takes a little over two hours, and when we arrive at LaGuardia airport, it is through a bank of gray, foggy clouds that seem to sit just fifty feet above every building. The terminal is old and still yellow from decades of cigarette smoke, but somehow this adds to the charm. In my mind, things here are supposed to be ancient, because no one can stop using them long enough for them to be replaced. I have no idea if it's really true, but I look forward to finding out. I've seen New York in movies. I know it's where the heart of publishing is in America. My father hates it. I already know I love it.

Sterling holds my hand as we exit the gangway, an unreadable expression on his face.

"Does it feel good to be home?" I ask.

"A little. Not the going home part. I'm excited to show you things." Guilt is written plainly on his face, and when he sees my quizzical look he explains, "Everything is still open today. Tomorrow, half of everything will be closed, and on Christmas we'll have our choice of bodegas and food carts, but not much else."

"Gotcha. So what's the plan?"

"Francie is at work. We're already in Queens, so it won't take long to get there and drop our stuff off. After that, we'll go into Manhattan and start eating."

"*Start* eating? How much eating are we going to be doing?" My stomach grumbles audibly, as if it agrees with Sterling.

He chuckles, his stubbly chin rubbing against my temple as he folds me into the space under his arm. "Don't worry, it's less than we'll be walking. In here," he says, pointing at a tram with a sign above it showing various transit symbols. "New York is an incredible food city. And I don't mean haute cuisine, although there's a lot of that, too. Food carts, pizza parlors who sell by the slice, literal holes in the wall. Every immigrant who comes here brings their food along with them, and if you're adventurous enough, you can have stuff from all over the world."

"And you're adventurous?" I ask, letting him take my rolling carry-on bag as I get on the tram.

"I want it all," he says simply, and I wonder if I can convince him to screw my brains out before we leave the apartment in Queens.

We end up taking a bus to a subway line marked with purple, then go a few stops west, getting off somewhere marked 40th Street - Lowery Street. When we climb the stairs to street level, I'm surprised to see that most of the buildings are small, about 10 stories at most, with most quite a bit shorter than that.

"I always thought everything in New York was a

skyscraper," I say, turning slow circles as I trail along the sidewalk behind Sterling, trying to take everything in.

"I guess that's normal. It's what all the movies show. Most of the tall stuff is in Manhattan, but there's a lot more to New York than Manhattan," Sterling explains, pointing with his chin at the forest of steel buildings in the distance while wheeling both our suitcases over the frequently broken pavement.

"Hey you," a man calls to me, unfolding his body from beneath a cardboard box in an alley which happens to be next to a very posh shoe store. "I told you. I *told YOU*."

I feel a little ashamed when realization dawns: this is a homeless person. I turn over a few phrases in my mind, trying to figure out what to say to diffuse his apparent anger, but Sterling reaches across my body and pulls me along after him. "Back off, buddy."

The man grumbles under his breath, and we're maybe another 40 yards down the street when I hear him yell the same thing at a different passer-by.

"Told you what?" I ask when we're well past, confused. "Did you know him before or something?"

He takes a moment to consider his response.

"We used to be best friends. But that was before she came between us," Sterling says wistfully as a grin twitches at the corners of his mouth.

"I guess not." I stick my tongue out at him.

"Don't be like that, Lucky. Your innocence is adorable." He pauses to pull me close, enjoying being with me. "It is a little surprising. I didn't think you had any innocence left."

Sterling stops in front of a modest brown-brick building

more or less like every other one on the block. "Wait out here while I drop the bags off."

"Can't I come up and look? I know you said Francie is at work, but do you really think she'd mind?" I am almost as curious to see the inside of Francie's place as I am to see everything in New York.

"Better not. We can't be trusted alone behind closed doors," Sterling says. He grabs our bags and heads in.

He's gone maybe two minutes, which gives me a little time to work out how to handle the money situation. I have plenty. My father and brother insisted I take my own weight in traveller's checks, as well as a credit card, and a taser. I left the taser under my bed, of course—there was no way I would get one on a plane.

My father wasn't happy when I told him I was going. He raged for five straight minutes about ruining Christmas before I told him I would go even if he didn't give permission. I expected him to give in at that point, as we both knew he didn't want me—or anyone else—around this year. And sure enough, after a moment's consideration he said 'fine' and walked away. I hadn't been completely honest about who I was going with or where I was staying. That's probably why Malcolm suggested I check into The Plaza.

I've never stayed anywhere like this before. All my travel has involved five-star resorts and chauffeurs. I want to experience Sterling's city, though. Still, I can't help worrying that Sterling will try to impress me. I know Sterling's pride won't permit me to pay for him. In fact, I suspect it won't allow me to pay for myself.

"Ready?" he asks, adjusting my Burberry scarf against the wind.

"I am." I've managed to figure out exactly how to work the money situation. It's the oldest trick in the arsenal: play dumb. After our run-in with the homeless man, it shouldn't be a hard sell.

I deploy my plan for the first time at the metro station not far from his apartment. It's easy enough to pretend I don't know what I'm doing at the automated terminal selling MetroCards, switching the setting from one to two *unlimited* level cards while Sterling isn't looking.

"I got you one," I say proudly. "Is it enough?"

"Lucky, this is an unlimited card—for a month. We're only here for a week," he says with a laugh. "Let me help you next time."

Maybe my plan is working a little too well.

We board the subway in Queens and take the purple line over to Manhattan. From there, we walk a few blocks to Rockefeller Square. We watch the ice skaters—mostly tourists in bright, puffy coats—attempt to stay upright. It's particularly fun to watch parents get pulled down by their children, both collapsing with laughter on the ice. My stomach grumbles, and I'm reminded of his plan to eat everything. "Didn't you say something about food?"

"Yeah, I did. It's a couple blocks away. I just thought we'd take a minute here. I've actually never bothered coming here before," Sterling says, his brow furrowing sheepishly.

"I can cross Rockefeller off my list now. But I want Sterling Ford's New York. Not everyone else's. Now take me to food!" I tug on his coat, ready to leave the tourist side of the city behind.

We hold hands as we walk, and after another few

blocks arrive at a park lined on one side with food carts. "You ever had Dosa?"

"Dough-what?"

"Do-sa. It's a stuffed savory pancake from southern India. I come here just for these," he explains.

I sniff the air. One aroma, blooming warm and spicy, rises above the others. "Is that what I'm smelling? It smells incredible."

That's actually understating it. The scent of chilies and cinnamon wafts toward us, and I can feel my stomach start doing flips. I am pretty sure the length of the line we're in means the food will be worth it—but not if I die of hunger first. Luckily, the line moves more quickly than I would have guessed, and within ten minutes the man behind the counter barks, "Order?"

"Two Special Pondicherry," Sterling says.

We stand to the side, watching the cook make our dosa. He scoops a bubbly white paste from a chilled vat in his cart, then uses the flat bottom of the scoop to distribute the gloppy batter in a large circle on his griddle, before repeating the whole process. Next, he grabs a bottle and squirts bright yellow liquid on top of the rapidly browning batter.

"That's clarified butter," Sterling says, and I turn to see him looking at the dosa exactly how he looks at me whenever we're alone.

"Wow" is all I can find to say. He means it when he says he loves food.

The dosa begin turning deep brown, and the cook reaches into his small fridge and takes out an industrial size vat of what looks like neon-yellow mashed potatoes and green vegetables. He puts two huge scoops on each dosa, then carefully rolls the pancake around its filling. Then, unceremoniously, he flips the dosa onto tiny, folded cardboard trays lined with napkins and hands them to us, already taking his next order.

We find a park bench nearby, and Sterling hands me my dosa, which overhangs its cardboard tray by a half foot on either end. Steam wafts up from it, warming me and making my mouth water.

"How did you find this place?" I ask, waiting for Sterling to take a bite so I can see how it's done.

"In New York, people look for lines," he explains, torn between taking his first bite and gratifying my curiosity. "They make fun of it in ads and stuff like that, but it's true all the same. If you see old, young, poor, rich, and immigrant people lining up for food, well, you should probably eat it."

He flattens one end of his rolled pancake enough to get it in his mouth and takes a huge bite.

So much for needing pointers.

"And you saw a line here?" I prompt before taking a huge bite of my own.

The flavor is almost beyond my comprehension. There are so many spices, so many distinct flavors, it doesn't seem possible it could all fit in one bite. The pancake is much crispier than I expect, shatter-y on the outside edge, but moist and springy inside. The filling reminds me of mashed potatoes, but only in texture. The flavor stings and soothes in equal measure. It's dizzying.

"Yeah. It's two p.m. now, so this is as short as his line gets."

"Holy shit, Sterling."

"I know."

"It's like everything I ate before this moment was saltine crackers."

"I know."

"Why isn't this everywhere?"

"That, I don't know."

We eat mostly in silence, but I can't help noticing how all the people leaving the dosa cart nod at us as they pass by, like we're members of the same secret club. And for the length of our meal, at least, I don't feel like an obnoxious, ignorant tourist, I feel like a New Yorker.

"What kind of dosa was this, again?" I ask, writing myself a note on my phone. I want to see if Felix can make it when I get back.

"Special Pondicherry."

"Got it."

He chuckles as he takes my trash and finds somewhere to toss it, then takes my hand and pulls me to my feet.

"Where to next?" I ask.

We take the subway again, this time the yellow line. After just two stops we hop off at the 23rd Street exit, and when we emerge on street level, I discover we're in the Flatiron District.

"This is a very posh area," Sterling explains. "Publishing, advertising, Fifth Avenue shopping runs that way."

He indicates a direction, but between the height of the buildings and the disorienting effects of traveling underground, he might as well save himself the trouble. I'll never keep it straight. It feels like I'm in a concrete and glass canyon. Everywhere I look there is a whole world to discover. Did I really imagine that after this I would tell people I'd seen New York? Which New York? Two people could live here for a decade and never do the same thing or eat at the same place.

And as I feel my world getting bigger, I realize how much smaller it makes Valmont and my life there. I planned to get a semester under my belt at home and then study abroad, but now there's Sterling. How can he be content in that sleepy college town, coming from this? If the world contains all of this—not through the pages of a book or a lesson in class—how can I ever be content to live out my life in Valmont?

Impossible.

Sterling watches as I spin like a top, shepherding me before I bump into oblivious, harried natives, and pointing out things I might miss. We go for a few more blocks until we reach The Strand. I've heard about it, but it's hard to believe it contains miles of books—until we step inside. We take an elevator to the fourth floor, where they keep a collection of rare or collectible books of every age, description—and price.

I don't buy anything, partly because I don't want to flash money in front of Sterling, but mostly because I don't want to lug heavy books around New York. After a half hour of flipping through antique books, Sterling decides to move on, plopping a copy of *The Sun Also Rises* back on the table with a wistful sigh.

"I'm going to run to the bathroom," he says. "Meet you downstairs."

As soon as he's gone, I buy the book and tuck it into my purse. I'll give it to him for Christmas, so he can't be mad.

It turns out that separating was a terrible idea, because it takes us twenty minutes to find each other again. He's carrying a brown paper sack when he finds me.

"Reading material for the plane home," he says. "I can't be left in a bookstore unattended."

"Noted."

"Can I put it in your bag?" He reaches for the flap.

"Let me!" I grab it and carefully tuck it next to his present so he can't see.

He leads me around another corner, and we find ourselves under massive scaffolding that covers one side of the street completely, even blocking the signs above businesses. We duck into a shop selling artisan meats and cheeses, and it takes me a moment to realize we're actually in a sort of shopping mall devoted to, well, eating.

It dawns on me where we are. "Wait, is this…"

"This is Eataly," Sterling says.

The day we visited my mom's grave together, he had told me about it. I push away a stab of sadness at the memory and focus on the moment. Mom would want me to make every day in New York a diamond. She loved the city, but never went after the disastrous family trip when I was four.

Eataly is a rabbit warren of artisan food, wine, and cooking gear. It's vaguely like a department store, but decorated like Old Europe, stuffed to the density of a Valmont football game crowd, and, best of all, sells everything from mini jam jars to entire casks of wine.

You don't just buy a cutting board here, you buy an African rosewood one crafted by a guy in Italy who makes three or four a year—and only if he feels like it. I understand this kind of luxury, even if this example is beyond my imagining.

For a moment I wonder why we're here, since it's so expensive, but the reason soon becomes apparent. They are aggressively sampling, hoping to move inventory in the last two days before Christmas. We hold hands, both of us grinning stupidly at each other as we pop whole new ways of experiencing the world into our mouths. My favorite is a cheese called Taleggio, which spreads like soft butter and tastes like the secret lovechild of brie and cream cheese.

I discover something about Sterling at Eataly. Whenever I take a bite of something, I notice he's almost nervous. At first I think it's because he wants to make sure I'm having a good time, but before long I realize he's studying me with the same careful concern he uses when we're alone. He wants me to enjoy this as much as he does.

But despite how much we're eating—more than I ever have, in fact—I want more. I'm ravenous for Sterling's New York. I don't want to go back to Valmont with regrets. I don't want to wonder how good the weird-looking buns in the Chinese corner stand are, or why a shop sells only baguettes. I want to *know*.

And that means trying everything.

And maybe that's why, after stumbling groggily back onto the street, and with Sterling holding a small bag of things I just couldn't help buying, I make a decision: for the rest of the trip, when I see something that scares or intimidates me, I'm going to try it.

Why not?

24

STERLING

She is completely fucking insane. Like, different person insane.

And I'm pretty sure I created this monster.

My carefully planned day has flown out the window—not that I'm disappointed. Ten minutes ago, we ate frog legs from a stall in Chinatown while holding NY-style soft pretzels in the other hand. I dragged her onto the subway after, and as I gave her a kiss, we both had to stifle oily, smoky burps. We were nearly hysterical with laughter, and—this being New York—no one even seemed to notice.

I'm nearly broke now, but I would consider robbing a bank if it kept this incredible day going. How often do you know, while it's happening, that you're having experiences that will last you the rest of your life? I've never felt that before. The stuff in my past—I wish I could forget a lot of it. I always imagined that if I got married or went on a trip to Europe, those memories would be the kind that last. Big, huge moments. The kind you're supposed to remember. I had no idea it could just... happen.

But that's what it's like with her. She keeps saying *my* New York, but it sure seems like it's all hers now. I steer us to Greenwich Village, with a vague eye on seeing if my favorite falafel place is still there. In New York, you just never know.

We climb the stairs up from the subway stop, emerging onto relaxed streets. It's a different side of the city than she's seen so far. Not as much bustle. It's a nice change of pace.

"Oh, it's *looove-ly,*" Adair coos—taking one look at the ample shade trees, their branches bare for winter and strung with lights, the cobbled alleys, the sleepier vibe—and falls in love with Greenwich.

"Planning your new life?" I tease, pulling her to me and kissing her beneath her ear.

"Tell me you wouldn't like to live here," she demands, pecking me on the cheek.

"I would *not* like to live here, Lucky. Hate to break it to you."

"Why not?"

"It's expensive, for one thing." I have to yell the words after her, because she is already off at breakneck pace, headed down a pedestrian-only alley full of red, cobbled bricks that match most of the buildings lining either side of the way.

"Exactly my point," she calls over her shoulder, refusing to slow down. "It's expensive because everyone wants to live here. Because it's awesome."

"For some."

"What's not to like? Look," she points at a Middle Eastern cafe, "they like hummus. We like hummus."

"True." I can't fight her, not when she's like this. Plus, hummus is delicious.

"Look, a sex shop. They like sex. And *we* like sex."

"I'm not sure—"

It's too late. She walks in like she owns the place.

I dip in right behind Adair, who has stopped dead in her tracks with her back to me.

"Hiya," a shop girl calls to us, striding out from behind the counter. She's got purple hair cut down to a severe bob, incredibly good ink, and the sort of perky disposition you expect in a kindergarten teacher on the first day of school—if Kindergarten teachers sold vibrators.

"What brings you in today?"

I can't see Adair's face, but I know she is overwhelmed because *I'm* overwhelmed. I've lived in New York my whole life, and I've never actually gone inside somewhere like this.

She backs up a few steps, careful to keep smiling at the clerk, and holds her hand out, searching for mine. "Oh, not much? I'm out with my boyfriend and I don't think he particularly wanted to come in here."

The clerk gives Adair the slightest eye roll and smiles knowingly. "That's too bad. We have lots of ways to have fun here."

"I bet," Adair agrees, like she's talking about the weather or something.

The fuck? They're best friends, already?

"Well," the shop girl waits for a suitably meaningful pause to develop, "I won't pry. Let me know if you have any questions. And you should. I don't even know what some of this stuff is for."

Adair finds my hand at last and leads me back into the narrow canyon of vice.

"You don't have to pretend like you want to be in here, you know," I say, trying not to sound judgmental while keeping my eyes on her. Finally, she sighs.

"Come on, lover," she says, pulling me along after her, out the door.

"Do stop in again. Maybe when you've had a chance to loosen him up?" the shop girl calls after us.

"Sooo... why don't we stick to eating?"

"Embarrassed, Ford?" she asks, even though her cheeks are faintly pink.

"I just don't think we need any help in that department." I eye the colorful window display. "Unless you're planning to replace me?"

"Never," she promises.

We don't get far before she slows down.

"How far have we walked today?" Adair says before waving away her own question. "Let's find someplace to sit down and eat, okay?"

I gawk at her. "More food?"

"Are you judging me?"

"Never," I promise.

I pull out my phone and check the listing for Levantine, my favorite falafel place. It's still there, just a couple blocks away, and open for another couple of hours. "I know just the place."

"Lead on, Ford." She points the way—although it is the wrong way—with the authority of a career general.

"Lucky, you are just full of surprises today," I marvel.

"Yeah, and it's all your fault. Showing me new things and what not."

"Good thing there is always new stuff to try," I say, using my hand to crush her body against mine.

"You can say that again. Now feed me or lose me forever."

ADAIR

Dinner with Francie is a casual affair, since I'm still stuffed from eating half of what New York has to offer. She tells me stories at the kitchen table, Sterling objecting every few seconds, until she looks at the clock on the microwave.

"I've got to be up early," she says.

"Are you working?" I can't help being surprised. Tomorrow is Christmas Eve, and I'd expected to spend the day with her.

"Tomorrow and the next day," she says with meaning. "Nurses don't get holidays."

This, however, is news to Sterling. "I thought you got time off."

"Two more shifts and then I have three days to spend with you," she promises. "It's better this way. I get holiday pay, and I had Thanksgiving off. Fair is fair."

She stands up and ruffles his hair affectionately before stretching her arms over her head. Looking down, she shakes her head. "I never even got out of these scrubs. I'll be out of the bathroom in a few. You two going to stay up longer?"

"We'll head to my room. I don't want to keep you up."

"Your room?" I repeat. "I thought I was sleeping on the couch."

Sterling and Francie share a look.

"Why would you sleep on the couch?" he asks.

"You don't mind?" I question Francie. Even now, a few months from getting married, after living together for a year, my brother and Ginny sleep in separate rooms when she spends the night. It's how things are done in Valmont.

"You can sleep on the couch if you want, sugar, but it's not very comfortable," she warns me before disappearing up the stairs.

"Worried I'll try something?" Sterling nuzzles against my ear, laughter in his voice.

"I know you'll try something," I mutter. "I guess I'm not used to..."

"Being treated like an adult?" Regret flashes in his eyes the moment it's out of his mouth. "I'm sorry, I shouldn't—"

"No, you're right," I stop him. "My father doesn't treat me like an adult. He's disinterested in everything but keeping up appearances." That's why he makes a big show of holiday parties and separate bedrooms. He cares more about what the world thinks of him and his family than he does about me.

We climb the steps to the upper floor, the stairs groaning under old shag carpeting. Sterling pushes open the first door in the small hallway.

"It's not much, but I spent most of my teen years in this

room—after I came to live with Francie, that is." Sterling looks nervous. I think he's afraid I'll take one look and declare I'm getting a room at the Ritz.

The room is tiny, about half the size of a Valmont dorm room. A small window looks out on the red brick building across the alley, and there's a twin bed in the corner next to it. The rest of the room is filled with books. Wherever there isn't room for a bookcase, shelves have been bolted onto the walls. I notice that most of the books are marked with white Dewey decimal stickers.

"Is there anything left at your local library?" I say without thinking.

"I didn't steal them," he says, a little wounded.

"I'm sorry. I didn't mean—"

"It's fair." He runs his fingers along the spines of a row of books, almost wistfully. "When the library around the corner closed, they moved most of their books to other branches. What was left over was sold four for a dollar. At that point, there wasn't a single book from a bestseller list this century. I spent every dollar I could get my hands on. I looked for change on my way to school. I went so many times over their last month that the librarians ended up letting me carry off entire boxes for free, just so they wouldn't have to take them to a landfill."

"I'm sure it had nothing to do with you loving books as much as they did," I say. "How many of them have you read?"

"Almost all of the fiction," he says evenly. "Older non-fiction is pretty hit-and-miss. Racist historians from the 50s get old pretty fast."

I almost can't believe he has read all these books. Did he

do anything else? I find an average looking shelf, count the number of books, and multiply it by the number of shelves I see. "Sterling, there are probably two thousand books here. You're telling me you've read almost all of them?"

"I've seen the library at Windfall. You've probably read even more than me."

"Uh, no. Not even close. What happens in this one?" I put my hand on a book at random. It turns out to be *Lady Chatterley's Lover,* by D.H. Lawrence. Whoops.

"Don't pretend like you don't know that one. You like the Brits, remember?"

"That doesn't mean I've all of British literature." I look around the room again. "I mean, you have."

"It's not great, anyway. Too stoically British for me. You should read it." A wry smile pops onto Sterling's face as he adds, "Might give you pointers on falling for someone beneath you."

I shake my head. I hate it when he says things like that, but I don't want to fight—so I pretend he means something else. "Are you saying you're a libertine?"

"Your virtue is not safe." He pulls me toward him, his hands greedy for my body.

Francie's voice sounds behind us in the hall as Sterling gives my earlobe a playful nip. "I'm going to bed. Good-night, you two."

She shuts the door, leaving us alone. "I still can't believe she's okay with me being in your room."

"Like people our age don't sleep together in Valmont?"

"We're raised to sneak around," I tell him. "It's the proper thing to do."

"Wait, where were we?"

"You were assailing my virtue."

"Right," he says, and his hands are on me again. "Where do you come down on opening presents before Christmas?"

He pops the top button of my red plaid pajamas.

"We always open presents on Christmas Eve."

"What about Christmas Eve's Eve? I'm not sure I can wait until Christmas morning," he explains. "You are my present, right?"

"As long as it won't ruin Christmas or anything."

He pops another button, just between my breasts, and I can feel the familiar electric throb of his hands on my body. I close my eyes and let it take over.

"See, that's your problem right there, Lucky."

I peek down at what he's talking about. "Huh?"

"The bow is supposed to go on the outside of the present." He points to the small silk bow sewn on my bra.

"You know, I wasn't sure I had it right. That's why there are two bows."

"Two?" He fiddles with the drawstring on my bottoms. "Where's the other one?"

"You'll have to look."

He bunches the fabric of my shirt in either hand and pulls me toward him. He peers down at my chest, inspecting my body carefully. "No, not here."

He drops on one knee, pulls up the loose flannel fabric of my bottoms. "Am I closer?"

"You're getting warmer."

His hands run up the backs of my thighs. When they

reach my ass, he takes his time, clearly enjoying the inspection process. "It's not here, either."

"You know, when I'm really excited for a present, I can't help ripping the wrapping off." It's not exactly true. Most of the Christmas presents I've received seem to have been picked off a shelf during a brisk walk through Nieman Marcus. I learned pretty quickly not to get my hopes up.

Sterling rises to his feet and fixes me with a hungry look. My eyes flutter again as I feel his hands grab the fabric around the clasped buttons of my top. A sharp yank separates one side from the other, and I hear the buttons cascade to the floor in every direction.

"What am I going to wear on Christmas?" I gasp, but Sterling distracts me immediately.

With two strong hands below my ribs, he lifts me from the ground. He's pinned the cuffs of my pant with his feet, and they slide free of my hips as he lifts, pooling beneath me. That's what I get for suggesting he rip open his gift.

"Found it," he says triumphantly. His teeth nip my skin as he bites down on the matching bow of my panties. When he gently lowers me to the small bed, his teeth are still clasped on it.

He draws my panties off with the bow between his teeth, and I nearly combust. Sterling smirks as my hips wiggle closer. Sliding his palms down my inner thighs, he coaxes them open before dipping to yoke himself with my knees.

I try to say something, but the feel of his breath there robs me of words.

His warm tongue incapacitates me further, and I hear myself moan in pleasure as if I were outside my own body.

He takes his time, moving slowly over a large area, then increases the tempo and pressure until I'm pulsing to his rhythm.

He sucks my clit into his mouth, and it's as if I can feel every drop of blood in my body go to meet him. I bite my lip, trying to stifle my pleasure. There's no way these walls can stand up to the pleasure threatening to spill out of me. There's a swirl and a nip and the first loud moan escapes.

Sterling's hand covers my mouth. Apparently, he's worried about traumatizing Francie, too.

His other hand spreads me, and then his tongue dips lower. I whimper against his palm, covering his hand with my own to help smother my noises. He seems to sense that I'm close, and his tongue thrusts into me while his hand clamps down on my cries.

The pleasure is tidal, drawing me out and pushing me back. But something's missing. The waves fade and I yank his hand away from my mouth. "I need you. Now."

"That bed is awfully squeaky." He shakes his head, and a painful throb fills the absence of his mouth.

"Then screw the bed." I shove him away and drop to the floor. He gets the idea, falling back on his heels, as I reach over to my bag beside the bed and remove a condom. He watches, his eyes narrow and hooded, as I roll it into place.

I climb onto him, straddling him just over the navel. I place his hands where I want them, one on my mouth, as before, the other on my hip, and then I lower myself until I feel the brief sting of latex followed by the sensation of every inch of him sliding into me. It only seems fair that it's my turn to control things. Sterling stares at me, his face wearing a look of awe, as I circle around him.

"Fuck," he groans.

My hips rise and fall in a tempo of their own choosing. When I can't hold my release another second I grab his hands and throw them onto my ass. He pushes our hips together with all his might. It sends me over the edge, and Sterling crushes his mouth to mine, swallowing my cries, as his own body tenses. We collapse into each other, sweaty and out of breath.

"If I live a hundred years," he says raggedly, "I'll never see something that hot again."

"Challenge accepted," I say, nuzzling into his chest.

The next morning I wake up to blinding light streaming through the window. My hand reaches behind me and finds nothing but an empty mattress. Hauling myself out of Sterling's bed, I rub my eyes, clearing the sleep enough to realize the light is so bright because it snowed.

Snow usually comes late to middle Tennessee, arriving after the holiday season. The last white Christmas I remember was five years ago. I dig in my suitcase, pulling on a thick pair of fleece leggings and an oversized Valmont University sweatshirt. Then I bounce down to find Sterling.

Rounding the bottom of the staircase, I pause to check out the house. We'd arrived so late last night that it was already dark out, and then we'd gotten caught in the kitchen with Francie. This is the first time I really get to see it. The living room is cramped, a miss-mash of old furniture from different decades pushed against the wall to make as much space to move as possible. An older television is propped on a cart in the corner—and there are books everywhere. I wonder if they're Francie's or Sterling's. But there's one thing missing.

A Christmas tree.

"Sterling," I call, retracing my way to the kitchen. "Where's the..." My question fades when I come around the corner. He's standing at the counter, rifling through a stack of envelopes while a black, plastic coffee machine brews a pot. That's not what stops me, though. He's standing there in nothing but boxers. No matter how many times I see him like this, I can't help stopping to admire him,.

He turns, a smirk twisting across his lips, stubble dusting his jawline. "Forget what you were saying, Lucky?"

I shake my head, trying to clear my brain, which is as blurry as the swirling snowfall outside the window. In the end, I'm forced to close my eyes to regain control of myself.

"Christmas tree," I say. "Where's the Christmas tree?"

"In Central Park," he says.

The spell is broken, and I'm able to look at him again, careful to keep my eyes above shoulder level. "Your Christmas tree?"

"We don't do that," he says.

"You... what?"

"Francie almost always works Christmas. No one else wants to," he says. "What's the point of putting up a tree for like five minutes?"

My own family always put up a tree despite leaving for

vacation on Christmas morning. I can't understand not having one. "It's tradition."

"We can decorate her cactus," he suggests pointing to the small potted plant on the window.

"Well, I know what we're doing today," I say.

"Lucky…"

"Nope." I cross to him and wrap my arms around my waist. "You've been all of my firsts, Sterling Ford. Let me be your first Christmas morning."

"Do I get to unwrap you?" he asks, his hand sliding around to grope my rear.

"Again?"

"Well, I could have sworn I already did it, but here's my present all covered up again."

"Get dressed," I order him with a swift kiss. "I want to go out in the snow, and then we can get a tree and…"

"Okay, slow down." He drops the envelopes on the counter, but his eyes linger on them. I see one from Valmont on top.

"Is everything okay?"

"Bills," he says tightly. "Looks like my scholarship didn't cover everything."

"What does that mean?" I ask.

"It's nothing for you to worry about. I'll talk with Francie. I just wish she'd told me. I should have been working this semester."

"You were going to school," I remind him.

A muscle twitches in his jaw, and his response is so even that I know he's calibrating it carefully. "Not everyone has the luxury of being a full-time student. It's not a big deal. I can find something on campus to help out."

He kisses me and dashes upstairs to get dressed. I stare at the envelope, fighting the urge to open it and see how much he owes. It would be easy for me to pay it off. I could even sweet talk someone in the administration to send me future bills by dropping my last name. Then, he wouldn't have to worry, and Francie wouldn't have to take holiday shifts. But if he ever found out...

The bill is still on the counter, untouched, and I'm finishing a cup of coffee when Sterling appears downstairs, fully dressed.

"Okay, show me how this Christmas thing is done, Lucky."

We head into the snow in search of a Christmas tree lot, but I can't quit thinking about that bill and wondering what to do about it.

The lot closest to Sterling's is already closed, and we have to go another block to find one with a few trees left. All of them are scraggly, scrawny pines that look like they've lost half their needles.

"I can see why you want one of these," Sterling says dryly. "Aren't these a fire hazard?"

I study the tree he's pointing to and am forced to agree he's right. It's clearly dead.

"Let's keep looking."

"Your lips are blue," he says, fixing my scarf for the tenth time. "Let's head back, and I'll warm you up."

The offer is tempting, and I'm on the verge of giving in, when I spot a few smaller trees near the lot's business office. The trees are only two or three feet tall, but they're healthy.

"There!" I point.

"You want a Charlie Brown tree?"

"A what?" I ask.

He stares at me. "And I'm the one who doesn't do Christmas, right?"

The lot gives us the tree, which pleases Sterling, and because it's so small it takes no effort to carry it back to his place. We spend the afternoon crafting ornaments from some of the old racist history books he never got rid of—it's obviously the best use for them—and watching the Charlie Brown Christmas Special.

When we're finished with our homemade decorations, we stand back to admire our work.

"It's actually awesome," Sterling says.

"It's perfect."

"What else am I supposed to do on Christmas?" he asks. "What do you do at home?"

"We unwrap presents on Christmas Eve, and then we have breakfast the next morning before we go on a trip. Mom always planned them." My voice breaks as I realize that this tradition is gone forever. Being in New York is distracting me, but it doesn't change it.

"Let's open presents then," he says.

"Really?" I say. "You got me a present?"

"Of course I got you a present," he says, groaning. "I'm not a complete amateur—but it's not much."

"I got you something, too. Something small," I say quickly.

"I haven't wrapped it yet."

"Me either."

"We're not very good at this, are we?" he asks.

"It's just practice for next year," I say.

"Keeping me around that long?" He manages to make this sound like a joke, but there's an edge of something to it.

"Give me a second to get yours."

We meet back in the living room a few minutes later and sit in front of our tree.

"You first." I thrust the bag from The Strand at him.

A bemused smile cracks his mouth.

"What?" I ask.

"You'll see." He takes out the novel slowly, and I can't get a read on him.

"I saw you looking at it," I say when he remains silent. "So I cheated and bought it."

"It's wonderful," he says in a quiet voice. "Better than my old library copy."

I can't tell if he actually likes it. Maybe he's disappointed to receive a book he already owns. Maybe I misread his interest. I break the silence, tugging on his hand. "My turn!"

"Um, I should really..." He scoots a little and I realize there's a brown paper bag next to him—and he's trying to hide it.

"Is that it?" I snatch it before he can stop me.

"Just... I thought of you, and it's stupid."

The brown paper bag is stamped with The Strand logo, and I realize it's the 'reading material for the plane.' Sneaky. That's what he found funny. We both found a way to buy each other a book without the other one noticing. I open the bag and draw out a used copy of The Great Gatsby. It's not a fancy one from the rare books room we visited. Most of its age is down to shelf-wear, like it had been sitting for a long time, unread. The cover is older, a simple illustration of eyes, and not much else. When I open it, I actually hear the spine crack. Inside the pages are slightly yellow but otherwise pristine save for notes scattered throughout.

"I did that," he admits. "This morning. I thought it would be cool for you to see what I thought. It's dumb."

"I love it," I say honestly.

"It's not nearly as nice as this," he says.

"It's the words that matter. That's what you gave me— its heart." I crawl over to him and kiss him.

"That's all, I'm afraid," he says. "Told you Christmas is pretty fast at my house."

"That's all?" I repeat, pretending to be confused. "I could have sworn you had something else to give me."

He catches on quickly, and we spend the rest of the day giving each other our hearts.

Francie's shift turns into a double and by the time she makes it home, Sterling has crashed on the couch. He doesn't even wake up when she tosses her keys loudly on the counter. I untangle myself, eager to have a minute alone with her.

"You're awake," she says when I walk into the kitchen.

"I've been watching Christmas movies. My mom loved them," I explain, grabbing a seat at the kitchen table. Somehow it helps me feel closer to her to remember the little traditions. The ones that didn't involve party guests and boarding passes. I'm finding she lives on in the spirit of the holiday more than in the grand gestures.

"Sterling around?" She opens the fridge and pulls out a plastic container.

"He fell asleep during *It's a Wonderful Life.*"

"You must have worn him out."

It takes me a second to realize she's talking about our day and not anything she might have overheard last night. "I made him get a tree."

"That will do it. Being happy always makes him tired," she says as she presses buttons on the microwave to reheat the leftovers. "He's not used to it."

She does know him.

"I'm hoping to change that," I confide in her.

"As long as you're realistic, hon. Sometimes love makes you a better person, but it always accepts you when you're not." She joins me at the table. "He's had a rough life."

"He told me—about his parents and his sister."

She seems surprised by this. "He doesn't like to talk about his family. Most of what I know is from files and court appearances," she says. "I'm glad he finally opened up about it with you."

"I was thinking that maybe I could help him find his sister while—"

"That's not a good idea," she cuts me off. When my face falls, she continues on, quickly, "He went looking for her a few years ago, and he found her."

"And?" I ask breathlessly. He'd left this part of the story out. "Was she okay? Are they in contact?"

"She wound up with a really nice family—well off, happy. It nearly broke him."

"What? Why?" It's exactly what he wanted for her. It's why he took her to CPS himself.

"I don't think he'd ever admit it, but he was hurt. Not because he wanted her to be lonely, but because she'd moved on. I don't think he's ever been able to do that. He was so much older than her when it happened. I think it scarred him."

And he'd been the one to find the body, the one to feed his starving kid sister, the one who walked into a social services office to give her up.

"That boy had to grow up before parts of him were ready, and he's angry," she says, spearing a bite of chicken on her fork. "Not because she has a better life. He wanted that for her. Because there's no one to forgive. His father never asked and his mama's gone, so he just carries around all that pain from those memories, bottling it up..."

Until he can't anymore. I'd witnessed how he could lash out. I'd seen him jump to the worst possible conclusion.

"But the real problem is that he hates pity," Francie continues. "If he thinks you feel sorry for him, he'll turn on you. Fast."

"That's why you were always hard on him," I guess. I'd heard about her rules and expectations.

"Tough love," she says.

"I don't know if I can do that," I admit.

"That's my job. He might not think of me the same way, but Sterling's my son. My job as his mama is to give him tough love. He needs something else from you."

Suddenly, I don't know if I'm doing any of this right. "What? How do I know if I'm giving him what he needs?"

"Because it's what you need, hon. That's what falling in

love is—give and take, acceptance and challenge, soft and hard. It's every kind of love you'll ever need. The right person is your family, your friend, your partner, your better and your worst. That's why so many people get it wrong," she says softly. "They get caught up in one kind of love and think that can carry them. Real love takes everything you have to give."

"But it's worth it." I know it. I feel it. "I don't need him to be perfect. I just need him to be mine."

"That's a good start." She hesitates for a minute. "Is he happy there? At Valmont?"

"Sometimes." I decide not to lie. "Not always. It's different than here."

"But he's got you."

"Sometimes," I say with a laugh. "We've had our moments."

"You'll have more of them."

"Francie." I'm not sure how to bring up the bills. "I hope this doesn't offend you—Sterling would kill me—but he saw the bill from school. I can help with that."

"You're sweet," she says, reaching over to pat my hand. "I've got it covered. It just came. I put aside some of the money I got from fostering him the last few years. I always knew he was too smart not to go to college."

"But Valmont is so expensive."

"And his scholarship covers most of it. The rest I can handle." She levels a serious gaze at me. "But if you want to help me out, just make sure you don't distract him too much. He needs to keep his grades up."

"Yes, ma'am." It's the least I can do.

"Now, how about some Christmas cookies?" she asks.

"I hid them earlier, so Sterling didn't eat them all while I was at work.

She pulls an old tin from a cabinet over the fridge and pries open the lid. She's just put them on the table in front of us when Sterling appears, rubbing sleep from his eyes.

"Did someone say cookies?"

He looks confused when we burst out laughing.

26

ADAIR

PRESENT DAY

When I was a child, Windfall stretched so far that I couldn't fathom it ending. It was my entire world, but I never quite belonged. Today, bathed in the warm light of June, it looks small. Maybe it's never been as impressive as I thought. Maybe my world is just so much larger now. I don't know. But despite its diminished effect, a pit grows in my stomach, hollowing out my core with dread, as I drive past the gates to the main house. I can't separate the two desires warring inside me: I want to leave, and I want to stay. I can't do both, and I'm uncertain I'm making the right decision.

I don't bother pulling around to the back. I have an hour before Ginny returns from dance lessons with Ellie, and Malcolm is at the office. I'd rather not drag boxes across two wings of the house and down the servant corridor. It feels strange, but somehow necessary, to pause at the front door and ring the bell. Felix answers it with record speed.

"You don't need to knock," he says.

"I think I do," I say. "If for no other reason then to train myself that this isn't home anymore."

"How does that feel?" He steps to the side, allowing me to enter.

"Strange, but not painful." I squint as I search for the right way to explain it. "It feels right. That's what's weird about it."

He nods, an understanding smile turning up his lips. "You've moved on."

"I don't think I ever felt at home here," I confess.

Felix pauses as if considering this, but he doesn't dwell. "And your new place at the Eaton? How does it feel?"

"Like I live in a hotel." I suspect it will always feel that way. I'm already considering whether I could sell it and find myself a little house somewhere near the Bluebird offices. Nothing fancy. Some place to call my own.

"It will get better."

"I should get going. I can't wear things like this to work," I say with a grin, gesturing to my linen shorts and thin tank top I'd worn to pack my belongings. "I'll probably take some things today, pack up the rest, and arrange for someone to come and get them. Did you get my message about boxes?" As much as I want my belongings, especially my underwear, I know there's no way I can get everything I own in the Roadster. I considered renting a truck, but given the restrictions I'll face moving things into the Eaton, I thought better of it. I already located a local moving company and got them scheduled.

"I did, but..." Felix hesitates, a slight hitch in his voice. "There's been a development."

I incline my head to the side and study him. His

Adam's apple bobs nervously. It's not like Felix to look so anxious.

"What is it?" I ask. I didn't think the pit in my stomach could get bigger. I was wrong.

"Your things have already been packed up and moved to storage." He shakes his head. "I tried to reach you as it was happening, but you weren't answering your phone. After Sterling came here looking for you, Malcolm had the staff do it. By the time your message reached me, it was done. I should have told you, but I worried you might not come back to the house."

"Are you serious?" I race up the stairs toward my rooms. I sure as hell wouldn't have come back to this house, not if I'd known my brother tried to entirely erase me from it. I'm breathless by the time I reach my bedroom. There's a handful of boxes, covered with a tarp, and a fresh coat of white paint on the walls. My feet won't move. I'm stuck in the doorway, staring at what my life to this point has been reduced to: an empty room and white walls.

I'm still there when Felix reaches me. He puts an arm around my shoulder.

"I wonder which box my underwear is in," I say dumbly. He squeezes me closer to him.

"The girls marked everything. I'll find it," he promises.

How could my brother do this? I'd given up everything for this family—for him and Ginny and Ellie. I'd put up with our father. I'd done everything asked of me. And the first time I took a step outside the boundaries they had given me, I'd been packed up and relegated to storage. I lurch forward, crossing to the tarp and tug it free. There's three boxes under it, all marked: garbage. Ripping off the packing tape, I open the first box to discover stacks and stacks of battered notebooks. Stomach acid burns my throat. I don't know what's more sickening: that he nearly threw away my old journals or that he likely read them. I open the other two and find books and photos, even a framed picture of me with mom a few months before she died.

"What did they pack?" My voice startles me. It sounds a million miles away. I turn to Felix, holding my memories in my hands.

"They said everything." He stares at the photographs and notebooks in horror. "If I had known..."

"I know," I stop him. There's no way Felix would have allowed them to toss my past aside like this if they had consulted him. I doubt any of the other household staff would, either. That can only mean one thing. "He ordered them to do it. He told them to throw this away."

Somewhere in storage, I'll find boxes of clothing and shoes. Things I need, but things I can replace. What Malcolm nearly took from me was priceless, and he knows it.

"Why does he hate me?" I ask Felix in a soft voice. "What did I ever do?"

"You had the courage to leave." Felix places his hands on my shoulders and turns me to face him. "Courage he has never had. His whole life has been following in your father's footsteps. Even now, he's still doing it. But you? You walked away from all of this. You struck out on your own."

"That's not the only reason." I dare a look at Felix. "We

both know it's about who isn't here any more. But how could they hate me for that?."

"Love is a tough concept for your family."

"It's a hard concept for me, too." My thoughts wander to Sterling. I know what love feels like, because not a day has gone by in the last five years where I haven't thought of him and felt it. The trouble is, like my family, I never understood what to do with those feelings.

"The trick is to find someone worth loving," Felix tells me. "Find someone that challenges you. Find someone that makes you a better version of yourself. Someone you want to come home to and tell about your day. Someone you can talk to about everything."

Emotion swells my throat, preventing me from speaking, and Felix sighs.

"I suppose I have no business giving anyone else relationship advice," he admits.

"I'm no expert, but that seemed like decent advice. Maybe you should call Maria," I say meaningfully.

Felix's eyes droop at the mention of his ex-paramour, a schoolteacher at Beautiful Valley Elementary. They'd been on and off again for years, but he hadn't spoken of her in months. "I'm afraid that ship sailed—off to Memphis."

"What?"

"I waited too long," he says. "She wanted a family, and I wasn't ready."

He's lying, and I know it. Felix might have left, moved on with his life, married Maria, and lived happily ever after. Instead, he'd stuck around to see me through my mother's death. Then Sterling left, and I went to London. "You gave your notice before I moved to England. Why didn't you leave then?"

"Your father asked me to stay on a little while longer while he looked for a replacement. It was a reasonable request," Felix says, "and Maria had no problem with it—until I changed my mind about leaving."

"But why did you change your mind?" Why didn't he leave? Why didn't he escape? He gave up the happy ending he might have had with Maria for years of suffering abuse at my father's hands.

"You know why," he whispers. "I couldn't bear making you come back here alone to face your family." He's never admitted to me what we both knew. I was the reason Felix stayed. He stayed for me and Ellie and Ginny and Malcolm —and where had that gotten him?

"You shouldn't have."

The corner of his mouth crooks. "I'd do it again in a heartbeat."

And now he's stuck here, nailed in place by my father's final edict naming Felix as the trustee of Windfall until Ellie was old enough to inherit it. "They're going to be terrible to you."

"I don't do it for them."

"Thank you." There's nothing else I can give him for the sacrifices he has made.

"Let's get these to your car," he suggests.

I take one box and Felix takes two. We're halfway down the main stairs when Malcolm bursts through the front door.

"What do you think you're doing?" he demands.

drags her daughter, still dressed in tights and leotard, toward us. "You didn't!"

"And lose the chance to take back what my family built?" Malcolm roars.

"But how?" Ginny stammers, shrinking a bit under his ferocious gaze. Ellie clings to her side, but her eyes are on me.

I smile, hoping to reassure her, but she hides her face against her mother's purse. Malcolm isn't the only one angry that I left.

"Once we sell the house, we'll be fine," Malcolm says, adjusting his tie. I resist the urge to grab it and strangle him with it.

"But where will we live, and how will we even do it? Did you give him permission?" Ginny turns wild eyes on Felix.

"No," Felix says firmly.

"The lawyers are working to remove Felix as Ellie's trustee," Malcolm explains. "It's better this way. We'll have control again. We'll find somewhere smaller and build the family name into what it was once."

And that's when I realize why he's doing this. I was wrong. Malcolm isn't following the script anymore. He's writing his own. He wants to make a name for himself, just like I do. That doesn't make what he's doing okay. Because even if he's fighting my father's crooked legacy, he's doing it using the MacLaine handbook. He'll bulldoze through each of us if we stand in his way. In his effort to free himself from our father, he's become something just as terrible.

"We should talk about this later," I say gently, still watching Ellie's frightened eyes half-hidden behind Ginny.

Malcolm turns to me, his face full of pure hatred. "You aren't part of this family anymore. There is nothing to talk about. Get out of our house."

"No!" Ellie jumps out from behind her mother and runs to me, wrapping her tiny arms around my leg. "Don't leave Auntie Dair!"

"See, how you confuse her by coming here?" Ginny accuses, grabbing Ellie's shoulder to pull her off me.

I push her hand off and curl my arm protectively around the little girl. "Don't."

Ellie looks up to Ginny, tears swimming in her eyes. "I'll be good, remember? Just like you said." She turns her pleading to me. "I promised. I told her I would behave so you don't have to leave again."

"What did you tell her?" I ask Ginny in horror.

"The truth. That her Aunt left her and wouldn't be coming back."

"How could you?"

"I'm her mother. I'm all she needs." Ginny yanks Ellie off me, but she kicks free and grabs hold of me again.

"Don't leave me," Ellie sobs against me.

I stare at my brother and his wife before turning my confusion to Felix. Finally, I look down to Ellie. Staying here can only make things worse for Ellie. At least, in the short term. But I realize now I have no choice. I can't let Malcolm sell Windfall any more than I can trust them to put Ellie's interests first.

Dropping to one knee, I wrap my arms around Ellie and look into her tear-stained eyes. Every ounce of me hurts, knowing I have to leave her here, even for a minute. "I have to go today, but I will be back for you. I will never leave you." I reach up to draw a small heart on her chest. "I'm always here."

She places a soft palm on my chest. "And I'm here?"

I choke back a sob. "Always." I hug her tightly, closing my eyes to the venomous expression on Ginny's face. "Felix will take care of you, and I will see you before you can even miss me."

"Promise?" she says in her tiny voice.

"Don't you dare," Ginny warns me. "Don't you dare say yes. You have no right."

I release Ellie and she runs over to Felix. Standing, I nod to him and he picks her up. "Let's go see about a cookie."

Thank God for Felix and his cookies. I wait until they're gone.

"I have every right," I tell her. Ginny opens her mouth to argue, but I cut her off, "Tell her, Malcolm."

The color drains from Ginny's face and she spins to face her husband. "What does she mean by that?"

Malcolm squares his shoulders, ignoring her to glare at me. "Get the fuck out of here."

"You'll hear from my lawyers," I say.

This actually makes him laugh. "You don't have lawyers. The family does, and I think I've made it pretty clear that you're no longer a member of this family."

"I've lived in Valmont my whole life," I remind him. "I know a lot of lawyers."

"I will bury you with litigation," he threatens me. "This will never see the light of day. You don't have the resources to fight me for this house."

"I don't want the house," I say softly. "I want what's

mine, and I know someone who has the resources to help me."

"Sterling Ford?" he guesses. "Who do you think is selling the company back to me? He's only looking out for himself."

"What?" I can't process what he's telling me. Why would Sterling give up his interest in MacLaine Media now? I had to stop him. I had to explain what's really at stake.

"You know what kind of man he is," Malcolm says. "I knew the moment I met him. He's ruthless, cold, manipulative. He would make a better MacLaine than you do."

I calmly walk to where Felix placed my boxes when he took Ellie to the kitchens. Picking them up, I carry them to join the box on the table. It's a little awkward, but I can't leave them behind. Not now. Not when I know he'll throw them out before I can come back for them.

When I reach the door, I fumble for the handle, barely opening it while Ginny and Malcolm look on.

I'm two steps out the door when Malcolm calls after me, "There's nothing you can say to change his mind. The deal is done."

I don't bother responding to him. I need to leave before he realizes he let me walk out of this house with everything I need to destroy him. He thinks there's nothing I can do to change Sterling's mind about selling the company? We'll see about that.

27

STERLING

I've lost my mind. It's the only way to account for what I've just done. Stepping out of Laird & Wharton, I ignore the cellphone buzzing in my pocket. It's probably Sutton trying to talk me out of signing the initial documents again. I can't blame her. If I told myself two months ago what I'd be doing today, I might have kicked my own ass.

"Mr. Ford." Cameron Laird, my new lawyer, rushes out, clutching a folder. "You left this. It has your copies of the initial documents. Once we receive final signatures, we'll be able to move forward."

I take the folder from her and tuck it under my arm. "Thank you, Ms. Laird. I'll wait for your call."

"May I call you Sterling?" she asks. She brushes a blonde strand of hair from her eyes and tucks it behind her ear. It's the only thing about Ms. Laird that's out of place. Everything from her no-nonsense black pant suit to her simple diamond earrings and carefully styled hair presents a business woman. It's why her question is so surprising.

"My friends do," I say.

"Sterling, as your friend," she begins, planting a hand on her hip, "Not as your lawyer, can I ask you if you're sure? I don't want to see you make a mistake. You'd make more going through a private broker to find an accredited investor."

"This isn't about money," I say to her.

"I thought everything was about money." Her crimson lips purse into a bemused smile. "If it's not about money, it must be about love. You're a fool if you go through with either option."

"Believe me, I'm a fool if I don't."

She checks her watch. "I need to get back to my next appointment. I'll be in touch." She takes a step and hesitates. "Think it over."

I nod, knowing there's no way she or anyone else is going to convince me to take another course of action. I bought into MacLaine Media to undermine it. It's what Angus and Malcolm MacLaine deserved. They still deserve it, but I can't go through with my plan without hurting Adair. So, I don't have any other options, and I have no interest in carrying around this albatross any more.

My phone rings for the third time, and I slide it from my pocket. It's time to face the music.

"Where have you been?" Sutton demands as soon as I answer.

"I was in a meeting." I continue down Market Street, pinning my phone against my ear with my shoulder so I can dig out my keys.

"Tell me you didn't just sign away millions of dollars."

"I didn't." It's the truth. I haven't signed away anything. Yet. "Who told you I did?"

"Luca told me where you were going," she says.

"Why are you talking to Luca?"

"Because he doesn't avoid my calls!"

I frown. I'm going to have a chat with my best friend about my kid sister. I know Luca enjoys having her around, but it's dangerous for her to get too close to a DeAngelo.

"You know what that family did," she continues. "Not just to you. They're terrible. They don't deserve a second chance."

I stop a few feet from my Aston Martin. "I'm not giving them a second chance."

I can't expect her to understand this. She's too young to have experience with this world. Before I can tell her that, a shadow casts itself in my path. I look up and meet an unwanted, but familiar, set of eyes set into a muscular six foot three inch frame.

Nikolai Koltsov. If you're going to happen upon a member of the Semsynovey Bratva on the street, he's the one you want. You're unlikely to walk away from an encounter with any of the other Koltsov brothers. Ink swirls on every exposed inch of his skin from the neck down, like the rest of his family. At least, the ones I've met. A lick of blond hair is slicked back from his face, the sides of his skull buzzed closely to reveal more tattoos. He crosses his arms, the seams of his blue suit jacket straining against muscles he built during his teen years when he was in and out of prison.

"Hey, I have to run," I say to Sutton, not daring to look

away from him. I hang up, ignoring her protests. "It's been a long time."

"And many miles." There's only the slightest tinge of an accent in his words. He spent nearly all his life in America, but his family business is conducted so frequently in Russian that the accent lingers.

"To think we both wound up here," I say. "Unless this isn't a coincidence." It's best to play dumb to give myself time to think. The worst thing I can do is draw the small 9mm I carry under my arm. There's no way Nikolai isn't armed, and he's likely as fast as I am.

"Not a coincidence," he says, "as I think you already know."

Trust a Koltsov to see through my bullshit. My index finger twitches. "What is it then?"

"A courtesy call," he says.

This, I'm not expecting. I blink. Noah seemed pretty sure the Koltsovs planned to kill me. Knowing what I do about the Bratva, I was inclined to agree.

"You've been named by an informant." He picks a piece of lint off his cuff, displaying four different crosses etched into his knuckles. "Normally, we would kill you."

I raise my eyebrows. This is definitely not going like I expected. "But it's my lucky day?"

"We're in your debt," he says.

"You are?" I search my brain for any reason why the Koltsovs would owe me shit and come up empty-handed.

"Some of us," he says. "Not all my brothers agree on this point, but they're willing to turn their heads, if you disappear. At least, until this matter is resolved."

"And how long will that be?" I ask tightly.

"Weeks. Years. Who knows?"

"I can't disappear," I say. "But I have no interest in hurting your family. You have my word."

Nikolai brushes his lip with his thumb, shaking his head. "Unfortunately, your word doesn't mean much. No offense."

"None taken." I can appreciate the business side of this arrangement. "If I don't go?"

"I'm afraid my brothers are very impatient. They've been learning a lot about you the past few weeks," he says. "They think they can provide strong motivation for you to change your mind."

"What kind of motivation?"

"Your family is here in Tennessee, right?"

"I wouldn't advise you to go after my sister," I say coolly. I make a mental note to get Sutton on a plane headed somewhere tropical within twenty-four hours.

"No, we respect a brother's love for his sister, but there are others you care for. Your blood, if you will," he says. "Your father, this woman, Adair MacLaine, and your—"

"I'd stop if I were you."

"And if I were you," he says, leaning closer, "I'd leave town. I hear London is lovely this time of year."

"London is hot this time of year," I say flatly.

He chuckles as he takes out a pair of sunglasses and slides them on. "Not as hot as hell, Mr. Ford."

Afternoon Nashville traffic is heavy on the best days, a parking lot on the worst. Today, it's somewhere in between: an agonizingly slow conveyor belt of cars. I slam my fist against the horn in frustration and the guy in front of me flips me off. For a brief second, I imagine getting out of the Vanquish, dragging the man from his shitty Kia, and pummeling him until the raging frustration churning inside me subsides. I force my attention away from him, gripping the steering wheel in a death lock, and spot an empty parking spot ahead. Laying on my horn, I rev the engine, nudging forward until I'm on the guy ahead's bumper. I can see him cursing at me, but I just honk again until he moves forward. It takes a few minutes, but gradually I get close enough to swerve into the spot, nearly scraping my front end against the Kia.

I jump out, ignoring the number of people who've rolled down their windows to yell at me. I peel off my suit jacket and toss it in the back. I start running, remembering only then that I've left my gun holster on. My 9mm knocks against my rib cage and I ignore it. The Eaton is only seven blocks north. That might be five minutes in running shoes. In Berlutis, it takes me ten.

The concierge pauses as I dash into the lobby, dripping from my impromptu jog in the southern heat. "May I help you, sir?"

But I'm already to the elevators. I punch the up button a couple times, calling over my shoulder. "I know where I'm going."

A couple waiting nearby move slowly away. The doors open and the passengers start to exit, freezing when they find me sweaty and waiting to board. I move to the side and slip in once it's empty. No one tries to board with me. Inside, I consider taking out my gun. Nikolai threatened Adair. That much I know. But it felt more like an ultimatum than an imminent threat. I won't relax until she's in my sights, though. Her hall is quiet when I arrive, and I'm forced to consider what to do if she doesn't answer. She could be at the publishing house or out with Poppy, but I wouldn't know that. She's not exactly answering my calls.

I bang on her door until I hear an annoyed "I'm coming" from inside. The relief is instant at the sound of her voice. She throws open the door—hands planted on her hips, hair spilling over her shoulders, feet bare—and opens her mouth to chew me out.

I don't have time for that.

She's in my arms in a split second. By the next, my mouth is on hers. Her palms flatten on my chest, but instead of pushing me away like I expect, her fingers grab hold of my shirt to pull me closer. She presses closer, her body molding to mine. No matter how much time passes— no matter how much she changes—we have always been and will always be a perfect fit. My hands slide under her ass, lifting her in one smooth motion and spinning us inside her suite. I kick the door closed behind us. The kiss deepens, as though we're both searching for something we lost inside each other. When we finally break apart, Adair's lips are swollen red and her forehead dewy.

"What was that for?" she asks breathlessly.

For being alive, I think. I decide it's best not to say this out loud. I rest my forehead against hers. "Because I needed to kiss you."

"Need, huh?" she murmurs.

"It's the best word I've got. They haven't coined one yet that encompasses the exact feeling. I suspect it's because no one has ever loved anyone this much before."

"You love me?" she says.

"You know I do." I steal another kiss, just so I can taste her again.

"I wasn't sure you knew."

"You didn't put up a fight," I say. I can't bring myself to let go of her.

"You had the element of surprise working in your favor." She studies me for a moment, her eyes scanning my disheveled appearance. "What happened...?"

"It's a long story." I loosen my hold on her a little. Then, I notice the mess in her living room. "What the hell happened here, Lucky?"

"Nothing," she says quickly, pulling free from me. "I picked up some things from Windfall. I've been going through them." She starts scooping things off the floor and dumping them into open cardboard boxes.

My eyebrow curves into a question mark. It doesn't look as much like organization as it does the aftermath of a hurricane. "Looking for something?"

"Yeah," she says absently before shaking her head. "I mean, not really. Malcolm... you know what? It's a long story, too." She stops her harried cleaning and turns on me. "Did you offer to sell Malcolm your shares of MacLaine Media?"

This wasn't how I planned to have this conversation with her, but judging from her tone, she already knows. "I told him to make an offer."

Adair closes her eyes, her hands gripping the back of a nearby chair. "Why would you do that?"

"I didn't say I would accept his offer." I cross to her, carefully stepping over the papers, books, and photographs strewn across the navy carpet. "In fact, I planned to reach out to another potential investor."

Her eyes snap open. "Who?"

"Isn't it obvious? You."

Adair continues to stare at me, jaw unhinged as she processes this. "Me?"

"It's what you've always wanted: control."

"Over my life. Not the company."

"You might not like it, Lucky, but you're a MacLaine. That company belongs to you as much as it belongs to him. You want control? Take it. Refuse it. I'm putting it in your hands," I say. "You get to choose what to do with it. You're every bit as much a MacLaine as Malcolm is. Your father shouldn't have made you feel otherwise."

A battle wages in her green eyes. It's not an easy choice. I knew it wouldn't be. But she has to be the one to make it. Maybe she will never trust me again. Maybe we're still doomed. But I can give her this, if nothing else.

"I already drew up the papers," I say to her.

"I don't have the money to buy it," she says softly. "You must know that."

"Lucky, it's yours. Your birthright. I'm not selling it to you. I'm giving it to you." I pause, realizing there are some other things she ought to know. "I don't hold all the shares, though. Jack and Luca do as well."

"I suspected." She does a fair job of looking put out by this. "I can't take the shares. They belong to you."

"That's what you don't get." I hook a finger in the waistband of her pants and draw her closer to me. "Everything I have—everything I am—is yours."

"Does the bank know that?" She laughs nervously. It fades when she sees that I'm serious.

"They're just waiting on your signatures."

Adair pushes away, her eyes widening. "What are you saying?"

"I'm all in," I tell her. "I meant it when I wrote it on that card. I always will be. Maybe this is a shitty way of showing you, but what's mine is yours. All of it. You can help me build more or ruin me, but I can't deny you belong with me, at my side. Equals. I know that compared to your family, it's nothing, but it's yours."

"It's everything," she whispers.

"I never thought a MacLaine would settle for so little," I tease.

"Sterling." She bites her bottom lip, her lashes fluttering as she gazes into my eyes. "What if I don't want to be a MacLaine anymore?"

My cock stiffens at the implication of her words. "What are you saying, Lucky?"

"There's so much I need to tell you, and I still have questions—"

"What are you saying?" I repeat before she can walk her words back any further.

She's so breathless, I can barely hear her. "I don't want to be a MacLaine anymore. I want a real family. I want you."

"Come here." I wrap her in my arms, holding her and savoring her completion of me. Her head fits into the hollow under my chin, and her scent—magnolias wafting through the southern summer heat—fills my nose, telling me I'm home.

For almost a month I've been driving myself crazy trying to prove my love to Adair. Now I've done it, and I'm not sure how. Since she's the one that saved me. From madness. From ruin. I spent five years telling myself it wasn't real, believing she deserved a reckoning and that it would finally sever her hold on me.

But now I recognize the truth. Our lives were never separate. There was only ever us. At the time we met, we were waiting—full of anger and frustration—for life to begin. Meeting her was no less than being born: confusing, exhilarating, intense. Life from nothing.

But others came between us, and we let them. Ever since then we've been pale shadows of real people, haunting our own lives like ghosts. Unable to move on. Unable to let go of the real life we once glimpsed.

I draw her head up and cup her chin. "I will always love you."

"Sterling, I love you," she purrs, nuzzling my earlobe with her nose.

"Does it feel good to say it again?" I lift her, cradling her body in my arms, and carry her towards the bedroom.

"God, yes," she says, her emerald eyes piercing through me to my soul.

"I'm going to worship you, Lucky. *Every fucking inch of you.*" I want to give her a taste of what awaits her for the rest of her life. I need to.

"Mmm?" She gives me a dreamy look, and the corners of her mouth curl into a satisfied grin. "Every inch, huh?."

"You are a goddess." I back through the door of her room and lay her on the bed. "Goddesses deserve to be worshipped."

"Should I be taking notes?" she says teasingly, but her eyelids are already heavy, her mouth the perfect, kissable pout.

I pull the knot of my tie and slide it free of my collar, dropping it on the bed next to her. This wakes her up a little. Her tongue flickers over her lower lip as my fingers close over the first button.

"Feel free to skip to the good part," she says, reaching to tug my shirt free. I push her hand away.

"Patience," I murmur. Her pout deepens, but I take my time with each button, never letting my eyes leave hers. "There's a ritual to worshipping, Adair," I explain. "Certain formalities."

This proclamation is met with a skeptical glare. "Fuck formalities!"

I kick off my shoes and bend to slowly pull off each sock. She watches, her hips wriggling restlessly. Her teeth bite down on her lower lip when my fingers reach for my belt buckle and my cock hardens at the greedy gleam in her eyes. "Oh, I don't know. I think you'll end up liking the formalities."

She blushes, ruddy patches of red glowing through the cream of her skin. I slide the belt off and abandon it next to my tie. Adair's breathing grows shallow as I unfasten my pants and let them fall to the floor. Those green eyes of hers zero in on the silhouette of my cock, straining to escape my boxers. I hook my thumbs under the elastic and pause to drink in the sight of her strewn across the bed, waiting for me. Her knees are raised, wedging her shorts around her shapely ass. There's a hand tucked where her thighs press together as her body writhes to the pulse of need overtaking her body. The straps of her threadbare tank fall over her shoulders. And the look on her face. Swollen lips. Pink cheeks. Her hair a tangled copper pool haloing her head. It's the goddamn sexiest thing I've seen in my entire life.

Circling to the foot of the bed, I drop onto the mattress and prowl toward her. I pause at her feet, slipping off her sandals and kissing each bit of exposed skin. My hands slide up her legs, reaching for her shorts. I quickly trail kisses from her feet to her knees, slowing as I reach her perfect thighs. She lifts her hips instinctively and I tug off her shorts to reveal a pair of black lace underwear.

My mouth teases down her thighs, tasting her soft skin, until I reach her panties, then it closes over the lace-covered mound. Her scent fills my nostrils, sending another rush of blood to my already painfully hard cock. I can taste her through the fabric and I can't help allowing myself one gentle suck. A hopeful moan slips from her lips, followed by another "I love you."

The curves of her body guides my lips to her navel as I push the hem of her shirt up to reveal more delicious flesh. Her bra is sheer black and trimmed with lace, and the promise of her luscious breasts makes my cock pulse. I lift her sharply to me, crushing her plump, pink mouth to mine. I suck her lower lip into my mouth, savoring not only the taste of her, but how she melts against me. I can do anything I want to her. She'll let me. She's given me her body completely. There's not an ounce of resistance in her, and I'm going to reward her for that abandon.

I release her lip to draw her top over her head. Her breath catches, then her chest deflates in a deep sigh. Unclasping her bra, I throw her clothes behind me onto the

floor. I want to make every part of her swollen and sensitive. I want every inch of her to experience the orgasm I'm
about to give her. It's what a goddess deserves.

Lowering her shoulders back onto the bed, my arm still
beneath them, I roll from between her legs to lie beside her.
My mouth finds her breast, kissing slow circles as my hand
caresses the other one. Drawing the furl of her nipple into
my mouth, I suck hard, eliciting a sharp hiss. I attend to her
other breast the same way, my hand gliding slowly down to
hover over her panties.

Adair's body responds instantly, her hips bucking as
she tries to create more friction between my hand and her
panties. For a moment I do nothing but let her circle
against me, in thrall to her body's response, powerless to her
perfection.

She groans as I abandon her nipple, and the sound
draws me to her mouth. I go there next, my lips finding
hers, then journeying to the soft curve where her shoulder
and neck meet. When I nip the tender, vulnerable flesh
there she jolts up, her teeth sinking into my shoulder for a
second before she moves on hungrily. Her fingernails dig
into my back as she clutches me tightly.

I'm lost to it, the feeling of her mouth, her teeth. She
sucks my ear, bites down hard into the sinew where neck
meets shoulder. She could eat me alive and I would
thank her.

But I can't stop myself from taking back control.
Angling my face over hers, I capture her lips again, sucking
until the slightest hint of pain escapes her. She releases me
and I plunge down, burying my face between her legs. Her

fingers tangle in my hair, caressing my scalp as I gather the fabric of her panties in my hands.

"I'd order you to stop wearing these," I say, "but I do like ripping them off you." I find the seam and pull, my efforts rewarded by the subtle pop of each thread giving way.

Lucky's whole body begins to vibrate in anticipation as the last barrier between us gives way. She whimpers, her fingers tugging my hair, her hips bucking closer. "Put your mouth on me. Worship me."

"Fuck yes," I say, so consumed that I don't know which one of us needs it more.

I thrust my tongue inside her as her hips roll up, opening all of her to me. Licking slowly, I savor her with long, intense strokes, building in pace along with the guidance of her hips.

"Oh my God." The words roll out of her like thunder when I take her clit into my mouth, sucking until it swells. The fingers in my hair grasp and pull. It's not a plea to stop, just a tether to grip as she rides out the pleasure.

The surges fade to aftershocks and the hands pulling my hair relax. I crawl forward, kissing her belly, her breasts, and appreciating the languid, trembling of her body.

"I need you inside me," she pleads, her voice a deep, aching thing. "Make love to me."

"I worship you," I say, kissing her collarbone as I lower my hips, nudging between her slick heat and lingering there. "I love you."

There's no resistance when I thrust forward. She takes all of me in one powerful stroke, and the look on her face is one I know I will see in my dreams forever, divine and profane at the same time. A goddess come to down to earth.

I can't be gentle or slow. I need to watch her unravel again. Grabbing her shoulders, I slam against her again and again, a throbbing pain echoing from my balls with each stroke.

"Yes!" she screams, all restraint gone, total abandon unlocked.

It spurs me on, driving me into a frenzy. "I love you," escapes my lips, the subconscious thoughts inside my head spilling out of me unfiltered, as easily as talking to myself.

"Don't leave me again," she sobs, hooking her heels behind my hips and adding their strength to my own. Her fingers dig into my back, and every time I pull away I feel their sharp sting, telling me the price of parting from her and inviting my return.

"Never," I promise. Our eyes meet, finding calm in the eye of the storm ravaging our bodies.

She surrenders first, her body tightening around me and I join her, my low, unending groan filling the room in chorus with her own.

Her body melts into the bed as her shaking subsides, and I pull from her gently, turning her onto her side and drawing her to me, back to chest, my chin on her shoulder, my arms wrapped around her, promising never to let her go.

The world feels tender and raw, as new and beautiful as the woman in my arms. I want to explore both. For now, though, I want only to hold her.

Life from nothing. Rapture from ruin. Us.

28

STERLING

THE PAST

I don't know how I wound up here.

A pin sticks my thigh, and I yelp, glaring down at the seamstress.

"Sorry," she says past a dozen more of the offending instruments clamped between her teeth.

"Do I really need my own tuxedo?" I ask Adair for what must be the twentieth time this week.

"Cyrus's does not fit you," she says firmly, "and why rent? I'm probably going to have to drag you to a million more of these things."

"Is your brother planning on getting married to a lot of women?" I cock an eyebrow at her reflection in the mirror.

"Him and everyone else I know," she teases. "It's our way of life."

The seamstress pops the final pin out of her mouth. "She's got a point."

It's strange how easily people laugh off weddings and divorces around here. The closer to Malcolm MacLaine's wedding we've come, the more jokes I've heard—from everyone. Cyrus. Adair. Even Poppy has made a crack or two, and she's the optimistic one, usually.

"Of course, you don't have to come," Adair says.

"I'm coming, Lucky. Done deal. Unless you want to take someone else."

She moves behind me, her delicate hands resting on my shoulders, and our eyes meet in the mirror. "Not with how you look in this. Damn, Ford."

At least she's pumping up my ego, since she's going to insist on buying me the suit. She started hinting at it before we left New York. Then, she mentioned the plans for the wedding: a formal afternoon ceremony at a large cathedral in Nashville followed by a reception at the Valmont Country Club. I said yes before I found out that she was in the wedding. She softened the blow by telling me Cyrus and Poppy would be there. We were three weeks into the new semester when she mentioned actually buying a tuxedo.

"You could have told me you were dragging me for a fitting, you know?"

"Would you have come?" she asks.

"I'm just saying that when you get all dolled up and wag your little finger at me to follow you—it gets my hopes up."

She showed up outside my Finance class wearing a denim skirt too short for January paired with thigh-high suede boots. I should have known she was up to something. That's what I get for letting my dick do the thinking.

Adair leans forward, lowering her voice so the seamstress doesn't hear her, "I'll make it up to you."

That's more like it.

Adair's eyes narrow, her lips flatten into a line, but she can't stop herself from laughing.

"Sorry, Lucky," I say, pulling her to me. "I'm trying."

"I know. Me, too. We'll get better at this."

"At what? Being from different sides of the track?"

"At just letting small stuff like this go," she says.

I open my mouth, about to tell her that I can't let five-thousand dollars go, but then I shut it. She's right. Money matters a lot more when you don't have it. Adair does. I can't change that. But it doesn't define who she is, and I know it.

"Now, I think you said something about making this up to me?" I remind her, my head dipping to her neck.

"What do you have in mind?" she murmurs.

"Let me show you."

I haven't been to a lot of weddings. Foster kids don't get invitations to things like that, but I suspect this is a bit crazier than most. Between a thousand guests and the release of live doves *inside* the church, I find myself wondering if Cirque de Soleil will be performing at the reception. Thankfully, it's just another extravagant party.

Ropes of pale pink roses and ivy drape elegantly across the ceiling, meeting in the center where a crystal chandelier hangs over the dance floor. A hundred tables cluster around it, each carefully set with bone china and silver flatware.

"Want something from the bar?" Cyrus asks when we find our table.

"Cyrus!" Poppy says sharply.

"Oh, sorry, man." My roommate looks flustered.

"It's okay." I grip the back of my chair and look around. "I think I'm going to find Adair."

I'm weaving my way through a crowd of Valmont elite, searching for her, when a hand closes over my arm. I pivot to find her standing behind me.

"I was just looking for..." Words fail me. I saw her walk down the aisle in her bridesmaid's dress, but there had been a crowd blocking my view. Up close? She's every dream I've forgotten in the morning, come back to me. Her dress is the palest pink, almost as fair as her skin. The gauzy fabric crosses delicately over her breasts and wraps around the curve of her shoulders, showcasing her freckles. Despite the hours of makeup, she looks like she does in the morning after we make love—lips pink, cheeks stained with a flush of red. I'll never remember exactly what she wore, but I will never forget this feeling.

"Did I do alright?" she says, laughter in her eyes. When I don't answer, she prompts, "Walking down the aisle? I hope my practice paid off."

I shake myself out of my fog and crook a finger at her. "You didn't trip once," I say, trying to sound natural. "That deserves a reward."

No one notices us kissing at a wedding. We blend in with the romantic atmosphere too well. So I take my time, showing her exactly how perfect she is to me. When I finally release her, we wander through the middle of the crowd, and apart from everyone.

The floor-to-ceiling windows of the country club ballroom look out over a large, picturesque lake. Banks of red-barked cypress trees, up-lit with gold, cluster around the shores, and wide swathes of green fairway dotted with white sand sweep in every direction. The lake itself is a mirror of the sky above, glowing with the incandescent oranges, reds, and purples of the setting sun.

I squeeze Adair's hand as an announcer's smooth baritone calls out from the P.A. system. "Please join us in the ballroom where Malcolm and Virginia will now share their first dance as a married couple."

The newlyweds stroll to the middle of the parquet dance floor, hand in hand, as a spotlight appears from above. Everyone applauds, even me. I couldn't care less about Malcolm and Ginny and the rest of the MacLaine family, honestly. It's more like I'm clapping for the idea that two people can give this much of themselves to each other.

Adair shoots me a surprised look.

"What?" I ask defensively. "This is pretty magical."

"Weddings are definitely romantic," Adair says with a sigh. She takes my hand in both of hers and rests her head on my shoulder as the first notes of their song start up.

It's a short song, and just as the next begins, the announcer invites everyone to join in the dancing.

Adair has other ideas, though, because she pulls me into the hallway.

"Where are we going, Lucky?"

"This way," she says with the easy smile of someone beginning to feel their champagne.

"I can see that. Where will we end up?"

"Shh. Shh." She places an index finger on my lips and looks around in exaggerated paranoia. "It's a secret."

Definitely feeling the champagne.

The country club building is huge, and the more stairs we climb, the fewer people we see.

"Don't you want to dance?" I ask.

"It's a kind of dancing, yes," she says with a devilish grin, pulling me into a room marked *linen*.

"I don't think this is a good idea, Lucky. I don't have protection, and there are people—"

"What's wrong with lots of people?" She says with the slow precision of a person determined to sound less tipsy than they really are. "There should be lots of people at a wedding. They're there to look at you and tell you how happy you look. Oh, and the presents. They give presents. Presents are good."

"We don't want a wedding like this, Lucky. Weddings should be small and intimate. Only the people you really care about should come."

Her breath hitches, her eyes sparkling with something other than champagne. "You're planning our wedding, huh?"

"Adair MacLaine, I've known you were it for me since the moment I first saw you." I cup her chin in my hand. "And then you were a bitch, and I was a dick—and maybe we just both knew and it scared us. But we couldn't fight it. We'll never be able to fight this."

"How can you...?" She searches my face.

"I've stopped thinking about *my* future. There's only *our* future. I can't see it any other way."

"Sterling, I..." she trails off, at a loss.

"I'm all in, Adair. I love you."

She pulls me to her like I'm the air she needs to breathe.

That's how it should be. Her need fills me with purpose: to live a better life, to be a better person, to make her happy, safe, fulfilled. And it's not just the obvious things—her sense of humor, her intelligence, her perfect body. It's the little things I can't get enough of. How the downy fuzz on the back of her neck stands up when I whisper in her ear. How the corners of her eyes crinkle when I tease her. How she opens for me when we make love, trusting me so completely. Each day there's a new discovery, a new detail I never noticed. I want to spend the rest of my life discovering as many of them as I can.

"I need you inside me." Her body hums with nervous energy. She tosses a pile of neatly folded towels to the ground, clearing space on a narrow counter set against the wall. There's a moment of frenzied movement as I hike her skirt to her hips and lift her onto the edge of the counter. Her fingers fumble with my belt, unbuckling it and shoving my pants open enough to free me. Everything happens on instinct, each movement as inexorable as gravity.

Her gaze meets mine, and I know I would do anything to have her look at me this way forever.

I thrust, instantly relieved to be inside her. Adair's arms coil around my shoulders as she melts against me. For a moment I wonder what I did to deserve her, how I could be lucky enough to be here now with her, promising each other forever with our bodies.

We're not in a linen closet. We're in our own special place, entirely within ourselves.

No one can find us here.

We have all the time we need.

And when we come down from our great heights, it is

to a world laying at our feet, waiting for us to make it what we will.

"It's so...much...better," Adair pants, "that way."

No, not better.

Perfect.

29

ADAIR

PRESENT DAY

"What is all this, anyway?" Sterling asks, tying his robe while we wait for room service. He glances at the boxes spilling over into the living room.

There's no danger in him looking, because it's not here. I've been through everything. I wouldn't have thrown it away, which means Malcolm must have taken it. Despite that, my heart still races. I squash the anxiety down and ignore it. He'll forgive me when the time comes, and I'll find it. Sterling will help me. But not today. Today I want to linger in us before dredging up the past. "I was looking for something. I don't know how much Malcolm has thrown away."

"He tried to throw away your things? He's such a dick." Sterling picks up a paper, his face rife with disgust. If he didn't like Malcolm before, he despises him now.

"My clothes are in storage somewhere." I roll my eyes. "It's so like my brother to toss a framed photo of mom and me away, but keep my prom dress. Sentimentality is lost on my family."

"But not on you." He picks up a stack of books and smiles. It's my old copy of *Pride and Prejudice*, the one he read and left notes in, along with a Steinbeck I borrowed from him, and the copy of *The Great Gatsby* he gave me for Christmas five years ago. His eyes flicker dangerously, and I feel my belly tighten. He's thinking about the past, too, and from the looks of it, feeling rather sentimental.

My ringtone shatters the moment, and I reach for it. "Don't tell anyone."

I reject the call as soon as I see the Caller ID. Malcolm's ears must be burning. "Speak of the devil."

"I thought I was the devil," Sterling says, thumbing through *Pride and Prejudice*.

"This is mine." He holds up *The Grapes of Wrath*.

"I've been meaning to give it back to you." My phone rings again and I reject the call.

"How long until room service arrives?" he asks, advancing a step closer.

"It's usually pretty fast." I hold up a finger in warning. "So don't get any ideas. We should wait."

He lowers his head to nuzzle my neck, his breath tickling across my earlobe. "But the things we shouldn't do are the most fun."

How am I going to survive this man? His mouth cruises along my jaw towards my lips, and I'm already resigning myself to cold food when there's a knock on the door.

"Hold that thought," he orders me, disappearing to sign for room service.

I tighten my robe and peek over to see it's Anthony, the poor kid who delivered the wrong screwdriver, with our order. He spots me and looks down at his feet, mumbling something to Sterling as he pushes the cart into the living room.

But I barely notice. The screwdriver. The drawer. I told myself to let it go, but now it occurs to me that my family has always been better at hiding dirty laundry. Maybe there's a reason that drawer is locked. Maybe there's a reason my dad left this suite, of all places, to me. I grab a butter knife off the room service cart and carry it to the desk.

"Um, thanks," Sterling says behind me.

I can feel them both staring at me, but it hardly matters if Anthony thinks I'm nuts. Sterling already knows I am. The suite door shuts and Sterling appears next to me. I continue trying to pry the drawer open. His hand closes over mine. "Allow me."

He takes the knife and pops the lock so quickly I'm not sure how he does it. We stare at each other for a minute. I don't know what I'll find in that drawer. I told him there were things I need to tell him, but what if this is how he finds out?

"I'm tired of secrets," I say. "I want to tell you everything, but you aren't going to like all of it."

"You're not the only one with bad news," he says. "Look, I promise to listen, and no matter what you need to tell me, it's not going to change how I feel about you."

God, I hope that's true.

"It might," I say faintly.

"You might change your mind when I tell you all my secrets," he reminds me.

"I doubt it." I don't just doubt it. I know I won't. I'm all in. Sterling might have done terrible things in impossible situations. He might have made bad calls. So have I. "We can't have a future if we keep getting dragged into the past."

"Then, let's open the drawer, Lucky."

I take a deep breath and steel myself for whatever my father felt was so important he locked it in a hotel drawer. I slide open the drawer, revealing a stack of yellowing paper. My gaze skips over the top page.

Untitled by Anne MacLaine

I pick up the stack, moving the first page and read the words: Chapter One.

"My mom wrote a book," I say it as much for my benefit as his.

"Why is it here?" He doesn't try to take it from me. Instead, he moves behind me, coiling his strong arms around my waist and looking over my shoulder.

"I don't know." I press the manuscript to my chest, a deep ache growing with each breath I take. "I didn't even know she wrote. Should I read it?"

"I think she'd want you to," he says.

It's not what I thought I might find in that drawer. It's not something I ever expected to find. What else don't I know about my family? My ringtone breaks the silence again and I drop the manuscript on the desk and race over to pick it up. "I'm sorry," I say to Sterling, seeing it's my brother for the third time. A familiar panic settles over me. The last time he called this repeatedly was the night our mom died. "It's him again. I should make sure nothing's wrong."

Sterling's face remains blank, but I know what he thinks. Still, no matter how broken my relationship is with Malcolm, I can't risk ignoring him. I answer, "What?"

"I could ask you the same thing," Malcolm storms.

Did I actually just interrupt a romantic interlude with a veritable sex god—and the love of my life—to get lectured by my brother?

"I have company. I need to go," I say.

"Have you seen the news? Been on Facebook?" he demands.

My thumb freezes over the end button. "No, why?"

"Is your company Sterling Ford?" he asks. "You might ask him. I don't know who else would do this to our family. But if I find out you had anything to do with it, I will make sure you not only never step foot inside this house again, but that you never see *your* family again."

"I have no fucking clue what you're talking about," I hiss, but he's already hung up on me.

Sterling plucks a fry from a plate on the dining cart. "Everything okay?"

"I'm not sure," I mutter, opening the news app on my phone.

Sterling doesn't press me for more information. Instead, he grabs another fry and *The Great Gatsby*. He thumbs it open at the same time that I see the first mention of MacLaine.

"Oh holy shit," I breathe, reading the headline. "Did you tell someone about the night my mom died?"

I look over to Sterling for an answer, but he's holding a

sheet of paper. It's creased from being stuck inside the novel for years, but, even from here, I recognize the City of Valmont watermark printed on the back. When he manages to tear his eyes from it, they find me. Neither of us speaks. We just stare at each other as the past comes back to destroy us once again.

THE RIVALS SAGA CONTINUES!

Sometimes the truth sets you free.

Sometimes it's a complete

BOMBSHELL

The explosive conclusion to Adair and Sterling's story.

Available
November 16, 2020

ACKNOWLEDGMENTS

I'd like to thank the characters in this book for giving me a place to escape during this crazy year!

Thanks to Louise, my fairy godmother, and the team at The Bent Agency. Not just for all your hard work, but also the integrity and ingenuity you showcase every single day.

Thank you to my foreign teams for all the hard work you do getting my books to readers all over the world. Thank you to Blanvalet for your enthusiasm regarding this new project.

Thank you to my endlessly patient assistants, Natasha and Shelby. You keep my shit together better than I do!

Thanks you to my Loves for being my safe place online. I'm so glad we have each other!

To my author friends, this has been an insane year and I am awed by your grace, motivation, and humor.

To my readers—thank you for loving Sterling as much as I do!

I couldn't do any of this without my family. Thank you

for being my cheerleaders, my accountability partners, my escape at the end of the day.

And to Josh, I'm all in. Always.

ABOUT THE AUTHOR

GENEVA LEE is the *New York Times, USA Today,* and internationally bestselling author of over a dozen novels, including the Royals Saga which has sold two million copies worldwide. She lives in Poulsbo Washington with her husband and three children, and she co-owns Away With Words Bookshop with her sister.

Geneva is married to her high school sweetheart. He's always the first person to read her books. Sometimes, he reads as she writes them. Last year, they were surprised by finding out Geneva was pregnant with their third child. They welcomed a beautiful baby girl in 2020.

When she isn't working or writing, Geneva likes to read, bake ridiculous cakes, run, and binge television seasons. She loves to travel and is always eager to go on a new adventure.

Learn more at GenevaLee.com

Made in the USA
Columbia, SC
24 September 2020

21369527R00231